Compulsive

Jim Nelson

To Mary—for all the years.

To Wendy and Mary Jean—for their love and encouragement.

To Jim and Chris—for believing in me.

Compulsive

ISBN 1-889459-16-X

·

Cheshire Moon Publications
1019 Fox Hills Drive
Fort Collins, CO 80526
(970) 226-8701

Foreword

I met Jim Nelson at the Glenwood Writers Conference in 1990, and there he showed me the manuscript of a novel he had written. Faculty at these conferences are overwhelmed with work and I didn't look forward to perusing a long piece that was not part of the requirements. But as I read the manuscript that would become *Compulsive,* I realized that I was enjoying myself, that I was in the grip of a work of sureness, authority, and directness, and that the writer had a topic about which he had profound knowledge and a strong will to communicate.

These features are not as common as one might think. Knowledge, experience, skill, and enthusiasm must blend to give the work a motive force that carries the reader along, supplying pleasure not only at the destination but all along the way. Nelson's work was doing that for me. The day went down and I was still reading.

I knew nothing about gambling and even less about why someone would want to come in out of the sunshine to do it. I had spent a week one night at the tables in Atlantic City and had had more than enough time there to last the rest of my life.

Yet, Nelson took me with Don Curtis on his odyssey, and neither romanticizing nor damning him, allowed me to see across the space between us, into that life and into the heart of that compulsion.

I *learned* a lot. I learned about point spread and the details of poker. I learned about the laws of chance as they work in gambling and about how the house figures, and I learned about the kind of biochemistry I suspect we all have to some degree, allowing us to get high and dope ourselves up on our own products, becoming chemically dependent without ever having made a single drug deal.

As I read the book, I watched this happen to Don Curtis in the swift, quiet way a fast river takes a rafter downstream beyond his skill and strength. I praised the book for its quiet, unassuming truths. Nelson doesn't see his protagonist as a tragic hero, but as an ordinary man who suddenly realizes his picnic blanket has been spread on quicksand.

I told Jim I admired *Compulsive* and wanted to show it to my agent. I sent it away. No luck. I tried other places. No luck. When I had no more ways of helping, I reluctantly gave up, but I never thought I had been mistaken. Now and then Jim would get in touch. He wrote other work and it was published. I would read it and say, "Yes, yes, but what about *Compulsive?*"

He called recently and told me he had found a home for the book. I'm delighted. I hope it sells a million copies and makes author and publisher rich. They both deserve it.

—*Joanne Greenberg*

Preface

Compulsive is fiction, but it deals with an addiction, a disease, an invisible disorder that affects as many as one in twenty-five of us. It drains bank accounts, takes money needed for food and shelter, and destroys families. Like drugs and alcohol, gambling produces a high that pulls the victim ever deeper into the disorder. Like other addictions, the initial experiences can be extremely pleasurable. It is only later, after the affliction has its grip, that the enormity of the need makes itself known.

It is estimated that several billion dollars are wagered, both legally and illegally, in the United States each year. With the growth in gambling "opportunities," *Compulsive* deals with a problem that will affect more and more of us in the years to come. Many readers will recognize their own feelings, their own emotions, in those of Don Curtis as he experiences the extraordinary highs, the crushing lows, and the ultimate devastation of his life because of his acquired compulsion to gamble.

After researching and writing the novel, I severely curtailed my own gambling activities.

I scared myself.

—Jim Nelson

Prologue

For a few seconds the exhilaration of the speed took him away from the real world, the world that had been beating up on him so badly. He braked hard, slammed the gearshift lever into third, and swerved around the truck. The rpms climbed into the turbo range, and the Saab accelerated briskly. The lane in front of him was clear, and he let it run, glancing quickly in the rear view mirror for any sign of a Denver police car. Seeing none, he walked it up to seventy-five before shifting back into fourth.
Then it came back. It all came back.

He was in extremely deep shit. He was deeply in debt, his wife was about to divorce him, and his business was going down the tubes. The few friends that he had left would cheerfully take his last dollar on a poker table. He owed a tremendous amount of money, and the creditors were at his heels, but they were a minor concern compared to the loan sharks. Those people you just didn't ignore.

He was traveling north on Interstate 25 through Denver. The digital speedometer read seventy-nine miles per hour, and he was weaving through the slower traffic. As he flashed beneath an underpass, he glanced at the concrete pillar which supported the cross street. It was easily ten feet in diameter. There were curving guard rails around the post on both sides, to ward off wayward traffic, but he noted that there was a space between the ends of the guard rails that appeared to be big enough to admit a small car. If a driver hit it just right, he could make it between the rails, and then there would be nothing between the car and the pillar. A person contemplating such a thing would want to be traveling at a high rate of speed, to eliminate any possibility of survival.

He shook his head, taking his eyes off the roadway for just an instant. He had frightened himself, and it took a few seconds to come to terms with the fact that he had even ... but one of the few things left from the fiasco of the previous year was several hundred thousand dollars worth of life insurance. That kind of money would allow Barbara and the boys to pick up the pieces, pay off the debts, and start over.

If only she could understand. He hadn't done it just for himself. When it started, it had been for her, for them, but then it had all gone wrong, and now there was nothing, nothing but the staggering debts and the memories of the losses. So many losses, so much money! He had been forced into the position of trying to win it back. There was no other place that kind of money could come from. But she didn't understand! She just kept yammering at him to go to the damned meetings, face up to his addiction, quit gambling.

He had tried, God how he had tried. But he felt trapped, cornered like some kind of a damned animal! He had stormed out of the house, screaming at her, "I'll go to the fucking meeting, if it means that much to you." He had no intention whatsoever of carrying out the promise, but maybe she would believe that he actually had gone to one of them, and get off his back!

He jockeyed for position on the freeway, and cut into the inside lane. As the highway curved, he could see another underpass ahead about three-quarters of a mile. From what he could see, there was an opening between the guard rails. He rammed the shift lever up into third and wound the little engine out to a high whine before he again hit fourth and slammed the accelerator back to the floor.

One

He leaned unconsciously to the right, using body English to force the flight of the ball back toward the green. The ball chose to ignore him and continued to hook toward the taller grass and trees to the left of the fairway. It hit at the edge of the fairway and bounced high before disappearing into the rough. He stared after it, mentally marking the spot where the ball had disappeared before going back into his stance, adjusting his feet slightly, and swinging again at the spot where the white sphere had perched seconds before. The second swing naturally felt perfect. He still must not be turning his hands over enough. He sighed and looked around for his tee.

"Nice long drive, slick." The sarcasm came from Jeff Stevens, the newest member of their weekly foursome. Stevens pretended to rummage through his big golf bag. "I think I've got a machete in here somewhere, if you want to borrow it."

Don Curtis turned to glare at the other man, his temper flaring. Stevens was still fumbling around in his bag, laughing to himself, so he missed the look. By the time he looked up, Don had composed his features into a lop-sided grin. "I've gotta do something to make up for your putting, slick!" He dropped his head and peered at Stevens over the top of his sunglasses, his eyebrows raised.

Jeff Stevens had been invited to join Don, Lou D'Amato, and Charlie Hardwick as the fourth in their Saturday morning golf outings. An opening had been created when Vic Gregory was transferred back east. Vic had been a regular member of the foursome for several years, and the other three missed him more than any one of them would care to admit. Vic had been a good, solid golfer with a seven handicap and the type of personality that really made him hard to dislike. The four golfers had developed a relationship which allowed them to pick on each other unmercifully, but yet not carry the harassment to the point of hurt feelings or anger. Vic had fit into the group very well. He possessed a dry, sarcastic sense of humor, and delighted in making comments which convulsed the other three. The four of them had frequently been the subjects of stares from other golfers when they would dissolve into gales of laughter over something or other that Vic had said.

Jeff Stevens was another matter. He was a large man, about six feet three and around two hundred twenty pounds, but he possessed none of the gentleness often associated with men of his size. Rather, he had more the temperament of the schoolyard bully. He had been introduced to the group by Lou D'Amato. Lou worked for Creative Software, a large company which sold computer programs of all types. There were two main sales divisions of the company, one dealing with business software, the other selling those programs used by educational institutions. Lou was the regional sales manager for the business products, and Jeff Stevens had recently taken over the comparable position in the educational division.

Jeff had been rather subdued on the first two Saturdays after he was asked to join them. He was very strong, and his big arms and shoulders could drive the ball a country mile. When he stepped up to the tee box, he had a habit of addressing the ball, setting his stance, and then closing his eyes for a few seconds, as if to summon up some sort of inner guidance. When he swung, the crack of the impact was almost painful. Unfortunately for his overall game, he tended to use the same approach with the other clubs in his bag. He tried to force shots through his strength, rather than coaxing or finessing the ball to the green and into the cup. If he hit a bad shot, nine times out of ten the ball would travel too far, rather than not far enough. The other three had seen him bury his club head in the turf in disgust at a botched pitch shot, and occasionally wondered if they had made the right choice in rounding out their little group.

As he apparently became more comfortable with the other three men, his true personality began to appear a little more each week. Don, Charlie, and Lou had continued their normal good-natured bickering, assuming that Jeff would eventually join in. When he did, his sense of humor turned out to be a bit caustic for their taste. He tended toward biting sarcasm rather than friendly bantering. If one of the other players screwed up a shot, he was quick to condemn. His remarks were almost taunting, as if he were trying to purposely start an argument. It did not seem to occur to him to make any comments which would be in any way self-deprecating.

While the others would cheerfully make fun of themselves as quickly as they would anyone else, that did not appear to be Jeff Steven's style. If any of the other members of the foursome made any disparaging remarks about his play, he was quick to come up with an excuse for his failure to execute the perfect shot. The grass would have been too long, too wet, too dry, or too something.

Don had taken to mildly criticizing the play of the big man, just to see what would happen. He would wait until Jeff had sliced one off into the woods and then wink at Lou and Charlie and say something like, "Well, that ought to wake up those squirrels!" He was usually rewarded by the reddening of the skin above the collar of his target, and some sort of excuse for the miscue. Don had thought several times that he would not be quite so quick to bait Stevens if it were not for the bigger man's habit of calling everyone "slick."

Don Curtis owned his own accounting business. He had met Lou about five years previously when Lou was one step below his present position and traveled the front range of the Rocky Mountains selling computerized business systems. He usually sold to the proliferation of computer stores which sprang up in the early eighties, but Lou and Don had met at a conference on income tax software, and Lou had agreed to get Don a price break on a new product. Lou had taken to dropping by Don's office periodically to check on the performance of the program, and they gradually became friends.

Charlie was, and Vic Gregory had been, a neighbor of Don's. Like most residents of a big city, Don's acquaintances came chiefly from his work or the immediate vicinity of his residence. Life was just too damned busy to branch out much further than that. The rest of the umpteen million residents of Denver and the surrounding suburbs were faces or voices, nothing more. Don did not know, nor did he have any desire to know, the persons behind the faces that briefly entered his life each day. The faces that passed him on the freeway every morning and night, the faces that served him his lunch and the faces that populated the elevator to his floor in the office building all blended together in his memory, and were, for all he knew or cared, interchangeable.

Barbara, his wife of twelve years, worked part time as a guidance counselor at John Quincy Adams High School, the school that served the area of Littleton in which they lived. It was located just a few blocks from their house. Barbara was the envy of most of the other working wives and mothers in their neighborhood, as she was able to ride a bike to work most days, if the weather permitted. A few of their friends had come from the contacts she made through her job, but like Don, her life was busy enough with two children and work to rule out much in the way of new friends.

Charlie Hardwick was next up to the tee box. He was resplendent in lime-green pants, a sport shirt which was a checkerboard of the same shade of green and a hot pink, and a Panama-style straw hat with a pink band. Charlie's mode of dress on the golf course was, as far as anyone could determine, his one break with conformity. He lived two houses to the west of Don and Barbara Curtis in a definitely upper-middle-class development known as Cherry Park. His house was remarkable only for its similarity to the other houses in the immediate area. He drove a gray four-door Honda and a Mercury station wagon, and made his living as a professor of psychology in the University of Denver Graduate School. He delighted in his golfing outfits and in the reactions which they elicited. Don was sure that the

Technicolor clothing was really some sort of bizarre psychological experiment, in which he was a reluctant participant, but he could never get Charlie to admit it.

Charlie played golf much like he lived. He placed the ball on the tee, placed the head of the driver behind the ball, and backed up until his hands were on the rubber grip. He tightened his hold on the club, brought it back over his right shoulder, and drove the ball about a hundred and forty yards right down the middle of the fairway. He wasn't long, but he was by God consistent!

As Charlie stepped back, Jeff couldn't resist a comment. "You know, Charlie, I'll bet those threads glow in the dark! Where do you buy that stuff, anyway?"

"I have it specially made to fit both my manly physique and my exquisite taste," replied Charlie.

Jeff snorted. "Well, Charles, I don't know how to break this to you, but either you or your tailor is operating under an extremely false impression!" He roared with laughter, punching Charlie lightly on the shoulder. The other three just smiled.

Lou caught the eyes of Don and Charlie for a second, shook his head slightly, and turned to tee up his ball. He hit a good, solid shot, a little high and to the right, but it stayed in the fairway and bounced to a stop about a hundred and sixty yards out.

When Jeff drove, the familiar crack of the club face against the ball pulled the eyes of the other three toward the distant green. As expected, the white ball sailed out and up, seeming to curve skywards in flight before it finally started its descent toward the middle of the green swath in front of them.

"Jesus!" The oath came from Lou. "Jeffrey, you may sell inferior computer products, but you can sure hit the shit out of a golf ball!"

"Yeah," said Don, "It's too bad the rest of his game sucks!"

"My game sucks! How about that beauty you just rattled the trees with, slick?"

"Don't you worry about my game!" Don said heatedly. "Who lost the last two holes for us? It sure as hell wasn't me!"

The foursome had made it a practice since soon after they started playing together to bet on each hole. They would form two teams, through the luck of a coin toss, and the team with the lowest combined score for each hole would win the bet for that hole. It had started as nothing more than friendly wagering, a way to build the competition a bit more. The bet had been five dollars per person per hole, so that the eighteen holes could conceivably cost one of the teams ninety dollars each, assuming they lost every hole. In reality, however, the golfers were pretty evenly matched, and the damage was seldom more that twenty-five or thirty dollars one way or the other. One of the first things suggested by Jeff when he joined them was to raise the stakes.

"What kind of money are you thinking about?" Charlie had asked.

"Well, twenty dollars a hole would make it worthwhile," Jeff had replied. "If you're gonna bet, why just fuck around with it? Bet something that's gonna mean something!"

They had finally agreed to raise the bet to ten dollars per man per hole. They reasoned that the bite shouldn't be more than double what it used to be, and each of them could certainly afford to lose fifty dollars or so a week. Don knew what Charlie made at the college because he did the professor's taxes each year. Charlie's wife didn't work, but she was the beneficiary of a small trust from her father's estate which kept her in the good graces of several of Denver's finer clothing stores. He had no idea what Lou and Jeff made as sales managers, but he suspected that they were both in at least the high five figure category, more likely the low sixes.

Don grossed about two hundred and fifty thousand in his practice, and after paying rent, salaries for his staff of three, and other office expenses, he took home about a hundred and thirty thousand dollars a year. He always felt a little guilty when he lost the weekly bet, even if it was only twenty dollars or so. The feeling never lasted long, as rationalization would set in and justify the loss as only the evening-out process over the long haul. He did, after all, win about as many bets as he lost, and over the space of a year, he knew that he had never gained or lost more than a hundred and fifty dollars or so. "Pocket change," as Jeff Stevens would refer to it.

The minor disappointment of losing was always overcome

by the thrill of winning. When he played well, and was lucky enough to draw a partner who also had a good day, he would drive home with the satisfaction that he had paid for his green fees and drinks, and was still money ahead.

The first two weeks after they raised the ante, Don had played as if inspired. The first week, he had had to overcome the mistakes of Charlie, who played poorly. The little psychologist had been recovering from the flu, and was not up to his game at all. Nonetheless, their team won ten of the eighteen holes, relieving Lou and Jeff of twenty dollars apiece.

The next week, he was teamed with Lou, and they both had one of the best days they were to have all season. They won seven of the first nine holes, and were ahead by fifty dollars each as they stopped for a drink. Jeff was not a happy man, bitching and moaning about his bad luck in the draw for partners and several shots of his own which had been ruined by everything from the groundskeepers to the manufacturer of his clubs. When he was reminded that he was the one who would have set the stakes at double the present rate, he mumbled something about making the wager worthwhile. Charlie played his usual solid game for the last nine holes, but Jeff swung at the ball as if he were killing snakes. At the end of the round, Don and Lou stood with their hands outstretched as Charlie and Jeff counted out ninety dollars apiece. Lou had been somewhat concerned about the amount of money involved.

"Ah . . . this is a lot of money." Lou held the bills in his palm, looking at the other three of them. "I'm not sure about this. I mean, a few bucks is okay, but . . ." The sentence trailed off.

"A lot of money? Lou, don't be such a wimp! What the hell are you whining about? You won!" Jeff was incredulous. "You don't see Charlie and me complaining, do you?" No one brought up the fact that he had spent most of the last nine holes doing just that. No more was said about the matter, and the stakes were left at ten dollars. After the first two weeks, everyone's game settled down to a more equal footing, and the losses and wins were averaging thirty to forty dollars per week.

Don experienced a real rush the week that he won the ninety dollars. He had never won that much before! He didn't spend a great deal of time thinking consciously about his feelings, but he attributed the elation partly to the fact that he had won the money from Jeff Stevens. He mentally put Jeff down for his highly competitive nature, but Don was himself quite competitive.

On the drive home that day, he had almost decided to stop and buy something for Barbara with his new-found wealth. He slowed and almost turned into the shopping center north of his housing development when he abruptly changed his mind. A new thought intruded. In the last two weeks, he had won a hundred and ten dollars! If he put that money aside, and added his future wins to it, he could eventually afford to buy her something really nice. That thought really appealed to him. He would have the opportunity to be a hero, with somebody else's money!

As they advanced toward the green, Jeff walked with Charlie down the middle of the fairway, Lou headed toward the right, and Don walked toward the left rough. He had seen the ball disappear just behind a tall poplar tree at the edge of the groomed grass, and he headed toward it, mentally reviewing his most recent confrontation with Jeff Stevens. Don knew that the other man's blustering and sarcasm was only his way of dealing with his world (God, he was starting to sound like Charlie!) but he still found it irritating. He wasn't sure which irritated him more, the actions and words of Stevens, or the fact that he allowed those actions and words to get under his skin. Who the hell was he mad at, anyway? It was all very confusing, and he did his best to put it out of his mind as he stepped into the taller grass and started the search for his ball.

He finally found it nestled in a depression next to a small tree, and punched it out onto the fairway with an eight-iron. As he walked out to the ball, he saw that the other three men had made it to the green and were waiting for him. He shouted "Incoming!", and hit a very nice pitching wedge shot to within about four feet of the pin. As he approached the putting surface he saw that his partner had once again overshot the pin, and was laying just barely on the green, about twenty feet past the hole. Jeff was the first to putt, and no one said a word as he stroked the ball firmly, a little too firmly, and left himself about an eight-footer back the other way. He swore and walked directly to the ball, ignoring the fact that Charlie and Lou were both further away from the hole than he was, and therefore should have been allowed to putt before him. He went through the procedure of lining up the putt, and again brought the head of the putter back and forward.

"Whoa, ball! Goddamnit!" He quickly walked to the other side of the hole and hit the ball again, finally holing it. He retrieved his ball and walked off the green toward his bag, mumbling to himself. Both Charlie and Lou sank their putts, and Don was pleased with his, the ball hitting the back of the hole with a small click. As the three of them walked toward Stevens, Don couldn't resist twisting the knife.

"Nice long putt, slick! There's another ten bucks down the dumper!" He was essentially needling Jeff, but deep down in his gut he had a tiny cold feeling. The hundred and ten bucks that he had squirreled away for Barbara's present had been whittled down to eighty over the past three weeks, and today's game looked to deplete it even more. He knew it was silly to worry about the money. For Christ's sake, he made a hundred and fifty bucks an hour for dealing with other people's financial situations, why should he be worried about that stinking hundred and ten? If he wanted to buy his wife a present, he could just do it. He could write a check or use one of the several credit cards in his wallet. Hell, he usually carried over a hundred with him in cash, so what was the big deal?

He knew what the big deal was. If he could use the money won from the golf game to buy something, it was like free money! It wasn't using money that should rightfully be used for the mortgage payment or the car payments or the kid's orthodontist or the savings account. What had the old guy said in that movie about pool hustlers? "Money won is twice as good as money earned"? Something like that. Of course, he had been talking about real money, not these little weekly golf bets. Don's background in accounting and financial planning had pretty much turned him into a conservative. He knew that he could never make the kind of bets necessary to win real money. That was the stuff of movies and television.

Jeff had, uncharacteristically, ignored Don's last jibe. He just picked up his golf bag and walked toward the next tee. Once there, he busied himself with the ball washer until he apparently cooled down. Not much was said as the four of them drove toward the next green. They all stayed within the boundaries of the fairway this time, and as Don started down off the tee area, Jeff fell into step beside him.

"Sorry about that last hole, Don. I know I kinda tend to be an asshole, and some people don't appreciate it much. I get a little upset sometimes, and I don't play very well when that happens. I'll spot you the ten, if you want."

Don was startled by the change in the big man's attitude, and just looked over at him for a minute. "No! Nonsense! Keep your money. I'm sorry, too. I shouldn't have . . . I shouldn't have criticized your putting." He glanced over at Stevens again. "Although it was pretty shitty!" He laughed and danced out of the way as the other man took a good-natured swing at him, the tension broken between them. Don looked over and saw that they had pulled even with Charlie's ball, and that the little man was about to take his second shot. As they waited, Jeff spoke again.

"You got any money down tomorrow?"

"Huh?" The question had caught Don off guard, and he wasn't sure what the big man meant.

Seeing Don's confusion, Jeff said, "Football! Football! You got any bets down on the games tomorrow?"

"Oh," said Don. "No, I don't. I'm in a football pool in my office building, but I don't do any betting other than that."

"Football pools!" Jeff said it like it was something disgusting. "Nickels and dimes! Football pools are for secretaries and office boys! I had a secretary once that picked the teams in a pool by whether she would like to visit the cities they were from, and she beat the crap out of all of the so-called experts in the office! I'm not talking about guessing, I'm talking about betting football!"

"No, I'm afraid I'm a little too conservative for much more than the betting we do on the golf game every week. If you'll remember, we were playing for five dollars a hole before you joined us."

"Yeah, I know. I guess I've just graduated away from the nickel-dime bullshit. I used to play for the coins, when I was in high school. When I joined the Army, I discovered that if I was gonna play, I was gonna have to play with the big boys, and the big boys don't play for small change. I don't know how it is for everybody else, but once I started playing poker and craps and such for bigger money, I just couldn't go back. There just wasn't the . . . I don't really know how to describe it . . . there wasn't the same feeling, the same rush, even when I won. If I won a few bucks, it didn't mean anything after I had been where I had won a few hundred or a few thousand."

"A few thousand?" Don looked at Stevens in amazement. "Did you say a few thousand?"

"Yeah, a few times I've gotten lucky at the right times. Of course, I've lost a few times, too."

Don shook his head. "Yeah, I guess that would give you a rush! I've never even made or lost that much in the stock market! Of course, the stuff I'm in is pretty stable . . ."

"The stock market? And you say you don't gamble! What the hell do you think Wall Street is? It's the biggest damn casino in the world, that's what it is! They don't have whorehouse wall-paper or bimbos serving drinks, but it's still nothing more than legalized gambling!"

They were approaching Don's ball. He put the conversation on the back burner of his mind for a minute, and focused on the small dimpled ball at his feet. He was, he estimated, about a hundred forty yards out. Don chose a seven-iron and raised a respectable divot as the steel club head sliced down through the ball and into the turf in front of it. The loft on the club sent the ball high into the air toward the green. The shot was a little short, and the backspin bounced it back away from the near edge of the green. Don bent and replaced the divot, and then turned toward Jeff.

As he again looked at the other man over the top of his glasses, Jeff raised both of his hands to shoulder level, palms out. He grinned and shook his head, indicating that he had nothing to say. Don grinned back and the two of them walked on toward the green.

Two

"Okay, how much have you had withheld? Federal withholding?" Don was working with an income tax client, estimating the client's tax position as of the next April fifteenth. The taxpayer, an auto mechanic, was calling from his workplace in North Denver, and his voice was coming out of the speakerphone on Don's desk. Don made a few keystrokes and watched the screen on his desk change as the income tax program digested the new bit of information.

"How about itemized deductions? Mortgage interest and house taxes and new tools and such. Do you foresee any big changes in those? Okay, how about other income, other than the wages and interest we've already talked about? Do you still have the rental? Are you charging any more than last year? How much more?" His fingers danced over the keys of his desk calculator, and he read the answer in the green figures of the calculator's display unit and entered the figure in the computer. He watched for a few seconds, hit a key, then two more, and sat back in the big chair.

"Well, Al, it looks like you'll be all right. With the figures we're using, you're set for a refund of about nine hundred from federal and . . . ah . . ." He leaned forward and touched two more keys. "About four hundred fifty from state. You could probably add an exemption on your W-4 form, but I'd suggest that you leave it as it is, just in case we're off on any of our estimates."

"Okay, Don. Thanks for the information. Send me a bill."

"You can depend on it!"

"I figured that. Well, we'll see you in January. Or February."

"Or March. You forget, I've done your taxes for. . ." He leafed quickly through Al's file. ". . . five years. When have you ever been in here before late March?"

"Yeah, well . . . like I said, we'll see you in March," said Al, chuckling.

"We'll be looking forward to it. See you then, Al."

"Right. Bye." The electronic sound of Al hanging up came through the small speaker, followed by the buzzing of what passed for a dial tone. Don reached forward and hit the button to terminate his end of the connection. He closed the client file, swiveled in his chair, and tossed the file into the box sitting on the credenza behind his desk. He leaned back again, taking a moment to gaze out of his office window. He had been lucky enough or persistent enough, he had never really been sure which, to find an affordable office on the west side of the sixth floor of an office building on the western edge of the downtown business area. The location gave him an unobstructed view of the Rocky Mountains, the foothills of which began just a few miles west of downtown Denver.

On the days when the wind blew, clearing out the smog which tended to collect along the Platte River, the air of the mile-high city almost sparkled. On such a day, the colors of blue and purple of the various layers of hills leading back to the white peaks stood out beautifully. At night, and he spent a great many nights in the office between January first and April fifteenth, the lights of the suburbs that had been gradually pushed up and over the nearest of the foothills twinkled at him, as if to try and lure him away from his labors. To add insult, his building sat under one of the traffic patterns leading away from Denver International Airport. He was accustomed to the sight of the big birds blasting their way through the thin air towards Los Angeles, Hawaii, and God knew where else, while he sat there trying to keep his clients out of trouble with the Internal Revenue Service.

"Fly on, you bastards!" he had been known to yell at the lights of the planes as they defied several laws of physics in their attempts to clear the fourteen thousand foot granite monoliths just to the west. "Fly on! My turn will come!"

And come it did. As a reward to both himself, for working twelve to fourteen hours a day for three and a half months, and to his family, for essentially getting along without him for most of that time, he and Barbara had, for the last several years, planned a vacation. The vacation began April sixteenth, and lasted from ten days to two weeks, depending on the office staff and the work load. He was usually exhausted, and wasn't worth a damn for about two days, but then he would dive into the vacation with the same dedication he had demonstrated during the previous three and a half months.

He had once calculated that, given the extended hours of "tax season," as of April fifteenth of each year, he had worked the equivalent of over six months. "Therefore," he had concluded, "some sonofabitch owes me eleven weeks!" Under that theory, he tried whenever possible to take long weekends and a number of short vacations during the rest of the year. Since he made at least half of his annual income during the intensity of tax season, he felt no guilt at all in leaving the office early, or in occasionally sleeping in. He had an excellent staff, and they were perfectly capable of handling most of the day-to-day activities of the office.

Don was feeling pretty good about his world. He had a thriving accounting practice, a nice home, a beautiful wife, and two strapping sons. The boys were five and seven, and were just as loud and obnoxious as five- and seven-year-olds are supposed to be. He had a little money set aside in some super-conservative mutual funds, and he had set up a profit-sharing plan for the office a couple of years ago which was growing nicely. He was the trustee of the plan and had invested the money in government securities. He knew that some, like Jeff Stevens, considered him to be way too conservative for his own good. Don supposed that might be true to some extent, but he had seen too many of his clients over the years who had taken flyers on everything from penny stocks to gold mines. The success stories were few, and the failures had been many. He would sit on his mutual funds and his Ginny-Maes, thank you very much, and let the others take the chances.

As he sat back forward, there was a light knock on the office door.

"Come in, please!" he said expansively, the good mood extending out to embrace whomever might be begging entrance to his quarters. "Who calls at my portals?"

Becky Marino walked into the room, looking at Don with one eyebrow raised. She had been his secretary, head bookkeeper, and second in command for three years. She was, from Don's viewpoint, quite attractive. She had long black hair and large brown eyes. She favored white blouses, which set off her dusky complexion quite nicely. He had often thought that if he were not happily married, and if she were not happily married, and if she did not work for him, he might just make a move on her. But he was, she was, she did, and he had not.

"Have I mentioned that there is a certain segment of the population who considers you just a trifle strange?" She asked.

"And who might that be, my dear?" he asked, taking the bait.

She grinned and said, "Just the ones who know you!"

"You're a cruel woman, you Aztec wench! Show me what you have brought, and begone from my sight!"

"Well, I hate to interrupt you when you're so busy," she said, looking pointedly at his empty desk, "but the football pool form just came in on the fax." She tossed the sheet of paper on the desk and turned to leave. As she went out the door, she turned back and said, "If your testosterone levels are low or something and you need help with that, let me know. I'll be out here filing my nails." She smiled sweetly at him and shut the door.

"I could probably use some help," he said to the door. He had picked an average of seven out of the weekly twelve games correctly so far this season. Not too good a record. He had paid twenty dollars to enter the pool, and there was the chance to win sixty-five dollars each week if he were the one out of forty-seven participants who had the most correct picks.

He knew something about most of the teams, and could predict the probable winners of quite a few of the weekly matchups, just from their reputations. If, for instance, the New York Giants were playing the San Francisco Forty-Niners, he had no idea what the hell to do. He usually picked the close calls by something scientific, like tossing a coin, but he seemed to always wind up on the wrong end of those choices. He had won once in the previous three years, and that had been about it.

He studied the new form, his pen poised to make the picks. Phoenix at New England. Phoenix. Atlanta at New Orleans. New Orleans, definitely! Denver at Chicago. The Broncos should win; they were presently sitting on top of their division, but they were so damned scary. If they were playing in Denver, there would be no question. Well, almost none. The visiting teams tended to run out of gas, oxygen to be exact, when they played in Denver. The rarefied air took its toll, usually during the second half. Denver. Out of loyalty, if nothing else.

As he was perusing the form, a stray thought intruded. He recalled the conversation of the previous Saturday with Jeff Stevens. Jeff obviously knew something about betting on football. Don knew nothing about sports betting, and he had always wondered if, say, Nebraska was playing, say, Slippery Rock Teacher's College, why one couldn't just bet the farm on Nebraska and clean up. He was smart enough to know that it couldn't be that easy, and he had heard about something called the "point spread." That was about the extent of his knowledge. He reached for the phone, and then stopped. Did he really want to talk to Stevens? He didn't really like him, although he had shown an almost human side after their confrontation last week. Oh, what the hell could it hurt?

He picked up the receiver, remembered that he didn't know the number, and opened his bottom desk drawer to haul out the three-inch thick Denver phone directory. And that was only one of the three phone books which covered the metropolitan area. The city was getting too damned big!

After he had made his way electronically through the switchboard at Creative Software and Jeff Stevens' secretary, he finally heard the voice of the big man on the other end of the line.

"Donald, my boy! How are you?" God, he sounded like a salesman! Well, at least he hadn't said "slick."

"I'm good, Jeff. Thanks. Do you have a minute?"

"All the time in the world. What can I help you with?"

Don wasn't really sure how to phrase his question. Finally he said, "We were talking last Saturday about betting football. I was just thinking about it, and I realized that I really don't know much about it, and I would like to."

"Well, sure! I ought to know a little about it, the number of bookmakers I've supported over the years! What do you want to know?"

Rather than simply say "everything," Don decided for some reason not to carry it to quite that extent. He guessed that he didn't want to confess complete ignorance to Stevens. "Well, could you tell me how the point spread works?"

"How does a point spread work? Well, let me see if I can . . ." There was silence as Jeff gathered his thoughts. "Well, the books, the bookmakers look at a game, let's say a football game. They know all of the teams inside out, their strengths, their weaknesses, who's hurt, all that. They compare the stats of the two teams, they look at their performance on grass, on artificial turf, how they play at home and on the road. Say Denver is playing the Vikings, and they're playing in Denver. We've got a grass field here, and Minnesota plays better on artificial turf, so that's against them. The Broncos always play better at home, but the Vikings are a helluva lot more consistent than Denver ever thought about being. If everybody's healthy, all of the big guns, they might decide that Denver ought to win by six points. So, they make Denver like minus six and a half. That means that you take the final score for Denver and subtract the points from it, and see if they would still have won. Does that make sense to you?"

" I . . . I think so."

"Meaning no. Okay, let me put it another way. If you take Denver and 'give' six and a half points, then they have to win by at least seven for you to win your bet. If the final score is twenty-one to fourteen, Denver, you win. If the score is twenty-one to fifteen or sixteen or anything more, you lose."

Don was beginning to see. "Yeah, okay. That makes sense. And if you bet on the Vikings?"

"If you bet on the Vikings and 'take' the points, then you win if the Vikings win or if Denver wins by less than seven points."

"Right. So it doesn't really matter who wins the game?"

"Only to them and to the suckers that screw around with football pools! Oh, sorry! I forgot that you're into that kind of bullshit."

Don knew that the other man was just kidding him, but his sense of pride made him say, "Well, that's why I'm trying to learn at the feet of the master, so I can mend my ways."

"Well, it's probably about time. Oh, and you can bet the over and under, too, but that's mostly a Vegas-type bet."

Don was out of his element again. "The what?"

"The over and under. You can bet that the total score of the game, both teams, will be either over or under a certain amount, like thirty-two and a half, for instance."

"Why all the half-points?"

"To eliminate ties with the bookmaker. You either win or lose. There are all kinds of bets you can make. Christ, you ought to see Vegas before the Superbowl! On that game, you can bet on the number of quarterback sacks, the first team to score, the scores by quarters, the first team to fumble, any Goddamned thing you can think of. Last year I played a thirteen-way parlay card that I paid twenty bucks for, and if all thirteen of the bets would have come in, I would have won like sixteen thousand dollars! I was just fucking around, something to make the game more interesting, and I think I lost out in the first quarter, but what the hell. It makes a good story!"

"All right, I give up. What's a parlay card?"

"All the sports books in Vegas have them. You pick teams and overs and unders, but you can pick up to twenty-four bets. If you pick two bets, bet five bucks and win both of them, they give you . . . I forget, it's like ten bucks. If you pick twenty-four and hit all of them, they give you the fucking casino!"

"Not a real good bet?"

"You got it! It's a real sucker bet, but it appeals to the masses, and the casinos make a ton of money on it."

"Well, how do you make the bets? Do you call Las Vegas, or what?"

"If you do, they'll hang up on you. It's against the law to place sports bets outside of Nevada. They'll throw your ass in the joint just for trying."

"But how about horse races? Isn't betting on horse races or greyhound races legal in Colorado?"

"Yeah, you can bet on the horses and the dogs in Colorado. But the law's entirely different for betting football or basketball, or whatever. You've got to know a guy."

"Know a guy?" Don repeated.

"Yeah. If you know the right people, you can get a bet down on just about any damned thing you want to. If you're really interested, I can put you on to a couple of people who can help you."

Don had visions of dark, faceless figures in alleyways, carrying briefcases stuffed with small, unmarked bills. "But if it's illegal . . ."

"Well shit, driving too fast is illegal! There's a lot of things that are illegal, but that doesn't stop people from doing them, and it never will! People love to gamble! Why do you think they opened those casinos in Central City and Blackhawk and Cripple Creek? Because they know that there are people all over the eastern slope of Colorado, plus about a bazillion tourists, who love to gamble! There are riverboats on the Mississippi River, filled with people who never see the water, because they're down in the bowels of the damned thing gambling! They call baseball the national pastime. Bullshit! Betting on baseball, maybe."

Don was still hesitant. "Well, I think I need to learn a little more about the teams and such before I actually make any bets . . ."

"Hell, get your feet wet, man! I'm going to be calling in some of my bets tomorrow. Why don't I put down a little something for you? You can pay me back Saturday when I see you."

"I don't know, Jeff, I don't have that much money that I can risk losing."

"Now that is exactly the wrong attitude! Don't even think about losing! Just tell me how much you want to win, and that's what I'll bet for you."

Don did some quick mental calculations. After Saturday's golf match, he had sixty dollars in winnings left. Would Jeff think that a twenty dollar bet was too little? He kept telling himself that he didn't care what Jeff Stevens thought about him, but he didn't want to appear to be . . . appear to be what? A sucker? Cheap? He wasn't sure what made him say it, but the next words out of his mouth were, "I've got sixty bucks that isn't doing anything! What would you recommend I bet it on?"

Sixty dollars! Was he out of his Goddamned mind? If he lost the sixty, he would be back where he started. Of course, it wasn't really his money. It was money that he had won from other people; it was free money. And what if he won? The vision of a small pile of twenties pushed to the front of his mind. Jeff was saying something.

". . . got the Raiders at minus two and a half, and I think it's one hell of a bet. They've been kickin' ass all over the league, and I think they'll cover easy."

"Okay, whatever you think, Jeff. So I'll be betting that the Raiders will win by at least three points, correct?"

The laughter coming through the phone didn't sound sarcastic. It sounded almost friendly. "You're a good student, slick. As the man says, there ain't no free lunch, but that's sure as hell the way I'm gonna bet."

Don thanked him and hung up the receiver. He turned again and looked out the window, but he really didn't focus on anything. He was wired! He felt a mixture of excitement and apprehension about the bet he had just arranged. If he lost, if the Raiders didn't . . . cover the point spread, that would be a downer. He'd be back to even. But if he won . . . God, if he won . . . !

Today was Thursday. Three more days until Sunday, game day for the National Football League. He usually watched the Bronco games simply because it was a sort of unwritten law in Denver that you had to do so. Any man seen in a grocery store during a Bronco game was looked upon with some degree of suspicion.

It suddenly occurred to him that he hadn't the foggiest notion who the Raiders were playing Sunday. He glanced at the football pool form, then reached into his wastebasket, retrieved the daily newspaper, and turned to the sports section. Another thought hit him. What if they were playing on Monday night? That would mean another entire day of waiting. As he scanned the newsprint, he saw that the Raiders were playing at eleven o'clock Denver time on Sunday, thank God, and that they would be up against the Buffalo Bills. He knew that the Raiders were presently in second place in the American League West Division, just behind Denver, and that was about all he knew. When Becky stuck her head in the door at five-fifteen to say goodnight, he still had the sports pages spread out over his desk, studying the statistics on the various teams.

* * * *

Saturday morning dawned very gray and got a lot grayer as sheets of rain swept down out of the mountains and drenched most of Denver and its suburbs. The phone rang at seven-thirty as Don was having his second cup of coffee and glaring out gloomily at the downpour. "Don? Lou. I guess we better hang it up for today, huh?"

"Yeah, I guess. It doesn't look to get much better, at least for a while. Have you called the other guys?"

"No, I haven't yet. Do you want to call Charlie?"

"Sure . . . no!" The sixty dollars jumped into his thoughts. "Why don't you call Charlie, and I'll call Jeff. I've got something I need to talk to him about."

"Well, sure, Don." Lou wondered what Don would have to talk about with Jeff Stevens, but he didn't want to ask. "'I guess I'll see you next week, okay?"

"Right, Lou. I think it's my turn to call for tee times, so I'll be talking to you sometime Friday."

"Gotcha! Have a good week."

"You too." He kept the phone cradled to his ear and hit the button to cut the connection. He dialed Jeff's number and waited while the phone rang four times. He was beginning to wonder if Stevens was home when what sounded like a young female voice answered.

"Stevens residence, this is Stacy speaking."

"Hi, Stacy. This is Don Curtis. Is your dad home?"

"My dad lives in Atlanta." The young voice was very formal. "Do you wish to speak to Jeff, my stepfather?"

" Ah... yes. I'm sorry, I didn't mean . . ." He heard the muffled sound of a hand being placed over the mouthpiece of the phone, and the voice hollering for Jeff.

"Hello?"

"Jeff?"

"Yeah. Is this Don?"

"Yes, it is. That's quite an answering service you've got there."

"Yeah, she's a peach. I'm fully convinced now that the shit music she listens to is effecting her hearing. I walked all the way in here from the garage wondering who the fuck Tom Curtis is. Anyway, what's up? I assume that the golf game is history."

"Afraid so. A little wet for my taste."

"Ah, well, it's probably a good thing as far as I'm concerned. I got a serious game tonight and these people like to stay up until all hours. Got to save my strength."

"What kind of a game? Poker?"

"Yeah. You a poker player?"

"Oh, I used to play a little in college, but that's about it. I haven't played in years."

"Well," Jeff said, "If you want to get into a game sometime, just let me know. I've got three different groups that I play with periodically. We're always looking for players. People have so damn many commitments!"

Don felt a small something stir way down in the back of his mind. It would be fun to play poker again! He had had his share of luck in college, but they were playing for pretty small change in those days. "Well, if you have an opening sometime, yeah, I'd like to play."

"Great! I'll let you know. Although, if you haven't played in years I wouldn't recommend starting with the bunch I'm playing with tonight. These guys are sharks! They've got fins . . . gill slits!"

Don laughed. "Sounds like a real pleasant bunch!"

"Oh, they are. I said 'guys', but two of them are women. One of those is the sweetest little grandmother you ever saw. All crinoline and soft wrinkles, but don't ever get in her way when she's got the cards! She'll run right over your ass, and while you're wiping the dust out of your eyes, she'll be stacking your chips in front of her. Vicious old broad!"

"You're kidding! Is she really a grandmother?"

"You bet your butt she is! She's got the pictures to prove it."

"I'd like to meet her sometime. She sounds delightful!"

Jeff snorted. "That's the trouble! She's so damned delightful, you just can't believe how good she really is. Last week when she caught the fourth three to beat my full house, I would have strangled her, but she's just so Goddamned cute!"

"You play every week?"

"Most weeks, two or three times. There's a three dollar game that usually runs Wednesday night, a ten dollar one on Fridays, and the one tonight varies from twenty dollar limit to pot limit."

"Pot limit?"

"Yeah. You know what pot limit is, don't you?"

"Well,....no."

"It just means that you can bet up to the size of the pot anytime during the game."

"Jesus! That sounds expensive!"

Jeff laughed. "It can be, but if you play it like you should, it can be damned profitable, too. Most of tonight's group are basically insane, so it's not unusual to see pots of several hundred dollars. I've kept track, and I'm way ahead over the couple of years I've played with them."

Don was amazed at Jeff's level of involvement in gambling. Amazed and, strangely enough, just a bit envious. He supposed that it was the romantic image of the gambler, the Wyatt Earp or the Doc Holliday, that appealed to him. It would have to be exciting to risk the kinds of money that the big man had been talking about.

"Oh, before I forget it, Jeff, I owe you sixty bucks for the bet you made. How about if I run it over to you later today?"

"Don't worry about it! You can pay me next Saturday, or better yet, I'll just take it out of your winnings."

"That sounds good! Okay, if you're sure."

"Sure I'm sure! It should be a good bet. Listen, I gotta run."

"Okay, Jeff. See you next week."

"You got it, sport. Take care."

"You too. Bye." Well, at least he had graduated to "sport."

Three

He knew it was silly, but he felt like a kid with a new toy as he waited impatiently for eleven o'clock to arrive. He had never before in his life wagered anything like the sixty dollars that was riding on the Raiders-Bills game. He found himself planning the watching of the game down to the last detail. The boys would probably want to watch at least part of it with him, but their attention spans were those of puppies. They could sit through most of a Broncos game by now, but again, that was the law.

He would have some difficulty explaining to them and to Barbara just why he was so interested in a game that did not involve Denver, but then they probably wouldn't care anyway. He was well stocked with non-alcoholic beer (the real stuff gave him a headache), and he was presently watching the bag of popcorn expand in the microwave like some sort of demented sea creature. Lunch was sort of a hit-or-miss affair around the Curtis household on Sundays, so that wouldn't interrupt the game.

"Hi, honey!" Barbara came in from living room in search of another cup of coffee. "Whatcha doin'?"

"Hi, baby. I'm just getting ready to watch a game. Comes on in about fifteen minutes."

"I thought the Broncos were on this afternoon."

"They are. This is the Raiders. And Buffalo. I thought it would be fun to watch." God, that sounded lame! But he didn't want to tell her about the bet until after he won, if in fact he did win. To tell her would spoil the surprise. And on the other hand, if he lost the sixty, there wouldn't be any surprise anyway, so it would be best to keep it to himself for right now.

"The Raiders and Denver are fighting for the conference lead, so I was interested to see how good they really look."

It was working! Her eyes were getting the glazed look which meant that she neither knew nor cared what he was talking about. She reserved that look for conversations about sports, fishing, or anything automotive. She was still nodding and smiling and making the appropriate noises, but the reasoning part of her mind was nowhere to be found. When she noticed that he had finished speaking, the eyes cleared immediately and she said, "Well, you have fun. I'm going to go get the grocery shopping done, and run over to Annie Brewster's for a little bit. Will you keep an eye on the monsters?"

"Sure! I'll try to keep them from destroying too much of the neighborhood before you get back. Are they Nintendo-ing?"

"They are. Fastest fingers west of the Mississippi! Well, I'm going to read some more of the paper, and then take off."

"Okay." The microwave dinged at him, and he took the bloated bag out and emptied it into a plastic bowl. He grabbed a beer, picked up the popcorn and a couple of napkins and headed for the den and the game. It was five till when he got his provisions placed properly, so he went in to check on the boys. They were sprawled in front of the big set in the living room, bombarding each other with electronic sights and sounds. He spoke to them, got no answer whatsoever, and turned back toward the den. He sat in the recliner, twisted the cap off the beer, and leaned back.

During the first quarter, the Raiders controlled the ball for the great majority of the time, coming out with a seven point lead. The teams had traded field goals early in the period, and the go-ahead touchdown came with about a minute and a half left, when the quarterback hit a little speedster by the name of Darnell Lacey right in the hands with a bomb down the left sidelines. Lacey was in full gallop when the ball arrived, and he high-stepped into the end zone. The resulting screech from Don brought both of the boys to the den door.

"Whatcha watchin', Dad?" It was David, the seven-year-old who spoke. He looked at the television screen. "That's not the Broncos. Is it?"

"No, it's not the Broncos. They're playing this afternoon."

"That's what I thought." Just then, the graphics on the screen told the world that the score was Raiders 10, Bills 3. "That's the Raiders and the Bills, isn't it?"

Don grinned. "Brilliant. Glad to see you can read. Want to watch some of the game with me?"

"You bet!" Ron, the youngest, didn't pass up too many chances to do something with his dad. He ran around to the other side of the chair, and clambered up onto the wide arm. As he leaned back against the chair, Don saw his hand dive into the popcorn bowl. David, too old for such silliness, chose to sit on the couch. They lasted almost until halftime. Not much happened in the second quarter, and the boys became bored with the defensive battle.

"Ronnie, you wanna see if you can beat me at Tunnel of the Trolls?"

"You bet!" Ron was down off the chair and out the door, followed closely by his brother. Don watched them go, and then looked at the popcorn bowl. Oh, well, he would make some more at halftime. The half ended with the same score, and he rounded the kids up and they made PBJs for lunch. There was a minor threat of mutiny when he informed them that they were to eat the extremely messy creations in the kitchen, but that was averted, and they all washed their sticky hands and stuffed the remains of the meal into the dishwasher.

He got back to the chair just as the second half started. The Bills ran the kickoff back to the Raider twenty, and went in two plays later on a swing pass. Two of the Raiders went the wrong way on the play, and that was just enough to open a hole in the defensive secondary through which someone could have driven a personnel carrier. Don felt a small discomfort as he saw the lead vanish. The defenses took over the game again, and things stayed the same into the middle of the fourth quarter.

Don wasn't sure when it happened, but he found himself sitting up in the chair, leaning toward the screen as if to somehow help the Raider offense get at least within field goal range. He was staring intently at the set, and his heart was beating a little more quickly than he would have liked. There were five minutes left, then four, then three. Finally, on second down, the Raiders quarterback again threw to Lacey, this time over the middle. The play was designed to gain the fifteen or so yards needed to put their kicker within easy range of the goal posts, but something went wrong. Lacey caught the ball, threw a magnificent head fake on a Bills middle linebacker easily twice his size, and danced around the defender to find himself trapped. The secondary was descending on him like a fleet of buses! Instead of taking the few yards gained, he spun and ran back almost to the line of scrimmage. His coach screamed at him. His teammates screamed at him. Don screamed at him, again bringing the boys on the run.

Ignoring all of them, Lacey turned and headed for the right sideline, with half of the Bills team in hot pursuit. As his own teammates threw themselves into the fray, he again reversed his field, dodging around and in back of the Raiders, who were now on the heels of the Bills. With his own team now between himself and the opposition, Lacey turned it on and ran a long curving pattern back across the field, almost to the left sideline, and into the end zone. When he crossed the goal line, there wasn't an opposing player within fifteen yards of him.

Don came out of the chair, his right fist punching upwards. "All fucking RIGHT!" he yelled. Too late, he remembered and turned to see the two young faces, shock and delight fighting for supremacy.

"Did the right guys win, Dad?" Ronnie was dancing around him, caught up in Don's excitement. David just stood and grinned at the two of them.

"Not quite yet, Ron, but there's only . . ." He glanced at the screen. "A little over a minute left, and the good guys are leading."

'By enough!' He added to himself.

The three of them sat down and watched the Bills try to mount some sort of comeback, but there was just not enough time left. As the game ended, the Raiders had Lacey in the air, tossing him around like a rag doll. The grin on the face of the little receiver went halfway around his head.

He had won! He couldn't believe it! God, that had been fun! He couldn't remember the last football game he had enjoyed as much. And he had made money doing it! He found himself wishing that he had a little something on the Bronco game that was just beginning. Oh, well, it should be a good game. The boys decided to watch at least the first part of the game with him. They were still excited by their father's outburst. Maybe it would happen again!

The phone rang just as the Broncos kicked off. The boys raced for it and wrestled briefly with the receiver. David won, and spoke into it. "Hello? Yeah. Just a minute." He handed the phone to Don, his attention back on the television.

"Hello? This is Don."

"Can that little sonofabitch Lacey run, or what?" The voice was that of Jeff Stevens.

"Hi, Jeff. Yeah, he sure as . . . heck can! We'll be seeing that one on the sports news for a couple of nights."

"You got that right. Well, do you feel richer?"

Don felt himself grinning at the phone. "I do indeed! How about you? You said that you were going to bet the same way, didn't you?"

"Absolutely! I said I thought it was a good bet. I won on the Patriots game too, but the Cowboys let me down. Bastards! They should have been able to cover six points against Detroit, but they kept fumbling the damned ball!"

"You had bets on three games?" Don asked. He felt a sort of warm tremor of excitement, a vicarious thrill at the gambling activities of the other man.

"Yeah, I'm ahead about five hundred for the day, but who the hell knows what will happen this afternoon. If Tampa Bay plays like they did last week and Denver can cover the spread, I'll be in fat city."

The sixty dollars that he had wagered on the earlier game suddenly seemed like an afterthought. He was amazed at the amounts of money about which Jeff was talking. "If you don't mind my asking, Jeff, how much money do you usually bet on the games?" He knew that the question wasn't proper, that it was none of his damned business, but he was fascinated.

There was silence on the line for a minute, and Don was about to take back the question and apologize when Jeff spoke. "No, I don't mind you asking. But you deal with the IRS, you know that I can't be too free with that kind of information. Between the college games on Saturday and the pros on Sunday and Monday night, I've probably got twenty-five hundred to three thousand in action on a given weekend."

"Holy . . ." Don glanced down at the two faces which immediately turned toward his, expecting another expletive. "Holy cow, Jeff! That's amazing! No wonder you wanted to bump the golf bet!"

"Yeah, well, I guess I was kind of an asshole about that. But if I'm going to bet on something, I like to bet enough to make a difference. Otherwise, it's kind of a waste of time."

"Nickels and dimes, right?"

"You got it. Nickels and dimes. I'm not bragging, but in a good year I'll pull down a hundred and twenty grand, with commissions and bonuses and all. I'm sure as shit not going to bet a dollar or two on anything. Why bother?"

Just then, the Denver quarterback disappeared under a mound of opposing uniforms. Don pulled the phone away from his ear slightly as Jeff exploded. "Jesus H. Christ! Where the fuck was the offensive line? You guys ever heard of blocking?" The boys looked up again, but all they heard were angry sounds from the phone.

"Idiots!" Jeff was still yelling at his television screen.

"What's the spread on the Denver game?" Don was pleased with himself, as if he had learned a few words of a foreign language, and had just used them in conversation.

"Denver is plus five and a half. Ordinarily that would be about right, but Reynolds is out because of that hamstring pull last week, and Chicago is hurting for receivers. Well, listen. I'll let you get back to the game. I'll see you Saturday, unless you need your money before that."

"No, no problem. Oh, wait a minute. Would . . . is it too late to make a bet on the Monday night game?" The excitement he felt during the Raiders game had felt good. Too good to pass up another chance.

"Well, yeah, it would be too late. Sorry." Jeff paused for a second, and then said, "But I've got three hundred on the Rams at minus four and a half. I could let you have a piece of that, if you want."

"Well, if you wouldn't mind . . ."

"Not at all! How much do you want?"

Don hesitated. He suddenly felt reluctant to risk any of his winnings, but he had pretty much committed himself. "I don't know. How good do you feel about the bet?"

"Well," Jeff said, "I don't think it's as good as the Raiders game was, but they ought to cover. If you don't feel good about it, don't bet it."

There it was. Stevens had given him an out, an excuse not to bet any of the money, if he didn't want to. His mind raced through a series of images. The excitement during the earlier game. The anticipated looks on the faces of Barbara and the boys as he presented them with surprises purchased with someone else's money. Himself sitting in his recliner on Monday night, watching something other than the football game, because the game meant next to nothing to him. Himself sitting in his recliner on Monday night, again experiencing the high that he had felt earlier. The possibility of reliving the heady experience of winning finally prevailed. After all, it was not like he was playing with money out of the food budget. He had won it, and it was his to do with as he wished! "How about seventy-five? Would that be okay?"

"Sure! Listen, if you want to bet on anything next weekend, you need to let me know by about Wednesday. That is, if you want me to take care of it for you. I could just give you the number of my bookie, but he gets a little nervous if too many people know about his activities."

"I appreciate it, Jeff. But I doubt very much if I'll be doing this on any sort of a regular basis."

"Whatever. Like I say, just let me know."

"I will. Thanks a lot."

"No problem. Talk to you later."

"Right. Bye." As he hung up the phone, Don was experiencing very mixed feelings. He was way ahead, but he had just agreed to risk about two-thirds of his winnings. Oh, well. If he lost the Monday night bet, he would still be ahead. And if he won again? God! If he won, he would be up close to two hundred dollars! That would mean dinner at The Renaissance for he and Barbara, with enough left over to buy some kind of electronic gizmo for the boys! He visualized his wife's delight at the chance to dine at her favorite restaurant. The Renaissance was very, very good, and they knew it. It was one of Denver's elite dining experiences, as they put it, and the prices reflected that attitude. Don and Barbara had celebrated a few special occasions there during their marriage, and he knew that she would relish the chance to go there again.

The sound of a horn in the driveway signaled him that Barbara had returned, and that she wanted help with the groceries. He decided not to disturb the boys, and walked through the kitchen to the side door. She asked him how the game had come out, and he told her that the Raiders had indeed looked impressive. They didn't talk football long enough for her eyes to glaze over completely, and they spent the next several moments chatting about nothing in particular as he helped her put the groceries away.

The Bronco game ended with Denver losing to the Bears by a field goal. Jeff had bet on the Broncos, so that was going to cut into his . . . wait! No! He had said that he had bet on Denver at plus five and a half, so adding five and a half to their score would mean that he had in fact won! Don found himself again wishing that he had bet on the Denver game. The boys had wandered off after the first half, and he had sat and watched the remainder of the game in a state of boredom, with none of the gusto, none of the enthusiasm which he had felt earlier.

Barbara had joined him in the den and was again reading the Sunday paper when Ronnie's voice sounded from the living room. "All fucking RIGHT!"

The outburst was followed by the sounds of his older brother shushing him and the crinkling of Barbara's paper as she lowered it to glare at her husband.

Four

"Your deal, Don." The cards were shoved toward him in an untidy pile. He picked them up, stood the stack on edge, and quickly straightened out the deck.

He shuffled five times, the edges of the cards snapping together, and then dropped the deck in front of the player at his right to be cut. As the top two-thirds of the cards were lifted from the deck and placed on the table toward him, he tossed two white poker chips into the bare middle of the table.

"Seven card high-low, eight or better." He put the thin part of the deck on top of the other cards, and started dealing. As he did, there were the usual random comments from the other players.

"Good game!"

"Did he say eight or better?"

"Gimme something I can play with, for Christ's sake!"

It was Wednesday night, and this was the third week that he had played with the three dollar limit group. Jeff Stevens had again mentioned the fact that they were always looking for "new blood," as he had put it, and Don had indicated a desire for an invitation. The group played at the homes of the various players, rotating in no particular order so that the regular players would each host the game about every eight weeks or so.

Don had not as yet played host to the group, but he was planning to do so the following week. He was a little concerned with Barbara's potential reaction, as three of the regulars were heavy smokers, and one of them favored cigars. He had quit smoking cigarettes five years previously, and Barbara had never smoked, so she was sure to be less than enthusiastic about the smell. Maybe he could rig up a fan in the window of the kitchen or something. Only one of the group owned a real honest-to-God poker table, with chip trays and drink holders and all, so they usually wound up playing on someone's kitchen table.

They played dealer's choice poker, with the deal rotating around the table to the left. The dealer was the only one of the players to ante each time, to avoid the built-in delays which would be caused by making everyone ante at each deal. The dealer would then choose the game to be played, and announce it to the table. This group played almost exclusively split games, where the highest hand and the lowest hand divided the pot.

They played that a straight, five cards in numerical sequence, or a flush, five cards of the same suit, did not eliminate a hand from contention for low. If the dealer called "eight or better," that meant that in order to qualify as a low hand, the player would have to hold five low cards, the largest denomination of which had to be an eight or lower. A wheel, or ace, two, three, four, and five was the best possible low hand. Since it was also a straight, it could conceivably win high also.

The group reasoned, rightly enough, that the high-low split games tended to keep more players in and build bigger pots, since each player had two chances to win at least half the money bet. The group had agreed to a maximum of three raises on each betting round, so that it could possibly cost twelve dollars to see the next card, but this rarely happened in practice.

The game Don had called and was now dealing started with each player receiving two cards face down and one face up. There was then a round of betting, with the highest card showing initiating the betting. Each player then had the opportunity, in turn, to fold, call, or raise. If a player didn't like the cards he had been dealt, he would fold by turning his "up" card over, and tossing his cards toward the middle of the table. If he chose to remain in the hand, he would either call, by matching the bet, or raise a maximum of three dollars by meeting the original bet and putting the additional money into the pot. After the first betting round, the dealer would then deal a fourth card face up, and the betting process would be repeated. This happened three more times, each of the remaining players receiving two more up cards, and then a last card face down.

After the last betting round, the players would turn all of their cards face up, and the highest hand would share the pot with the lowest one. Many times, there would only be two players at the end of the game, and unless one of them had the necessary cards to "scoop" the pot, or take the entire thing, they would then split the chips in the middle of the table. After each hand was completed, there was usually another round of comments, rehashing the hand and playing "what if?"

"If I'd stayed in, I'd have caught the flush."

"You didn't want the flush. The queen that he caught on the last card gives me the full house."

"I caught two, three, five, six on the first four cards! Chased that sonofabitch clear to the end, and do you think I could find another low card?"

"Well, I had two of your aces, but I could never improve. Whose deal?"

"Jeff's deal. What kind of garbage are you gonna deal, Jeff?"

The first week that Don played with the group, he had been quite hesitant. After being assured by Jeff Stevens that "kitchen-table" poker was actually legal in Colorado, as long as the players knew each other and the "house" didn't profit from hosting the game in any way, he had dug out his old copy of *Poker For Fun and Profit*. He had purchased the book at a garage sale some years previously, and had no more than leafed through it prior to now. He spent some time studying the types of games, rememorized the chart of hand values, and also committed to memory the author's three cardinal rules:

"If your first cards don't fit together in some way, fold!"

"If your opponents draw cards that obviously beat you, fold!"

"If you've got the winning hand at a given point, make them pay to draw out on you! Don't try to be cute and build the pot up by betting less than the maximum. You do, and somebody will stay in and beat you on the last card!"

Don had ridden to the game with Jeff that first week. He had two hundred dollars hidden in a compartment of his wallet. The rest of his "stash," as he now thought of it, was in an envelope in the back of the locked middle drawer of his desk.

The envelope now contained some five hundred and eight dollars. He had won the bet on the Monday night game when the Los Angeles Rams ran all over the Philadelphia Eagles, and had spent some time on the phone the next day with Stevens, discussing the games of the following weekend. He had wound up betting two college games and three pro contests, and had come out of the second weekend with an overall profit of two hundred and twenty-five dollars.

They had been able to play golf that next Saturday, and the two of them had pretty well dominated the conversation with things football. He and Charlie had been again teamed against Lou and Jeff, and had lost thirty dollars each. He jumped at the chance to recoup part of his losses when Jeff challenged him to a game of gin rummy after the golf game. He had played a great deal of gin in his college years, and managed to relieve the other man of eighteen dollars before they broke it up and Don headed home to watch the remainder of the second college game on which he had a bet. He had lost the first one, and needed Syracuse to come through for him. At least that would break him even for the day.

He had bet on at least two or three of the weekend games each week since his baptism with the Raiders game. He spent more and more time in front of the television set, reliving the feelings of triumph when his teams won or lost by the proper margins to insure him a winner. When he chose the wrong side in a contest and lost, either on his own or with the help of Jeff, he would feel dejected, almost betrayed, but these feelings never lasted very long. He was winning more than he lost, and those wins buoyed his confidence that the next contest would go his way.

The purchase of the "surprises" for Barbara and the boys had been put off several times. He reasoned that the money in his stash was necessary to make the bets. If he went ahead and spent the money on presents and such, there would not be enough of a cushion if he had a string of losses. Once he had built his bankroll up a bit more, there would be plenty of money for presents without endangering his ability to continue the wagering that was giving him so much pleasure.

The first Wednesday night with this group had been interesting, to say the least. He and Jeff had been the last to arrive at the ranch-style home in south Denver. The neighborhood appeared nice enough, sort of a middle-class Americana kind of area, but was obviously a couple of steps below Cherry Park in status and price range. There had been several cars parked either on the street or in the driveway leading to the single car garage. They ranged in age from what appeared to be a brand new Pontiac to an elderly Ford, about an eighty-four. As Jeff pulled up behind the Ford to park, he warned Don, "Watch out for a guy in a Hawaiian shirt and a baseball cap. He drives the Ford." He gestured out through the windshield of his car. "Good player, super aggressive. If you get in a pot with him, make sure you've got the cards!"

The other five players had already started playing. The dealer looked up briefly as they entered, said hello to Jeff, and smiled at Don. "Be right with you, guys. Grab a seat!" They sat down, taking chairs which were separated by a small man in a baseball cap advertising the Colorado Rockies, and the ugliest shirt Don had ever seen. The background color was kind of a mustard yellow, and it was covered with an array of palm trees in various attitudes and various shades of purple and lavender. Don caught Jeff's eye, glanced briefly at the man between them, and frowned. Jeff nodded.

The hand had finished and two of the players were dividing up the chips when the man who had been dealing rose and stuck his hand out toward Don. "Hi. I'm Paul Hammond." He indicated the woman sitting two places to his left. "This is my wife, Ginny. This is our abode in which we are playing this evening."

Don half stood and shook hands with Paul and then with Ginny. "I'm Don. Don Curtis." He almost added that he was an accountant, but didn't. He was used to being identified at business meetings and cocktail parties by his profession, but he had a feeling that these people really didn't care what he did for a living. "I appreciate your hospitality."

He was introduced to the other three at the table. The first was a middle-aged scholarly-looking man by the name of Brian Moulton, who was balding and who peered at Don over the tops of his half-glasses. Sitting next to him and on the immediate right of Don was another lady by the name of Shirley Campbell. She was attractive, with long, brown hair and brown eyes, and appeared to be in her middle thirties. She was intent on dividing the previous pot, and didn't look up at Don until she was finished. When she did, she flashed him a smile that somehow reminded him of toothpaste commercials.

The small man to his left was also preoccupied with his half of the pot, and finally looked over at the newcomer. Don felt for a few seconds that he was being examined. The man frowned at him for what felt like a long time, and then extended his hand. "I'm Tony."

Don waited for more, but that seemed to be it. He shook hands with the little man. "Don. Don Curtis. Nice to meet you, Tony." But the man's attention had turned to Paul, who was shuffling the cards.

Don did fairly well that first night, coming away losing only fifteen dollars. He had tried to adhere to the dictates of the book, folding hand after hand when he was dealt "rags," as the other players referred to bad cards. He had been a little tentative at first about betting the few good cards he saw, feeling a little strange about trying to take the money of these strangers. The bitching and crying that went on when one of the other players raised made him think that the people around the table were taking the actions personally. However, when he noticed that Brian, who had been doing most of the moaning, cheerfully reraised the bet the next time he caught five low cards in a row, he decided that the complaining was just a part of the game.

He found himself joining in with gusto. As the evening wore on, he caught himself "chasing," or staying in longer than he really should, in hopes of catching the right cards to give him at least half the pot. This seemed to be the norm for the group, which resulted in some impressive pots. Ginny and Tony had split one monster which must have contained over a hundred dollars. Ginny had caught a four on her sixth card, giving her a wheel, and Tony had started with three kings, made the full house on the fifth card, and had bet all the way. As luck would have it, Jeff had been betting a six-high straight, and Shirley and Don had both had flushes. The bitching approached record levels.

Don had not played the second week because Ronnie had been involved in a piano recital and he didn't want to miss it. He had briefly toyed with the idea of going to the game after the recital, but he dismissed the thought as soon as it had come into his head. As the week passed, however, he found himself looking forward to the Wednesday night game. It was an odd assortment of people, to be sure, but they all had a love of the game of poker in common. The conversation around the table centered on the game, and little else. As far as he could remember, the first night he had played with them there had been absolutely no mention of jobs, families, or children.

He and Jeff had spent the time between a few of the hands discussing sports and the bets which had been made for the upcoming weekend. That conversation brought up the slot machines and blackjack tables at Central City and Blackhawk, which led to a discussion of lotteries, which reminded someone of a story about a recent visit to Las Vegas. Gambling was all that these people seemed to talk about.

Don dealt the cards around the table, three per customer, and laid the remainder of the deck down in front of him. Ginny opened the betting for a dollar, Shirley called, Don called, and Tony raised it to four dollars. Amid comments of "There he goes again!" and "What's he so damned proud of?", the little man made a show of rechecking his two hole cards, and settled back to see what would happen. Jeff folded, as did Paul and Brian. Ginny called the raise, neatly rolling three one dollar chips into the middle of the table, where they lost momentum and fell into the pot. Shirley also called. Don looked at Tony's up card again. It had not changed. It was still the five of hearts. Ginny was showing the ace of diamonds, and Shirley had the queen of spades. Don had two queens down, and the jack of hearts as an up card. Against his better judgment, he called and picked up the deck.

On the second round, he dealt Tony another heart, a three, Ginny a seven of hearts, and Shirley a nine of spades. Don caught another jack. Two pair! Not bad for the first four cards. He was now high on the board, so he bet three dollars. Tony didn't hesitate at all as he pushed two stacks of three chips into the pot.

"Raise."

What the hell did he have? With the three and the five showing, it looked like a low hand, but he needed to catch another low card to qualify for the "eight or better." Tony didn't normally raise unless he had a sure thing, so did he have three fives? Ginny called the six dollars, and Shirley hesitated for a bit before she resignedly threw in two chips, a five and a one. Don briefly considered reraising, but the threat of the three fives stopped him. He just called.

"Okay, pot right?" He had picked up the habit of calling out the cards as they were dealt.

"Good low hand." He had dealt an ace of hearts to Tony.

"Possible straight flush wheel. Ten to the low hand, no help."

Ginny flinched as she saw the ten, a pretty good indication that she had been drawing to a low hand.

"Nines a pair." Shirley caught a second nine up, and peeked at her hole cards again. "And... a six to the jacks. Check to the low hand." He rapped his knuckles on the table in front of him and looked to his left. Tony, as expected, bet the three dollars. Ginny folded, and Shirley called, as did Don.

"Okay, an eight to the low, a king to the pair of nines, and another six." Wonderful! Three pair, and he could only play five cards! No help at all.

Don checked, Tony bet three, and Shirley gave up the chase and folded. Don called again, and dealt each of them their last card face down. He picked up all three of his hole cards, the last one on top, and held them up in front of him. He leaned away from Tony just a bit, to eliminate the possibility of the other man peeking at his cards, and slowly spread the cards out. When the last card finally appeared, it was the deuce of hearts. Well, at least the little man didn't have the straight flush. It would probably be a split pot, but just in case Tony had somehow missed his low hand, he bet the three. Tony raised! Oh, shit! He could only call, a sinking feeling beginning in his gut. The feeling was justified when Tony turned over his cards.

"I just got an eight for low, but I missed the full house and the flush." He had indeed missed the big hands, but he had three aces. Three aces which beat the hell out of any two of the pairs which Don held.

Well, that was stupid! Don knew that he should have put Tony on a high hand when he first started betting, but no! He had to hang on to his damned two pair till the end, hoping! He glanced down at the chips remaining in front of him. That had been expensive! He was down about fifty-five dollars for the evening, and he had just five chips left.

"Another stack, Jeff." He dug out his wallet and tossed the fourth twenty of the night toward their host. Jeff reached behind himself, turned back, and pushed a short stack of multi-colored chips across the table. Don added the five lonely chips to the new stack, and turned toward Tony. "You gonna deal, or you gonna play with your money?" The little man patiently finished arranging the chips from the last pot, turned toward Don, and favored him with one of the few smiles anyone had ever seen on his face.

"Same game!"

Five

Barbara walked into the bathroom as he was shaving. She carried two cups of black coffee and set one of them down on the counter next to Don's sink. She looked at Don in the mirror until he glanced toward her. "Mornin', sunshine!" He smiled at her and went back to scraping the lather off his chin.

"Morning yourself. What time did you get home last night? Your eyes look like you're about to bleed to death!"

He stopped for a second and peered at his reflection. The whites of his eyes were in fact laced with tiny red capillaries. The corners of his eyes looked red and sore. "I don't know, I guess about one or so, why?" He looked at her image in the mirror.

"Don, I looked at the clock at one twenty, and you weren't home then." Her voice was flat, unemotional. Just stating the facts.

He looked at her for a few more seconds, and then rinsed the razor under the faucet and went back to shaving. His voice was just a bit strained as he stretched his head up to tighten the skin of his neck. "I told you I didn't know. Maybe it was one thirty. Maybe it was a quarter till two. I really don't know."

He finished shaving, rinsed the remaining bits of lather off of his face and neck, and reached for the coffee. He took a sip of it, then another, and set the cup back down. Barbara was just leaning against the door frame, studying him. He finally turned to her. "What?"

"What do you mean, 'What?'"

"What are you staring at me for? Is there a problem? Are you pissed off because I got home late?"

She met his gaze for a few seconds, and then dropped her eyes. "No, I'm not pissed off. But it seems like you've been playing poker a lot lately. When you first mentioned playing on Wednesdays, I thought that it would be good for you to get out with the boys once in a while. You know, male bonding and all that crap. But you played two nights last week, and wound up sleeping most of Saturday morning."

"So? Is that a problem? I got the stuff done around here that you wanted, didn't I?"

"That's not the point. I've never known you to miss your weekly golf game unless you had a hundred and seven fever or it was snowing."

"Now that's not true! Besides, I just didn't feel up to playing golf last week."

Her eyes met his again. "Why not?"

"What the hell is this, an inquisition? I just didn't! Can't I decide for myself how I want to spend my Saturday mornings?"

She looked down at her coffee cup again and took a deep breath. "Of course you can. I didn't mean to imply that you couldn't. But I guess I just worry sometimes."

"Worry about what? My playing poker?"

"No, it's not the playing poker as such, but . . . I don't know, it's just a combination of things. I really don't mind your playing poker, but I hate to think of you being gone two nights every week. Plus, when you're here, you're not really here."

"What, pray tell, is that supposed to mean?" He had leaned back against the counter, and was standing with his arms crossed, looking at her.

"I don't know. You seem preoccupied. I've never seen you spend so much time in front of the television. What is this sudden fascination with football?"

"What do you mean? I've always watched football!"

"You've always watched the Bronco games, but you've told me yourself that you couldn't care less about college football. But if I want you on Saturday afternoons, that's where you'll be!"

He opened his mouth to reply, and suddenly realized that he hadn't the faintest idea what to say, so he closed it again. He turned and picked up the coffee cup. As he did, they heard the voice of David from downstairs.

"Mom, we got any grape jelly?"

Don reached for his wife's hand as she started to turn. She stopped and looked at him, her eyes sad. He held out his arms, and she stepped into his embrace, both of them careful not to spill their coffee. "I'm sorry, honey. I haven't meant to be preoccupied. I'll stay home this Friday, if you like."

She looked up at him. "Were you planning on playing Friday night?"

"Well, yeah, I was . . . " He saw that she was looking at him intently again. "But I'll cancel out. They can find somebody else."

"Well, if they are depending on you . . ." She left it open.

"No. No, that's okay. I'll call Al today, and tell him that I can't be there. Why don't you get a sitter, and we'll go see a movie or something?"

She stretched up on tiptoe and kissed him full on the mouth. "Thanks, sweetie! I might just do that." She turned and started toward the kitchen as David yelled again.

Don turned on the water in the bathtub and adjusted the temperature before he lifted the knob for the shower. He stepped out of his shorts and tossed then into the hamper. He was feeling good about the conversation with Barbara until he started remembering the game of the previous Friday night. That had been a game! He had thought that the Wednesday night group was made up of serious poker players, but the previous Friday night when Jeff had led him into the paneled den of Al Brainard, he thought for a minute that he had somehow stumbled upon a Hollywood sound stage, upon which was setting some director's idea of what a poker game should look like.

The table was oak, with plum-colored felt covering the playing surface. The eight positions around the big table were each favored with a chip tray, a drink holder, and an ash tray. The wood of the chairs matched the table, and they were upholstered in a shade of leather or vinyl which matched the felt. The piles of chips sitting in front of one of the three vacant chairs were in red, white, and blue, and each had a small "AB" etched in its center in gold.

As Al shook hands with Don and moved back around the table to sit behind the piles of chips, Don and Jeff took the two available seats. Don introduced himself around the table, trying not to smile at the thought which had immediately come to him. The other men, and they were all men, sitting around the table each looked like a caricature of a poker player. There was Al himself, a big man who was starting to go to fat, but who still had the shoulders and upper arms of the much younger Al staring down at them from the black and white photographs of his former life as a college football player. As they all traded a hundred dollars for one of the stacks in front of Al, Don studied the rest of the players. There was a small man by the name of Murray who sported the biggest cigar Don had ever seen. The damned thing looked like one of the kid's plastic bats. Looking back, however, he couldn't recall the man ever lighting it.

There was a lean, lanky cowboy-looking gentleman sitting on the immediate left of Al. He wore a western shirt, snap buttons and all, and a Stetson perched on the back of his head. As soon as he got his stack of chips, he took two stacks of six chips each and began shuffling them together with one hand. He would blend the chips into a stack of twelve, remove the top six and set them beside the other stack, and shuffle them together again. "Neat trick!" thought Don, vowing to practice it when he could do so unobserved.

There was a man in an expensive looking suit and shirt, who looked like he had never been outdoors. His hair was black and slicked back, accentuating his hawk-like nose and his high cheekbones. The only imperfection he had permitted in his appearance was the undoing of the top button on his shirt, and the slight loosening of his silk tie. He had long, very bony fingers, and it had felt like shaking hands with a skeleton.

The other two men could have been brothers. Had they not had the same first name, Don would have bet that they were. They were both big and looked Italian. Although they had both introduced themselves by the name of Vic, everyone else at the table referred to one of them as "Guido." Don decided that it must be a middle name or something.

The game had been ten dollar limit, so Don figured that the pots would be roughly three times the size of the ones at the three dollar limit Wednesday night game. He was mildly surprised, therefore, when the second hand of the evening produced a split pot which must have had four hundred dollars in it. He had dropped out early, to try and get a feel for the other players, but there were five people still throwing chips at the center of the table after the last card fell. Three of the players had been going for low hands, and two for high, and Guido and the cowboy had ended up with the pot. The other three players who had bet to the end each reached for more money. Don could clearly remember the buildup of excitement as he watched the proceedings. He remembered glancing over at Jeff, to see him grinning at Don's reaction. "What did I tell you?" he had said, and two of the other players looked up curiously at him for a second. But then the next hand was being dealt, and their attention went back to the cards.

Don had played what he felt was a good, solid game that night, and caught some good cards at the right times. When the game finally broke up at about three fifteen in the morning, Don cashed in five hundred and forty dollars worth of chips. He thought about getting up in about three and a half hours to play golf, and told Jeff on the way home that he didn't think he would make it. Jeff had called him a wimp, but Don really didn't care at that point. He had just won over four hundred dollars, he had close to eight hundred in his "stash," and he had four good bets going this weekend.

He felt like he had discovered a brand new life. If his luck continued, he would be able to build up to the point that he could make some serious bets, without seriously damaging the bankroll. He had been betting far more than he would have ever imagined he would, but he was still a piker compared to Jeff. Not that he wanted to pattern himself after the big man in any way. Stevens still got on his nerves at times, but the man did know his football betting!

Damn, he would like to play in that Friday night game again this week! Those guys were money trees, just waiting for him to

. . . but Barb did have a point. She deserved some of his time, too. She had been very supportive when he started playing on Wednesday nights several weeks ago. She hadn't even griped too much when the group played at his house, the smoke drifting up from the table to hang close to the ceiling before the fan caught it and blew it out the window. She had still worked the kitchen over pretty well with spray deodorizer the next morning. When he came down for breakfast, the kitchen smelled like someone had brutally killed a pine tree.

Maybe he could slip over to Al's after the movie and play a few hands. If, that is, Barb didn't get romantic. She did that sometimes after the two of them had spent a couple of hours holding hands in a theater. Some sort of togetherness thing, or something. Not that he objected! Not at all. Barb had accused him of having the hormone level of a high school junior on more than one occasion. He had undergone a vasectomy just before Ronnie was born, and the removal of the threat of another pregnancy had for a time given both of them the attitudes of rabbits. They slowed down some after the first couple of months, but sex was still a very regular part of their lives. "What a choice to have to make," he thought, "playing poker with a bunch of people with no regard whatsoever for money, or getting laid by someone who is very, very good at it."

That Friday evening, he and Barb did in fact go to a movie, one they had both been wanting to see. It was an action adventure set in the outback of Australia, and it had some wonderful scenes of the native animals. During one scene late in the movie, a love scene between the hero and the second female lead brought Barbara's hand over to rest on his inner thigh, some distance up from the knee. He could feel himself responding, and he looked over at her, but her eyes were riveted on the screen. He did indeed get laid that night, and by the time she was done with him, the thoughts of poker were pretty faint. They were still there, but they were pretty faint.

He played golf the next morning, and for the first time, the foursome broke exactly even. He and Lou had been up by two holes on the front nine, but they dropped back on the second half of the course when, for some unfathomable reason, Jeff actually started putting the ball properly. He sank a fifteen-footer on the sixteenth green, and a twelve-footer on the eighteenth. He was as surprised as the other three men.

Don was surprised and somewhat pleased that he didn't really mind not winning. He had enjoyed the extra spice added to the game by the bet, and that seemed to be enough. Of course, ten dollars per hole was a little tame compared to some of the sports bets and poker hands in which he had been involved lately. Perhaps that was the reason for the lack of disappointment. Whatever the reason, he was in excellent spirits as they headed home in Charlie's Honda. The red fuel light was blinking at them from Charlie's dash, so they pulled up to the gas pumps of a convenience store. As Charlie was filling the car, Don wandered inside in search of a little something for the boys.

He came up with a couple little plastic beasts from the planet something-or-other, and went to the counter to pay for them. There was a man ahead of him, and he heard him say, "Three quick picks, please." The clerk took the man's three one dollar bills, and punched something into the large computer terminal looking thing to her right. The thing made a ratcheting noise and spit forth a small slip of paper, which she handed to the man.

"Good luck!" She said at the man's back. There was no response.

"Hi! Can I help you?" God, she was cheerful! Well, that was all right. So was he.

"What's a 'quick pick'?"

"You don't know what a quick pick is?" She was incredulous. Still cheerful, but incredulous.

He glanced down at the grotesque little creatures in his hand. "No, I'm from the planet Zormoon, and I just got here. What's a quick pick?"

Her laughter was like a bell. She was pretty when she laughed. He decided not to tell her that, for fear that she would take him for just another horny middle-aged customer. "Well, it's like for the Lotto, y'know?" She pointed to Don's right, where a couple of cardboard containers held some red and white pieces of paper with a series of numbered spaces on them. One said

"Lotto" across the top, the other said "Keno." Don took one of the Lotto tickets and looked at it as his instructor continued.

"You can either pick your own numbers, like six of them, or you can get a 'quick pick' and let the computer do it for you. Y'know? The Lotto is at six million right now."

"So, if I pick six numbers, or let your friend there pick six numbers, and all six of them come up, I win six million?"

"Yeah." She looked at him closely. "Where are you from, really?"

He laughed. "I'm from here, really. I've seen the Lotto drawings on TV, but I really never paid that much attention. The odds have to be incredible!"

"The what?"

"Never mind. Do you have any favorite numbers?" He picked up one of the stubby little pencils and poised it over the form.

"Me?"

"Yeah, you. Give me some numbers, and if I win the six mil on those numbers, I'll split it with you."

"Really? God! I've never had anybody do that for me before!"

"You'd do it for me, wouldn't you?"

"What? Ah . . . well, yeah, I guess." She wasn't so sure.

"Well, I mean it! Gimme numbers!"

She thought. "Seven. And twenty-one. And thirteen and thirty and eighteen. How many is that?"

"One more."

"Ah . . . three. No! Make that four. You'd really split it with me?"

"If those numbers come up, Darlin', I will really split it with you." He handed the ticket to her, and dug out a twenty dollar bill. "Give me nineteen of those quick picks, too." She inserted the sheet he had filled out into the optical reader of the unit, punched a few buttons, and the machine spit out four tickets with five numbers each printed on them. She started to hand the penciled sheet back to him, and then stopped.

"Can I keep this, to check my . . . our numbers?"

"Sure." He folded the four tickets and slipped them into one of the credit card slots in his wallet. He was already looking forward to the next Lotto drawing. He realized that he didn't know when that was to take place. "When is the next drawing?"

"Umm . . . tonight! They have drawings on Wednesday and Saturday at ten o 'clock. At night."

"Great. Good luck!"

"Good luck to you, mister!"

"Thanks." He started for the door, glanced down, and returned to pay for the two little neon-colored beasties.

Six

He rechecked his figures. That couldn't be right! If there were forty two numbers, and they picked six of them, then the odds of any one number coming up would have to be one in seven. Not real good! But then, if one of the numbers picked did come up, then the odds of one of the other numbers also being picked would be . . .

His fingers danced over the keys of the calculator as he figured the odds of winning the Lotto. He watched the green numbers on the display screen increase as he continued the calculation. The numbers were coming out the same the second time. The odds of hitting three numbers out of six were thirty seven to one! And for that you got what? Three dollars? Helluva deal! The odds of picking four out of six were over five hundred to one, five out of six was slightly over twenty four thousand to one, and six out of six, the grand prize, the whole banana, was really a killer! Five million, two hundred forty thousand, seven hundred eighty six to one! And then they paid you off over twenty five years if you chose the annuity option.

He opened one of the drawers of his desk and found the little blue book with the annuity tables. That meant that they were really paying you about thirty seven percent of the total prize. The rest would be interest that the thing would earn over the years of the payout. Of course, you could choose an immediate lump sum payment, in which case they paid you forty percent of the total.

He went back to the calculator. He divided the five million and change by five, and then by fifty two, and chuckled to himself as he looked at the resulting figure. That meant that if a person spent five dollars a week on Lotto tickets, that person could reasonably expect to win the grand prize once every twenty thousand years or so. In that time, of course, he would have spent over five million dollars on Lotto tickets, but what the hell!

Of course, Don reasoned, there was always an eventual winner, and whoever won the thing probably didn't really give much of a damn about the odds. The fact that the odds of being struck by lightning were almost twice as good (or bad) probably wouldn't deter many people from throwing their few dollars a week into the well, blithely ignoring the fact that it was, statistically at least, impossible for them to win.

Don had, after his introduction to the game by the convenience store clerk, developed the habit of buying ten dollars worth of the little computerized tickets twice a week. He and the clerk only hit one number that first week, and he had not gone back to that particular store. She obviously didn't pick numbers very well. After his calculations, he laughingly rationalized that his weekly twenty dollar investment was cutting his odds down to winning once every five thousand years.

He did catch himself occasionally daydreaming about what it would be like to win several million dollars. He supposed that was normal. The chance to spend a few bucks and win that much money was, to be sure, seductive. The basic human desire to obtain something for nothing was strong, stronger, it seemed, than logic.

His thoughts were interrupted by the buzzing of the intercom. Becky's voice came from the instrument on his desk.

"Don, the bookkeeper from Samuelson's Furniture is on line two. She wants to know if we have everything we need to finish their corporate tax return. Do you want to talk to her?"

Don grimaced and looked at the stack of files, check stubs, and computer printouts on the corner of his desk which represented the past year's activity for the furniture company. The stuff had come in over a week ago, and he still hadn't touched it. Where the hell had all the time gone? He had always prided himself on the efficiency of the office, but lately things just didn't seem to be getting done.

He had thought about talking to Becky and the rest of the staff about it, but when he began analyzing the situation, it appeared that the problem was not with the other people in the office. The preliminary work was getting done. Becky was doing her usual good job of running the office and solving all but the most major of the day to day problems. The hang-up in productivity seemed to be in his own office. There just didn't seem to be enough time to get everything done anymore. The office had picked up a couple of new clients in the past couple of months, and he knew that it had taken some time to get them up and running, but it still appeared that he would have to delegate some more of the responsibility of the office.

"Ah . . . no. Just tell her that I'm in the middle of it, and I'll call her."

Becky's voice was just a bit hesitant. "Okay, I will. I think she's getting concerned that it won't be ready by the due date."

"Assure her that it will be ready, if I have to work all weekend to finish it."

"I'll tell her." She broke the connection.

Don sighed and pulled the stack of papers toward him. He was just opening the top file when there was a knock on the door and Becky stuck her head in. "Don, is there anything I can do to help you? You seem kind of harassed lately, and . . . well, I just wanted to see if I could help." She came on into the office and closed the door behind her. She knew that the outer office had big ears, and she didn't consider their conversation to be any of their business. She felt a very proprietary interest in the office, and she had noticed the change in her employer over the past several weeks.

Don frowned at her. "What do you mean, 'harassed'?"

"Well, I don't know . . . you've just seemed to be kind of preoccupied, or something. You've been putting off talking to clients, and I was just afraid that . . ." Becky felt that she was on dangerous ground, and she wasn't comfortable at all talking to her boss this way. She had hesitated saying anything at all, but the other people in the office were starting to talk about the change in Don, so she felt that she had to do something. "I was just afraid that you were unhappy with me, with my work." She finished lamely.

The lines in Don's face softened a little. "Becky, I am in no way unhappy with you! You know how much I depend on you to help me run this place! I'm sorry if I've worried you, but really, there is nothing wrong. I've just been spending some time on other things, things not really related to the office. I guess I'm just trying to break out of the traditional image of an accountant." He grinned at her.

"If you don't mind my asking, what kind of 'other things' are you spending time on? Or is it something I don't really want to know about?" She sat on the edge of one of the guest chairs, a little more relaxed.

Don just looked at her for a moment, considering. "Can you keep a secret, Becky my child?"

It was her turn to grin. "Have I not kept my mouth shut all these years about some of your clients and their dealings, or perhaps I should say lack of dealings, with the IRS?"

"That you have. Pardon me for asking, I should have known better." He suddenly appeared to be in a very good mood. He rolled his chair back a few inches and opened his center desk drawer. He reached into the back of the drawer and withdrew a white legal-sized envelope. As he did so, he watched her face. She was frowning, trying to guess the contents. With a flourish, he emptied the envelope onto the desktop. An untidy pile of bills, mostly hundreds with a few fifties and twenties, brought a sudden intake of breath from Becky. She looked at the money, up at Don's beaming face, and back at the money. She swallowed, and finally spoke.

"Well, at least now I know what you've been doing when you're not in the office. You've been knocking over liquor stores!"

He laughed. "Well, it's not quite that bad, although that might be easier on the nerves!" He picked up the wad of currency and began stacking it in denominations. Becky watched, fascinated.

"Okay, Don. Just what have you been up to? And how much do you have there?"

His voice dropped into his best W. C. Fields imitation, which was none too good. "Just a few well-placed wagers, my dear! Just the results of the consummation of a love affair with the lady known as Luck!" He finished sorting through the bills, and consulted a strip of adding machine tape which had also fallen out of the envelope. "And, in answer to your second question, exactly two thousand seven hundred and four dollars."

"Twenty seven hundred dollars? You made twenty seven hundred dollars gambling? Don! You don't gamble!"

"Not entirely true. That should be, I didn't gamble. Up until several weeks ago I didn't. Didn't know anything about it. But I've gotten lucky a few times."

"Apparently! What have you been betting on? Horses, dogs, what?" She couldn't take her eyes off the stacks of money.

"Nothing so mundane, I assure you!" Don was really enjoying himself, sharing his good fortune with someone. He felt a kind of a rush, a warm excited feeling, not entirely unlike the rush he felt when he was actually gambling. "I've won some of it playing poker and golf, but the majority has come from betting on football games."

"Football games!" Becky was incredulous. "Don, forgive me for saying so, but I know more about football than you do!"

"That was once true. And, I guess it might still be true, but that does not negate the fact that my ill-gotten gains have exceeded my ill-gotten losses!"

"This is unbelievable! It just doesn't seem like you to . . . to risk that kind of money. What does Barbara think of all this?" She swept her hand over the front of his desk, indicating the currency.

"Well . . . she doesn't really know." Don's manner changed slightly. He appeared to lose a little of the exuberance and seemed to be almost reluctant to say more. He looked at the money for a moment, and then finally raised his eyes to Becky's. "Well, of course she knows about my playing poker, I mean I'm gone one night a week, sometimes two, but we've never talked about the stakes in the poker games. And," he added, "she doesn't know about the football betting at all."

There was a new look in his eyes now, almost a look of pleading, as if he was asking for acceptance for something he knew to be wrong. The look disturbed Becky a great deal. She had never before seen this side of her employer. The two of them had worked side by side for over three years, and she thought that she knew him pretty well. But this gambling thing had seemed to change him, change him into someone she barely knew. She had liked the old Don very much. She wasn't so sure about the new one.

Suddenly, his face brightened again, as he said, "As soon as I can build this up a little more, I'm going to surprise Barbara with a trip to . . . somewhere, I'm not really sure where as yet. It depends on how I do. Maybe Hawaii, maybe Europe. She's never been to either place." He was smiling again, the promise of the surprise for Barbara outweighing any possible adverse reaction that his wife might have.

"Well, I'm sure that will please her. So . . . you are going to tell her where the money came from?"

"Sure I will! I would have told her about it before now, but I didn't want to spoil the surprise! You see?" He was looking to her for affirmation. "It may sound funny for me to say this, but I've really been conservative about it. I consider myself to be a good, solid poker player, and I won't bet any long shots on the football games. I've planned it just like I would plan an invest-ment. Sure, I've lost sometimes, but all in all, I ain't done bad!" He spread his arms toward his bankroll.

Becky was about to reply when he spoke again. "And, even if I lose all of this, it's really no big deal! Don't you see, it's other people's money! It's not money I worked for, it's not money that's earmarked for anything!"

She looked at him for a long moment. He was trying to convince her, but she got the feeling that he was also trying to convince himself. He had all the arguments down pat, and he sounded like he really believed what he was saying. But did he? "So you are saying that you really wouldn't mind if you lost it all back?"

He frowned. "Well, of course I would mind some, but it's not like I took the money out of our savings or our retirement fund to bet on football. It's free money! Any money is nice to have, but if by some chance I did lose it, I would just be right back where I started from. And," he added, "I've had a hell of a good time accumulating it!"

"Don, why are you sharing this with me? I really didn't mean to pry into your . . ."

"No, no!" he interrupted, "Don't worry about it. I appreciate your concern, I really do! And . . . I don't know, it's kind of nice to share this with someone. I guess it's just bragging, but that's sort of human nature, isn't it?"

"Yes, I guess it is. And I'm happy that you've won so much money, but I would really hate to see you lose it all again. I know I would be extremely upset if it happened to me." She got up and moved toward the door of the office. "You know that your secret is safe with me. I'll be anxious to hear Barbara's reaction when she finds . . . when you tell her about the trip. Do you think that is safe here?" She pointed at the stacks of bills.

"Sure. I keep it locked in my desk, and anyway, I like to keep it handy so I can take it out and spread it around on the floor and run through it barefooted occasionally."

She couldn't suppress a smile. "That's a great mental picture! You will let me know when you're going to do that so that I don't bring any clients into the office just then, won't you?"

"Why? Don't you think that they would appreciate seeing their accountant enjoy himself?"

"Enjoy himself, yes. Running around barefoot through piles of money, I seriously have my doubts!"

As she left the office, she thought, "And, I have my doubts whether those clients would like their accountant to spend quite so much time gambling!"

Seven

Don was about fifteen miles over the speed limit as he piloted the car around the curves of Clear Creek Canyon. He didn't feel in a particular hurry, but he had always enjoyed driving fast, pushing himself and his vehicle to experience the heightened sensation of mild danger. He was no daredevil, and he always drove carefully when Barbara or the boys were with him, but he considered himself to be a good driver and the feeling of pitting himself against the road was pleasurable.

As he drifted slightly over the center line of the road in rounding a blind curve, he kept his eyes glued to the edge of the rock wall which blocked his view of the road ahead. It was his concentration that saved him, as he spotted the fender of something red coming toward him. The driver of the approaching vehicle was also using a little more than his share of the road, and Don had to jerk the steering wheel and allow the centrifugal force of the curve to pull his car abruptly to the right. His side window was down, and he could hear the tires of the red car howl as the other driver also cranked his wheel over. Don's car headed for the trees at the right side of the road, and he was forced to cut the wheel back left to stay on the roadway. Luckily, he was past the other car by that time, as the back wheels broke loose, and he needed almost the entire road to correct the fish-tailing vehicle.

It was all over, the entire incident taking no more than three or four seconds, but his heart was still pounding several minutes later. Strangely, the adrenaline rush that he felt was rather enjoyable, once his mind told him that he was out of immediate danger. The aftermath of the feeling seemed to heighten the colors of the fall foliage which surrounded him. He had experimented with marijuana in college, but discounting cigarettes and alcohol, he had never done any other kind of drug. He wondered if this was the type of sensation that cocaine users experienced. If this was anything akin to the feeling they gained, he could understand the attraction. He did, however, stick closer to the speed limit for the rest of the drive.

He was headed for Central City, about forty five miles west of Denver. The former gold mining town had fallen on hard times in recent years, and in an effort to revitalize the almost nonexistent economy, the city fathers had chosen to join Blackhawk and Cripple Creek in initiating limited stakes gambling in Colorado. The constitutional amendment that would allow such activities had been put to a vote of the Colorado population, and had passed resoundingly. The proximity of Central City and Blackhawk to Denver and of Cripple Creek to Colorado Springs helped to insure a steady flow of money into the three towns.

He had not visited any of the three mountain towns since the inception of "gaming." "Gaming" was a term which had been adopted from the casinos of Nevada, supposedly in an effort to legitimize the activities in the minds of those who considered "gambling" to be inherently evil. It didn't work, of course, but Don thought that it was nice of them to make the effort.

Several of his fellow poker players had talked at length about the advent of gaming in the Rocky Mountains. Most of them had been to Las Vegas or one of the other Meccas of gambling, and there were the inevitable comparisons.

"It's close, but it ain't Vegas!"

"Well, I like it better! It's friendly. The people in Vegas are too damned impersonal!"

"Too crowded! I ain't gonna stand in line to play anything! When they first opened, they had people around the blackjack tables three deep!"

"You can't shoot craps! Or play roulette! And there sure ain't enough poker tables to go around."

Jeff Stevens had taken a slightly different slant. "Christ, I wish I owned a piece of one of those casinos! They got a captive audience or what? Six million people in the Denver area? They have to drive for over an hour to get there, and they're normally just up there on a day trip, so what are they gonna do? Gamble! And if they lose all the money they brought with them, they're gonna go to one of those idiot credit card machines, and get some more money, and gamble some more! They buck the traffic to get to the Goddamned casinos, and then they finally find a parking place, and they finally sit down at a blackjack table, and, win or lose, they aren't gonna give up that seat for anything, just 'cause it took them so long to get there in the first place.

"And the way those people play! They stay on fourteen or fifteen against a dealer's ten, they double down on twelve, and they split tens! Most of the tables have a five dollar minimum and a five dollar maximum, so you can't use any kind of a betting system. The casino owners ought to at least have the decency to wear masks! Any other self-respecting bandit would!"

So, Don was on his way to Central City to try his luck. It was Tuesday afternoon, and he had told Becky that he would be out of the office for the rest of the day. He had not volunteered any information as to his destination, and she had not felt that she should ask. She did note, however, that he had not taken his briefcase. She wondered how much was left in the white envelope.

As he turned on the street leading through Blackhawk and to Central City, he smiled at the sight of a figure dressed as a mountain man, complete with fringed buckskin shirt and coonskin cap, waving at the passing cars. People were waving back and honking at him. As he pulled past the first two casinos, he heard the clanging sounds of coins falling into the hoppers of slot machines. "Suckers!" he thought. "Stand there and feed your dollars into those things!" He felt superior to the slot players because he was on his way to do battle with the blackjack tables. He had purchased a couple of books on the subject, and he had spent several hours memorizing the "basic strategy" which determined when a player should stay with the cards they were dealt, take more cards, or increase their bets by splitting pairs or doubling down. He had learned that, if a player used the proper techniques, the house would only have an advantage of only about four percent. However, he had also read that most people didn't really have much of a clue as to the proper moves, and the normal house percentage was therefore much higher.

As he pulled through the narrow streets of Central City, he saw a group of people just entering the Teller House Bar and Casino. He wanted to see what they had done to the Teller House, as he remembered the old building as being one of the nicer examples of Victorian architecture in the mining town. But right now, he was here to gamble! The sightseeing could wait.

He found room to park in one of the lots not too far from the casino area, and walked back down the sidewalk. He went into two small casinos before he found one, the Long Branch Saloon, which had a couple of blackjack tables on the second floor. As he climbed the stairs, he was assailed by the tinny sound of coins falling into hoppers and the strange electronic music given off by the massed slot machines, sounding like a calliope gone mad.

As he gained the second floor, he could feel the familiar excitement beginning. He was about to play blackjack at a real live blackjack table for the first time in his life, and he could feel his palms sweating slightly. He put both hands in his pockets, drying them on the pocket linings. He saw that there were indeed two tables, and that they were both filled. Not only that, but each of the tables had a few people standing behind the players, almost hovering, obviously waiting for a seat.

He was disappointed. He had brought five hundred dollars with him, and he was ready to play. They were not, obviously, ready for him. He thought of moving on, looking for another table in one of the other casinos, but figured that the situation would be no different anywhere else. He moved to a position behind one of the players, and looked up to meet the glares of the other aspirants. It was obvious that there was to be a degree of competition for the seats themselves.

As he stood there watching the play at the table, he heard a squeal from behind him, followed by a ringing sound, followed by the sounds of a slot machine regurgitating coins. Everyone around the table turned to see that a young lady in a stylized cowboy hat had hit a three hundred dollar jackpot. She continued to squeal and bounce up and down as the colorful machine spewed out her winnings. As soon as the flow stopped, she dug into the hopper and began to shovel the coins back into the coin slot, three at a time. The people playing the slots on either side of her continued playing their respective machines with renewed vigor.

As he stood there with the others, he looked around the room, marveling at the mixture of eras represented. The mirror in the antique back bar reflected the flashing lights of the slots and the video poker machines. The closed circuit security cameras mounted above each of the two blackjack tables looked incongruous against the ancient pressed tin ceiling. The old mining town was certainly no virgin when it came to gambling, as well as vices of other sorts, but the clash of old and new was humorous.

He had stood there for some twenty minutes, during which time all of one player had given up his seat, when he decided to give it up and wander back over toward the Teller House. As he turned away from the table, however, his eyes lit upon the dollar slot machine on which the young lady had hit the jackpot earlier. She was now gone, and it was vacant. On a whim he stepped in front of it, neatly blocking the advance of a middle aged woman who called him an unattractive name and veered off to the right, searching for another empty machine. He pulled a twenty out of his wallet and signaled to the change girl who was circulating through the small area.

As he began feeding the silver dollar-sized tokens into the maw of the machine, he found himself trying by sheer force of will to control the movement of the wheels. He hit a few small payoffs, enough to keep him going for about fifteen minutes, but then the thing seemed to turn against him, and the last of the twenty disappeared down the slot. He hesitated for a few seconds, but when he turned and saw two people take a step toward him, expectation on their faces, he again hailed the change girl.

As he walked toward the Teller House, he was upset with himself for chasing that damned slot machine as far as he did. It had kept pimping him, showing him two of the three symbols necessary for the jackpot. He had pumped . . . what? Eighty bucks into the stupid thing? He stopped in a doorway and counted the remainder of the cash in his pocket. "Shit!" he said, turning the heads of an elderly couple on the sidewalk. There was only four hundred left! He couldn't have put a hundred dollars into that accursed machine! But he must have! Well, he would have to make it up at the blackjack table, if in fact he ever got to a black-jack table!

He was encouraged by the fact that the people leaving the Teller House seemed happy, smiling and shouting back and forth to each other. He knew that their mood meant basically nothing to his chances, but he was ready to take any omen that appeared favorable. He was ushered into the building by a large man in a tuxedo who wished him the very best of luck.

Don ignored him and walked into another cacophony of electronic slot machine sounds. He shouldered his way through the crowd and was pleased to find, in one of the rooms of the old building, six blackjack tables. There was the ubiquitous crowd around each of the tables, but he was determined to wait this time until he got a seat, if it took an hour. As he waited, he watched the money flow into and out of the slot machines which lined every wall. It appeared that more money was flowing in than the other way around. He would occasionally see someone head toward the cashier's cage with a cup full of quarters or a rack of dollar tokens, but that was a rare occurrence.

The six blackjack tables were arranged in a long oval, the inner circle forming the "pit." Every available foot of floor space which was not occupied by the blackjack area or the narrow aisles was covered by slots and video poker machines. The room had been nicely redecorated, but the primary colors of the slot machine signs clashed rather badly with the sedate Victorian wall-paper.

As it turned out, it was only ten minutes later when the rising young executive type to the left of the dealer finally went broke again and did not, this time, go to his pocket for more money. As he stood up, Don stepped into the space between the two tables, totally blocking the pathway to the chair. He waited until the man had gathered his cigarettes and lighter and turned to leave before he moved, letting the man pass and slipping into the chair in the same motion. He scooted the chair up to the table and reached for his money.

Here he was at last! Don bought in for two hundred, and placed one of the red five dollar chips in the small circle ahead of his position as he had seen done probably a hundred times while he was waiting. The dealer was in the middle of shuffling the six decks of cards, which gave him time to relax at last and ready himself for the battle to come. He noticed that the chips were decorated with a representation of the famous "Face on the Barroom Floor," for which the Teller House was famous. The face, that of an attractive young lady, had apparently been drawn sometime in the early part of the century by some lovesick drunk. That was about all he could remember of the story, but he thought that it was a nice touch, anyway.

The first hand came out. The dealers were all dealing the player's cards face up, so the players used hand signals to indicate their wishes. A beckoning motion got them another card, and a hand extended palm downward over the cards indicated "no more." If a player wanted to "double down," he would add another chip to his bet, and receive one more card. If he wanted to split a pair, he would again add another chip, and create two hands out of one.

The cards were fickle, at best. He would win slowly but steadily for a half hour or forty-five minutes, and then they would seem to turn against him for a period of time. If he doubled down or split pairs, he would catch cards which were of no use whatsoever. If he drew to a fourteen or a fifteen, he would get a facecard. If he had nineteen or twenty, the dealer would draw whatever was necessary to bring the dealer's hand to twenty-one. On two occasions, he had a blackjack, an ace and a ten-value card on the first two cards, only to have the dealer turn over his or her own blackjack to tie him.

As time passed, he began to become acquainted with the others at the table. The lady next to him was from Denver, and had ridden up on a charter bus tour. She was somewhat ahead, and was having a wonderful time. Next to her was a small gentleman who looked to have seen better days. His clothing was clean, but worn, and his fingers bore the scars of a lifetime of working with knives. He revealed that he had retired recently from one of the packing houses in North Denver. To his left was a biker, or what was dressed to pass for a biker. The long hair and beard, the tattoos and the black Harley shirt earned him quite a few sidelong glances, but it turned out that he was the owner of a liquor distributorship and rode the big bikes as a hobby, delighting in people's reaction to his appearance.

Rounding out the table was a couple who were on vacation from Ohio, and who had been in those seats, with the occasional necessary trip to the restroom, since the casino had opened at eight o'clock that morning. They were playing very badly, having a great time doing it, and had gone through God only knew how much money. They really didn't seem to care.

Don bought in twice more, a hundred at a shot, bringing his cash reserve to nothing. He had only about twelve chips left when he glanced at his watch. "Holy . . . ." He stopped in mid oath when the lady next to him looked up. It was six fifteen! He should have been home by now, even allowing for traffic. He had always been very conscientious about calling home if he was going to be late. He was a good hour and forty-five minutes away from his house! How the hell had it gotten so late? He had planned to play for a couple of hours at the most, and be home about now. What was he going to tell Barbara? He slid his chair back and said to the dealer, "Where's a phone?"

As he moved his chair, two people stepped quickly toward him, saw that there were still chips on the table in front of him, and backed off. He got off the chair, surprised at his stiffness. He had been sitting there for over four hours! As he sought out the phone, his bladder also spoke up, complaining about the bottled water he had been sipping. He saw a restroom sign, and moved toward it. As he relieved himself, he wondered what he should do.

He was down, down about four fifty for the day! He couldn't walk away from that without trying to win at least some of it back. His mind just wouldn't accept that as a possible action. He had gone bust almost every time he had taken a hit on a fifteen or sixteen. Many of those times, the dealer had then busted, so that he would have won, had he not taken the extra card. Maybe the "Basic Strategy" was wrong. It certainly seemed that way. Well, by God, he wasn't going to bust any more of those hands. He would just sit tight and let the dealer . . . but he was getting low on funds. He couldn't sustain another period of losing unless he had more of a stake.

He thought that he had seen one of the "instant cash" credit card machines outside the restroom door. He could get another hundred or two, increase his stake to the point where he had a chance to get some of his money back, and then simply earmark the money to go against the credit card bill when it came. He paid all of the bills at the office anyway, so Barbara wouldn't have to see the transaction and worry. He left the restroom and found the machine. He chuckled when he saw that he was even going to have to stand in line to use it. After he completed his transaction he started back toward the table, four hundred dollars in his pocket.

When he got back to the table, it appeared that the young couple had finally called it a day. They had been replaced at the table by a well dressed black man and a slim young girl who looked almost old enough to vote. They each bought a hundred dollars worth of chips and placed their bets. The man looked and acted like someone who had done this many times before. He counted the chips as they were given to him by the dealer, quickly forming four stacks of five, and just as quickly shuffling the small stacks back together. Don watched, reminded of the tricks that the cowboy had performed with his chips the first night he played in the ten dollar limit poker game. He had been practicing the move occasionally, but he was a long way from perfecting it.

The girl was just glad to be there, and her attitude showed it. She was smiling, smiling at no one in particular. She closely examined the chips, pulled a package of cigarettes out of her purse, and dug for a lighter. The pit boss appeared at her elbow, lit the cigarette for her, and produced an ashtray. Her smile got bigger for a second as she thanked him, but he was unsuccessful in keeping her attention for long, as the cards were coming.

As Don expected, the man was a good, solid player. He made his needs known with a minimum of movement, and showed no emotion at all as he won or lost. The girl was a different matter. When, on her second hand, she was dealt a queen of clubs and an ace of hearts on her first two cards, she turned heads from as far away as the next room with her scream of delight. When she looked up she caught Don's eye, then looked around the room to see the attention she had attracted. She looked quickly back down. When she looked up again, Don was still grinning at her. She smiled prettily at him and quieted down for all of four minutes or so, until the biker was favored with a blackjack. Her scream was almost as loud that time.

She soon had the entire table involved to a greater or lesser degree. The lady to Don's left was the first to join in, followed by Don, the biker, the little meat cutter, and finally even the stoic black man was cheering when one of the other players caught good cards. They were all having a wonderful time and chatting like old friends. Don had purchased another two hundred dollars worth of chips when he returned to the table, and he barely noticed them dwindling.

The dealers were on a twenty minute rotation, and it was therefore almost two hours later when the dealer who had been at the table when Don had left finally returned. As he was shuffling, he looked around at the players and asked Don, "You find the phone all right?"

He felt for a few seconds as if his entire existence had taken a hard right turn, and he was having trouble following the maneuver. The phone! He had called Barbara . . . hadn't he? Oh, Christ! He must have called her . . . but he had no memory of doing so! He had left the table, and gone to take a . . . and the money machine, and then back here! Oh, no! How the hell could he have forgotten? She was going to be sorely pissed, or scared to death, or both!

He bailed off the chair, almost knocking over an old man who was trying to make his way through the crowd. He looked at his watch as he pushed through the throngs of people. Eight thirty! He couldn't believe it! As he approached the public phone near the entrance, he saw that it was in use. He spotted the tuxedo at the entrance and grabbed him by the arm. The man turned his head quickly and almost jerked his arm away from Don's grasp, but apparently decided that the smaller man posed no threat.

"May I help you, sir?"

"Is there another phone anywhere close?"

"Well, let's see. Most of the shops will be closed by now, but I think there's a pay phone in front of the restaurant just around that corner." He pointed down the street to the right.

"Thanks!" Don walked quickly down the sidewalk away from the casino. As the sound of the slot machines faded, it occurred to him that it might be a good thing that the phone in the casino was busy. It might make it a little easier.

"Hello?" Barbara's voice sounded anxious, strained. "Hello?"

"Hi, Barb."

"Don! Where are you? Why didn't you call? I've been worried sick!"

"Now just calm down. I'm fine! I really am. I just had a little . . . a little car trouble."

"What happened? Are you all right?"

"Yes, yes. I told you I'm okay. I was just out at a client's office this afternoon, and I left there late, and . . . the car just quit on me on the way back. I messed with it for quite a while, and then finally I walked to a station, and . . . and I just got to a phone. I'm sorry if you were worried."

"Thank God! I was afraid that you had been in an accident or something. I was really starting to get scared!" He could hear the muffled sound of her voice as she put her hand over the phone and spoke. "It's Daddy. He's all right. He just had some trouble with the car." She spoke directly to him again. "Where are you? Do you need us to come get you?"

"No! No, the mechanic thinks it's just a clogged fuel filter or something simple. I should be able to head home in a little bit." He took a deep breath. "It might take a little time, though. It will probably take him some time to fix it, and I'm way the hell up in north Denver, so it will take me a while to drive on home."

"I understand. Thanks so much for calling. I really was getting nervous, and so were the boys. Drive carefully, and call me if you are going to be real late. It's about a quarter to nine now, do you want to go ahead and tell the boys goodnight?"

"Yeah, I'd better. They'll be sound asleep by the time I get home. Sorry again about worrying you."

"Thanks, but it's not your fault. Here are the boys. I'll see you when you get home. Oh, have you eaten?"

"Ah . . . no. Save something for me, will you?"

"I will. Love you."

"Love you too. See you in a couple of hours."

After he told the boys goodnight, he hung up the receiver and just looked at it for a second. He had never been unfaithful to Barbara. He had done his share of lusting and flirting, to be sure, but he had never had an extramarital affair, or even a one night stand. If he had done so, he imagined that he would feel very much as he felt at that moment. He had just flat lied to her! Of course, he had not told her about the sports betting, and they had never discussed the fact that he had won or lost several hundred dollars on several different evenings of poker, but that wasn't really lying. This had been.

He turned and walked slowly back up the street toward the Teller House, feeling like a real shit. He seriously considered going back to the phone and calling her back and confessing the lie to her. As he was about to do so, the music of the slots again came to him. He paused and stood on the sidewalk for a short time, weighing his options. When he looked back down toward the phone, he got a cold, heavy feeling in the pit of his stomach. When he turned toward the lighted doorway of the casino, he was not conscious of the subtle quickening of his pulse, but it was that quickening that propelled him up the street and back to the blackjack table.

As he pulled away from the stoplight and back onto the highway which would lead him down out of the mountains and back to Denver, he was thoroughly disgusted. He had been forced to lie to Barbara, and that upset him a great deal. What had started out as an innocent adventure, a little afternoon of relaxation and cards, had turned sour. Really sour! Over seven hundred dollars worth of sour! If the damned cards would have just fallen his way, he could have quit several hours ago, and been home on time. But his luck had seemed to keep getting worse as the day and evening wore on!

Finally, in an effort to make up at least some of his losses, he had started doubling down on twelves and thirteens, praying that he wouldn't catch a face card, or splitting pairs of ten-value cards, praying that he would. He knew that he was not been playing his cards properly, but he had not had a choice! With the damned five dollar limit, they wouldn't let him bet enough to win it back, so he had been forced to split and double to raise his bet. And then they gave him just the cards he didn't need! When he returned to the table after his phone call, his demeanor had quieted the table down somewhat. They soon began to ignore his obviously black mood, however, and went back to enjoying themselves.

He had played for another half hour before he finally forced himself to quit. He grudgingly relinquished his seat and left the table. As he walked toward the entrance, he noticed that the meter on the progressive slot machine was rapidly approaching four thousand dollars, and he was sorely tempted to take the remaining money in his pocket and try for the jackpot. Had all of the machines not been occupied, he probably would have.

As he came around a corner a little too fast, he was concentrating on holding the car in his lane. He had no desire to repeat the little fiasco of earlier when he had almost clipped the red car. He saw the lights of an approaching vehicle reflected on the trees at the side of the road, and dimmed his lights as he completed the curve. The other car went past him, and he had just flipped the high beams back on when the deer stepped out of the trees and froze in the middle of his lane.

It was a doe, a good-sized one. She stood like a light brown statue, her head turned toward him, the headlights giving her eyes a bright blue glow. All he could do was grip the steering wheel and stare at the twin blue spots as his right foot mashed the brake pedal. The wheels of the car locked up, bawling as they left four thick black stripes on the asphalt. Just before he hit her, the doe broke the hypnosis and tried to leap on across the road, but she was a split second too late.

Eight

There were several other people around the table. He could see them dimly, dark figures in the edge of his vision. He wondered who they were, but for some reason he was unable to turn toward them. They were not involved in the action, but he could feel them watching him, watching his performance. It was as though there was a spotlight centered on him, with the rest of the players, the rest of the room, the rest of existence, in the gray half-light outside the bright circle.

He was able to focus on his opponent who sat directly opposite, across the green felt tabletop. Don found himself staring at the cards in the hands of the other man, trying somehow to read them, to see through the backs and discern their values. The hands that held the unknown cards were thin, the fingers bony and pinkish-gray. The fingernails were long and unkempt, the edges ragged and discolored.

The only evidence of softness displayed by the hands at all were the veins which snaked under the translucent skin, branching and joining and branching again with no apparent pattern. As he watched, fascinated, the fingers moved, extracting one of the cards from the middle of the group of five and replacing it at one end. The hands then pushed the cards together and slowly spread them again, as if to see if any changes had occurred. One hand then left the cards and slowly pushed a stack of chips toward the center of the table. As the bottom of the stack touched the edge of the multicolored mound of chips already on the table, the stack tipped toward Don, spreading itself onto the pot almost like an embrace.

He looked down and saw that the felt in front of him was bare. All of the chips that had been there earlier were now in the center of the table, mixed with the chips of the other man. He wanted, needed desperately to call the bet and to raise, to bet more. He looked again at his own cards. They were beginning to be stained where his fingers gripped them. He was sweating profusely, and the salty liquid was running down across his temples onto his cheeks. He licked the corner of his mouth and tasted the bitterness.

Four aces! Four aces and a king! He had never before held such a hand, and he knew that it had to be a winner! The aces in his hand made a royal flush impossible, and the only other hand that could beat him would be a straight flush. But he didn't see how the other hand could be that good, because his adversary had started betting after receiving his first three cards. The other hand had to be three of a kind, a full house, or maybe it had improved to four of a kind. Whatever it was, he had it beat!

But he had no more chips! What could he . . . suddenly, he felt an awful pain deep down in his gut. There was a tearing sensation, followed by the biting of bitter cold as if frigid air had rushed into a hole in his being; it felt like he had always imagined a knife wound would feel.

He involuntarily looked down toward the source of the pain, but his eyes were stopped by the two stacks of chips that were now sitting on the table just in front of his hands. The pain forgotten, he jerked his head up toward the face of the man across from him. The face was dominated by the eyes and by the smile that leered back at him. The eyes did not blink, but held his in a harsh grip. The smile had nothing at all to do with humor or friendliness, but rather was feral, almost predatory. The eyes tore away from his for a second and glanced down at the chips which had appeared, then back up at him, as if to taunt him.

He hesitated no longer. His right hand moved to a position behind the chips, and he pushed them into the pot.

"Raise!" The sound was faint, scratchy. He cleared his throat and was about to speak again when the voice of the man stopped him. It sounded quiet and very far away, but he had no trouble understanding it.

"Reraise!"

The skeletal hand moved, pushing two more stacks of chips forward. Don again looked down at the bare space in front of him, and as he did so, the pain and tearing began again. It doubled him over, his head dropping toward the edge of the table. The blast of pain squeezed his eyes closed and brought tears. When he was able to open them again, he was looking directly down at two more stacks of chips!

The appearance of the chips seemed to ease the pain, and he straightened up in his chair and grabbed them, lifting them and slamming them back down, scattering some of the chips already in the pot. He said nothing this time, only glared at the dark visage on the other side of the table. The thin gray fingers moved.

"Reraise!"

He didn't even watch this time as his nemesis moved the bet in. He found himself hunching over, eagerly awaiting the sharp rending that he now knew would result in the magical appearance of more chips, enabling him to build up the pot. There was no doubt in his mind now that he held the winning hand. He had no idea how he knew it, but he was somehow sure.

When the pain savaged him this time, he tried to hold his eyes open, to watch the miracle. He was forced to squint, but he was able to see them materialize. The image shimmered for a few seconds and began to fade. In a panic he tightened his muscles, using pure will to bring back the hurt, the searing sensation. It did return, with a vengeance. When he was again able to sit upright, the chips were there. He understood that each new stake was somehow being wrenched from him, from the core of his being, and that the cold sensation which followed the pain was the atmosphere filling the vacuum left as part of him disappeared. He was not sure whether the pieces would be replaced after he won the pot, but it didn't seem to matter.

The reraises kept building the pot, building it to the point that there was little clear space left on the top of the table. He could hear excited murmuring from the dim figures to his right and left as the pile of chips grew. He could feel more and more of himself being ripped away, but that did not matter. What mattered was whether he could last long enough to deplete the diminishing stacks of chips in front of the other man. He was feeling weaker and weaker, but he was eating away at the reserves of the dark man, and . . . there! The last of the man's stacks were being moved into the pot! He had been able to do it. He faintly heard the voice say, "Call."

He used most of his remaining strength to slam his cards down on the table. "Four aces!" His voice sounded stronger than he expected as he felt himself grinning, waiting to see the losing hand.

The fingers picked one card out of the group of five, and tossed it face up onto the table. The seven of diamonds. Don quickly ran through the possibilities in his mind. Four sevens? The only hand that could beat him, a straight flush? Anything else was of no importance. The second card came down.

The queen of hearts! He had won! There was no poker hand possible with those two cards that would beat four aces! The re-lief washed over him like a soft, friendly surf. The third card landed on top of the other two. The deuce of hearts! What the hell? He couldn't believe it. The other man had been bluffing all along! He held garbage!

As the other two cards, the eight of spades and the jack of diamonds hit the table, he could hear the muffled exclamations of the other players. He couldn't help but admire the guts of his opponent, raising and reraising with absolutely nothing in his hand. He was still weak, but he was elated at winning the mon-strous pot. He started to lean forward to begin scooping in the giant heap of chips.

He couldn't move! Try as he might, he simply couldn't raise either of his arms. He tried to lean forward, but it was as if he were glued to the back of the chair. He lowered his head and tried to concentrate on gathering his strength, but he had appar-ently gone too far, used up too much of himself in building the pot.

He raised his head in desperation, to ask for help from the other players, and was horrified to see that the dark figure was raking in the pot! He opened his mouth to protest, to scream at the injustice of the act, but no sound came out. It was as if there was no air left in his lungs. He could open his mouth and move his lips and tongue, but that was all.

The man was standing now, laughing as he dragged the chips toward him. They had filled his chip tray, and were spilling over the far edge of the table onto the floor, his chair, his feet. He continued to laugh and to drag the colorful disks away from the center of the table.

Don turned his head to plead with the other players, and saw that they were also laughing, laughing with the dark man and laughing at him. He twisted within himself, trying to break free from the bondage. Finally, finally, he was able to take a deep breath and cry out against them.

"NO! NO! DON'T! IT'S NOT . . ." The pain grabbed him and jerked him back again. He felt a hand on his shoulder, holding him back, keeping him away from what was rightly his!

The player to his left was leaning toward him, shaking his shoulder slightly and saying something. Don fought to get free, but it was simply no use. He had used up too much, there was not enough . . .

"Mr. Curtis! It's okay, Mr. Curtis!"

It was NOT okay! They were taking . . . *"No! You can't . . ."*

"Mr. Curtis! You're safe now! No one is going to hurt you!"

He closed his eyes again, trying desperately to summon enough strength to resist the restraining hand. When he opened them, the room had suddenly grown light. He had somehow fallen onto his back, and was staring at the ceiling. But the darkness at the sides of the table was gone, and he jerked his head to the side to see . . . no one! The other players were gone! But who was holding him back? Whose hand was on his shoulder?

He jerked his head the other way, and was instantly sorry. The new pain in the side of his head overpowered the pain which remained in his midsection. He again blinked from the pain, and this time his eyes opened to see a woman whom he did not know.

He was surprised to see her, as he had not remembered any women in the game. The game! He looked up to see . . . the game was gone! The table, the other players, the mountain of chips, they were all . . ."What the hell?"

"It's okay, Mr. Curtis. You were dreaming. Just stay still."

"Where . . . where . . . ?"

"You're in Central Hospital, Mr. Curtis. You were involved in an automobile accident, and . . ."

"What?" He was still confused, the last shreds of the dream still drifting around in his mind.

"But I was . . ." Suddenly it was all there! Everything, that is, up to the moment of impact with the deer. He must have wrecked the car when the deer ran out in front of him on the road down from . . . Oh, shit! He had wrecked the car on the road down from Central City! After he had called Barbara and lied to her! Great! Just great! How the hell was he going to talk his way out of this one?

"How . . . how bad was it? How bad am I . . . hurt?" He wasn't really sure he wanted to know.

"I'll let the doctor discuss it with you, but I can tell you that you cracked a couple of ribs and got a pretty good bump on the side of your head. They thought for a while that you might have a skull fracture, but apparently the X-rays didn't show any real problem."

"Barbara . . . my wife . . . has she been here? Does she . . ."

"She was here last night, I think. I didn't come on duty until eight this morning, so I'm not sure, but the doctor will know, I'm sure. Unless you need anything, I'll let him know that you are awake."

As she left the room, Don gingerly laid his head back on the pillow, a real mosaic of thoughts bumping against each other in his mind. The deer. The pounding he had taken at the table in Central City. The dream. Barbara. The lies. He looked up as the door opened, thankful for the interruption of the doctor.

But it was not the doctor who walked into the room. It was Barbara. She looked pretty bad, her eyes red and puffy and her mouth tight. She saw that he was awake, and almost ran to the side of the bed.

"Oh, Don! Thank God! I was so afraid . . . you looked so . . . so hurt last night." She put her hands on his cheeks gently and buried her face in his shoulder. He could feel her shaking as she sobbed.

"I'm sorry, baby! I'm sorry I . . . I worried you." He had his arms around her shoulders and he held her tightly, adding his tears to hers.

"I was just . . . when you didn't show up . . . they called me at about midnight, and said that you had . . . that you were in an ambulance, on the way to the hospital." She sat up and looked at his face, the tears still running down her cheeks. "They didn't know how badly you were hurt when they called, only that you were unconscious, and that there . . . there was some kind of a head injury . . ."

She looked like she was ready to break down again. He reached up and put his hand on her cheek, wiping the tears away with his thumb. She leaned her head over to cradle the side of her face in his palm and closed her eyes. "I'm glad you're still here. I was afraid for a while that you might not be. When you didn't call back, and you didn't show up, and then when they called and said that there was some kind of a head thing . . . . It just scared the hell out of me!"

"The nurse said that there apparently wasn't anything broken, as far as my head is concerned." He touched his ribs gently with the tips of his fingers, and winced. "I wish I could say the same thing for my ribs."

"Yes, the doctor called early this morning and said that the head films were okay, but that you had done about three ribs. Apparently you hit your head on the side window and the shoulder harness got your ribs when the car rolled."

"I rolled it? Jesus! No wonder I feel like a bunch of buffalo stampeded over me!"

She sniffed and sat up straighter, dabbing at her eyes with a tissue. "Yes, you certainly did roll it. Apparently you hit a deer and ran off the road and rolled down an embankment. You wound up between the road and the creek. I haven't seen it yet, I don't think I want to, but they say that you wadded the Toyota up pretty good. Thank God you had your seat belt on!"

"Yeah. I'm glad I did. I'll have to be sure and tell the boys that the seat belt saved me. Maybe that will drive it into their little heads." He looked at her.

She finished drying her eyes and looked back at him. "Don?"

"Yes?"

"Don . . . what . . . what were you doing on that road?"

Here it was. "What do you mean?"

Oh, that was good! 'What do you mean?' What kind of a lame response was that?

"I mean, what were you doing on that road? You called me, you said you called me, from north Denver." Her voice was quiet, as if she were talking to a frightened child.

"I . . . okay, I wasn't in north Denver. I called you from Central City."

"Central City? What were you doing in Central City?" Her voice was not quite so soft now.

"Well, I . . . I didn't want you to worry, to worry about my driving down through the mountains at night . . ." It wasn't getting any better.

"What were you doing in Central City?"

"Well, there's a lot of activity up there now, with the gambling and all, and I thought that I could maybe pick up a client or two . . ."

"Don, please . . ."

"So I took the afternoon and drove up there to check it out and then the damned car quit on me as I was . . ."

"Bullshit! That's bullshit, Don, and I won't listen to it! You went up there to gamble, didn't you?"

"No! No, Barb! Honest to God, I . . ."

She jumped up from the bed and waved him into silence. He lay there, his mouth still open and his teeth clenched, waiting. She paced around to the other side of the bed, her head down and her hands closing and opening, closing and opening. Finally she turned on him and pointed a long index finger at his face. "You lied to me! You lied to me last night, and you're lying to me now! I've been worried half to death for the last eighteen hours or so, and what do I get from you? Lies! I know you're hurt, and I'm really sorry about that. I probably shouldn't be talking to you like this right now, but damn it, I will not be lied to!"

He found the control button and raised the head of the bed.

The movement didn't do his head any good, but he ignored the pounding. "Barbara, listen. Listen to me."

"Why should I listen to you? So you can lie to me some more? I've been worrying about the time you spent playing poker. I know, I know, you enjoy it, but most weeks you've been playing two nights, and last week you played three times! Don't you think that's a bit much?" He began to reply, but she cut him off. "And every weekend you're in front of that damned TV set, watching football. We used to do fun things on weekends, you and I and the boys, but now between golf and football, I hardly get to talk to you!" She had walked over and was leaning on the window-sill, staring out the window.

"I did gamble a little bit in Central City." As she turned to look at him, he looked down at the sheet and thin blanket that covered the lower half of his body. Then he looked up and met her eyes. "But that wasn't the only reason I went up there. I was caught up at the office, and I wanted to see what they had done with the old town. It was a nice day, and I decided to drive up and see for myself what everybody has been talking about." He could see that her anger had dissipated somewhat, and he was warming to his subject. "We'll have to drive up there some after-noon when you aren't working. You wouldn't believe what they've done to the Teller House!"

"How much money did you lose, Don?"

"How do you know I lost?" He tried a grin on her. It didn't seem to have much effect.

"How much?"

"I don't know, maybe . . . maybe fifty, seventy five bucks. But," he added quickly, "It was money I had won at poker and . . . at poker!" He studied her eyes, but he could tell nothing. "I really didn't play that long. I'm sorry if I worried you," he repeated.

She came back toward him and again sat on the edge of the bed. "I'm sorry, too. I must sound like a real bitch, screaming at you while you're laying there in a hospital bed! But I have been worried. You've been so distant sometimes I've been afraid that you were having an affair!" Her eyes were growing moist again.

"An affair! Good God, woman! Do you really think that I'd have the energy for an affair after you get done with me?" He had finally said the right thing. She leaned over and kissed him gently.

"Well, I would hope not! I do my best!"

"You certainly do! After we make love, I usually can't make a fist for three days!"

She giggled and kissed him again, slightly harder. As she did so, she let her left hand drag over the covers until it was at his crotch. He opened his eyes in surprise just in time to see the doctor walk into the room.

Nine

"Yeah, I think I finally got Sid convinced that you're a stand-up guy. In his business, I suppose you gotta be careful, but this guy is paranoid!"

"What does he think I am, a cop?" Don asked.

"No, he doesn't think you're a cop! He knows I'm not that dumb, but he told me that a friend of his, another bookie, got himself in the middle of a sting operation from not checking on the credentials of the people he did business with. All of a sudden he found himself up to his ass in vice cops, IRS agents, you name it. Sid said that it was too bad, 'cause the guy had a real nice operation going. Of course, Sid picked up some of his business, so he wasn't really too unhappy."

"So this Sid person thinks he's ready to deal with me personally?"

"Yeah, I talked to him about you. He knows that you've been betting through me for quite a while, and he and I go way back. I'm gonna be traveling a little more, so I didn't want you to be without a source."

"I appreciate that, Jeff. I really do!" He really did. The thought of going through a weekend without having three or four bets down was very uncomfortable for him. He hadn't really thought about it in any depth, but he wouldn't have even considered watching a game on which he didn't have a bet. What a waste of time that would be! "So . . . are you going to give me his number, or what?"

"Yeah, I'll give you his number, but don't you ever even think about giving it to anybody else without his express permission! You can write it down, but do it in some kind of a code so only you can figure out what the number is. Sorry for all the spy shit, but I told you he's paranoid! Now, one more thing. This guy Sid has some connections that are better not mentioned, except to say that you had better never try to fuck him! You do, you renege on him just once, and both you and I are walkin' funny, if we're walkin' at all. You because you tried to fuck him, and me because I introduced you to him. You understand me?"

"Are you serious? You make it sound like the mob!"

"I don't know who these guys are, and I don't want to know. I've heard some stories. Are you sure you still want the number?"

Don was somewhat taken aback. What had seemed like a simple matter of eliminating the middleman in what had become a weekly transaction had suddenly taken on quite ominous overtones. He almost backed down, not relishing the idea of involving himself in any way with the type of people that Jeff was describing. Maybe he should reconsider Jeff's offer, lay back a bit and just not make any bets on the weeks when Jeff would be unavailable.

As soon as the thought occurred to him, he dismissed it. He was building his bankroll up again after the disaster in Central City, and this was no time to back off. The World Series was coming up, and it would be very handy to be able to place bets on a daily basis, if he wanted to do so. Besides, he wasn't out to "fuck" anybody. If he kept his part of the agreement, if he was straight with this "Sid," there wouldn't be any problem.

Besides, he was feeling just a small touch of excitement at the suggestion that he might be actually dealing with a member of the underworld. He wondered if the term "underworld" was outdated.

"Of course I want his number! And don't worry, Jeff. I'm not going to do anything that would get either one of us in trouble."

"I sincerely hope not, Donald. I sincerely hope not!" As Jeff read the number to him, he punched it into his calculator and hit the total key. The numbers printed out on the tape, and he tore it off and laid it on the desk in front of him.

Jeff spoke again. "Oh, by the way, a couple of friends of mine and I have been flying out to Vegas over Superbowl weekend for the past couple of years. you want to go along?"

Don thought for a moment. The Superbowl was held when? The latter part of January, as he recalled. "Jesus, Jeff! I'd love to, but that's in the middle of tax season! I'll be up to my butt in tax returns, W-2 forms, payroll tax returns, you name it. I work about fourteen hours a day from the first of January to April fifteenth. I don't see how I could break away."

"Well, it's just terrible that so many people want to give you money that time of the year! Poor baby!"

"Yeah, it's a bitch!"

"Well, it was just an idea. Think about it. We'll fly down on Friday and back on Monday, so you wouldn't miss that much time in the office. We do have a helluva lot of fun!"

"You bastard! Rub it in, why don't you? I'll tell you, it's tempting, but I just don't see how I could do it."

"Like I say, think it over. It wouldn't cost you much for the flight and the room. The flights out of here are pretty cheap, and I get my room comped. So does one of the other guys that goes, so you could stay in my room. As long as you behave yourself!"

"Let that be the least of your worries! You get your room what?" Don asked.

"Comped. Paid for. Given to me at no charge. Just 'cause they like me."

"Who do you have to know to get a free room?"

"Nobody, really. I just make sure I have at least fifty on the table whenever the pit boss wanders by, and they treat me like a long lost rich uncle. Shit, I'm a piker! I know of guys that get everything comped! First class airfare, limo, a suite, broads, everything! Of course, they play a little higher stakes than I do."

"Broads?"

"Sure, broads! Hookers! There's more beautiful hookers in Vegas than you ever saw anywhere. When was the last time you were there?"

Don hesitated. He didn't want to seem like a neophyte to Jeff Stevens, but he had only been to Las Vegas once, many years ago. He and a couple of classmates had driven all night to get there, and he had wound up drunk from the free drinks that the cocktail waitresses in the slot machine area kept offering him.

He had been playing quarter machines, as he remembered. Not too long after they had arrived in town, he hit a five hundred dollar jackpot, and it took him all of about five hours to put every bit of it back. By the time he had finally run out of money, his right hand was black from handling the coins and pulling the handle. The rest of the trip had been mostly a blur, capped off by a world class hangover during the long ride back home. "It's been a while, Jeff. We usually go on vacation with the kids, so we wind up at Disney World, or some such."

"You haven't been there for a while, have you? They've got enough crap for kids to do to keep them out of your hair for days! There are several places that I know of that literally have acres of carnival games and video games and rides and everything you can think of to keep the kiddies busy so Mommy and Daddy can gamble.

"Of course, the kids are gambling too, but instead of giving them money or chips if they win, they give them stuffed animals and plastic swords and shit. It's really a neat deal! By the time Junior decides that he's had enough of stuffed Wiley Coyotes and high scores on a video game, they've got him convinced that putting your money out there and trying to win something is fun! Which, of course, it is!"

Don laughed. "Sounds like the ideal family vacation spot!"

"Honest to God, Don, it ain't that bad! If you can tear your ass away from the casinos, there's a lot to do in Vegas. There's Lake Mead, and some fabulous golf courses, and some of the best entertainment you ever saw."

"You sound like the Las Vegas Chamber of Commerce!"

Now Jeff chuckled. "What can I tell you? I'm a salesman! I get excited about something, I try to sell it. Kind of comes with the territory."

"Well, you've got me convinced, but I'm really gonna have to think about the Superbowl thing. I'll let you know."

"Okay, Don. No problem either way. The room is there if you want it, but you'll have to make the plane reservations before too long. That's a busy weekend for Vegas."

"I hear you. I'll give it some real thought."

"See you Saturday morning?"

"If it doesn't snow. That north wind at lunchtime really felt like fall!"

"Yeah, it did. Be careful with Sid's number!"

"I will! I will! I promise! See you Saturday."

"Right. Bye."

As he hung up the phone, he could feel the excitement. He sat up a little straighter and his eyes involuntarily darted around the room, as if he was about to spring into action of some sort. Las Vegas on Superbowl weekend! God, that would be fun! From what Jeff and the other poker players had said, the sports books in Vegas were really something to see. And the ability to simply walk up to a counter and place a bet on damned near anything having to do with sports! That would be so incredible! He had thought about the legal gambling houses of Nevada several times since he had begun playing poker and betting on the weekend games. He had daydreamed about the twenty-four hour a day availability of poker games, blackjack, craps, and all the rest.

It had seemed like a wonderland. The occasional television program or movie which had scenes filmed in Vegas had made it seem like the town he remembered from his youthful trip. It looked big and loud and flashy and slightly out of focus.

There was, of course, one big, make that giant, obstacle to his even thinking about such a trip. Since the accident a month ago, he had been mostly on his good behavior. The scene in the hospital was to be only the first of two or three "talks" that he and Barbara had had regarding his gambling. He had cut out the Wednesday night poker game, and had really concentrated on spending more time with his family on the weekends. He hadn't bet any less on the football and now baseball games, and the poker game that he gave up was by far the cheaper of the two, but of course Barbara was not aware of those facts. She was pleased with his efforts, and made it a point to tell him so.

As soon as his ribs healed a bit, she was somewhat more demonstrative with her feelings. The headache had gone away in a couple of days, but the ache in his rib cage stayed with him, and even now bit him once in a while when he moved wrong, just to remind him. He had not been back to Central City since the "Night of the Deer," as they referred to it. However, Barbara was planning to take the kids and go visit her mother in Cheyenne a couple of weekends from now, and he had been thinking about checking out Cripple Creek, seeing what they had done with the limited stakes "gaming."

He picked up the phone again and dialed the number of the Denver Daily News. Asking for the sports desk, he ascertained that the Super Bowl was scheduled for Sunday, January twenty-second. Don hung up and leafed through his "Executive Planner" calendar. He leaned back in his chair, tapping a pen against his chin. That would be three weeks into January, before the real crunch of personal income tax returns hit. They should have quite a few of the payroll tax returns done by then, and besides, the outer office staff did most of the work on those anyway. . .

Jeff had said that they usually flew down on Friday, which would be the twentieth, and back on Monday, so he would miss part of Friday, all day Saturday, and part of Monday. He didn't work Sundays anyway, as protection against burnout rather than for any religious reasons, so he would miss two, two and a half days at the most! Big deal! He worked his ass off during tax season, and it would probably be good for him to take a short break before February, when all the tax forms in the world came down on him.

He almost reached for the phone to call Jeff Stevens back, but his hand stopped part way there. Barbara had really seemed concerned when they "talked" about his gambling. Don loved her very much, and he certainly didn't want to do anything that would hurt or worry her. He had not revealed the extent of his involvement in poker and sports betting, because he was still in the process of building up his winnings. There still wasn't enough of a cushion to enable him to reveal the plans for the trip to her. What kind of reaction would she have when he finally was able to disclose the surprise vacation? The scene of drawing out the suspense and then laying the tickets on her had played out several times in his imagination.

He had decided on Hawaii, and even stopped in a travel agency on a lunch hour and inquired about fares, accommodations, and activities. Most of an hour had been spent talking to an agent by the name of Susan Goodwin whose husband, it turned out, was an attorney specializing in income tax law. She loaded him down with brochures, all of them featuring blue water, palm trees, and extremely attractive south sea island types with bare midriffs.

The brochures were still living in the bottom left drawer of his desk, and Don had the entire trip pretty well planned by now. His envelope contained somewhat in excess of four thousand dollars at this point, and he was considering renting a safety deposit box somewhere close to the office. He was becoming a little nervous having that much money laying around. Becky was the only other person who had any knowledge of the contents of his center drawer, but nonetheless he was apprehensive.

Of course, the big hurdle would be getting out of town on Super Bowl weekend without Barbara coming completely unglued at him. Once back from the trip, she could be mollified with the fact that he had not really gambled that much, and that he had won. He could flash a few hundred at her and she would never know the difference whether he had actually won or lost. She might or might not believe him about the amount of gambling he had done, but by that time it wouldn't make any difference.

Don realized that he might have to lie to her, but he had been skirting the truth, embellishing here and there, and omitting details for several months now, and the prospect of falsifying the results of a trip to Vegas seemed, if not natural, at least inevitable. It would be different, after all, if he were doing all of this for himself. That was not, and never had been the case, in his mind. He had started gambling, at least serious gambling, with the dream of buying something nice for Barbara and the boys, and that was still his intention. The only change had been the size of his dream. As he won, and kept winning more than he lost, he had dismissed the earlier visions of philanthropy as paltry. His priorities had also changed slightly.

There was still the determination to present his family with wonderful things, but he knew by now that he wasn't about to give up gambling when he reached the monetary level which would allow him to buy those things. That being the case, he would have to keep at least some money for his bankroll, so that he could continue to play without the worry of going "broke" during a losing streak. Losing streaks happened to the best of them, and he was no exception.

He had won more money in the last few months than he had ever imagined, but he knew from conversations with Jeff and the others that that was pretty small potatoes. They talked of "knowing a guy" or "knowing somebody who knew a guy" who bet tens of thousands of dollars every weekend. Don heard tales of no limit poker games where it was possible to win or lose a year's income on one hand. There was a kind of envy, almost a form of hero worship toward these mythical figures. After the rush, the buzz he got from betting a few hundred dollars, he couldn't imagine how it would feel to multiply his bets by ten or twenty or a hundred. It must be unbelievable!

Jeff had often talked about playing craps. Other than the fact that the game involved a pair of dice and sums of money, Don knew very little about it. He had gathered that sevens were good sometimes and bad sometimes, and that eleven was good most of the time, and that two and twelve were bad, unless you had a "field" bet, whatever that was. He did know, however, that it was a very fast-paced game, and that it was possible to make a great deal of money in a short period of time if the dice were rolling right. He would have to get together with Jeff and learn more about the game before the trip in January.

It occurred to him that he was already starting to make plans to go on the Super Bowl weekend trip. But really, why not? Did he need permission from his wife to take a long weekend trip with his friends? It was true that he had always checked with her before making any sort of major decision, but this wasn't really a very major decision, was it? After all, he did bring in the vast majority of the income for their household, and that should be worth something, shouldn't it? He had taken off on a couple of trips with the guys since they had been married, one fishing trip and one trip to Nebraska to hunt pheasants, and Barbara hadn't seemed to mind. Why should this be any different? Well, to be honest with himself, he knew why this one would be different in her mind. She really seemed to be concerned with his gambling. She had made that very clear the night in the hospital and in the discussions since then.

Well, damn it, she was just going to have to get over being so worried. He had found something that he enjoyed very much, something that gave him feelings of excitement and stimulation that he had never found in any other activity. The sensations which were brought on by gambling, and sometimes even by just the thought of gambling, were difficult for him to define, even to himself. They were like the feelings generated by sex, in that they gave him an attitude of comfort and confidence in his abilities. However, the feelings of belonging and of security which he felt when he was sitting at a poker table had no comparison in the activities of sex.

The feelings were, he supposed, somewhat like an addiction, because he looked forward to his next gambling encounter with a great deal of anticipation, but his activities had certainly not been self destructive in any way. Besides, there was no question that he would be able to quit gambling if he wanted to do so. He had quit smoking cigarettes, hadn't he? If he could get through that, he could definitely quit playing poker and betting on sports. There was, of course, no reason why he should quit. He was making money at the activity, and enjoying the hell out of it in the meantime.

The phone rang just once. "Creative Software. May I help you?"

"Could I speak to Jeff Stevens, please?"

"Mr. Steven's office, this is Jan."

"Hi, Jan. This is Don Curtis. Is Jeff available?"

"I believe so, Mr. Curtis. Please hold."

"Donald, my boy! How are you? It must be fifteen minutes since I talked to you."

"All of that! Tell me more about this alleged trip to Vegas."

"So, I whetted your appetite, did I? I thought that might happen. What do you want to know?"

"Well, you said that you flew out of here on Friday and came back Monday, is that right?"

"Yeah, just a minute. I've got it all written down here somewhere." Don could hear the other man shuffling papers. "Here it is! Yeah, we leave DIA at nine twenty A.M., and arrive in Vegas at ten fifteen. It's not quite a two hour flight, but we pick up an hour going out. Then we leave there at ten fifty A.M. on Monday and get back into Denver at one thirty. That gives us most of the day Friday, Friday night, Saturday, Sunday, and part of the day Monday. Plenty of time to have a few laughs and place a bet or two. Why? Have you decided that you can go?"

"I think I can work it out," Don said. "You said that you already have your reservations for the plane?"

"We do. Let me call them and I'll see if I can get you a seat. This far ahead, it shouldn't be a problem."

"Great! Listen, Jeff. I want to get together with you sometime prior to the trip and have you teach me how to play craps. I've never done that, and it sounds interesting."

Jeff chuckled. "It's interesting, all right. And the first thing you need to know is that the term is 'shooting craps.' You say 'playing craps' to anybody in Vegas and they'll know you just fell off the turnip truck. Tell you what. I've got a couple of books on craps that give you the basic setup, the types of bets, and like that. I'll bring them along Saturday, and you can study them for a bit, and then we'll get together and I can show you some of the finer points."

"Sounds great. Ah . . . from what you've said, it's possible to win quite a bit on a craps table, isn't it?"

"You bet it is, no pun intended." Jeff said. "If you get on a shooter who's rolling a bunch of numbers, and you keep increasing your bets, you can do real well. I heard about a guy from Japan that held the dice for twenty five minutes and walked away with a hundred and twenty thousand. That's the kind of a roll you dream about. But you gotta know how to bet! I was playing in downtown Vegas last year, and a little sweetie at the other end of the table was rolling numbers like you wouldn't believe and clapping her little hands and screaming and betting a dollar at a time. When she sevened out, she had won about forty bucks, and I had won thirty seven hundred. You just gotta know how to bet!"

"A hundred and twenty thousand?" Don's mind had hung up on the first part of Jeff's story, and he barely heard about the dollar bettor. "Jesus! That's a bunch of money!"

"Yeah, it is, but that sort of thing does happen. Well, listen, I'll call you back and let you know about the plane reservations."

"Okay. Thanks, Jeff."

"No problem. I'm glad you're going along. It'll be a kick!"

As he hung up the phone and again looked at his calendar, he felt like a kid counting the days until Christmas. The twenty second of January was over three months away! That seemed like an eternity! Well, that would give him time to further build up his bankroll, time to study the game of craps, and time to get Barbara used to the idea. He really didn't want her to worry.

Ten

Don was just finishing his breakfast when the boys appeared, in high gear as usual. David was holding some sort of a toy vehicle high in the air, and running for all he was worth to escape his younger brother.

Ronnie was in hot pursuit, screaming about thievery and injustice in general. They rounded the corner into the kitchen and flirted briefly with disaster as they both slid on the tile floor. They closely resembled one of their Saturday morning cartoons as their little legs churned, their stocking feet slipping, in their attempt to gain purchase on the polished floor.

Don grabbed Ronnie around the waist as he went by his chair, and swung him off the floor and into his lap, amidst the loud protests of the wronged one. David, having lost the incentive for further flight, slid to a halt and hopped up into his usual chair, grinning wickedly at his sibling. Don said nothing as Ronnie continued to kick and scream, but simply wrapped his hands around the boy's waist and moved the tips of his fingers against the small ribs. The shouts of anger dissolved into peals of laughter, and David was about to get back down off his chair and join in the melee when Barbara put a stop to it all.

"Now stop it, both of you! I've told you not to run in the kitchen! David! Sit still! Don, stop that!"

"Ah, Mom!" said David.

"Ah, Mom!" said Ronnie.

"Ah, Mom!" said Don.

She tried to glare at all three of them, but she was missing that tone in her voice that meant she was really serious. She tried again, but they all knew by then that she had already lost. "Don, I'm going to have to be penned up in the car with these two for two hours, and I'd like their adrenaline level to be somewhere near normal!" She glared at him. "If you don't mind!"

Don put Ronnie down and patted him on the rump. The boy circled around the other end of the table and made a half-hearted grab at the toy car. He missed, and climbed up into his own chair. "Sorry, Mommy." He looked up at his father and grinned.

"Me too, Mom." In a gesture of good faith, David placed the toy on the table between himself and Ronnie. Ronnie studiously ignored it.

"What time are you planning to take off?" asked Don.

"I don't know, probably before too long. I'd like to get to Mom's by lunchtime, if we can. She said that she would wait for us to eat lunch, so I took that as a rather broad hint."

Don smiled. "I think you're right. She doesn't like to change her schedule a lot, does she?"

"No, not really, but she is sure looking forward to seeing the boys again. I think we will head back Monday afternoon, so these guys will only miss two days of school. What are you planning to do while we're gone? Besides play golf and poker, that is."

Don looked up sharply, but she was busying herself getting the boys their breakfast. He had still been holding the poker games to one a week, and Barbara hadn't seemed too concerned with his gambling activities. At least she hadn't said anything in the last couple of weeks.

He had not as yet broached the subject of the planned Las Vegas trip. He figured that there was plenty of time for that, and the proper moment had not presented itself. Maybe if he won a significant amount of money this weekend, he would share that fact with her. That would enable him to use the argument that he would only be using those winnings on the Vegas trip. He assumed that there would be an argument over the trip, and he had been trying to think how best to come out of it with a whole skin.

"Well, I'll probably play tonight, and the weather is supposed to be pretty good, so golf on Saturday morning, but other than that, I haven't really planned that much. Probably just hang around, watch a little football, whatever comes to mind. Maybe cruise around downtown and see if I can get lucky." He kept his head down, but looked at her out from under his eyebrows.

She slowly turned toward him and said, "If you do, get lucky that is, be sure to call me from wherever you choose to live from then on. Just leave your house keys here on the table, because you won't be needing them anymore." She smiled at him, but he could see from the look in her eyes that she wasn't really joking.

"Ah . . . right! I'll remember that."

"You'd better!"

Ronnie looked up from his cereal. "What does 'get lucky' mean, Daddy?"

David also looked up at his father, waiting for an answer.

"Yes, Don. What does that mean? Tell us." Barbara sat down at the table and sipped at her coffee, waiting and smiling.

"I was . . . I was talking about playing poker! If you get lucky, you win!" Don said, glaring at his wife.

"You gonna go downtown and play poker?" David asked.

"Mommy said that if you did, and you got lucky, you would have to live somewhere else!" His brow furrowed as he tried to understand his parent's conversation.

"I don't want you to live someplace else, Daddy!" Ronnie was close to tears, his blue eyes round and staring as he looked from one parent to the other.

"Daddy isn't going to live anywhere else, guys! We were just kidding!" Barbara reached over and squeezed the hands of both boys. "I wasn't serious! I'm sorry. I didn't mean to scare you."

"Are you sure?" David was still trying to make some sense of it all.

Don reached over and put his hand on David's shoulder. "Yes, we're sure, Dave. Mom was just being silly!" That earned him another glare from Barbara, but the boys were settling down again, and they both relaxed.

"Nice going, Mom!" The corners of Don's mouth turned up slightly as he said it.

"You started it, you dummy!" She picked her coffee cup up and made as if to dump it in his lap. The reaction was everything she could have hoped for. He jumped up and back, knocking the chair over, and then tripped over the extended legs as he tried to regain his balance. He fell toward the kitchen counter and wound up hanging on the edge of the sink from his elbows, his legs splayed out. The rest of his family of course found it to be absolutely hilarious. Barbara had her head down on the table, her shoulders shaking with laughter, and the boys were almost falling out of their chairs.

Don wasn't sure how much of the hysterical laughter was the result of relief from the tense situation in which they had found themselves a few minutes earlier, but it was good to hear them. He stood back up, raised his index finger into the air, and said, "For my next trick . . ." Barbara just smiled this time, but that set the boys off again.

Barbara looked at her two sons, and then at Don, who was straightening his chair, and said, "Well, thanks for helping me keep them calm for the trip to Grandma's. Would you want to maybe call the vet's office and see if we can borrow a tranquilizer gun and a couple of darts?"

"That's a great idea!" said Don, sitting back down.

"What's a tran . . . tranalizer gun?" asked Ronnie.

His parents spoke almost in unison. "Never mind!"

He helped Barbara get the bags into the car before he left for work. She was taking the minivan, to give the three of them a little more room for the trip to Cheyenne. The boys had picked out most of their vast collection of toys to take along, and Barbara had succeeded in talking them out of the majority of them, so that the collection in the back of the van was merely ridiculous. As they carried the third load of stuff to the driveway, Don said, "So, you're going to be gone for what? Six months?"

Barbara looked at the piles of luggage and toys and shook her head. "It looks like it, doesn't it? And the sad part of it is that ninety percent of this stuff will never be touched until it gets back here. Oh, well!"

He walked back into the house and said good-bye to the boys. Barbara walked him back out to the driveway, and he kissed her hard. She pulled away and looked quickly around.

"Don! The neighbors!"

"Let them get their own!" He said as he grabbed her again. She gave in and kissed him back, and watched as he climbed into the Saab they had purchased to replace the car that he had totaled on "The Night of the Deer." Having admonished each other to drive carefully, she waved as he backed out into the street and headed for work. As she walked back past the van, she again shook her head at the assemblage of absolutely essential playthings in the vehicle.

As Don pulled out of the subdivision onto Arapahoe Road and headed for the interstate highway that would take him to the downtown area, he punched the Saab and listened to the faint whine of the turbo as it kicked in. The car was a four cylinder, and was fairly mild-mannered until it reached about 2,200 rpm. At that point, the turbo boost changed the performance remarkably. He wound the motor out in first and went for second, glancing in the rear view mirror for police cars. He was slow on the shift and the little car bogged just a bit as it dropped back down out of turbo range. He was going to have to work on that shift. He went for third, and then backed off as the digital speedometer passed sixty. God, this thing was fun to drive! He hit heavier traffic as he approached the interstate entrance, and his thoughts shifted to the coming weekend.

Don had his bets down for three college games on Saturday, three pro games on Sunday, and the baseball championships, which were also in progress. He had laid out a total of $1,600 on the various sporting events. He had been placing his own bets with the disembodied voice known as "Sid" for three weeks now, and he was convinced that the bookie had chosen his profession because it was one in which a person could succeed without having any trace of a personality. Don had tried to draw the other man into conversation a couple of times, and had finally given up. Sid's voice never changed. It was the same dull monotone every time Don called, win or lose.

Don had basically set up an "account" with Sid, and his wins or losses were added to or deducted from it. He was thus able to place a bet with just a phone call, and not have to worry about transferring money. He wouldn't have discussed it with anybody, but his new association with the bookie gave him a feeling of importance that he had not before experienced. He felt, for lack of a better term, superior. Don now had the ability to get "into the action" at his whim, and he did love being in the action.

He had the ten dollar limit game tonight, and of course golf in the morning, if the weather held. Glancing up to his left as he cruised north on the interstate, Don saw that there was a thin band of clouds over the mountains to the west of Denver, which could mean anything at all. The rest of the sky was blue, the blue that is only seen at the higher elevations. The "brown cloud," as Denver referred to its smog problem, was building up over the downtown area, and partly spoiled the visibility.

Since Don had been playing with the Friday night poker group, he had been becoming less and less enthusiastic about getting up at the crack of dawn to play golf. The poker game usually broke up around one or one thirty in the morning, which limited him to around five hours of sleep. His body kept insisting that five hours was simply not enough, but he usually was able to catch up a little on Sunday morning. He had begged off on a couple of occasions, claiming illness. Charlie and Lou apparently bought it, but Jeff had given him hell.

"You wimp! Can't take it, huh? Play a little poker, and you can't drag your ass out of bed the next morning!" Jeff had ragged on him, but he apparently hadn't said anything to the other two. Jeff seemed to be one of those rare individuals who could survive on very little sleep; Don envied that ability. He had always required eight or more hours a night, and he had been known to sleep for ten or more hours at a stretch, if nothing woke him. Of course, since the birth of David, neither he nor Barbara had gotten very many chances to sleep late. There seemed to be something about young boys that required sound to accompany any movement. It was a phenomenon which they had discussed with acquaintances who also had young children, and it appeared from their research that it was a characteristic of the species. At any rate, both Don and Barbara had spent quite a bit of their parental years in a constant state of mild sleep deprivation.

So, if the game was late tonight, and the weather tomorrow morning was conducive to golfing, he could take a nap Saturday afternoon. He would have the house to himself, and he could use the VCR to tape the college games while he was asleep. He would have to get some rest sometime, because he had plans for Saturday night. He had managed to get himself invited to the other poker game in which Jeff was involved, but in which Don had not as yet played.

The Saturday night game had been described as much the same as the others, as far as the types of games played and the general rules. The big difference was that this was a "pot limit" game. That meant that the only limit to the size of bet which could be made was the size of the pot at that time. As Jeff had described it, each hand started with everyone anteing a dollar. Therefore, if there were eight players, the first person to bet could bet anything up to that eight dollar limit. Assuming that the first bettor made a three dollar bet, that would bring the total of the pot to ten dollars. The next player would then have the option to fold his hand, call the three dollar bet, or call the three dollars and then raise up to thirteen dollars, as that would then be the size of the pot. Since the pot would then contain twenty six dollars, the next bettor could then call the thirteen dollar bet, making the total thirty nine, and then raise that amount.

As Jeff described the game, Don visualized a poker table groaning under the weight of huge pots, the amounts doubling with each successive bet. "The pots must be enormous! What kind of a bankroll do you need to come into the game with?"

"It's not as bad as you might think," Jeff had told him. "If somebody bets the size of the pot every time, it will usually get down to two players pretty quickly. People simply can't afford to hang around and hope to catch the cards they need on the end. Gets too expensive. So if somebody makes a big bet early in the hand, he's probably trying to eliminate competition before they draw out on him. If somebody bets the size of the pot late in the hand, they're probably bluffing, trying to blow everybody else out so they can steal the pot. If somebody has a lock, an unbeatable hand, they're not going to bet the maximum, because they want to keep people in. So you will see a lot of bets that are nowhere near the size of the pot. It plays a lot like the regular limit games, with the exception that there is always that giant bet available to you."

"And to everybody else!"

"Damn straight! The best thing to do when you're just starting to play pot limit is to hang back, wait for the good hands, and then try to figure out how much of a bet your opponent can stand. If you bet too much, they'll just drop, and you lose money. If you bet too little, and they call, you always wonder if they would have called a bigger bet."

"So it sounds like you need to play pretty tight, and not do much chasing?" asked Don.

"Well, of course you can really say that for any poker game, but you do have to be pretty conservative, unless you can stand swings of several hundred dollars. There are always a couple of people that don't seem to have much of a regard for money, and they keep things lively, but I try to lay back more than I would in, say, the ten dollar game. On the other hand, if you play like a 'rock,' play nothing but cinch hands, the other players are going to notice that pretty soon, and you'll find people throwing big raises at you because they know you'll fold anything but an absolute lock hand."

"Which would be great, if you had the nuts, but that's a little rare. By the way, where did the expression 'the nuts' ever come from, anyway?"

Jeff had thought for a minute. "I don't really know. It's an expression I picked up in Vegas. I've heard a cinch hand referred to as a lock, as the nuts, and even as the 'absolute Brazilians,' but I have no idea where it came from. Maybe from the old saying of 'having somebody by the nuts.' How does that go?"

"You mean, 'If you have them by the nuts, their hearts and minds will follow'?" said Don.

"That's the one. Anyway, to answer your other question, we usually buy into the pot limit game for two or three hundred. You want to have some money on the table in front of you, in case you do catch something good, and they play table stakes. You can't go into your pocket for more money during a hand. I usually take five hundred to a thousand with me, depending on how flush I feel. My best advice would be not to take any more than you want to lose!"

"Now what the hell kind of an attitude is that? Aren't you the one who told me not to think about losing?"

"Yeah, I know," said Jeff, "but strange things can happen. You can be sitting there with four of a kind, only one of them showing, betting your ass off, and some bastard with a possible ace-high flush bets into you. So you raise a couple of hundred, the pot's four hundred or so, and what looks like a flush makes it eight hundred. What are you gonna do with four of a kind? You gotta call, which is gonna cost you another four hundred, but what do you do then? You can raise twelve hundred, but if you do, you're exposing yourself to a possible twenty four hundred dollar raise. That's the kind of situation that sends you away talking to yourself. If you just call, and you wind up winning, you cuss yourself for not taking the raise. If you raise, get reraised, and raise again, which would be the natural thing to do with four of a kind, and then find out that the asshole actually has four aces or a straight flush, all you can do is cry while he rakes in the biggest damn pot you've ever seen, a lot of which is your money."

"Ouch!"

"Yeah, ouch! The thing is, in pot limit, you don't have to win a lot of pots to stay ahead, but you've gotta be careful. When some sonofabitch throws a monster raise at you and you don't call it, and then find out it was a bluff, it tends to keep you in the next time, when it might not be a bluff."

"Well," Don had replied, "'It sounds interesting. What time Saturday night?"

"They usually get started around seven-thirty, but they tend to play pretty late."

"What does 'pretty late' mean?"

"Well, for instance, last week I got home at about four Sunday morning."

"That's pretty late, but it shouldn't be a problem. Barb's out of town with the boys until Monday, so it can go as late as it wants to."

So, he had Friday night, Saturday, and, from the sounds of

it, the early hours of Sunday planned. Sunday afternoon the pro games and the baseball playoffs would be on. That left Sunday night. He supposed that he could just plan on relaxing and resting up for the beginning of the work week, but he hated to waste the free night. Barbara wouldn't be here to worry about him, and . . . wait a minute!

When she originally talked about going to her mother's, he had considered taking that time to check out the other mountain town with limited stakes gambling. Cripple Creek was only a little over two hours from Denver, and they had a few poker tables. Colorado law limited the maximum bet to five dollars, but he had heard that they allowed three raises, so it would be possible to build some fairly respectable pots. It might be fun to drive down there Sunday afternoon, listen to the Bronco game on the car radio, and play a little poker, maybe even try his luck at blackjack again.

It still pissed him off whenever he thought about the abortive trip to Central City. He had been totally devoid of luck that day, for sure. If he hadn't lost the hundred in the stupid slot machine, if he hadn't had the world's worst run of cards at the blackjack table, he wouldn't have had to stay so late, he wouldn't have been in such a hurry to get home, and that damned deer would have been in some other part of the forest! If all that hadn't happened, Barbara would have never known about the trip to Central City at all, and he wouldn't be quite so hampered in his gambling activities.

As he had told himself several times, he really didn't want to worry his wife. He knew that she was somewhat apprehensive about his poker playing, but she had pretty much reconciled herself to the fact that he was gone one night a week. She always made it a point to ask him if he had had fun playing, and he always answered in the affirmative. Most of the time, it was true. He really did have fun. He really enjoyed the game, he enjoyed the talk around the table, which ran the gamut from business dealings to some of the most truly raunchy jokes he had ever heard.

The conversations inevitably came back around to gambling, however, as that was the one thing that all of the players were sure to have in common. He was playing every week with attorneys, salespeople, retirees, and any number of other pursuits or professions. There were even a couple of people who drifted in and out of the weekly games whose form of livelihood never really became clear. Don had asked one of them, a large young man by the name of Andy, what he did for a living. Andy had replied, "I work for a guy, and he has me do stuff." For some reason, Don felt that he was not going to get a lot more out of Andy, and he had let it drop.

It was only when he suffered a heavy loss that he could say honestly that he had not enjoyed himself. He had a tendency, a tendency he had noticed early in his gambling "career," to chase. That is, he usually played a good conservative game of poker, using his mathematical abilities to quickly calculate the odds of improving a particular hand against the relationship of the required bet as compared to the size of the pot. If the "pot odds" were favorable, he would continue the hand. If not, he would fold and wait patiently for the next hand. As long as he was ahead for the night or close to even, he would play this steady, solid game.

But, if he suffered a big loss on a hand, either through the luck or stubbornness of another player, he tended to lose that waiting ability, that patience that had kept him even or enabled him to win. When that happened, he would find himself "chasing," or staying in hands too long. There was always the hope, even though he knew it was illogical, that the next card would be the one miracle he needed to win that pot, or the next one, or possibly the next, and bring him back to the winning side. A few times when he was chasing, the right cards did fall, and he would experience the elation of raking in the mound of chips.

More often than not, however, the cards he needed obstinately refused to appear, and he would end the hand by watching someone else stacking what had been his chips. The deeper the hole he dug for himself by playing substandard hands, the more desperate he became, until he either ran out of money or the other players called it a night, leaving him to drive home alone, mentally licking his wounds. He had railed at himself on several occasions, calling himself all kinds of stupid, and vowing to never again chase his money.

That resolve would usually last until the next time he found himself coming in second best on a big pot, and looking down to find that his stacks of chips were dwindling. Then, all of his good intentions would dissipate, and he would be off again on the quest for the elation which came with winning.

As Don pulled into the parking lot just down the street from his office, the thought occurred to him that he really had all day free, if he wanted to take it. He sat in the car for a moment, toying with the new thought. This was a slower time of the year in the office, and things were pretty well caught up. He had solved the earlier problem of productivity in the office through the delegation of more authority and responsibility to Becky and the staff. He had three clients which he had always handled himself, due to the complexity of their particular situations. Don had decided that, in order to give himself more time to accomplish the things he needed to accomplish in the office, he should assign two of those clients to Becky, and have her train someone else to take over part of her workload. If necessary, they could hire a part-time person to fill in. When he approached Becky with the idea, she had not seemed exactly thrilled. Her attitude had worried him a little.

"Don," she had said hesitantly, "do you really think that's a good idea? Those people are used to working with you, and I don't know that they would accept me."

"What do you mean? Why wouldn't they accept you?"

"Well, like I said, they are used to working with you. Besides, that one guy, Marv Lewis, doesn't think that anything in a skirt can possibly have a brain. If you look in the dictionary under 'chauvinist,' you'll find his picture!"

Don smiled and said, "I can't dispute that, but maybe it's time for old Marv to learn a lesson. You'll have him eating out of your hand in no time at all!"

"I doubt it! If you recall, besides being female, I'm not exactly what you would call a WASP, either. My last name is Marino, and my maiden name was Trijillo. Those ain't exactly Irish names, and Marv Lewis ain't exactly a liberal when it comes to races other than his own! I've heard some of his comments!"

Don knew that Becky was right. Marv Lewis was pretty much your classic bigot, but his account was time consuming, and he needed to get it off his desk. "Well, I'm sorry, Becky, but I'm afraid that the two of you are just going to have to put up with each other. Give a couple of your clients to somebody else in the office, so you'll have enough time. Hire a part-timer, if you have to."

Becky had stood then, and walked to the door of his office. She put her hand on the knob and turned back to look at him, her features set. "You're the boss, Don. But I think you're making a big mistake."

He had looked back at her, holding her eyes. "That's right, Becky. I am the boss! And it would be a good idea if you remembered that! And just how do you think I'm making a mistake?"

"I told you, Lewis is never going to be willing to work with me! Don, I'm sorry if I'm out of line, but you never used to have any trouble getting everything done! It's just since . . . since you started . . . gambling that things have gotten so far behind! I've tried to take up the slack, and so has everybody else in the office, but . . . I don't know, you're out of the office so much anymore, and . . ."

He had exploded then. "Just a Goddamned minute! It is none of your business, and it is none of their business," he swung his arm to indicate the outer office, "what I do or do not do! If I make a decision, I expect you to abide by it, whether you happen to like it or not! If Marv Lewis doesn't like it, he can go to hell! He's a pain in the ass anyway!" He wound up standing, his hands flat on the desk, leaning toward her.

She just stared at him for a few seconds, and then dropped her head and took a deep breath. She turned then and left the room, closing the door quietly behind her. It had been the worst confrontation the two of them had been involved in since she had started working for him. Nothing more had been said about the changes, and they returned to almost the same casual, friendly attitude toward each other, but it was not quite the same as before.

He regretted the change in their relationship, but the shifts in responsibility had allowed him to catch up with his own work. He had been spending some of his newfound free time studying the books on craps which Jeff had given him, and he was getting anxious to try some of the systems recommended in the books. It was too bad that there wasn't someplace around Denver that you could legally play craps, but he guessed he would just have to wait until the Superbowl weekend trip.

Eleven

The high-pitched beep of the radar detector jerked his right foot off of the accelerator. His eyes went to the rear view mirror, back to the road ahead, then to the speedometer, which read eighty-seven, then eighty-two, then seventy-four. Safely back under the speed limit, he relaxed again, and set the cruise control. The little electronic speeding device increased the frequency of its beeps until it was screaming at him, the red lights flashing insistently. He reached over and turned it down just as he spotted the highway patrol car on the other side of the interstate highway. It was one of the new little go-fast Chevy Camaros that were, according to those who were supposed to know, very quick. It certainly looked official, with its wide tires and hunkering silhouette. It paid him no attention and continued on north, searching for prey.

It was about ten thirty on Friday morning, and he had the Saab in fifth gear, headed south toward Colorado Springs and then Cripple Creek. He had made the two phone calls to clients that he knew had to be made, and then called Becky into his office.

"Tell me, Rebecca my dear, is there any abiding reason for my presence in the office today? I have things to do, missions to accomplish, dragons to slay!" He had grinned up at her from behind his desk, looking like a kid about to play hooky from school.

Becky was beginning to feel like the mother of a wayward adolescent. She was watching something happen, something over which she had very little control, and she wasn't sure what to do about it. She had worked for Don for a long time, and she really liked the job. In truth, she really liked Don. He had always been wonderful to work with, and he had made her feel more like an equal than an employee. He had given her more and more responsibility as time went on, and he had raised her salary periodically to compensate her for her hard work and loyalty. She would never have admitted it to Don or to anyone else, but her feelings for him were a little more than those of an employee or even a business associate. She was happily married, but if he had ever made an advance toward her, she knew that she would at least think twice before she turned him down. But that had been the old Don. The Don Curtis she had grown to respect and almost love was not the man who was presently grinning at her like an idiot, in reality asking permission from her to go play.

"Well, there's nothing on your calendar for today, but I thought that you might want to talk to Marv Lewis. I was right about his attitude toward me. He is very unhappy that he is sup-posed to deal with, as he put it, a 'Mexican girl.' At least he didn't call me a 'Spic broad', but he might as well have! He as much as said that he was going to take his business somewhere else if he couldn't work directly with you. I can't deal with him! If you want to keep him as a client, you're going to have to talk to him, and soon!" She was obviously upset, her hands clenched in her lap, and the color of her cheeks a reddish-bronze.

Don glanced at his watch as he spoke. "When did you talk to him last? What did he say?"

"I've called him three times in the past two days, trying to smooth things over, and I've gotten absolutely nowhere! He just refuses to work with me at all! I checked back, and we've billed him a little over nine thousand dollars in the past year. Like I said, I thought you would like to talk to him, maybe go over to his office and see him face to face."

Don had frowned and said, "Well, if he refuses to deal with you, maybe we're better off without him, or his business!"

"But Don! He's been a client for what? Four years? You don't want to throw away all that just because he doesn't like people with brown skin. Or black skin. Or any other color skin but white!" She was getting upset again, just thinking about it. "And that's a lot of money!"

"The money isn't the point! I will not stand for him, or anyone else, treating you like that! If he wants to go somewhere else, let him!"

She had noticed him glance at his watch again. He was upset by the bigotry of the client, but he obviously had something else on his mind. She tried again. "Don't you think you should call him?"

"No, I don't! Marv Lewis can go to hell, as far as I'm concerned! Now, is there anything else you need me for?"

Becky had been almost speechless. Yes, the client was a bigot, but she knew that Don couldn't just kiss off nine thousand dollars a year. Whatever was on his mind must be very important to him. She watched him leave the office, and stared at the closed door for several seconds. She had the uneasy feeling that she knew exactly what had him so preoccupied.

The patrol car safely behind him, he turned the fuzz buster back up and, just for the hell of it, shifted down to fourth gear. That brought the tachometer up into the range of the turbocharger, and the little car accelerated enthusiastically. Don's thoughts returned to the situation with Marv Lewis, and he experienced a moment of guilt for his failure to deal with it. He knew that he should have stayed in Denver and gone to see the client, or at least called him, but he really didn't want to take the time.

He had decided that he might as well take the opportunity to check out Cripple Creek today, rather than wait until Sunday. He was caught up at the office, and there was really no reason why he shouldn't take the day off and see what kind of action Cripple Creek really had. Don had heard quite a bit of talk about the loose poker games in the old gold mining town, and he was anxious to see for himself. Maybe he would give Lewis a call on Monday. Maybe he wouldn't. He had been a client for a long time, and he paid his bill every month, but the guy was a pain in the ass, and a bigot. Don cared a lot for Becky, and he wasn't going to let any sonofabitch treat her like she was in any way inferior. Well, whatever happened with Mr. Lewis, it would just have to happen next week. He had things to do.

Don figured that he should be in Cripple Creek by eleven forty-five at the latest, and the ten dollar limit game tonight wouldn't start until about eight, so he would have at least six hours to play before he had to head back to Denver. He felt good, alive. The weekend was shaping up very nicely, to his way of thinking. He could warm up on the boys in Cripple Creek, and then use the people in the ten dollar game tonight to build up a stake for the pot limit game tomorrow night. He should certainly have his fill of poker by the time this weekend was over! Although, he thought to himself, he doubted if he could ever really get his fill of poker. He absolutely loved the game. He had purchased a few books on the subject, and had studied the game from the viewpoint of several former world champions.

Don had learned that a casino in Las Vegas by the name of Binion's Horseshoe held an annual event known as the World Series of Poker. The buy-in for the tournament was ten thousand dollars, but the winner of the three day event could plan on taking home over a million dollars in prize money. There were several hundred entrants each year. Several of the former winners had published books on the game of poker, concentrating on their particular techniques. Don had adopted many of the tips given in the books, and his game had gradually improved. He still had some trouble with chasing, staying in hands too long, but he was trying to work on his patience.

The drive from Colorado Springs up into the mountains surrounding Cripple Creek was spectacular, with several vistas where he could see for fifty miles or more out across the high ridges and canyons of the Rockies. Don gave each of the views no more than a glance as he piloted the Saab around the curves of the two lane road. He knew he was pushing the car a little hard for the road, but he couldn't help it. The knowledge that there were poker games in progress ahead of him trickled adrenaline into his bloodstream. His blood pressure went up a couple of notches and his pulse eased into the nineties as he rounded a curve and finally saw the little town laid out before him in the high mountain valley.

As he pulled down the hill onto the main street, he could see that the street was lined with cars, and there were quite a few people wandering the sidewalks. It didn't seem to be quite as crowded as Central City, but the town was busy, to be sure. Don drove the length of the street, made a U-turn, and saw the back-up lights of a parked car come on ahead of him. He slowed and pulled into the space left by the departing vehicle. Hopping out of the car, he noticed the chill in the mountain air. He reached back in and grabbed his suit jacket, and locked the car. As he did so, the music of the slot machines came to him again.

He checked a couple of smaller casinos and found that the first had no poker tables, and that the second had a list of people waiting for seats. He was in no mood to wait, and asked the poker manager where he might find another table. He was directed to a big, two story structure which he had driven past on his way through town. The building housed the Midnight Rose Hotel and Casino. As he entered, Don stopped and looked around at the interior. The bottom floor was taken up by what appeared to be about an acre of slots and video poker machines. A stairway curved off to the right, and a one word sign at the top of the stairs said "POKER." Don took the stairs two at a time. He was mildly surprised to find himself breathing a little faster than normal at the top, then he remembered that Cripple Creek sits at somewhere between nine and ten thousand feet in elevation.

He looked around the second floor and saw a bar, a few restaurant tables, several blackjack tables, and most importantly, six . . . no, seven poker tables!

"Care to play a little poker, Sir?"

"What? I'm sorry?" Don had been headed for the tables, looking for an empty seat.

"I said, would . . ."

Don turned to see a dapper gentleman in a white, collarless western shirt and a red brocade vest. The man was holding a clipboard with what appeared to be a list of names on it. Most of the names had been crossed out.

"Yeah! Poker!" said Don, feeling more or less illiterate.

"Well, we have a short list on all of the games. What would you like to play?"

"Ahh . . . you have seven-card stud?"

"Yes, Sir. We have three ahead of you on that game. We only have two names on Holdem . . . ?

"Sure! Put me down on both of them!"

"Your name?"

"Don Curt . . ." Don glanced down at the list. The majority of the list was first names only, with a few last initials. "Don," he said, "Don C."

"Thanks, Don. I'll call you as soon as we have an opening!"

He stood back to watch the action and try to get a feel for the games. He had never played in a casino poker game, and as he watched, he decided that the main difference from the home games in which he had been participating was the presence of the house dealers. The dealer was the only one at the table to handle the deck, and he was taking a percentage out of each pot for the casino. Since the dealer did not play a hand, but only dealt to the players and controlled the game, that was the way the casino made money on the game. The house did not actually win any money from the players, as was done at the other casino games, but they certainly took a share of each pot. The game itself seemed to be fairly friendly and relaxed, with most of the players chatting and seemingly having a good time. It appeared that several of the players were locals, as they knew each other and the dealers on a first name basis.

Don was getting antsy and was just starting to consider looking for an open slot machine when a seat opened up at one of the blackjack tables, and he was unable to resist. He slid into the seat and dug into his pocket. He had taken a thousand dollars out of the envelope before he left the office, and he peeled off one of the hundreds and tossed it toward the dealer.

He had only played for about twenty minutes when two of the poker players at one of the Holdem tables, apparently friends, decided to call it quits and got up. The floorman called the two names which were ahead of him, but only one of them showed up, so he called, "Don!"

He was ahead of the blackjack game about thirty bucks, and he picked up the stack of red chips and walked over to the poker table. As he sat down, he nodded to the people sitting next to him, a stout young man in blue jeans and a sweatshirt which advertised someplace called Captiva Island, and a rather thin lady who appeared to be somewhere on the far side of sixty. The young man smiled openly at him, but the woman looked at him suspiciously. She apparently decided that he wasn't an immediate threat, because she turned her head back toward the table and lit what was apparently the next in a long line of cigarettes, judging by the overflowing ashtray at her elbow. Don had noticed that poker players were among the last of the holdouts when it came to cigarette smoking. Must have something to do with the tension.

The game was called Texas Holdem. Each player was dealt two cards, there was a round of betting, then three cards were dealt face up in the middle of the table. The three cards played in everyone's hand. After another round of betting, another card was dealt up, then another bet, then a last up card. The five common cards were called the "board." The best five card hand out of the seven available to each player won the hand.

The game sounded simplistic when Don had first been introduced to it, but the more he played it, the more he realized just how complex it could be. Like most poker games, proper play called for a great deal of patience. There were ten places at the table, and logic dictated that, in the long run, each player would have the best cards only once in ten hands. The players, of course, believed no such thing. According to the books, a conservative player would play maybe fifteen percent of the hands, but the assortment of players that Don now faced obviously were not interested in conservatism. Most of the players stayed to see the "flop," as the first three up cards were called, and you could depend on fully half of the table staying to see the last card.

Don had learned that poker games can be classified as either "tight," in which everyone patiently waits for good cards before committing themselves, "loose," where all of the players are either tired of waiting or just out to have a good time, or a combination of the two. The combination was naturally the most common situation, with a few tight players and a few loose ones.

This game could only be identified as loose. The money flowed freely, the raises were frequent, and the pots grew to a very respectable size for a five dollar limit game. Don knew from his study and playing experience that the best strategy is to play loose in a tight game, and tight in a loose one.

He started out doing just that, throwing away hand after hand, waiting for high cards or pairs before committing any of his money to the pots. He caught an ace and queen of hearts, raised before the flop, got six takers, and picked up the fifth heart on the fourth up card for the "nut" flush. He bet the maximum all the way through the hand, and picked up a very nice pot. He tossed a dollar chip to the dealer, which seemed to be the custom, and added the winnings to his stacks. About four hands later, he started with a pair of tens in his hand, picked up a third one on the flop, and wound up with a full house when a pair of fours appeared on the board.

Again the pot was a nice one, and Don found himself wishing that he still smoked cigarettes; a congratulatory smoke would go well just now. He briefly considered offering to buy a cigarette from the lady next to him, but thought better of it, and settled for a scotch and water from the cocktail waitress. She was a small, bubbly blond, and he earned a pretty smile from her when he tipped her two dollar chips. Knowing he had to drive back to Denver and stay sharp for the other game, he vowed to himself to have only one drink. It was early, and the alcohol would wear off long before he had to head back.

He threw away several more hands, leaning back and sipping his drink. Then, he lifted the corners of his two cards to see a pair of aces! He had been blessed with the best possible starting hand in Holdem. He leaned forward, his elbows on the edge of the table, and waited for the betting to get around to him. When it did, he raised. The next three players folded, the next two called the raise, and three more folded. The smoker to his right reraised! Don glanced over at her, but she was busy lighting another cigarette. He had the best hand at that point, so he reraised. One more player tossed his cards toward the dealer, but the rest called. Don could feel his state of relaxation begin to dissipate. This was going to be some pot!

The flop was the queen of spades, the nine of spades, and the ace of hearts. He still had the best possible hand at that point, so he again waited to raise. To his surprise, the lady raised! He hesitated just a beat, and then reraised. The other remaining player called the fifteen dollars, and she raised again. The limit was three raises, so the Don just called, as did the other player. The next card came out. The eight of spades. That made three spades on the board, which meant that someone could have a flush.

Suddenly, the tables had turned, and Don realized that he was probably going to have to improve his hand to win! The man across the table bet, the lady raised again, and Don just called. That did him little good, because the man reraised, as did the woman. Don called, and stared at the spot in the middle of the table where the last card was to appear. It seemed to take a long time for the dealer to turn it up. The queen of clubs! Now that was more like it! He had aces full of queens! Who cared about the damned flush! To his delight, the man bet, and the nice lady to his right raised. Don of course reraised, and was a bit surprised when the man also raised. He had read the man as having the flush because of the way he bet, but he couldn't believe that he would reraise with a possible full house showing.

As the last bet hit the table, so did Don's cards. "Aces full!" he said.

"DAMN it!" said the lady to his right. She threw her cards in the general direction of the dealer. They turned face up, revealing an ace and a queen. She had been betting two pair, and had caught queens full of aces, the second-best full house. The dealer looked at her cards and then turned them face down and pushed them into the discard pile.

Don waited patiently to see the flush and experienced a small uneasy feeling as he noticed that the man across the table was smiling. His eyes were drawn back to the middle of the table. Queen of spades, nine of spades, and eight of spades. The uneasiness changed to a vague feeling of dread as he now saw what he had missed in his excitement. Just as he saw the possibility, his remaining opponent turned up the ten and jack of spades! The sonofabitch had caught the straight flush!

It was like a physical blow. Don watched helplessly as the dealer picked up the useless aces and buried them in the discards. It took the dealer two shoves to push the monster pot toward the beaming man. There were exclamations all around the table at the size of the pot and at the "bad beat" taken by Don and the lady. Then the next hand was coming out, and the fiasco became history.

The woman to his right looked at her cards, and without waiting for her turn to act, threw them toward the dealer and stood up, gathering her cigarettes, her lighter, and her few remaining chips. The floorman saw the movement, and reached for his list. She was replaced by a large man in a black felt cowboy hat and a full beard.

Don was still reeling from the previous hand. He had been so sure that he had a winner! He had just flat missed the straight flush threat. But even so, what were the chances? He peeked at his new cards, garbage, and tossed them in. He quickly counted his remaining chips and found that the disaster had pretty well put him back where he had been when he sat down. Ah, well. He reached for his scotch and water, found it empty, and looked around for the cocktail girl. It was still early. He resisted his usual penchant for chasing cards after a big loss, and forced himself to sit back and relax. He got his new drink and looked around the casino as he sipped it. It was obvious that someone had spent a great deal of money on the restoration of the old building. It had been very nicely done.

He threw away another pair of worthless cards and looked at his watch. Almost two thirty. He would have to leave by six at the latest if he hoped to be back in Denver in time for the start of tonight's game. He noticed that he was feeling the effects of the second drink a bit, and it occurred to him that he had not eaten since breakfast. There was a nice looking restaurant just a few steps away, and he considered leaving the table for long enough to eat, as he had seen others do. It seemed to be acceptable to leave a seat at the poker table for up to half an hour or so, without incurring the wrath of the casino personnel or the other players. He thought about it, but he didn't really want to leave the table. He was still trying to decide when he caught a couple of good cards and got involved in another good-sized pot. He lost again, and this loss did tip him over into the chasing syndrome.

For the next two hours, he was involved in almost every hand. He was staying to look at the flop with almost anything in his hand, praying that the first three common cards would somehow fit his. For a change, luck seemed to be with him, and more often than not, he did catch the cards he needed to win. As the chips piled up in front of him, the other players tended to give his hand more respect, usually more respect than it really deserved. He found himself raising the bet just to see what would happen, and he took several pots when all of the other players folded.

He knew that he was not playing nearly as conservatively as he should, but by God, whatever he was doing was working. With each successive win, his confidence grew. All thoughts of eating forgotten, he continued to throw chips at the center of the table, glorying in the feeling of control. He had, through the aggressive style of play into which he had fallen, taken control of the table, and it was an incredible rush! If he did lose a hand, he was getting comments like, "Well, that's a miracle! He lost one!"

If he called the opening bet, or raised before the flop, more and more of the players would simply throw their cards in, saying, "If he's in, I'm out!" or "I can't beat him!"

The bearded man to his right leaned over and said, "That's a helluva rush you got goin', partner! But if I was you, I'd back off a bit. You ain't gettin' full value on your good hands."

Don looked at the man. The pale blue eyes looked back at him from under shaggy eyebrows. He seemed sincere. "Excuse me?" Don said.

"You ain't gettin' full value. You got everybody so Goddamned scared, nobody's gonna stay in and pay you off when you do get a good hand."

Don looked back at him, considering what the man had said. He was probably right. He remembered reading in the books about "shifting gears," or varying your style of play to keep your opponents guessing. It was good, logical advice. What the big man didn't realize, however, was that Don was on a high, a rush brought on by the feelings of power and control which he would not, could not, relinquish. At this point, he probably couldn't have stayed out of any hand with even the slimmest possibility of winning if he had tried.

This was it. This was what it was all about. The euphoria which he was feeling was the reason he was here, rather than back in Denver in his office dealing with assholes like Mr. Marvin Lewis.

"Yeah, well," he said, turning back to his cards. He peeked at them, waited until the bet got around to him, and rolled two five dollar chips toward the dealer.

"Raise," he said. The bearded man just took a deep breath and shook his head.

Twelve

He had the Saab wound up again, trying to make up time. He had really had a hard time tearing himself away from the game in Cripple Creek. It had been unbelievable! The cards had finally returned to a more equal distribution of luck, and, after losing three hands in a row, he had calmed down and gone back to a somewhat more conservative style of play. At about a quarter to six, he had prepared to leave. He asked the floorman for a rack, a plastic chip tray that holds a hundred chips, and began filling it from the stacks in front of him. As he was doing so, the dealer dealt him two more cards. He lifted the corners and saw a pair of kings. He waited for his turn to bet, and raised.

"Oh, Christ, there he goes again!" from the other end of the table.

"I thought you were leaving!" from the beard next to him.

Don had grinned and pointed toward the dealer. "Well, he keeps giving me cards! It's not my fault!"

The man across the table who had stomped on his aces full with the straight flush had been almost devoid of luck since then, and most of his chips were gone. "If he ever does leave, I want that seat!" He glared at the other players, as if daring anyone to contradict him.

Don had won that hand, and added the new supply of chips to the rack. It was almost full of the red five dollar chips! He was damned near four hundred dollars ahead for the session! Not half bad for a five dollar limit game! He had been ready to stand up when the dealer spun two more cards in his direction. Almost every head at the table turned in his direction as he peeked at the cards. He realized what was happening, and made the most of it. He lifted the corners of the cards, put them back down, frowned, and lifted them again. Then, he slowly squared the cards up in front of the rack and pulled one of the stacks of chips back out and set it on the table in front of him, as if getting ready to bet. Then he innocently looked up. Everyone folded. He looked around the table, peeked at his cards again, shrugged, and tossed them in, face down. There were grumbles from the others, and he had again started to rise, but the dealer was too quick for him.

When the cards again turned against him, he looked at his watch and discovered that almost another hour had gone by. Don almost jumped out of the chair. As he did so, the man across the table grabbed his chips and stood, again daring anyone to contest him for the lucky chair.

Don had cashed in five hundred and sixty five dollars. He had five seventy in total, but at the last minute he pulled one of the five dollar chips back from the cashier and looked at the stylized image of a rose. He flipped the chip into the air, caught it, and slipped it into his pocket. He wanted a souvenir of this day, of his first attempt at casino poker, and of his incredible . . . what? Luck? Skill? Surely a combination of both, but really, what did it matter? He had won! Not only had he won more that anyone could reasonably expect to win in a five dollar game, but he had also been in control! He had owned that damned table! Those people had been looking to him to see what he was going to do before they acted! God, that had been a good feeling!

He had felt somewhat light-headed when he walked out into the mountain air on his way to the car, and he remembered again that he hadn't eaten. He figured that he would grab something from a convenience store or a drive-in on his way back to Denver, as he was already going to be late. That was really no problem, except that he found himself resenting the two hours or so that it would take to get there. He would have stayed in the Cripple Creek game, but the way he had been doing, the five dollar limit had begun to feel restrictive. Don just hoped that his luck, or skill, or whatever held for a while longer. If he could experience anything approaching the game today when he got into the pot limit game tomorrow night, he could make a fortune! With his winnings today, he would be going into the game tonight with almost fifteen hundred, and he fully expected to continue to build up his bankroll. He planned to go into the pot limit game with at least two thousand in his pocket, and it looked like that would be no problem whatsoever.

The only reason he finally got anything to eat was the fact that he had to stop for gas in Castle Rock, and he took the two minutes necessary to heat a couple of microwave sandwiches and grab a cup of coffee. He grabbed a handful of napkins and trotted back out to the car. As he sped on north toward Denver, he noted that the sandwiches had the taste and consistency of cardboard. The food and black coffee hit his empty stomach like a bomb, and the excess of stomach acid tried to back up into his throat. He got only about halfway through the second sandwich, and gave up. He would have to see if Al Brainard had any antacid.

He wound up about an hour late. As he pulled up to Brainard's house, he saw most of the familiar vehicles. This group was pretty consistent, and it was rare that they had to scare up a substitute player. As he walked into the den, most of the players looked up and greeted him. The Italian that everyone called Guido had nicknamed Don "Numbers," and it had caught on with the group. As he sat down at what had become his customary chair, the cowboy, whose name had turned out to be Ben, said, "How's it hangin', Numbers?"

"Good, Ben! Damned good, as a matter of fact!" Don said, as he tossed a hundred toward Al and received his allotment of monogrammed chips.

Murray spoke around his cigar. "What are you so damned cheerful about? You look like you just got laid!"

"Not exactly, Murray. Not exactly. I decided to drive down to Cripple Creek this morning, and I had a little fun at a poker table."

"That's just five dollar limit, isn't it?" asked Vic.

"Yeah, but they get some pretty good pots. I came out ahead about five hundred."

"Jesus!" said Jeff, "That ain't bad! You must have run all over them!"

Don grinned. "Yeah, I caught a few cards, but you wouldn't believe what this guy did to my aces full . . ."

The game broke up at three. Don was exhausted, and he had put away a few drinks during the course of the evening, so his play was getting pretty sloppy by then, and he gave back some of his winnings. Even at that, his luck had continued. He had dearly loved the feelings generated by the aggressive play earlier in the day, and he had continued that style, with occasional shifts to a more conservative style. And, by God, it worked! Just when the others figured out that he had been bluffing, and quit folding whenever he bet, Don would back off and play only good hands. After they became convinced that he had come to his senses and was betting quality cards, he would switch back to exaggerating his strength, and blow them out once more.

When they cashed in, he was up nine hundred and twenty seven dollars! What a day he had experienced! He had won fourteen hundred dollars! He couldn't have a drop of adrenaline left in his adrenal glands, or wherever the hell it came from! He felt drained, totally used up, but he wouldn't have traded today for anything in the world. As he pulled into his driveway, he remembered to get the empty coffee cup, the napkins, and the remains of the sandwiches, and drop them into the trash can.

It seemed strange to be walking into a totally empty house. By this time, Don was used to coming into the house late at night, but he always knew that the family was there. Asleep, but there. He didn't dwell on the thought, but it was a different feeling. As he entered the master bedroom, the glowing green figures on the clock radio said three fifty. He debated whether he really wanted to get up in three and a half hours to play golf. He had ducked the weekly game two or three times in the last month or so, and he knew that Charlie and Lou were beginning to wonder about him. Jeff, of course, had given him hell about it. Don knew that Jeff played every Friday night, but he was always at the golf course bright and early, raring to go. He just seemed to have boundless energy and little need for sleep.

Don sat on the side of the bed and set the alarm for seven thirty. He could sleep tomorrow afternoon. He wished that he could start the golf game now! He was whipped, but he was still jazzed from his fantastic day of poker, and he was a little concerned that he might not be able to go to sleep at all. He went back downstairs and poured himself a generous portion of scotch, tossed in a couple of ice cubes, and sipped it as he climbed back to the second floor. He undressed, climbed into bed, and lay back. He was asleep before he even thought of finishing the scotch.

Don looked at his hand, puzzled. There was something red on it, some kind of stain. He pulled his handkerchief out and wiped his fingers on it. Some of the red color came off, but not quite all. A bit of the stain had seeped into the ridges of his fingertips, and refused to wipe off. He thought no more of it, and made his next bet. The cards came face down, and he lifted the corners to see if he needed any more. He had an ace and a nine. The dealer's up card was an eight, and he decided to play the hand as twenty, and stand. He signaled his intentions by sliding the cards under the stack of chips which he had bet.

As he released the cards, he saw that there were red splotches on the corners that he had just touched. He turned his hand over again and saw that the ends of his fingers were again covered with the red substance. He frowned and touched his thumb and his first two fingers together.

Whatever the liquid was, it was somewhat thick and just a little sticky. Don glanced quickly around him and saw that no one else, the dealer or the other blackjack players, seemed to notice. He brought the tips of his fingers to his nose and sniffed. There was no discernible odor. He again wiped his fingers off, and studied them for a few seconds, trying to see if he had injured himself in some way. Nothing new appeared, only the residual stain. It was very strange.

The dealer wound up with eighteen, and paid him, stacking chips next to his bet until the two piles were equal. Don decided to increase his bet slightly, and split his winnings, placing half of the chips on top of his original bet, and pulling the other half toward him. As he did, he left a trail of red droplets on the felt tabletop.

His breath caught and his hand shook slightly as he again looked at the crimson fluid, now running down his upraised fingers onto his hand. He pulled the handkerchief back out and wiped furiously at his hand. Where was it coming from?

He took a clean section of the cloth and wrapped it around his index finger. He touched it to the top of one of the stacks of chips in front of him, and sure enough, it came away soaked. It was the chips! It was coming from the chips! He looked up at the dealer in wonderment, but the dealer was waiting for one of the other players to make up their mind.

"There's something on these chips!" Don said, holding up the soiled square of cloth.

The dealer looked up at him, smiled, and said, ". . . with a hundred and twenty people aboard. It appeared that the plane may have lost power during the takeoff, and . . ."

Don looked at him incredulously. "What?"

" . . . reports of casualties are sketchy at this time, but we will bring you updates as we receive them."

Don rolled over and opened his eyes wide, trying to focus on the clock radio. The image would not come together. When he closed his eyes again, the image of the red chips came back, but then seemed to dissolve into small wisps of mist. He tried to understand, tried to bring back the situation so that he . . . but it was gone. The green numbers cheerfully informed him that it was now seven thirty, and the radio droned on.

He flopped over on his back and groggily took inventory. He felt like crap. His head ached, his eyes burned, and the back of his neck and the tops of his shoulders felt like they were tied in somewhat complicated knots. He briefly considered saying to hell with it, silencing the radio and sinking back down into the pillow. His bladder was full, however, and would not hear of it.

By the time he stumbled into the bathroom and relieved himself, he began to relive the previous day and night, and the blood started pumping just a little bit faster. He leaned on the sink and stared at the bloodshot, stubbled face that was staring back at him. He went back into the bedroom, took his wallet out of his suitcoat, and pulled the wad of money out of it. He held it up and allowed the hundred dollar bills to trickle through his fingers and flutter down onto the bed. He looked at the bills for a few seconds and then threw his head back and cackled. He was still chuckling to himself as he started down the stairs to make coffee.

"Hey, easy money!" Jeff yelled at him from the practice green as he pulled his clubs out of the back of the Saab. Don looked up to see the big man coming toward him, smiling. "Did you have to make two trips to carry all of your money into the house after last night? You were hot!"

It was incredible! He knew that Jeff Stevens hadn't gotten any more sleep than he had, but here he was, hale and hearty. Not only that, but he had obviously been here for at least a little while, waiting for the rest of them. As Don fell into step with Jeff and they headed for the area of the first tee, he said, "Well, you know, even a blind pig finds an acorn once in a while."

"Blind pig my ass! You were playing like you were inspired! Yeah, okay, you caught some nice cards when you needed them, but you went through that game like grease through a goose! I finally just sat back and watched the fun. Where the hell did you learn to play like that?"

"Well, I've done a little reading, and I finally tried to put some of the recommendations into action yesterday in Cripple Creek, and they worked!"

Jeff snorted. "I guess they worked! Of course, not to take anything away from your performance, but if you point at something, most of those guys will look at your finger."

"Are you saying that they aren't exactly nuclear physicists?" Don laughed as he pulled out his driver and swung it, trying to loosen up his shoulders.

"Are you kidding me?" Jeff turned and waved to Lou, who was making his way toward them from the parking lot. "Most of those people are barely literate! I mean, look around the table! You got a midget Jew that wishes that his dick was as big as his cigar, you got a cowboy, and you got a former jock. Then, there's Alec, who looks like he's been dead for about a year, and the two Mafia rejects. Why do you think I play with that group? It sure as hell ain't because of their scholastic averages!"

Don was still laughing when Lou got to them, and he saw Charlie trotting in their direction, almost glowing in his neon green and orange outfit. Jeff had started telling Lou about the previous evening's game, but he stopped short when he caught sight of the little psychiatrist.

"By the gods!" he shouted, gaining the attention of the foursome on the first tee, "Are thy garments, perchance, radioactive?"

Charlie smiled and said, "Have no fear, mortals. 'Tis only I, your mentor, come again to enlighten you in the ways of things golf."

"Enlighten this, you iridescent little fuck!" Jeff said, grabbing his crotch. Don and Lou cracked up, laughing hard enough to again draw glares from the golfers ahead of them.

The four of them, still snickering, began walking toward the tee. The last of the other foursome drove, and moved off down the fairway. Lou looked at Don and said, "You look like you been rode hard, son! You okay?"

Charlie chimed in. "Yeah, Donald. In my professional opinion, you look like shit!"

"What the hell is this?" said Don, "I know for a fact that this itinerant software peddler here didn't get any more sleep than I did, and I'm the one that gets accused of looking like shit!"

"Yeah," said Lou, "But Jeff always looks like shit! There's no way to tell the difference!"

"That's true," said Don, "Ah, well, I suppose I must put up with this kind of verbal abuse in order to avail myself of your money. Speaking of that, would anyone be interested in raising the stakes a bit?"

"I would!" said Jeff.

"We just raised the bet a few months ago!" protested Charlie. "Ten dollars a hole is just fine with me."

"Yeah," said Lou, "I don't see any reason to change it. This has always been a friendly group, and I would hate to see . . ."

"Okay, Okay! If you guys want to play for nickels and dimes, go right ahead!" Don turned to Jeff. "What say you and I sweeten up the pot a little, just between the two of us? We can stick with the usual bet with the foursome, and you and I can..."

"You got it, slick! You want to go fifty a hole?"

"Sure! Sounds good to me!" Don was tired, physically exhausted, but he could now feel the energy level rising, the blood beginning to flow. Suddenly, the fun was back! Why hadn't he thought of this before? He had been growing almost bored with the weekly game, had found himself wishing that he were somewhere else, doing something else. More and more, that something else revolved around wagering. Now he could have both the companionship and sport of the golf game, and the excitement of gambling on it.

They went through the ritual of flipping coins, Charlie coming up heads and the other three tails. Charlie put his quarter back in his pocket, and Don, Jeff, and Lou flipped again. This time, Lou had tails and Don and Jeff both had heads, so they wound up as partners. Jeff fished around in the pocket of his bag for a new ball, and said to Don, "You still got anything left from last night, Numbers?"

"You just watch, sucker, you just watch! I finally figured out a way to win money from all three of you at once, so just watch the hell out!"

Jeff grinned at him, but the other two didn't. Charlie frowned as Don turned away and prepared to tee up his ball. The brightly colored little man tried to catch Lou's eye to see his reaction, but he failed. He would have to get Lou aside later during the round. He was becoming concerned.

Charlie didn't get his chance until the fourth hole, a long dog-leg to the right. Lou and Charlie drove to the middle of the fairway, and Jeff cut the dog-leg, driving over the trees at the right edge of the groomed pathway, trying to take a shortcut to the green. Don knew that he couldn't follow the shot of the bigger man, so he attempted to drive to the extreme right edge of the fairway, hoping for a good roll that would take him beyond the corner and give him a clear shot at the green. He was almost successful, but the shot sliced just a bit, and wound up in the edge of the trees. As Don and Jeff took off toward the right, Charlie touched Lou on the arm and motioned for him to hang back a bit.

"Lou, it's probably none of my damned business, I know it's none of my damned business, but I'm worried about the change in Don."

Lou nodded, watching the other two golfers walking ahead of them, talking animatedly.

"You mean the gambling?"

"Right. It seems to be the only thing he talks about any-more. Jeff is bad enough, but Don seems, and I hate to say it, almost compulsive."

Lou was quiet for a few seconds, thinking. "That's kinda like alcoholism, isn't it?"

Charlie nodded. "It sure is. The parallels are remarkable. Almost everybody drinks once in a while, whether it's a glass of wine with dinner, a beer after mowing the lawn, or something more. Only a small percentage ever get to the point where they can't control it, where they have to have it. When that happens, the person doesn't have the control any more."

"So they can't stop."

"Right. The alcohol, or the effects of the alcohol are in con-trol. It's the same way with gambling. Almost everybody does it, flipping a coin for coffee, buying a lotto ticket, or," he grinned and swung his arm to indicate their surroundings, "betting on a golf game. Most of it is perfectly harmless, just a way of trying to add a little extra dimension, a little more fun to life. But again, a certain number of people get 'hooked,' in the vernacular, and then the same thing happens."

"The gambling takes over."

"Exactly! It's a psychological addiction. Most addictions, heroin and cocaine and the like, are chemical dependencies. The body grows to crave the drug, the effects of the drug. With gam-bling it's different. The only chemicals involved are the ones pro-duced by the body itself."

"Kinda like adrenaline?" asked Lou.

"Very much like that. The person gambles, which produces something very similar to an adrenaline rush. As long as the ac-tivity goes on, the rush continues, win or lose. When the gambler quits playing, the rush goes away, and with it go the feelings of excitement and control, the euphoria that the action brought on. Everyone experiences those feelings."

Lou grinned. "Well, winning's a lot more fun than losing, that's for sure!"

"Sure," said Charlie, "That's why Las Vegas and Atlantic City bring people and money in by the busloads! But, again like alcohol, a few can't just enjoy the feeling and let it go. They have, or develop, a need to experience the rush over and over. And unfortunately, like other addictions, the gambler builds up what could be called a tolerance. The cocaine freak needs more and more coke to achieve the same high, and the compulsive gambler needs more and more action as time goes on."

"Jesus! And you think that's happening to Don?"

They were approaching Charlie's ball, and he took out a two iron and addressed it. He took a slow, careful backswing, and shanked it. Instead of cutting across the corner of the dogleg as planned, he dribbled it on down the middle of the fairway about fifty yards. He looked at the club and shoved it back into his bag. As they started toward Lou's ball a few yards away, Charlie said, "Lou, have you heard why, if you're ever caught out on the golf course in a lightning storm, you should hold a two iron over your head?"

"No, why?"

"'Cause not even God can hit a two iron!"

They laughed, but as Lou stepped up to his ball, he looked up to see Don disappearing into the woods and he frowned again. He hit a beautiful shot that rose nicely and then sliced slightly, carrying the ball around the bend in the fairway. He turned back to Charlie. "So, anyway, you think that Don might be getting . . . what? Compulsive?"

"Right. Compulsive. I've got no proof, and I suppose I should talk to him about it, but I just wanted to get someone else's opinion."

"Well, I'm sure as hell no expert, but I know that he has been talking more and more about the poker games and betting on football, and all that, but I guess I just put it down to Jeff's influence. I know that Jeff is kind of a high roller, and he and Don have gotten to be pretty good friends."

They came to Charlie's ball, and this time he hit a solid three iron which put him in pretty good position. As they started walking again, he said, "I'm really not sure what I should do. I hate to see something like this get its hooks into Don, but I have no proof one way or the other. He's a friend and a neighbor, and I don't want to seem like I'm trying to run his life for him."

Again Lou thought for a moment, and said, "Maybe you should talk to his wife. What's her name?"

"Barbara."

"Right, Barbara. Do you think it would do any good to talk to her?"

Charlie considered the possibility. "I don't know! I don't have any idea how much she knows about what he's doing. I suspect that we might know more than she does, simply from listening to him and Jeff talk. I don't want to screw up their relationship. If what I suspect is true, he's going to need some help, but . . . dammit, I don't really have anything more than suspicions at this point! Maybe he's handling it just fine, for all I know! I'm just concerned."

"Well, to hear him talk, he has been winning," said Lou.

"Yeah, apparently he has. Hell, I would gamble more if I knew I could win!"

"Wouldn't we all, Charles. Wouldn't we all."

Thirteen

By the time he got home from the golf game, Don was really beginning to drag. The lack of sleep was beginning to catch up, and his eyes were burning. He was feeling somewhat smug, in that his luck was continuing, and he had driven away from the golf course ninety dollars richer. He and Jeff had won thirty dollars apiece from Charlie and Lou, and he had won an additional sixty dollars from Jeff. He was up almost fifteen hundred dollars for the weekend, and it was only about noon on Saturday! It felt good.

It was nice to have been able to gamble when and where he had wanted yesterday. He had actually had a choice as to whether he wished to stay in the game in Cripple Creek or move on to the one in Denver. The golf game had been kind of small potatoes after the stakes he had played the previous day, but it had been fun listening to Jeff bitch about losing to him.

His mind was still on the game when he unlocked the front door and walked into the house, so the silence surprised him for a few seconds. He had stopped and listened for some sign on life before it dawned on him that the rest of his family was in Cheyenne. It also occurred to him that he had not spoken to Barbara since their departure Friday morning. Don walked into the den and saw that the light on the answering machine was blinking. As he reached for the message button, a sudden thought froze his hand in midair.

Barbara would have called the office yesterday morning to let him know that she had arrived safely at her mother's home. She would have called at about the time he was on his way to Cripple Creek. Becky would have told her that he had taken the rest of the day off, and Barbara would probably have assumed that he was off somewhere gambling! Dammit, he had a right to do what he wanted to do! He knew that he should have called her yesterday or last night, but he had been too . . . he just hadn't done it. She was going to be upset with him, and he hated the thought of once again being put in the position of having to defend his actions.

The little red light on the answering machine was blinking in a pattern of four, indicating four messages. He took a deep breath and punched the button. Barbara's voice came out of the tiny speaker.

"Hi, Honey! We made it just fine. Mom says hi. I tried to call you at the office, but Becky said that you had taken off. Give me a call here when you get home, okay? Love you." The beep signaled the end of the message. Then the same voice spoke again.

"Hi, Don. It's seven thirty Friday night, and I haven't heard from you, and I was getting just a little worried. If you are playing poker tonight, I know that you won't be home for hours, but please call me first thing in the morning, will you? I love you."

Again, the beep. This time, there was only silence on the machine, and then the sound of someone hanging up. The last message was the same voice. "Don, it's ten o'clock Saturday morning." Her voice sounded tight, angry. "I know you're alive, because I called the golf course and they said that you were signed in and on the course. I would really appreciate it if you could take the time out of your busy schedule to call me. If it's not too much trouble!" Even the final beep of the little machine sounded pissed off.

Don just stood there, listening to the sounds of the tape dutifully rewinding and resetting itself for the next call. He suddenly felt more tired than he had before. All he wanted to do was sleep. He had the pot limit game tonight, and he had to be sharp for that. He thought of grabbing a long nap and dealing with Barbara later, but as attractive as that sounded, he knew that he couldn't do it.

He sat down at the desk and found his mother-in-law's number. He dialed it, and waited. The phone at the other end of the line rang three times, four, five. Don thought for a moment that he might have a reprieve, that he could in fact put off the confrontation. But then he heard the receiver lifted in the middle of the sixth ring and he recognized Barbara's mother's voice.

"Hello?"

"Hello, Helen. How are you?"

"Don? I'm fine. Are you okay? Barbara has been worried. Let me get her!"

He had opened his mouth to reply. He closed it again and waited.

"Don?" Barbara's voice had a bit of an edge to it.

"Hi, Hon! I'm sorry I didn't call you yesterday, but I got tied up with something and I just . . . I just didn't get it done. I'm sorry." He finished lamely.

"What did you get tied up with, Don?"

He did his best to stall. "What do you mean?"

"I mean, what were you doing all day yesterday? What were you so 'tied up' with that you couldn't find two minutes to call me?"

"Barb, I said I was sorry! What do you want from me?" He replied heatedly, trying to take the offensive.

Her voice was rising slightly. "What I want from you is for you to tell me what you were doing yesterday!"

He waited, but so did she. Finally, she said, "Don?"

"What?"

"You were gambling, weren't you?"

Again he hesitated. No matter what he said now, he was going to be wrong. He hated that situation, hated the helpless feeling it gave him, and, at that moment, hated Barbara for trapping him into it.

Again, he tried to take the offensive position. "Well, what if I was? I think I'm old enough to make my own decisions! If I decide to take some time off from the office, I think I have that right! And, if I decide to play poker or something, I think I have the right to do that, too! I haven't noticed that my gambling once in a while has effected you to any great extent! I believe, if I'm not mistaken, that I'm still making the mortgage payment, paying your credit card bills!"

"Dammit, Don, it's not about the money! I have no idea how much money you've won or lost, and I don't care. I know that you would never risk enough of our money on gambling to make any difference. That's just not you. But I am concerned about the fact that when you are thinking about playing poker or whatever, that's all you can seem to think about! It's like the gambling is all that's important to you. I'm sorry, but you act as if the boys and I don't exist!"

"What?" He was yelling at the phone by now. "What the hell do you mean? When have I ever . . ." He knew that was a mistake. He had given her an opening, and she pounced.

"How about yesterday, Don?" Her voice was quieter now, almost flat. "What about yesterday? Why didn't you call me yesterday to see if we had made it to Mom's okay?"

"I didn't say I was gambling yesterday!" He was so damned tired, he just couldn't think of anything else to say to defend himself. "You're the one who said . . ."

"Don, I was worried sick about you! I was really surprised when I called your office and found out that you had taken off somewhere. You hadn't said a thing about not working yesterday. And then when you didn't call . . . I was afraid that you were gambling somewhere, and I was afraid that you weren't, that something had happened to you, that you had been in another accident!"

He had lost. He knew that he was standing on indefensible ground, had no weapons left. He felt weak, emasculated. All of the thrill of the winning, the excitement of the action was gone now, and he was left debilitated. He just felt empty, and so tired.

"Don? Did you hear me?"

He took a deep breath. He was leaning forward now, his head in his hand and his eyes closed. "I heard you. I'm sorry. I'm sorry I didn't call. There just wasn't . . ." He paused and went on. "I don't know what else to say to you. I'm just really, really sorry!"

"I'm sorry too, Don." Her voice was softer now. The argument was almost over, but there was no doubt as to which way it had gone. "I was just so scared! It's not like you to forget to call me, and I was afraid that something had happened."

"I know, Barb, and I really am sorry. It won't happen again. I promise! I love you."

"I love you too. I'm sorry I got so upset."

He knew what he was supposed to say, and he said it. "That's okay. I didn't mean to upset you."

"Well, you take care of yourself for the rest of the weekend, and we'll see you on Monday."

"Okay. You drive carefully on the way back."

"I will. I do love you, you know."

"I know. And I love you too. I'm sorry I worried you."

"Thanks. Bye."

"Bye." He hung up the phone and knew instantly that he should have asked to talk to the boys, or at least asked about them. He briefly considered calling back, but he was so tired that his body felt heavy, and he just couldn't make the effort. He felt badly about forgetting his sons, but Barbara hadn't bothered to ask whether he had won or lost. She said that it wasn't important to her, and that might well be, but it was sure as hell important to him! He felt somewhat vindicated, and stood up to go to bed and get the sorely needed sleep. As he did, his eyes lit on the television set. He really should set up the VCR to tape the sports channel. He had money down on some of the college games, and it would be nice to be able to review the results when he woke up.

However, the effort involved in finding a blank tape just seemed to be too much. He instead turned and made his way to the stairs. His stomach complained briefly, trying to remind him that he had not eaten since God only knew when, but he ignored the mild pangs and went on up to the bedroom. He didn't bother to undress. He just kicked off his shoes and sat down on the edge of the bed. He set the clock radio for six thirty. The poker game was to begin at eight, and he would want to clean up and get something to eat before then. If he went right to sleep, and there seemed to be little doubt of that, he could get about six hours. He would have to sleep most of tomorrow to catch up, but he had nothing else planned. He could tape the results of the pro games, and have a relaxed, easy day. The way he felt right now, he was going to need it.

The number four horse broke for the outside at the last turn of the track, and the jockey started using the whip. They had been running fifth, blocked by the leaders around much of the circuit, but as the big beasts pounded down the straightaway for the finish, the four horse seemed to stretch just a little further with each lunge. The beat of the collective hooves sounded like sustained thunder, but the four horse seemed to move just a little quicker, the wrapped legs flashing ahead to pull the body forward.

He was on his feet, screaming. "Number four! Number four! Run, you beautiful sonofabitch!" He was surrounded by other bettors, themselves trying to urge their own favorite to the front of the pack through their verbal imploring.

He had felt the dejection of the loser as he saw the horse on which he had wagered get himself trapped against the rail. He could not, for some reason, remember exactly how much he had bet on the horse, but he knew that he had bet the horse to win. Second or third place would mean nothing. All he remembered of the bet was that he had handed over a handful of bills and received in return the bright yellow ticket which he now held tightly in his hand. He supposed that the ticket would probably tell him the amount bet, but he couldn't take his eyes off the straining horses.

He had never bet on the ponies before, and he was having a wonderful time. The excitement of the crowd was infectious. He had arrived just after the second race, and the ground was already almost covered with discarded losing tickets. He had seen countless movies and television programs in which the hopeful bettors were crowded against the rail, intently watching the race, and that is where he now found himself. He clutched the ticket and waved it at the charging pack of horses, still yelling at the top of his lungs. The nasal voice of the track announcer competed with the noise of the crowd.

". . . and number three is leading by half a length, number six is gaining on the inside, and here comes number four . . ."

God, this is great! Why had he waited so long to start coming to the horse races? The atmosphere was absolutely electric! He felt larger than life, almost intoxicated with the thrill of watching his horse drive for the finish. He glanced quickly at the electronic board which gave the odds to be paid on each entrant in the race. They varied from two dollars and thirty cents on the number two horse to twenty six dollars and eighty cents on the number seven.

His horse, the number four, was scheduled to pay four dollars and twenty cents for every dollar bet, if he did in fact win. And, if he kept gaining on the leaders at his present rate, there was a very good chance of his doing just that! It almost seemed as if they were moving in slow motion, the heads of the horses and the jockeys bobbing up and down with the impact of the hooves on the dirt. The blue silk shirt of the number four jockey shimmered as the wind currents ruffled the material. The whip rose and fell with the movements of the big muscles of the horse as they continued to gain on the field.

They were just pulling ahead of the second place horse when something happened. At first, there was just a flicker of something different. He couldn't tell what it had been, as it happened so quickly that it was over almost before it had begun. The rhythm had seemed to change for just an instant, but now everything seemed the same as before. He had just started to yell again when all hell broke loose. The four horse stumbled, tried to recover, and then went down in a heap. The jockey, still moving at the pace of the running horse, was catapulted forward like a rag doll. He ducked just before he hit, rolled, and lay still. The animal was also still, the rest of the horses passing the big body on their way to the finish.

Strangely, the announcer's voice droned on, detailing the positions of the various horses, but no mention was made of the fallen horse or rider. He couldn't tear his eyes away from the two mounds laying on the track, the one looking huge, the other brightly colored but pitifully small. When he could look away, he turned to the people surrounding him to see their reaction to the terrible accident.

He was mystified to see no reaction at all. The crowd continued to turn with the movement of the pack, yelling either praise or expletives as their own choices either won or lost. Somehow, he seemed to be the only one aware of the catastrophe. He grabbed the arm of the man next to him and began to point at the apparently dead horse, but the man paid no attention whatsoever to him. He had turned away from the track toward the man for a second, and when he turned back, the track was empty. The other horses had gone on around the curve of the track, slowing after the sprint to the finish line.

He blinked several times and again looked toward the area where the accident had occurred, but there was so sign of either horse or rider. Had he imagined the fall? He turned toward the results board, to learn that number three had finished first, number six had been second, and the seven horse was third. No mention of the four horse. He looked back to the odds board, and was shocked to see that the number four position no longer existed! It was not only just blank, there was simply no space for it! The numbers ran one, two, three, five.

Don was very confused. He could have sworn that ... suddenly, he heard the bugle signaling the start of the next race. He spun around to see the gate spring open and the horses lunge out, beginning their battle to be the first to circle the track and cross the finish line. His disappointment at not getting a bet down on this race caused him to look down at the yellow ticket which he still held. Only it wasn't yellow, like the new layer of discards which now covered the ground at his feet. It was green, and there were four more of them under it.

He studied the top one, and found that it was for the fourth race, the one just beginning. It represented a bet of a hundred dollars on the number two horse. The other tickets were identical. His eyes went to the odds board, and he saw that the two horse had started the race at six dollars and ten cents. He did a quick mental calculation and come up with the fact that, if the two horse came through for him, he would win over three thousand dollars!

Before he looked back to the track, he noticed that the number four position had somehow reappeared, and that the board looked normal. That bothered him a little, but his attention was now on the new contest, and it didn't seem to matter so much any more. As the horses came around the fourth turn and headed for the finish pole, the crowd again came alive, clamoring for their choice to prevail. He joined in, waving his arms and actually jumping up and down as the big number two horse with the green silks surged to the front of the pack and began to pull away. It was a beautiful thing to watch as the muscles of the animal bunched and extended, bunched and extended, driving it forward and away from the rest of the pack.

He was screaming, "Yes! Yes! Yes!" his hands gripping the rail, as it happened again. This time, there was no warning at all. Suddenly, the horse was down, the jockey's body whipping forward and down as his feet refused to leave the stirrups. Instead of the frantic evasive maneuvers he expected by the rest of the horses and riders, they just pounded straight ahead as if nothing had happened. Had the fallen team simply been trampled, run over?

It took only seconds for the rest of the field to pass the spot where he had seen the big horse go down. As the last horse passed, the clods of dirt thrown up and back by the racing hooves fell back to the track surface. There was no trace of either the horse or the jockey. He turned slowly towards the odds board, afraid of what he was going to see there. The numbers read one, three, four, five . . .

As the music slowly intruded on his consciousness, he realized that he had been asleep. As he rolled over and looked at the clock, he was momentarily confused as to what had been a dream and what had not. He was pretty sure about the horse race, but what about the poker games? It was not until he pulled out his wallet and looked at the wads of currency that he was sure.

He felt groggy, still half asleep as he stumbled into the bathroom. He peered into the mirror and saw that he looked pretty much like he felt. He stripped and turned the shower on full force. The water began to revive him, and his thoughts turned to the conversation, argument, or whatever the hell it had been with Barbara. He was going to have to be more careful about calling her. She had always insisted on his keeping in touch, and until now it had never been a problem. He had every intention of continuing his gambling activities, and he certainly didn't need her on his case about it.

He thought that it would be a good idea to call her before he left for the game, just to tell her that he loved her and to make some points for possible future use. He would call her, and make sure to at least ask about Ronnie and David, and set her mind at ease that he hadn't gone completely over the edge.

Feeling self-righteous about the decision to call Barbara, he turned his thoughts to the game. Jeff Stevens would be there, but he didn't know any of the other players. He would have to hang back, wait until he could get some sort of a handle on their styles of play before he committed a great deal of money to the game. He had learned over the months of play that poker players will, if closely observed, give clues, or "tells," as to the strength of their hands. If a player looked at a new card and then quickly glanced at his chips or made any sort of hand movement toward them, it meant that he had improved his hand and was mentally preparing to bet or raise. Staring at a new card or flop meant little or no improvement, while looking away from the action as if disinterested meant exactly the opposite.

Often, the opponents at a poker game would act strong or aggressive with a weak hand, and discouraged and ready to fold with a strong one. Weak meant strong and strong meant weak. The knowledge had proven to be helpful on several occasions, and had helped him win several pots that he might otherwise have kissed off.

Don shaved and brushed his teeth, and dressed in faded jeans, running shoes, and a sweat jacket. Might as well be comfortable. He again checked the bankroll and went down to the kitchen to find something to eat. He had eaten very little in the last two days, and he was ready to devour just about anything that crossed his path. He set up the coffee maker to make four or five cups, and proceeded to make himself a huge sandwich. He carried the meal into the den and grabbed the remote control for the TV.

While he ate and sipped the coffee, he learned that one of his teams had all but failed to show up, and suffered a very decisive defeat. The point spread turned out to be a joke, and they had cost him two hundred bucks. Luckily, the other two colleges listened to reason and covered the spread nicely, so he had won two hundred dollars while he slept. Not too bad, but he would have been up six hundred if a particular southern college had paid attention. Oh, well. He glanced at the clock on the VCR and saw that it was twenty minutes till eight.

It was a good twenty minute drive to the house where the game was to be held, so he put his dish and cup in the sink, shut off the coffee maker, and headed for the driveway. As he headed the Saab out of the subdivision, he could once again feel the start of the excitement, the increased alertness brought on by the anticipation of the game to come. He was feeling good, feeling ready. He was way ahead for the weekend, and he had high expectations of adding to his winnings tonight. His concentration on the game was total, and all thoughts of calling Barbara were gone.

Fourteen

Don had locked his car and was walking toward the big two story house when he heard a beep and looked up to see Jeff's BMW pulling to the curb. He turned and walked over, watching as Jeff locked the car and activated the car alarm. "Well, are you ready, slick?" he asked.

"Damned right! I slept all afternoon, and I am very ready! I hope you brought a lot of money, because you're gonna need it." Don slapped the big man on the shoulder.

"Well, just remember what I told you about this group. They aren't exactly pushovers. Pot limit is a different kind of poker. There's a lot of waiting for nut hands, but there can be a lot of bluffing, too. You gotta watch the other players, watch for tells. Somebody comes at you with a monster raise lookin' like he considers you to be a couple of links below him in the food chain, he's probably got shit for cards. If, on the other hand, somebody checks into you while he's checkin' his watch, yawning, and changing the channel on the TV, you might want to check right back at him. He's probably loaded!"

Don smiled, but he also nodded, appreciating the other man's advice. "I'll watch myself. Thanks, slick!" he added, punching Stevens on the shoulder and dancing away, the adrenaline beginning to ooze into his bloodstream. Jeff had seen the display of vigor before in his friend, the almost infectious display of vitality brought on by the expectation of the action to come. As they walked to the door, they saw two more cars pull up and park just across the street.

They had been playing for about an hour before Don and Jeff found themselves in contention for a pot. As they were both reasonably conservative poker players, Jeff more than Don, it was rare that the two of them got involved in the same pot. When it did happen, they played against each other as if they were the bitterest of enemies. They delighted in taking each other's money, and the loser of the battle could count on hearing about it repeatedly. Of course, it had never before happened in a pot limit game.

Don had been somewhat surprised at the small size of the pots, given the betting structure. The players, including himself, were playing pretty tight. He was spending his time between playable hands studying the others, and he knew that they were in turn trying to get a line on him. There had seemed to be, up to now, little or no bluffing. If someone got a lock hand, they knew that if they bet heavily, they would drive out possible contributors, so the raises were usually for much less than the limit imposed by the pot size.

He picked up the corners of his hole cards to find two kings. His first up card was a seven. The seven wasn't too exciting, but the kings held promise. He looked around the table to see a two, an eight, an ace, a jack, a ten, and another ace. The aces were split between two of the other hands, and that was good. That would make it just a bit harder for someone to catch a pair of aces.

There was a round of betting, and Don threw in a small raise, just to get a feel for what was going on. The two and the eight folded, and the other four hands just called. His second card was another seven. Two pair in four cards. The first ace caught a queen, the jack got a three, the ten got an eight, and the second ace caught a nine. There was little doubt that he had the best hand at this point, and it was his bet. He considered laying back and luring more money into the pot, but he had been drawn out on too many times, and he knew that the correct play at this point was to bet as much as possible to try and drive people out of the hand before they could catch up with him.

"How much is in there?" Don asked the table in general, nodding toward the pot. One of the players who had dropped out sorted through the pot, and came up with a total of twenty-nine dollars.

"Twenty-nine!" said Don, shoving the chips into the middle of the table. The ace queen called, the jack three folded, as did the ten eight, and the ace nine, which happened to be Jeff, called and then raised. Since the pot, including his call, now contained one hundred sixteen dollars, that had become the new raise limit. Jeff contented himself with throwing in one black chip, representing a hundred dollars.

"Raise a hundred." He didn't look at Don or the other remaining player, but just sat still and gazed at the pile of chips in the center of the playing surface, doing his best to betray nothing. Don frowned and hesitated before making any move. Two pair! The big man had to have two pair, aces and nines. One ace was in use, but the others had not made an appearance, and there were three nines still hidden somewhere. Of course, he could have three of a kind, either aces or nines, but . . . he hadn't raised on the first round of betting, so it was doubtful that he had three aces. Probably three nines, or two pair. Either way, he was now at least second best. Of course, Jeff had been known to bluff, but . . . better just call.

He did so, tossing the chip into the pot. Surprisingly, the other player also called. The ace queen were not suited, so what the hell was he going for, a straight? Of course, he could also have three of a kind or two pair, but he wasn't betting as though he had anything special.

On the next round, Don caught another king! He concentrated on showing no emotion. He almost looked away from the table unconsciously, but he caught himself in time and looked to see the new cards of his opponents. Jeff now showed ace, nine, queen, and the other player, who Don knew only as "Luke," now had a ten to go with his ace and queen. Don was still high with the pair of sevens showing, so it was his bet. "Four sixteen in the pot," said one of the watchers.

Again, he knew what he should do. The full house obviously was the best hand at this point, but either of the other players could conceivably catch the cards necessary to beat him. He should go ahead and bet the maximum, try to eliminate them before they had the chance to draw out on him. But, if he did bet the maximum, they would probably both fold, and he would have missed out on at least a couple hundred dollars in winnings. Even if Jeff was sitting on two pair, as he suspected, he would have to catch an ace on one of the next two cards to beat Don's made hand. If in fact Jeff had two aces already, there was only one ace left. If he caught a nine and made three nines and two aces, Don's full house would still beat him. He decided to compromise and tossed in three black chips.

"Just three hundred," he said, smiling at Jeff and Luke.

Luke looked up at him, studying his face. "The king look that good to you, son?" The man's eyes were steady and unblinking, and seemed to bore into Don's. He continued the glare for what seemed like a long time, but finally he averted his gaze and peered again at his down cards. He looked back at Don for another second, and then picked up the exposed cards and threw them face down into the pot. He then picked up his two down cards and did the same thing, muttering, "SonofaBITCH!" His outburst over, he sat back and lit a cigarette, joining the onlookers to watch the rest of the hand.

Don turned to Jeff and said, "And how about you, Sir? Would you care to match my wager, or shall I just take the pot as it sits and put these little beauties back in the deck so that you will never, ever know what I had?"

Jeff looked sideways at Don, shook his head, and silently rolled three black chips into the pot. "Call, you fucking bean counter!"

The last up card came out. Don was watching Jeff for reactions, so he saw the ace at the same time Jeff did. Goddamnit! Aces full! The big bastard had to have three aces and two nines! But wait a minute. If he had started with two nines in the hole, he would have three nines and two aces, and Don would still have a winner. What to do? He really wasn't sure. He had gotten a ten for his last up card, no help at all. Dammit, he should have bet the maximum earlier when he had the chance and maybe . . . he rapped his knuckles on the table, checking to Jeff.

"So, you ain't quite so cocky now, huh? Well, let's just see how much you really liked that last king!" He studied the stacks of chips in front of him, and bet four hundred dollars.

Don said nothing, just took a deep breath. His heart was racing, and a cold trickle of sweat ran down his ribs on the right side, making him shiver inside. He call the four hundred.

The final two cards were dealt face down, and both Don and Jeff lifted the corners and peeked at them. At this point, there was over eighteen hundred dollars in the pot. Jeff only had about five hundred left in front of him, and Don a little over six hundred. They were playing "table stakes," meaning that during any one hand, the players could only bet the amount of money in front of them. No one could go to their pocket for more money during a hand. If a player went "all in," or ran out of chips during a hand, he was still eligible to win the amount that was in the pot at that time. Any further bets among the remaining players were kept separate in a "side pot." If, as was now the case, there were only two players, and one went "all in," there could be no more betting, and the players would just show their hands to determine the winner.

Don now had a three to go with his other cards, and he again checked. He either had a winner or he didn't, and he figured that Jeff was going to wind up putting the remainder of his chips in regardless of the outcome. There would be no way of bluffing the other man at this point, so it was sort of a run for the border. As he expected, Jeff carefully counted out the five hundred and thirty chips in front of him and pushed them in. "All in," he said.

Don had no choice at that point. This was actually the easiest decision of the entire hand. He quite possible had the winner, and he was risking an additional five hundred and thirty to win over twenty three hundred! He quietly pushed the stacks of chips in with his left hand, and turned over the other two kings with his right. He was almost afraid to look up. When he did, he saw that Jeff was just staring at the kings and sevens, his jaw clenched. Jeff picked up all of his cards and put them together, then spread them open and looked at them, holding them so that no one else could see them. He stared at them for a long moment, and then brought his right hand across his body and threw the cards across the table. They hit and skipped across the large mound of chips, and the top one flipped over to reveal a single nine.

"Nines full, Jeff?" asked one of the other players.

"Of course, nines full! I was just praying that dipshit here had sevens full of kings, rather than the other way around." He turned toward Don and said, "Enjoy my money while you can, you rotten little rat bastard! I take my valuable time, teach your ugly ass to play poker, introduce you to these fine gentlemen," he swept his arm around the table, "and what do you do? You have the unmitigated balls to stay in the biggest pot I've seen since a year ago August, just because you had the winning hand! Ungrateful little prick!"

Don had figured out about halfway through the tirade that Jeff wasn't serious, and he waited patiently while the big man blew off steam. When Jeff finished, Don was still stacking chips from the huge pot. He couldn't believe it! What a pot! He tried to review the play and the betting, but he was so excited that it was all just a jumble. Maybe he could straighten it all out in his mind later. Jeff had run out of chips, so he obviously wouldn't have gotten any more of his money, but maybe if he had bet less, he could have kept Luke in for a while longer . . .

The rest of the players were rehashing the hand and waiting for Luke to finish shuffling and deal the next round of cards. Don finished arranging his new supply of chips and turned to Jeff. "If you care to learn more about the game, I would be glad to teach you. I think you'll find that my lessons are relatively inexpensive. Although, I must admit, that last one was a bit pricey." He was pretty sure what the response would be, and Jeff didn't disappoint him.

"Teach this!" he said.

The rest of the evening was not nearly as rewarding for Don. It was as if he had used all of his luck up on the monster pot. He had trouble staying out of the next few hands, simply because the blood was still rushing. Don had really been on a high during the hand, and winning it had sent him damned near through the roof. He had been glad at the time that he had the chips to mess with, because his hands had been shaking quite badly. He kept telling himself that he was chasing cards and that he had to quit, he had to conserve the winnings.

Don kept vowing that he would quit chasing on the next hand, but he just had to see one more card. Finally, he dropped out of a hand in which the first four cards were total garbage, and his accountant's mind demanded that he count the chips in front of him. The stacks were still impressive, but there was only a little over two thousand left! After the big win, there had been over twenty nine hundred! He had pissed away damned nine hundred dollars just screwing around, paying to see just one more card, just one more card . . .

Well, that was enough of that! He was a better player than that, and all he had to do was play tight, like he knew he should, and wait for the nuts. If he could just settle down. He was still feeling jittery. He looked across the room and turned to their host. "Johnny, would you mind if I mixed myself a drink?"

Johnny Gambello, the owner of the house and the normal host of the game, looked like an extra from "The Godfather." He was large, dark, and extremely Italian. His hair was thick and black, just beginning to gray at the temples, and he wore dark shirts and suspenders.

"Sure, Kid!" he said, looking up at Don over his half-glasses. "Help yourself, or wait until I win this hand, and I'll get you something myself."

"No, thanks. I'll get it." Don got up, said, "Deal me in the next hand," and walked to the bar. He stepped behind it, found a short, heavy drink glass, and dropped a couple of ice cubes into it. He looked over the shelves, and was impressed by the assortment of expensive booze. He looked for scotch, and all he could find was Glenheather, a single malt scotch whiskey famed for its smoky flavor. He felt a little guilty for drinking anything that expensive, but it was the only scotch he could see. He filled the glass about halfway with the amber liquid and swirled it around the ice cubes for a few seconds.

He looked over to see that the hand was finishing, said, "Deal me in," again, and sipped the scotch. It was wonderful! He held a small amount of the liquor in his mouth, allowing the fumes to flow upwards into the back of his nose. It burned his tongue and made his eyes water, but it was wonderful! He glanced toward the table again and tilted the bottle once more, filling the glass to about the two-thirds level this time.

As he sat back down at the table and took another drink, he could feel his shoulder and neck muscles begin to relax. That was more like it! He had, up to now, made it a practice to abstain from drinking much of anything when he was playing poker. He knew that alcohol tended to blur the judgment process, and he wanted to be as sharp as possible when he was trying to take advantage of his fellow man. (Or woman.) He also knew that the streets were relatively empty during the early morning hours when he was driving home from the games, and he didn't want to chance a summons for "driving under the influence."

But now, the night was still young, and any effects of the drink would have plenty of time to wear off before he hit the streets. The drinks he had consumed in Cripple Creek had hit him a bit, but that had been on an empty stomach, and he had eaten a good meal earlier this evening. Not only that, but he had been munching on honey roasted peanuts since arriving at Johnny's house, so he felt comfortable with the imbibing. Maybe he should have a drink once in a while, loosen up a little. As the alcohol worked its way into his bloodstream, he certainly felt more relaxed, more confident. He raised his glass, now some-what depleted, toward his host.

"Good scotch, Johnny! Thanks."

"Welcome. I like it. I made myself a promise a bunch of years ago when I was in the joint that I would never, ever drink cheap booze again. When all you've got to drink is some crap made out of potatoes or raisins, you get your fill of rotgut real fast!"

Don got involved in a hand just then, but his curiosity had been aroused. The next time the two of them were just watching the action, Don asked, "Johnny, you said something about being in jail?"

The other man was watching the action on the table, so he talked to Don while his eyes were on the remaining players. "Prison, yeah. I was in for three years. Got my ass busted on a drug charge."

Don was amazed. He must have led a pretty protected life, but he had never known anyone who had actually been in prison. He felt, strangely, like a kid in the presence of a rock star or some damned thing. A drug bust! He looked around the well-appointed den. The upholstery of the furniture and the bindings of the books in the shelves to the right of the bar were leather. It must have wiped out most of a herd of cattle to furnish this room! He couldn't help but wonder how much of the house and all it contained had been purchased with drug money. It occurred to him that he had no idea what Johnny did for a living, and he wasn't sure how to ask.

He looked at his next cards and discovered an ace, queen and nine of hearts. He played the hand to the end, winding up with a heart flush which beat Johnny's straight and Luke's smaller flush. He raked in a two hundred dollar pot and reached for his drink. The liquor was gone, and the glass contained only a couple of lonely chunks of ice. Johnny saw the movement, caught Don's eye, and jerked his thumb toward the bar. Don considered for a moment, then shrugged and got up.

He was feeling great. He had won back some of the money he had thrown away earlier, and he had effectively anesthetized the jittery feeling. He was playing high stakes poker with an ex-con, as well as God only knew what else. He was ahead . . . he wasn't sure how far ahead he was for the weekend, but he was ahead a helluva lot. What a life this was! It beat the hell out of accounting! If he could depend on winning like this all the time, he could give up the nine to five bullshit, give up all the stress and ridiculous hours of tax season.

Accounting was a good way to make a living, but it was boring! B-O-R-I-N-G! There weren't a lot of adrenaline rushes in the accounting game.

He drove home carefully. Against his better judgment, he had gotten into the scotch a bit more than he planned. He wasn't sure how many drinks he had wound up having, but it had been several. His poker playing, unfortunately, had not improved with the infusion of alcohol.

He had begun chasing again, staying in hands for the pure joy of playing. He regretted the losses, but not enough to slow him down. All told, he had given back almost two thousand of the winnings, and wound up only about three hundred ahead for the night. Oh, well, what the hell! He was still way ahead overall, so who the fuck cared? He parked in the driveway, staggered a bit as he made his way into the house, and took four aspirin in anticipation of the hangover he knew was to come.

Fifteen

The pilot nailed the throttles of the 737 and the big bird abruptly nosed up. Don had flown quite a bit, and this was like every other takeoff he could remember. He had no sensation of the plane lifting off the runway, only of the change in the angle of the fuselage. He tensed as he always did, not really able to convince himself that the tail wasn't going to drag. It never had, of course, but you never really knew.

He turned away from the window, and saw Jeff Stevens grinning at him. "What?" asked Don.

"Excited, slick?"

"Well . . . I guess, a little. Why?"

"Oh, nothing," said Jeff, "It's just that you look like a kid on his way to Grandma's house for Christmas, that's all."

Don started to reply, but he knew that the big man was right. He contented himself with elbowing his seat mate in the ribs. He turned back toward the window and was treated to a panoramic view of the front range of the Rockies, glowing white in the morning sun. It had been a good snow year, and Don knew that the ski areas scattered throughout the Rocky Mountains were busy with brightly-clad skiers and snowboarders gliding with various degrees of dexterity over the packed slopes.

Don was tired, tired from three weeks of wrestling with corporate tax returns, payroll records, and sundry other bookkeeping nightmares. He had been working until ten or eleven o'clock every night, six days a week, since the first of the year. Well, that was mostly true. He had, for several months, been playing in the pot limit game on Saturday nights. He had become quite adept at sneaking into the house in the wee hours without disturbing Barbara's slumbers. The boys were usually up and running by about eight on Sundays, so he didn't get a lot of sleep on Saturday nights. He could sometimes grab a nap on Sunday afternoons, but that was somewhat of a rarity. He had nodded off at his desk on a couple of occasions, but since he habitually kept his office door closed, no one was the wiser.

He had finally broached the subject of the Super Bowl weekend trip with Barbara. He put it off for as long as he thought he could, and chose New Year's Eve for the announcement. They were at a party and Barb had ingested four drinks, which was about two over her limit. She was becoming quite mellow, and he decided that the time was right.

"By the way," he had begun, "I'm going to be out of town on the weekend of the twenty-first of January."

"Oh?" she had been grazing the hors d'oeuvres table, and she stopped with a toothpick-impaled shrimp halfway to her mouth. "Where do you have to go?"

"Well, it's Superbowl weekend, and some guys are going to leave on Friday and come back on Monday, and . . ."

She had frowned, chewing on the shrimp. She swallowed, and interrupted. "You're going to the Superbowl?" She knew very little about football, but the knowledge that she did possess included the fact that the Superbowl was almost always held somewhere warm. The outside temperature that evening hovered around five above zero, and the wind chill was about twelve below. Denver was usually quite temperate during the winter, considering the elevation, but the warm weather would not really return for several months yet.

"Without me?" She continued to frown, and her lower lip protruded ever so slightly.

Don laughed. The laugh sounded normal from the outside, but it felt a little nervous. "No. No, we're not going to the Superbowl. We're going to Vegas." There. It was out in the open, laying there between them, waiting.

She had turned half away from him, searching the array of tiny foods for something else to sample. She hesitated for just a second, and then turned back to him. "Vegas? As in Las Vegas?"

"Well . . . yeah. We'll leave on Friday and fly back on Monday, so I won't miss that much time at the office, and I'd be watching the game anyway on Sunday, so it shouldn't make much difference to you." He was talking fast, trying unconsciously to overpower her with words.

"Oh, Don." Her face had fallen slightly. The frown was pretty much gone, but there were still twin furrows between her brows. "Do you think you should?" She was trying very hard to be sober, to think clearly. It seemed to suddenly be very important that she do so, but the alcohol had a grip on her mind and her tongue and didn't seem to be willing to let go.

"Well, just why the hell shouldn't I? I work my ass off at that office, and I really think I deserve to . . ."

She interrupted again. His voice was increasing in volume, and a couple of people on the other side of the table glanced up and moved away slightly to indicate their desire to ignore the argument, whatever it was about. Of course, they also carefully stayed within earshot.

Barbara had brought her finger to her lips, trying to keep the discussion to themselves.

"Don! Keep you voice down!" She had taken his arm and led him away from the table and the disappointed ears. "I didn't . . . I didn't say you didn't deserve it. I know how hard you work and you know I appreciate it! What . . ." She stopped and took a deep breath, trying to collect her thoughts. "What I meant was . . . I'm sorry, Honey, but I still worry about you gambling."

He had no defense. He knew it, and he resorted to anger. "Jesus Christ! Just because I play a little poker on Saturday night, that makes me some sort of a . . . a degenerate? It's not as if I couldn't quit if I wanted to, you know! I'm not that far gone yet, you know! Is that what you want? Do you want me to just quit, prove to you that I can?" Now why the hell had he said that? What if she would call him on it? Luckily, she didn't seize the opportunity.

"Don, please! I'm not . . . I don't think . . . I don't think anything of the kind! It's just what we've talked about before, that you seem to get so . . . I don't know, so involved with it. It just scares me! And Las Vegas is so . . . so . . . "

"Las Vegas is so what?" he challenged, "Have you ever been there?"

"No, but . . . I've heard about . . . about all the gambling, and about people losing lots of money, and . . ."

"Well, is that what you think I'm going to do? Go down there and lose all of our money? Is that what worries you? Are you afraid that I can't control myself?" He was pushing her, pushing as hard as he could. His tone was sarcastic, biting. If someone had asked him at that moment why he was punishing his wife, he would have been at a loss to explain it. All he knew was that, for some reason, he felt threatened, and he was lashing out to protect . . . something.

She had broken off the discussion at that point, refusing to discuss it any further. Since then, they had really seen very little of each other, due to his work schedule. They had breakfast together, but they were usually joined by the boys. He had not been getting home until around ten thirty or eleven, and by that time he was usually ready for nothing more than a stiff drink and sleep. She had asked a couple questions about the trip, just informational stuff, hoping to reopen the conversation, but he had given her nothing more than the answers. She had finally accepted the trip as fact, and tried not to worry. Don was working hard, and he certainly deserved some time off. It would probably be good for him to get away from the office and relax, but the damned gambling . . . Still, what he had said before was true. He had not, at least to her knowledge, used money for gambling that should have gone to pay bills, or buy food, or . . . of course, Don paid the bills from the office so she really didn't know . . . No! That was not even a consideration! That was simply not something Don would do! She had put the thought out of her mind, almost completely.

The stewardess was serving drinks, and Jeff ordered a screwdriver, Don a bloody Mary. Don felt like a kid on his way to Disneyland. He had worked late the previous night, and

Barbara had insisted on their making love. She was determined, as she put it, "Not to have you go off to Las Vegas in a horny condition." It had been wonderful, maybe even better than normal. He was already hyper from the thought of the trip to the Mecca of gambling, and his excited state did nothing to take away from his performance. Afterwards, Barb had held him close to her for a long time, finally drifting off in his arms. He had lain awake for what seemed like hours, and finally slept himself. If there were any dreams, he did not remember them.

The other two members of their foursome were sitting across the aisle from them. To Don's delight, one of the other members of the little group had turned out to be Johnny Gambello, their host for the pot-limit game. Don had learned that Johnny was involved in "investments." Whenever Don had tried to get more specific, Johnny had proven to be somewhat evasive.

The man sitting beside Johnny was about six feet three, two hundred forty pounds, and was the color of a chocolate bar. Wes Davidson was, among other things, Johnny's attorney. One of the "other things" was an ex-running back for the Denver Broncos. He had played for four years and had been well on his way to breaking some rushing records when a blindside tackle had ruined both his left knee and his football career. He had used some of his extraordinary earnings from football to finance a law degree from Denver University. Don had met him several weeks ago when he filled in for a vacancy in the poker game. All of the players were football fans to one degree or another, so Wes had been an instant celebrity. By the end of the evening, he wasn't quite so popular with some of the group. He was a solid, opportunistic poker player.

Don had won some, lost some on the poker games and sports betting in the past several months, but in general he had increased his bankroll. He had six thousand dollars earmarked for the trip. He had no intention of risking all of it, or even a significant part, but he wanted to be able to ride out any losing streaks that might occur. He had been betting on football and the end of the baseball season and was just beginning to dabble in betting basketball. Each of the pro basketball teams seemed to have about forty games a day, so there was no scarcity of betting possibilities.

Jeff finished his drink and leaned back, snoring softly within minutes. Don tried to relax and grab a few minutes of sleep, but it was impossible; he was just too keyed up. He leafed through the in-flight magazine for a bit, and finally resorted to watching the white landscape slide by, thirty thousand feet below. The peaks and canyons of the Rockies gradually gave way to the rolling hills of the southwestern desert. The snow cover became thinner, patchy, and finally disappeared altogether, to be replaced by the dark tan of the sand.

The monotony of the scenery had almost lulled him to the point of sleep when the pitch of the engines changed fractionally. The sound of the big jets had receded into the unconscious minds of the passengers, and had gone mostly unheard, until the change in tone once again made it evident as the pilot throttled back just a bit to begin his descent into Las Vegas. They were apparently not the only people in the world who had decided to spend Superbowl weekend in Vegas. There were a great number of planes clamoring for landing space, and they were placed in a holding pattern which took them over the city and back out over the blue waters of Lake Mead.

The city itself seemed to sprawl in all directions, filling the shallow valley floor. Two areas of high-rise buildings marked the downtown area and the strip hotels. Between the two sectors of multi-story structures, sort of by itself, was what appeared to be a giant tower. It was obviously the tallest thing in the city, and it was topped with a large round pod which looked as if it could contain a restaurant. There was something wrapped around the top of the thing, something red and . . . Don squinted his eyes through the plane window, trying to make out what it was.

"See the tower?" Jeff was leaning forward, peering out the window past Don's head.

"Yeah! What the hell . . . ?"

"Tallest thing west of the Mississippi, I hear," said Jeff, "See that red thing around the top?"

"I do! What is it?"

"A roller coaster!"

"A what?"

"A roller coaster! Can you even imagine? You wouldn't get me up there with a gun!"

"God, no! People actually ride that thing?" Don felt a kind of crawly feeling deep down in his abdomen.

"I guess! Not this kid!" Jeff 's gaze shifted away from the tower as the plane banked. "Jesus, look at the smog! Not that anybody gives much of a shit. The air in the casinos is conditioned and filtered. Filled with cigarette smoke, but conditioned and filtered."

As they circled and finally lined up with the runway to land, Don tried to imagine the action going on below them. Jeff had described literally acres of slot machines, blackjack tables, crap tables, poker tables, roulette wheels, every kind of gambling imaginable. As the wheels touched the runway, Don was sitting straight, staring out the window as if to catch sight of something wonderful.

Jeff poked him on the arm. "Ready, slick?"

"Oh, Christ, yes! Lead me to the tables! I am so ready!"

Jeff turned to Johnny and Wes and said, "Somebody want to get a bucket of cold water and throw it on our boy here? Cool him down a bit?"

The other two men laughed and Wes said, "Y'all better chill, Bro. Y'all go runnin' off here wavin' money around, they gonna take it away from y'all, and slap yo lily-white ass and send y'all home to momma!"

Johnny turned to the big black man and said, "Where the hell you get that corn pone accent, boy?"

"I will have you know, Sir, that I come from a long line of black people, and black people have been known to draw out a syllable or two. I'm just trying to honor my ancestors."

Johnny smiled and shook his head. "Yeah, well, I'm not sure your ancestors would appreciate it. That's the worst accent I ever heard! You better stick to talkin' attorney."

They were up and moving into the aisle now, preparing to leave the plane. For the benefit of everyone around them, Wes turned to Johnny and said loudly, "And watch who you callin' 'boy'!"

To the delight of the four of them, the passengers within hearing distance gave them a wide berth as they moved off the plane.

As the four men walked up the concourse toward the main terminal, Don thought he heard a familiar sound ahead of them. It took him only an instant to identify it. Slot machines! There was no sound like it in the world! He turned to Jeff and pointed to the source of the sound. "Even here?"

"You better believe it! I think it's right nice of the folks here in Vegas to provide the departing passengers one last chance to get even, don't you?"

"I wonder if anyone's ever flown in here, lost all their money at the airport, and flown back home?" Don asked, laughing.

"I'd bet on it!"

"Is that a pun?" asked Wes.

"Probably."

They had all used small, carry-on luggage, so there was no delay in waiting for the baggage fairies. Don noted that almost everyone on the moving sidewalks, or "people carriers" was walking forward, instead of waiting for the mechanical devices to propel them to the terminal. That is, those on the arriving side were walking. The departing passengers seemed to be in no great hurry.

He had no idea where they were headed, so he just followed the lead of the others. They walked out to the taxi area, and Jeff led them past the multi-colored vehicles to an area which held more stretch limousines than Don had ever seen in one place. Jeff held a brief conversation with the driver of a white stretch Lincoln with "Bedouin" on the door in gold leaf. The driver popped out and opened the back door, and the four men entered the obscenely plush interior.

"Jesus!" exclaimed Wes, "You white folks know how to live! This sucker is better equipped than my house!"

It was, indeed, equipped. A small bar in one corner appeared to be well stocked, and there was a miniature color television, a VCR, and a stereo system. There was room to seat six people comfortably, and enough floor space to hold a dance. Johnny surveyed the bar and said, "There doesn't seem to be any Glenheather, Don. Will Callanish do?"

"Well, hell!" Don said, "I'll see if I can choke it down."

As they sipped their drinks, Don watched Las Vegas slide

by the windows of the limo. At first, it looked like any other large city, shopping centers, filling stations, apartment houses. But then, as they approached Las Vegas Boulevard, he began to see the word "casino" repeated more and more often in the signs. The palm trees became more frequent and appeared larger and more well groomed. A right turn, and suddenly they were on the Strip! He began to see the big ones, the huge casino hotels that were famous in song and legend. The bigger properties were set back from the street, giving room for exotic plantings, fountains, and, for God's sake, a working volcano! The strip was crowded with cars, buses, taxis, and other limos. The weather felt almost balmy after the freezing temperature they had left behind only a couple of hours ago.

As they entered the main lobby of the Bedouin, Don was amazed at the opulence of the furnishings and appointments of the massive room. The gold and white color scheme of the limo was carried over to the hotel itself. If overdone, the gold accents could have looked cheap, garish, but they were not, and did not. There were lines in front of each of the registration windows, but Jeff led them past the crowd to a window marked "For VIP Guests Only." A very attractive blond with a name tag reading "Melody" looked up and smiled as they approached.

"May I help you?"

"You can indeed, my dear. I'm Jeff Stevens."

She leafed quickly through a small file box, and withdrew a card. "Welcome back to the Bedouin, Mr. Stevens. We have you in one of our large rooms with two king-sized beds. Will that be satisfactory?"

"That will be eminently satisfactory, Darlin'."

"How many keys will you need?"

"Two will be just fine, unless you want one for yourself."

It was obvious that Jeff was not the first man to make a proposal of that sort to Melody. She smiled sweetly, and said, "But then we would need four, one for me and one for my husband."

Jeff asked, "Does Don here look like his type?"

Melody looked past Jeff at Don. "No, I'm afraid not."

"Well, then, I guess two will be enough." Jeff sighed and

signed the card. She pushed a button at the side of the window and a bellman immediately appeared at their sides. She handed him the keys.

"Enjoy your stay, gentlemen. And good luck!" As they turned away, they heard her say to Johnny, "May I help you?"

The other men were barely able to contain Don long enough to get settled in the rooms and grab some lunch. They ate in a coffee shop that overlooked the casino floor, which did nothing at all for Don's patience. He would have skipped eating and gone directly to the tables, had the other three not almost carried him to the restaurant. As it was, he barely tasted the sandwich as he looked out over the thousands of square feet of casino action. The ubiquitous slot machines provided most of the noise, but intermixed were the cries of the craps dealers and the delighted shouts and screams of successful players. The sounds and the sights of the action spread out below him had him by the scruff of the neck and was shaking gently. His pulse was markedly higher than normal, the familiar feeling of the adrenaline rush beginning.

Jeff finished his meal and leaned back. "Well, Donald, what would you like to try first? And," he added, "quit drooling! It's unseemly!"

Don was about to reply when his eyes lit on a sign which he had not seen before. It was like some of the signs he had seen above what were called "progressive" slot machines, which added a small percentage of each bet to the jackpot until someone eventually hit the right combination of symbols on the slot machine reels. This sign, however, presently read four million seven hundred thirty thousand six hundred fifty something. The digits in the dollar and cents positions were changing too fast to read. Another sign above the numbers read "Megabucks."

"What the hell is that?"

"What the hell is what?" asked Johnny.

"What the hell is Megabucks?"

"Oh, that's a progressive dollar slot that's tied in with other machines all over the state. The total just keeps getting bigger until somebody hits it."

"You mean you could actually win over four million dollars?" Don was fascinated.

"Sure! And you could get struck by lightning, too!" said Wes. "Yeah, somebody hits the thing once in a while, but that's because, any hour of the day or night, there's about a bazillion people playing it."

Jeff added, "Somebody eventually hits the lottery back home, too, but that doesn't mean the odds are worth a shit! Anyway, what do you want to play? The tables await! Unless, of course, you want to try the Megabucks? Like I said, the odds suck, but on the other hand, it's hard to win four million bucks on a blackjack table. It can take just forever!"

"Well," said Don, "How about craps? You showed me how to bet, sorta, and I'd like to try it!"

"You're on! You guys want to shoot some craps?"

"Sure!

"Why not? Let's get 'em!"

They charged the meal to Jeff's room, and headed for the casino floor. There were four crap tables in operation, three of them fairly crowded, and one with only the dealers and four players. Don headed for one of the empty spaces at the sparsely populated table, but Jeff caught his arm. "Cold table." he said.

"Beg pardon?"

"Never go to a cold table. The dice been runnin' cold on that table, otherwise it would be as crowded as the others. When it warms up, it'll draw a crowd again." He led Don to one of the other tables, and they squeezed in at the end between what looked like Joe college and an incredibly old oriental man. The dice were presently being rolled by a middle aged lady at the other end of the table, and she had apparently been rolling for a while, as the other players were cheering her on. Don looked at the surface of the table, and was immediately intimidated. There seemed to be stacks of chips everywhere! He had seen pictures of a craps layout, showing the various betting areas, but the real thing somehow looked much more complicated. He decided to just watch Jeff for a bit, and see what happened.

Jeff took a large roll of bills out of his front pants pocket, and peeled off ten hundreds. He tossed them in front of the dealer nearest him. The dealer spread the bills out on the table surface, said "Change a thousand," to the man in the suit sitting at the middle of the table, and the man nodded. The dealer took ten black chips from the stacks in front of him and placed them in front of Jeff.

Jeff took five of the chips and tossed them back to the dealer, saying, "Quarters." The dealer replaced the hundred dollar chips with a stack of green twenty five dollar chips, and Jeff began placing his bets. The shooter had just made her point, to the delight of the crowd, and Jeff placed three of the green chips on the "pass" line. The lady rolled a five, and Jeff immediately placed one of the hundred dollar chips behind the green chips. Don reviewed the rules that Jeff had tried to drill into him. He knew that, if the shooter rolled another five before she rolled a seven, Jeff would win. If a seven showed first, he would lose. Simple enough so far!

The pass line bet was, he knew, one of the better bets in Vegas, the odds only being about one point four percent against the bettor. The other bet, the "odds" bet, as it was known, was actually an even-money bet. That meant that, in the case of Jeff's bet, the odds against the number coming up before a seven was three to two, and that's what the bet paid. Jeff had bet a hundred dollars on the odds bet, and he would be paid a hundred fifty dollars if he won. The pass line bet paid even money. Seventy five dollars bet would win seventy five dollars.

Jeff made another bet, this time on the "come" line, and the lady threw a four. He tossed another three green chips to the dealer, and, without a word being spoken between them, the dealer picked up the come bet, put it on the four, and placed the second bet on top of the first. That was as far as Don could follow the action. The lady kept rolling the dice for several more minutes, and the chips were flying! Don worked with numbers every day, but he marveled at the ability of the dealers to keep track of who had made what bets, and the payoffs on each bet. On every roll of the dice, chips changed hands. There seemed to be hundreds of different types of bets available, and it appeared that almost every one of them were being used.

The small oriental man was betting with black chips exclusively, and the line of chips in the rack in front of him grew slowly. Jeff's fortunes also seemed to be building slightly, but for every bet he won, he seemed to make another bet. Don couldn't keep track, but the big man must be ahead over a thousand. However, most of it was out there on the table in the form of additional bets.

The lady rolled an eleven. Jeff straightened up, glanced quickly at the line of chips in the rack in front of him, and said, "Take me down!" The dealer's hands flew as he gathered several of Jeff's bets and gave the chips back. Jeff gathered the chips and put them in the rack with the others. He began to count them, but he noticed that Don was staring at him, and he smiled. "Superstition!" he said. "A lot of times, a seven will follow an eleven." He noticed the skeptical look from Don and added, "Of course, a lot of times it doesn't, but she can't roll forever."

The old gentleman to their right had apparently also decided that a seven was due, as he motioned to the dealer to take him down, too. The dealer again removed a large number of black chips from the betting surface, and Jeff said, "Good move, Pops!"

The oriental ignored him.

"How come they let you take back part of your bets?" Don was trying hard to understand, but it was not coming.

"Certain bets, like the odds bets, don't hold any advantage for the casino, so they don't have any objection to your taking them off anytime you want to." They watched as the woman rolled another number, a six, and then a seven. There was a collective groan around the table as all action came to a halt and the dealers collected the majority of the bets on the table and placed them in the stacks along the back wall of the table, the stacks belonging to the casino. The dice were passed to the player to the left of the lady, and the action began again.

Don watched as Jeff counted the chips in front of him, and was amazed to find that his friend had won over seventeen hundred dollars in a little more than ten minutes. A thought occurred to him, and he glanced at the racks in front of the old man. Where Jeff had been betting green chips, twenty five dollar chips, the little man had been betting hundreds. He must be up several thousand. Don almost ripped his pocket getting his money out.

Sixteen

 Don remembered the initial lecture that Jeff had given him after Don digested the rules of craps from the books.

"Money can be made at a craps table. Significant money. All it takes is a reasonable amount of cooperation from the dice, and some sort of halfway intelligent betting system. If someone throws a series of winning numbers, say a series of eight, and bets a dollar each time, he'll win the first eight bets and lose the ninth, for a net gain of eight dollars. Right?"

"Yeah, makes sense."

"If another bettor also begins with a dollar bet, but lets each win ride, essentially doubling the bet each time with the winnings from the previous roll, he'll have won two hundred and fifty five dollars by the end of the eighth bet, and will then lose it all on the ninth roll. Okay?"

"I'm with you so far."

"So, obviously, the ideal betting system lies somewhere between those two extremes. The big boys say that you should only increase the amount of a bet after a win. This makes sense, if only for the reason that the additional money wagered comes from the casino's money, not your own. If the shooter makes several of the right numbers, the increase in bets and the ability to make several different kinds of bets enables the bettor to wager a great deal of money, most of it winnings. Every shooter will eventually lose. When that happens, a lot of bets which have carefully been built up over the period of the shooter's 'hand' will be lost, but the bettor will hopefully have taken off some of each win and will therefore be ahead of the game when the inevitable does happen."

Don nodded. "Yeah. That does make sense. So, if you're playing with their money, it doesn't hurt as much when you do lose!"

"Right. You can also bet "against" the dice, or bet that the shooter won't win. If the dice are 'cold,' if the shooter is constantly rolling the wrong numbers, money can also be made, using the same logic. A lot of players refuse to bet against the dice. They figure it's unlucky. Possibly it is, but then so's losing.

"The worst thing, the crap that will move the chips from the player's stacks to the casino's with the most efficiency is if the dice start 'chopping.' When the dice chop, they'll come up with the right numbers for two or three bets running, just enough to get the bettors excited into pressing their bets, taking odds, and making new bets. Then, almost like they have some kind of a perverse mind of their own, exactly the wrong number will come up. The players bitch and moan, the dealers rake in the bets, the dice will pass to the next shooter, and the whole thing starts over."

Don had the misfortune to jump into the game just as the dice were, for some damned reason, about to begin an extended period of chopping. He had also bought a thousand dollars worth of chips, and he bet seventy five dollars on the pass line. The new shooter rolled an eight, one of the easier numbers to make. Don took odds on the eight, betting a hundred and twenty-five dollars. He also made a "come" bet. The shooter threw a five, and Don again took odds. He backed off at that point, realizing that he had just bet three hundred and seventy-five dollars. His points were the eight and the five, and he needed those two numbers to appear before a seven was thrown. As he was calculating, the dice came hopping down the table toward him, and he looked down to see a four and a three. Well, shit!

He watched as his chips were added to the stacks in front of the dealer, and bet again. The next shooter declined the opportunity to roll the dice, and the oriental man was next up.

He placed three black chips on the pass line, selected two of the dice, and quickly threw them backhanded. They hit the end of the table, bounced once, and were still. "Seven! A winner, seven."

The dealer placed three green chips beside Don's bet, and Don pressed the bet, taking two chips and leaving one, increasing the bet to a hundred dollars. The elderly man rolled a six, a nine, and an eight. Don bet on each of the rolls, and took odds on each bet. The old man promptly rolled a seven.

Don looked down to see what he had left of the thousand dollars, and was shocked to see four green chips. He had blown nine hundred dollars on two shooters! Un-fucking-believable! Goddamned dice! He turned to glare at the little old man, but he was gone. He had pocketed his remaining chips and melted into the crowd milling through the big gaming area.

He looked up to see that the attention of the entire table was now on him.

"Would you like to shoot, sir?" The stickman, the dealer who used a long, hooked stick to control the dice, had pushed six dice to a position just in front of him, and everyone was waiting for him to act.

"Shoot 'em or pass 'em!" From the other end of the table.

"Sir? Do you want the dice?" The players were getting restless, and the stickman was getting just a little testy. Don picked up two of the dice and began the motion of throwing them at the other end of the table, but the stickman and one of the other dealers both yelled.

"Hold it!"

"You have to have a bet down, Sir."

"What the hell's the holdup? Shoot the fuckin' dice!" This from the man who had filled the space vacated by the oriental.

Don was mad about the losses and embarrassed by the delay he had caused. He looked at the lonely green chips and started for his pocket. He'd show them! They weren't dealing with a complete greenhorn! As his hand came up with the roll of bills in it, its motion was stopped by the big hand of Jeff Stevens.

"Easy, Son. Let's take a walk."

"Bullshit!" Don spat back at him, "They've got . . ."

Jeff interrupted him. "I know what they've got, Don. Bet the hundred if you have to, but then we're gonna take a walk. They're not likely to close the casino if we take a break. They'll still be here."

Don looked at his friend and saw that he was serious. Jeff was, he knew, fully capable of picking him up and carrying him away from the table if he so desired. Don's shoulders dropped, and he reached down and placed one of the twenty-five dollar chips on the pass line.

"Are you gonna roll the dice, or not?"

"What the hell is his problem?"

"We're ready now, Sir!" Sarcastically, from the stickman.

"Just shoot the Goddamned things!"

Don threw the dice, a trifle harder than he had intended, but they hit the other end of the table and fell back onto the playing surface.

"Eleven!" cried the stickman, hooking the dice and sliding them to the middle of the table. "Pay the front line!" The dealer placed another green chip beside Don's bet, and the dice were again shoved toward him.

"Now that's more like it!" The man to his right had just won a pass line bet of three hundred dollars, and Don was suddenly his best friend. "Do it again, shooter!"

Don increased his bet to fifty and threw the dice again. "Seven! A winner, seven."

"Yeah! "

"He's slow, but he's hot!"

"One more time, shooter!"

He bet three green chips and glanced over at Jeff. The big man was grinning now, holding a number of chips in his hand, ready to bet. The dice were on their way again.

"Six! Mark the six!" The dealers slid markers to the numbers printed across the top of the table and placed them on the six. The chips were beginning to fly again. The bettors were now convinced that the tall young man at the end of the table was on his way to a hot hand, and they were poised to take full advantage of the casino. And, as if to reward them for their faith, the dice rolled to a stop and displayed another six!

"Six! A winner!"

"All fuckin' right!"

"Oh, yes! Yes!"

"Same shooter, coming out with a new number!"

"Give 'em hell, kid!"

"Get your bets down!"

"How 'bout another eleven?"

"Yeah! Eleven never hurt nobody!"

He rolled a five, a twelve, an eight, a four, and another five. The table was going nuts by this time, and the dealers' hands were flying, collecting or paying off bets. No person at the table was over ten feet away from any other person, but everyone was yelling.

"Five dollar hard eight!"

"It's a bet!"

"Thirty two across, dealer!"

"You want odds on your four, ma'am?"

"Press the four!"

"Field bets, come bets!"

"Shooter coming out again!"

Don continued to roll. The table was about three deep now, disembodied arms reaching between players to place bets. The din was awesome. Don had won steadily, and had increased his bet with each win. He also made more bets, different bets, trying to gain back the earlier losses. The table was his now, the other bettors cheering him on, slapping him on the shoulder. He was costing the casino a considerable amount of money, and his table-mates appreciated it.

He kept increasing the size and amounts of his bets until he was almost back to even. He made one more bet, and saw that the rack in front of him was empty. He was well ahead of where he had been when he started rolling the dice, but it was all out there on the table. He felt a small, cold stirring deep down in his gut, and he almost told the dealer to take his odds bets down, as he had seen Jeff do earlier, but that would mean cutting into his winnings if those numbers came up, so he didn't do it.

He picked up the dice again and looked quickly at his bets. He had just about everything covered. If anything other than a seven came up, he would win at least one of the bets. He made a promise to himself that he would start taking back his winnings, stockpiling against the time when the seven would finally . . .

"Seven out!"

No! No! Not a seven! Anything but . . .

There was the usual groan from the other bettors, but there were also shouts of congratulation and commiseration.

"Good hand!"

"Way to go, shooter!"

Jeff was busily counting his chips. He finished and turned to Don with a grin. "Helluva hand, slick! How did you . . ." His eyes moved to the empty racks in front of Don. "Oh, shit! All of it? You had it all out there?"

Don took a deep breath, pursed his lips and blew it back out. "Yeah. It was going so well, the numbers were really coming, and . . ." He turned away from the table and smacked the top of the elbow cushion with his hand. The stickman pushed the dice toward Jeff, but he waved them away.

"You ready for that walk now?" Jeff strained up on his toes, trying to see if Johnny and Wes were still at one of the other crap tables, but they were nowhere to be seen.

Don looked back at the table, at the action beginning again, and hesitated. Jeff said, "Come on! This isn't the only game in town, for Christ's sake! Let's try something else!"

Don allowed himself to be led away from the table then. Their vacant spaces were immediately filled with two other bettors, eager for battle. A cheer went up as the stickman yelled, "Seven. Seven, a winner!"

As they walked away from the craps area, the noise level dropped considerably, and Jeff asked, "Do you mind a little advice?"

Don snorted. "Are you gonna give me a lecture on money management?"

Jeff flared. "No, I'm not gonna give you a lecture! I'm trying to help, Goddammit! If you don't want my help, you can . . . "

Don put his hand on the other man's shoulder. "I'm sorry. I know you're trying to help. I'm just pissed off!"

"Well, sure you are! You just dropped . . . what? A grand?"

Don nodded.

"Okay. First, you started too heavy. You should take it easy bettin' at first, see which way the wind blows before you commit any real money. When you lost the first bets, you should have backed off, bet less. Instead, you jumped in deeper, trying to get your money back. You should have walked the first time I mentioned it, but you were chasing that money. As it turned out, you had one hell of a roll. I made damned near two grand on it, but I was takin' back part of each win. You got greedy, and put it all back out there. What do you think built this place, and all the others like it?" He swept his arm up to indicate the cavernous interior of the casino.

Don followed the gesture, not sure what Jeff meant. "I don't know. What?"

"Greed, my boy! Greed paid for every brick, every light bulb, every stick of furniture in this mother! Greed is what brings several million dollars a day into this town, and greed is what keeps the vast majority of that money here. No matter what happens, they got you! If you win, you see how easy it is and how good it feels, and you try to win more. Greed. If you lose, you think, 'Hey, wait a minute! I had that money a minute ago, and I want it back!' That's greed, too. Either way, you play some more, and the house percentages get you sooner or later. If you are one of the very few that leave town ahead, they don't care. There will have been many others that didn't, and they know that you'll eventually be back, and they'll get you then."

"Yeah, I suppose that's true. Somebody has to pay for all this shit!"

"Right. When the Mirage opened, the word was that they had to win a million dollars a day, just to pay the overhead. Just to break even!"

"Jesus! A million a day?"

"That's what the word was. Oh, speaking of the Mirage, we gotta go over there and play some poker. They've got the damnedest poker room you've ever seen!"

"Big?"

"The biggest in town! Like twenty-five or thirty tables, and everything from low limit up to pot limit. Some of the big boys play there."

"The big boys?"

"Yeah, the pros. The people who play poker for a living."

Since the first time Don had learned that there was such a thing as a professional poker player, he had fantasized about it. What a life that must be! He loved playing poker, and he considered himself to be fairly good at the game. He had certainly won more than he had lost over the past several months, and the idea of doing something that was as much fun as playing poker for a living was intriguing. He knew that his family required more security than something like that could possible offer, but it didn't hurt to dream, did it?

As they walked through the casino, they approached the blackjack area. As they did, they saw Wes stand up from one of the tables and wave at them. He held up two fingers and pointed down at the blackjack table, indicating two open chairs. They waved back and walked toward him.

The table had a twenty five dollar minimum bet, so Don and Jeff both bought in for five hundred. Johnny and Wes were both playing at the table, and Wes had a respectable pile of green chips in front of him. Johnny, on the other hand, only had a few chips left.

"How was the craps table?" asked Wes.

Jeff hesitated, looking at Don. Don was feeling better already, just the fact of being back in the action pumping him like a shot of caffeine. "The teacher did okay. The student didn't do so hot!"

"Oops! Get in your shorts a bit, did they?" Wes turned to the attractive young lady sitting next to him. "Pardon my language, Ma'am."

She smiled prettily at Wes and laid her hand on his big forearm. "No need to apologize. I just love it when you talk dirty!" She left her hand on his arm for a bit longer than necessary, and the other three men exchanged glances, grinning and raising their eyebrows.

Wes winked at Don with the eye that was away from the young woman, and said, "You want to hear dirty language, just hang around until I start losing!"

Johnny looked up at her and said, "If you're impatient,

Honey, I have been losing. I could whisper some sweet swear words in your ear. Matter of fact, that would probably be a hell of a lot more fun than this has been!" He glared at the dealer. Both the dealer and the young lady ignored him, and he shook his head and looked at his next two cards. A queen and a three. The dealer's up card was a ten. He signaled for another card, caught a nine, and watched another fifty bucks go down the drain.

Don decided that he admired the taste of the person who designed the uniforms or costumes of the cocktail waitresses. They were modeled after the saris worn by the real desert dwellers of the middle east, but there the resemblance ended. The purpose of the real sari is to protect the wearer from the sun and from the eyes of others. The purpose of these outfits was somewhat different. They would have offered very little protection from the sun, and almost none from the eyes of the observer. One shoulder was bare, the other covered by the thinnest of white fabric, which drifted down in front and back and was held at the waist by a sash of the same fabric in gold. The white fabric ended just below the crotch of the wearer, and the overall effect was that the waitresses were wearing layers of gauze, and nothing more. The veil which they wore was all but transparent, and did little to hide their lips, but it did tend to accentuate their eyes. Don stuck to drinking coffee, but he fell in love about three times while they were playing blackjack.

They played for about an hour and a half, Wes and his admirer winning, and Johnny, Don, Jeff, and the other player losing. Don was down a couple hundred, and was considering seeking greener pastures, but he was enjoying watching the woman put moves on Wes. Her intentions were quite obvious, but Wes was playing dumb, pretending not to pick up on her signals. She still had both hands above the table, but no one would have been surprised to see one of them disappear. It turned out that her name was Jessica, she was from San Francisco, and she was in Vegas for the weekend with her older sister and her sister's husband. She was, in real life, a mortgage broker.

Wes finally tired of stringing her along and began, to her delight, to respond. The two of them became chummier and chummier, whispering and giggling like two teenagers. They had pretty much shut out the rest of the world, and were playing their cards mechanically, absorbed in the age-old mating ritual.

Jeff looked at Johnny and Don and said, "This is about all of this fun I can take. What say we mosey over to the sports book and make a bet or two on the game?"

Johnny stood up and gathered the few remaining chips in front of him. "Good idea! Better make some bets before I go broke completely."

"Do they have one here?" asked Don.

"They certainly do! Come with me, my son, and allow me to show you something that will make your little heart go pitty-pat!" They left Wes and his pending conquest, or Jessica and her pending conquest, depending on the point of view, and the three of them wove through the crowds toward the other side of the casino floor. As they were approaching the sports book area, Don caught an occasional glimpse of television screens, but he was totally unprepared for the sports betting setup.

The ceiling disappeared, and the far wall of the area looked to be about three stories tall. It was covered with scoreboards and television screens. Dominating the wall were the two giant screens, one of which was blank, the other showing the finish of a horse race from somewhere. There wasn't a lot of live sports coverage going on in the middle of Friday afternoon, so many of the small screens were also blank. The initial effect was mind-boggling, and it took Don a couple of minutes to find the listings which gave the matchups and the point spread on each of the college and pro basketball games for the weekend. And of course, the Superbowl. There was, as Jeff had promised, a long list of bets which could be made on the game.

The game itself was to be played between the Buffalo Bills, the American Football League champions, and the Washington Redskins, of the National Football League. The Bills were favored, and the point spread put them at minus six and a half. You could, of course, bet on the outcome of the game itself, and almost everybody did, just out of form, but that was by no means the only bet that could be made.

Because of the general silliness which surrounds the Superbowl, and also because it tended to line the pockets of the casino owners, the bettors could wager on which team would score first, score last, commit the first fumble, have the most punts or field goals or penalties or whatever. Thus, it was possible to make fifteen or so different wagers on the same game.

It appeared that every sporting event in the known universe was being watched, monitored, and bet upon. The nasal monotone of a horse race announcer competed with the sounds of the slot machines behind them. There was seating for several hundred people, and each seat had a little desk to one side of it, presumably for one's betting slips, racing forms, or whatever. There were fifty or so people sitting in the sports book area, apparently intent on one of the horse races.

Jeff and Don had discussed the upcoming game, and they agreed that Buffalo should win by ten points. They both placed bets on Buffalo. Don had hoped to use his Vegas winnings to bet on the game, but thus far, there didn't seem to be any such thing. He bet a thousand on the game itself, and also bet a parlay ticket which would pay off if Buffalo scored the first field goal, Washington gave up the first fumble and suffered the first quarterback sack, Buffalo outscored Washington in the second quarter, and there were less than ten points scored in the first quarter. He knew it was a sucker bet, so he only risked a hundred on it. If it would somehow come through for him, however, he would collect thirty two hundred dollars! Besides, it would make the game a lot more fun to watch.

Jeff and Johnny had finished their transactions with the betting windows, and they started back toward the main casino. Johnny had also bet on the Bills, and they congratulated each other on their betting expertise. They walked toward the blackjack area again, and saw that the chairs which had been occupied by Jennifer and Wes were now vacant.

Johnny said, "Well, looks like ol' Wesley is getting his watch wound!"

"Does he make a habit of . . . of this sort of thing?" asked Don, waving his hand to indicate something, he wasn't really sure what.

"If by 'this sort of thing,' you mean getting laid at odd times of the day, yes he does. Women simply seem to fall all over him.

I mean he's big, and not bad looking, I guess, but there's just something about him . . ."

"Is it true what they say about black men?" asked Jeff.

"Well, I certainly wouldn't know!" said Johnny.

Don said, "You mean about the rhythm?"

"Yeah, right!" said Jeff.

Johnny decided that he wanted to shoot some more craps, so the three of them drifted back over to the crap table area. This time, Don bought in for five hundred and played much more conservatively. They played for a period of two hours, and the dice let Don get ahead by nearly two thousand before a vicious series of chops took it all back away, plus another seven hundred. He had done it again, he had chased the losses, trying to regain both the money and the feelings which had gone along with winning.

He felt more comfortable at the table this time, more familiar with the mysterious goings-on. He had actually been able to follow the betting of Johnny, and Johnny made every bet there was to make. This characteristic surprised Don, because Johnny was a fairly conservative poker player, which took great patience. Here on the crap table, he exhibited none of that patience. He wanted action on every roll of the dice, and that is exactly what he got. A single number could generate payoffs on two or three different bets, or losses on the same number of bets. Don couldn't see that the betting method was particularly profitable, but it was certainly fun.

Don had truly enjoyed playing, notwithstanding the fact that he lost another seven hundred dollars. The money meant really very little to him; it was simply a method of keeping score.

The only problem was that he needed money to continue playing. He told Jeff that he would be right back, and he walked quickly to the men's room and locked himself in one of the stalls. He took out his bankroll and counted it. There was three thousand and change left. That couldn't be right! Could it? He had lost a thousand at the first craps table, seven hundred just now, and two hundred playing blackjack. That was just nineteen hundred. Where the hell . . . Of course! He had bet a grand on the game and another hundred on the parlay card. That wasn't really money lost, yet, but he had gone through three thousand dollars in . . . he looked at his watch . . . in just over seven hours. At this rate, he would be totally out of money by about two o'clock tomorrow morning. He couldn't let that happen! The craps tables hadn't been very good to him, and the blackjack seemed too mechanical. What he needed was a game where he had some degree of expertise, where he could afford to wait until fate swung his way again. He walked back out to the crap table, got Jeff's attention, and said, "You want to show me that poker room at the Mirage?"

They decided to walk the few blocks from the Bedouin to the Mirage. As they left the front entrance of the hotel-casino complex, Don was almost dazzled by the display of lighting on the strip. Each property along the length of the strip had done its best to outdo its neighbors in the display of neon, colored lights, blinking lights, lights that moved, lights that spun and danced and exploded. The overall effect, of course, was one of almost outlandish garishness.

Jeff said, "You are now entering Las Vegas. Please check your good taste at the city limits."

"It is kinda spectacular, though," said Don. He spotted the blue Mirage sign in the distance, and pointed. "There?"

"There!"

The evening air was chilly, but it felt good against their faces after the biting cold of Colorado in January. There weren't a great many pedestrians about, but the street itself was solid with vehicular traffic. They went in the main entrance of the Mirage, after stopping and witnessing the eruptions of fire and steam which spewed out of the working volcano outside the entrance. The thing was rumored to have cost many millions of dollars, and covered a couple of acres. A great deal of water flowed down the sides of the mountain day and night, cascading over waterfalls into pools at the base. Every fifteen minutes, after dark, the thing erupted! It was difficult for Don to believe not only that someone could build something like this, but also that they would build it. After the display died down, they walked on into the long hallway leading to the casino. There was a large crowd lined up along one wall, the wall being composed of floor to ceiling glass. Don stretched up on his toes to see what the attraction was, and saw two of the most beautiful animals he had ever seen.

Lounging in a setting of white marble, green plants, and shallow pools with fountains were two big cats that had to be albino tigers! The area they were in was large and immaculate, and the animals looked like they were used to the lap of luxury. They tended toward fat, but they were nonetheless magnificent! He was still exclaiming about the cats when Jeff led him into the casino area. They walked past another huge sports book to the poker room. As soon as he laid eyes on the tables and the action on them, all thoughts of the cats were gone.

Seventeen

"Where y'all from, son?" The question came from the man sitting to Don's left. Don had noticed him when the man sat down at the poker table. It would have been hard not to notice him. He appeared to be somewhere in his sixties, and the lined, tan skin of his face was set off by a magnificent handlebar mustache and bushy eyebrows. The facial hair was white, as was the hair sticking out from under a Stetson which looked like it had actually seen service outdoors. Don had been playing in the twenty dollar limit game for about three hours when the old man entered the card room. He was obviously well known, as he was greeted by the floorman, two of the dealers, and several of the players. They referred to him as "Slats."

"Colorado. Denver. How about you?"

"Oh, we live here now. We sold a little hunk of land down in Texas a few years back and decided to move here to retire. We used to come here 'bout three or four times a year, so we just finally decided to make it permanent."

"You play here a lot?"

The man laughed. "I 'spect you could say that. I play 'bout every day, at least for a while."

"Doesn't your wife object? To your playing so much, I mean."

"Nope. She sure don't. That's her over there at the stud table." He pointed at a matronly lady two tables over, who looked like anybody's grandmother. She looked up, saw him looking at her, and waggled her fingers at him.

"Pretty lady!" said Don.

"Yeah, she's a good ol' gal. When she goes, I'm gonna make a wallet out of her."

Don had been sipping a cup of coffee when Slats made the comment, and it was all he could do to keep from spewing coffee all over his end of the table. As it was, he snorted, got coffee into the back of his nose, and almost choked. He scooted back from the table and bent over, coughing. When he could finally glare up at the Texan through tear-filled eyes, he saw that the eyes of the man were sparkling, and the ends of his mustache twitched as he tried not to laugh.

The older man appeared to be an excellent poker player. He was very patient, and filled the time between playable hands either studying the habits of the other players or chatting. When he did get involved in a hand, his concentration was total. On two occasions, He had been in the middle of a sentence when he had looked at his first cards and decided to play the hand. He would be totally silent during the battle, but he would then return to complete the thought. When he did play, he used a style that was quite aggressive, and the other players seemed to respect him and his cards.

Don had also been playing a pretty tight game, trying to get a feel for the competition. He soon learned that these people made the home poker players with whom he was familiar seem like so many amateurs. At any one time, the table would consist of one, maybe two tourists like himself, a couple of off duty poker dealers, and a number of "locals." The locals consisted of three types; retirees, such as Slats and his wife, residents of Vegas who had real jobs, and the odd professional poker player. It was difficult to tell one type of local from another, but he was pretty sure that the tall young man at the other end of the table was a pro. He talked mostly of his recent experiences in tournament play, and a couple of people dropped by the table to congratulate him on taking second place in some contest or other.

Don counted his chips again. Once an accountant, always an accountant, he thought to himself. He was down about four hundred since he started, but the pots had been averaging three hundred or so. Given a couple of decent hands, he could make that up in a hurry. They were playing Texas Holdem. Jeff had elected to play seven card stud, and played for about four hours before he got antsy. He cashed in and came over to see if Don was ready to leave.

"How you doin', slick? You hurtin' them?"

"Well, not exactly. I strongly suspect that some of these people have played poker before!"

Slats couldn't resist chiming in. "Yeah, there's a few of 'em that maybe played a hand or two, but ain't none of 'em ever been worth a damn."

As he fully expected, the statement earned him about a minute and a half of good natured verbal abuse from several of the other players.

"Just watch yourself, Pops!"

"Is the light okay at that end of the table, Grandpa?"

"Isn't it about time for your nap, you old fart?"

Don grinned and said, "Jeff, this is Slats."

The two men shook hands, and Slats said, "You boys havin' a good time?"

"Absolutely!" said Jeff. "This town is unbelievable!"

"Ya makin' any money?"

"Well, I'm doing okay, but I can't speak for my friend Donald." Jeff stopped talking as the next round of cards came out. When the bet came around to Don, he raised. Slats folded his cards and he and Jeff watched the action. Most of the way through the hand, Don bet or raised every chance he got. Two other players went with him all the way, and the pot grew to a very respectable size. Before the last card hit the table, the board, or the cards in the center of the table which all of the players used, consisted of the deuce, ten, and jack of hearts, and the queen of spades. Don lifted the corners of his cards, and Jeff and Slats both saw that he had the ace and king of hearts. Barring something disastrous, like a pair showing in the middle of the table, he had the nuts, the lock hand.

The dust settled from the round of betting, and the dealer put out the last card. The queen of clubs. Don's shoulders dropped fractionally, but the other two players checked to him! Maybe the flush was good! They could be laying back, planning to raise, but that didn't seem likely. He bet twenty, and sat back to see what was going to happen. The next player in turn hesitated, looked at his cards, and raised twenty! The third player frowned, looked at the cards in the middle of the table, at his own two cards, and re-raised! Well, there it was. One of them, maybe both of them, had a full house! He knew it, everyone knew it. It was obvious. The full house had not been possible until the second queen had appeared. But now, if one of the other players had, for example, a queen and a deuce, he now had three queens and two deuces. If one of them had a pair of jacks, he had three jacks and two queens.

Don stalled for as long as he thought he could. Logically, he should fold, throw the cards in and cut his losses. He had tried to bet as much as he could, to either blow the others out of the hand or to make it as expensive as possible for them to draw out on him. He had made it expensive, for sure, but now his hand was the underdog.

But, what if they were bluffing? What if the flush was still good? They could be betting on two pair or three of a kind. With the cards showing, one of them could have an ace-high straight or a smaller flush. He should fold, get the hell out, but he just couldn't. He could feel the palms of his hands growing moist.

"Forty dollars to you, sir." The dealer, as well as the rest of the table, was looking at him, waiting for him to act.

"Yeah, I know!" Don's hand moved toward his chips, stopped, and then he grabbed a green chip and three red ones and threw them toward the pot. "Call!"

This time, there was no hesitation. The next player raised again. The table limit on raises was three, so the third man just called, as did Don. The third player was the first to show his down cards. He had a queen and a ten.

"Not good enough!" said the other player. Predictably, he showed the other queen and a jack. Don didn't even show his hand to the rest of the table. He just pitched the cards toward the dealer, face down.

He felt Jeff's hand on his shoulder. "Tough break! If the damned board hadn't paired . . . well, I'm gonna take off. You want to come?"

Again, Don knew what he should do. He should get his ass up, go walk it off, shake off the effects of the defeat, take a nap, anything but sit there and try to get the money back. But he was not capable of doing any of those things. He had lost a lot of money since they flew into town earlier that day, and he had just been embarrassed in front of Jeff and the Texan. Don cursed himself for staying in the hand longer than he should have, for chasing, for letting pride and greed rule his actions.

"Ah . . . no. No, Jeff, I think I'll stick around here for a while. You go ahead. Give 'em hell!"

"I'll do my best! You too! Be careful." Jeff raised his eyebrows as he said the last words, trying to warn Don to watch out for the predators with which he was playing.

Don caught the look. "Don't worry about me, Dad! I'll be okay!" He said it just a little sarcastically. Jeff held his eyes for a second longer, and then looked away and turned to leave the poker room.

As Don turned back to the table, he thought, "Jesus! He's getting as bad as my damned wife! 'Be careful! Don't gamble so much! Do this! Don't do that!' Well, I can fucking well take care of myself, thank you very much! Just kindly leave me the fuck alone, and let me do what I want to do!"

He looked at his next cards, searching for any excuse to get involved in another pot. He called the bet and the raise before the flop, and threw the cards away when the first three up cards had absolutely no relationship to his hand. He looked around and caught the eye of the cocktail waitress. She was very tall and very pretty, and her name, according to her name tag, was Lori. She smiled at him and he said, "Do you have any Glenheather, Lori?"

"No, sir. I'm sorry. Would Callanish do?"

"Admirably! On the rocks, please."

"I'll be right back with your drink, sir. Would anyone else care for a cocktail?"

She took orders from the rest of the table, and as she was making her way back toward the service bar, Don reached out and caught her arm. She looked back at him, and he said,

"Make that a double, would you? Thanks!"

"That was a bad beat you took there, son!" said Slats, "Those pairs will kill ya!"

"That's no shit! I should have folded when the second queen showed, but it's hard to lay down an ace-high flush!"

"That's for damned sure! 'Course, I'll bet that you never caught a full house on the last card to beat some poor bastard who was pushing his flush for all it was worth."

Don grinned. "Why, Heavens no! I would never do such a thing!"

The next cards came out, and Don watched as the Texan battled three other players for a monster pot. Again, a pair showed on the last card, and Slats checked. The next two players also checked, but the other one bet twenty. Without any hesitation at all, Slats raised! The other two players folded instantly, and the bettor studied his cards and the board for a long time, and finally threw his cards in. The dealer shoved the pile of chips toward the older man, and he showed his hand to Don before he threw it in, face down.

He had garbage! He had been bluffing! Don couldn't help but laugh, which drew the glares of the three players who Slats had blown out with the raise. He leaned over and whispered, "You old bastard! You had no business at all in that hand! How did you know that the pair didn't help him? And, while I'm at it, how did you know that the pair was going to show up? If they hadn't been convinced that you had the full house . . ." He ran down, and just sat and shook his head.

Slats just grinned and stacked his chips. Finally he said, "Well, I just kinda took advantage of a situation there. They all saw you get your ass kicked a while ago when the pair showed on the end, so I figured they might of learned a lesson. Sure enough, it looks like they did."

Don's double Callanish came, and he tipped Lori a dollar. The drink was of course free. The casinos of Nevada seemed to have no qualms whatsoever about buying the players whatever they wanted to drink, and all they wanted to drink. He sipped the Callanish and wished for just a second that he still smoked cigarettes. Many of the poker players smoked, and he knew that the effects of the nicotine would help in dealing with the stresses of poker. Ah, well, the scotch would have somewhat the same effect. The trouble with alcohol was that it tended to cloud the judgment after a time. He had no intention of having more than one or two drinks. If he was going to play with these folks, he would have to be as sharp as possible.

As the game progressed, the players changed periodically. He was able to pretty well peg who was a local and who was not, and he was quietly proud of the fact that he had lasted longer than any of the other tourists who wandered into the game. The locals were really incredible to watch in action. They were patient. They could afford to be patient, as they would be here tomorrow and the day after tomorrow and the day after that. If they had to wait for an hour to get a playable hand, they waited an hour.

Don realized that, as a tourist, he had no such luxury. He was only in town for a very few days. If he wanted to play a decent amount of hands during the time allotted to him, he necessarily had to be less selective about the hands he played. He knew that the locals were also aware of this, and that they would take full advantage of the fact. The attitude toward money also had to be completely different between tourists and the locals. No one, unless he was very wealthy, could afford to play medium stakes poker day after day and hope to survive, unless he was quite conservative. The locals seemed to be, on the whole, very careful with their money. Whether they are playing with money budgeted from wages or investment income, or are depending on their winnings to support them, Don reasoned that they had to be careful.

He knew that the average tourist, on the other hand, realistically couldn't care less about the money. He was in town to have a good time, and if playing a few hands of poker helped to provide that, so be it. Everyone likes to win, of course, and if by chance he came out ahead at the end of the trip, great! That would be the frosting! But deep down in his little tourist heart he knows that he is going to lie about his wins or losses when he gets home anyway, so what the hell difference does it make? He has found a place where, for the expenditure of a few hundred or a few thousand bucks, he can be treated like royalty!

He can have breakfast in bed at any time of the day or night, he can rub shoulders with stars of the world of movies or boxing or what have you, he can engage in acts of a sexual nature that would boggle the mind! He has found, in a word, paradise! And there is always the chance, however slight, that he will engage in all of the aforementioned activities and actually win money in the meantime! It could happen! They didn't build Caesar's Palace or the Mirage or the Excaliber because a lot of people took home more money than they brought with them, but it could happen! And, Don reasoned, it could happen to him!

However, he thought to himself that if he was going to take any excess money home, he was going to have to get his butt in gear! He had lost steadily since Jeff left, and he was down close to eight hundred for the session. That meant he had . . . what? Only about twenty two hundred left! GodDAMNit! What had happened to all the dreams, the visions of taking Vegas by the neck and shaking it until it showed him the respect he was due? He felt angry, depressed, but keyed up at the same time. He knew that he was a better gambler than this.

He had just had a horrible run of luck. For Christ's sake, he stood at the crap table and watched Jeff win a ton of money, and as soon as his money hit the table, the stupid dice had turned nasty. The blackjack was no better, and the second session of craps was another disaster! All right, maybe he should have played it a little easier, taken back some of the winnings, but dammit, you had to bet money to win money, didn't you? And now he was sitting at a table with seven vultures and one lonely tourist from Tulsa or someplace. The tourist was the target of everyone at the table, Don included. Before he finally left, Don had gotten a small piece of him, but the others had divided him up pretty well.

Slats stretched and signaled the floorman for a rack. He began stacking his chips in the carrier, and nodded to his wife. She gathered her chips and came over to their table.

"You're not leaving?" Don had enjoyed the company of the old cowboy, and he was truly sorry to see him go.

"It's our bedtime, youngster. We gotta get our beauty sleep. Amy here don't really need it, but I could sure use some!" Amy smiled at her mate, and the two of them made ready to leave. Just before they left, Slats leaned over, his hand on Don's shoulder. "If you don't mind a little advice, Son?" Without waiting for a reply, he continued, "No offense, but you might consider playin' in one of the lower limit games," Don looked up at him sharply, "just till you get the feel of playin' here! These people are carnivorous as hell, and I don't want to come back here tomorrow and find nothin' but a pile of gnawed bones!" He patted Don on the shoulder once, and turned away. Don just stared after them as they made their way out of the room.

He couldn't believe it! Did he have a sign on him somewhere that said, 'I need mothering!'? What business was it of Slats, or Jeff, or Barbara, or anybody what stakes he played at? What was he, a fucking ten year old? Play at a lower limit? Horseshit! This damned town had several thousand of his dollars, and he wasn't going to get it back playing for nickels and dimes! In fact, there was a pot limit game going on two tables over, and he had been considering putting his name on the list for that game. The pots in this game were okay, but if he hoped to recoup his losses, he was going to have to move up to where the serious money was. He had glimpsed a couple of the pots on that table, and they had been, to say the least, impressive.

He glanced at his watch, and had to look again to confirm what he had seen. The digital timepiece, still set on Denver time, read three forty A.M.! But that wasn't possible! It felt like it should be about nine o'clock, maybe ten at the most! There were no windows in the casino, and no clocks were visible, but he thought he had a better sense of time than that! He had been tired when he got on the plane this morning . . . correction, yesterday morning . . . and he had been gambling heavily for . . . what? Thirteen, fourteen hours? When had he eaten last? He had taken time for dinner, hadn't . . . no, he hadn't. The vaguely remembered lunch was the last food he had eaten.

He was going to have to . . . Oh, shit! GodDAMNit! He was supposed to have called Barbara when they landed! She was going to be rabid! Why did she always insist that he keep in such close touch? She acted like she didn't trust him, didn't think he was capable of living his own life, didn't want him doing anything at all on his own. Why the hell was everybody trying to be his mother? He was, for Christ's sake, thirty four years old, he had built a successful accounting practice, he owned a house in one of the nicer subdivisions in Denver, and he had accomplished all that without someone dogging his every Goddamned step! Well, she could just fucking well wait until he got ready to call her tomorrow . . . today.

He got up from the table, asked the floorman where the gift shop was located, and headed in that direction. After taking a couple of wrong turns and winding through a section of the hotel which appeared to be a rain forest, complete with birds, he finally found the shop. He purchased two chocolate bars, and thus fortified, made his way back toward the poker room. He giggled slightly. Chocolate and Callanish! It was true! You could eat like a king in Vegas!

On his way back into the poker room, he inquired as to the availability of seats in the pot-limit game, and was informed that there was a vacant seat now, if he would like to move over. He said that he indeed would.

As he sat down at the new table, he had just a brief hint of what a scuba diver must feel when he looks around and suddenly finds himself surrounded by shadowy shapes. None of the players at the table actually had the bad taste to salivate, but a couple of them looked close to it. He had assumed that the game was Holdem, the same as the game he had just left, because he had seen the five cards dealt up in the middle of the table. However, when he got his first cards from the dealer, he was surprised that there were four of them, instead of just two. He looked quickly around the table and saw that all of the other players had also gotten four cards. He must have frowned, because the dealer said to him, "Omaha."

"I beg your pardon?" said Don.

"Omaha. You do know that the game is Omaha, don't you?"

Two of the other players looked at each other, their faces expressionless.

"Well, yeah! No! I'm sorry, did you say Omaha?" Don knew that he had stumbled into something, something which would be better left alone, but he didn't want to appear a complete idiot. His pride wouldn't allow it.

"Yeah. Omaha. Omaha high only. You ever played Omaha before?"

"Well, no. Not exactly. I've played Holdem, but . . ."

"Well, it's just like Holdem, except that you get four cards instead of two, and you have to play two cards out of your hand in any hand you play."

"Two cards out of my hand."

"Right. In any hand you play, you have to play two cards out of your hand. No more than two, no less than two. Just two."

A couple more of the players looked at each other. One of them was having trouble suppressing a grin, and the other just didn't even try. Don noticed the exchange, and silently vowed revenge on the two players. So you had to play two cards out of your hand! He had four cards to work with, so how tough could that be?

He soon found out. Even though the game was pot limit, he was surprised at the number of players who stayed active on each hand. After watching a couple of hands played, he saw that the two extra cards in each hand really multiplied the possible combinations. Of the first five hands played after he sat down, three of them were decided on the last card. This seemed to be a peculiarity of the game, and many of the players were willing to chase, to invest the money necessary to see the last card. Consequently, the game offered a lot more action than the Holdem game. Don, as tired as he was, felt somewhat of a resurgence of the rush which seemed to accompany his involvement in the "action," whatever it might be. He held back for a brief period, trying to play it smart and get a feel for the other players, but it seemed that they were just content to get their cards, throw a great deal of their money at the pot, and wait to see who won. It wasn't long before Don was in the thick of it, betting and raising along with the rest.

He actually won for a while, raking in two big pots. The first one occurred when he got a full house on the flop and no one else improved their hand, and the second when he caught a fifth diamond on the last card to make his flush, beating out two straights. The two hands put him ahead of the game by about six hundred, and he was almost hovering over his chair in his excitement. The tiredness was forgotten, hunger was a distant memory, and a tall black girl by the name of Ginny had taken Lori's place as his supplier of Callanish. Life, for the moment, was good.

Eighteen

The game resembled craps, but it was being played outside. The playing surface was green, and sections of it were marked off in white. Each of the sections had a number or a symbol of some sort marked in it, and the markings seemed to disappear over the horizon. There were stacks of huge chips, apparently bets, in various places on the immense field, and a pair of dice lay at his feet. He looked around for guidance, and it came in the form of shouted commands.

"Shoot the fuckin' dice!"

"You gonna take all day?"

"What's your Goddamned problem? Shoot!"

"You gonna look at 'em or you gonna roll 'em?"

"Shoot the dice!"

"Shoot!"

"Shoot!"

He bent and picked up the dice. They appeared to be slightly larger than he remembered them being, and they were warm to the touch and very heavy. He swung his arm back and forward like a pendulum and released the cubes. They flew away from him in a shallow arc and hit the green surface. They each rolled once, and stopped.

"Three, craps! The shooter loses!" The voice seemed to come from somewhere above him. He looked up, but could see nothing.

For some reason, he couldn't remember the size of his bet. He looked to see what he had lost, and for the first time, he saw that the shapes which he had taken for stacks of chips were actually human figures! As he watched, the figures, who had been standing quietly in their proper places, began to move slowly away. Just before the figure nearest him turned away, he caught sight of its face, and was shocked to see Charlie Hardwick, his neighbor and golfing partner. Then, Charlie followed the rest of the figures. As they walked further away, the figures seemed to waver, flicker, and then fade until they were just hazy forms. Then they were gone.

What the hell kind of a game was this? He was a gambler, he had no objection to wagering money, even large sums of money, but this . . .

Movement pulled his head to the left, and he saw that new figures were slowly walking onto the playing surface, headed for the betting spaces. There didn't seem to be anyone he knew . . . wait! The large figure just to the right . . . it looked like . . . it was! Jeff! Jeff Stevens!

This was too much! He would refuse to . . . but if he did refuse, what of Charlie? Was this the only way to get Charlie back? He was about to turn away from the game, to demand some sort of an explanation, some delineation of the rules, when the shouts began again.

"Shoot!"

"You gonna shoot or not?"

"What the hell's your problem?"

The dice were back at his feet. He picked them up and threw them again.

"Twelve, craps! A loser!"

He reached out toward Jeff and tried to speak, to tell his friend not to worry, that he would win him back, him and Charlie both, but for some reason, no sound came out. He strained until he thought his throat might burst, but nothing was forthcoming. He could only stand there, his hand outstretched, as Jeff looked at him with eyes bright with fear. Then his gaze dropped, he turned his head toward the other retreating figures, and he reluctantly joined them. As his figure faded, Don looked around fearfully to see who was . . . Oh, my God! Oh, for God's sake, no!

Ronnie tried to make his way to his father's side, but it was as if he was guided by some sort of invisible hand. He walked past Don, on his way to the betting area, but his eyes never left those of his parent. The eyes looked young and frightened, but there was an undercurrent of trust, of confidence that somehow his Daddy would make everything all right. When he reached the proper spot he stopped and stood nervously, trying to look brave and unconcerned. He waited for Don to fix it, stuffing his hands into his pockets, taking them back out, scratching, wiping his nose on the back of his hand and the back of his hand on his jeans. His eyes only left those of his father when the shouting started again.

"Come on! Shoot!"

"DO something, will you!"

"NO!" Don screamed back at them, finding his voice at last. "No! I can't! Not Ronnie! Not my son . . ."

"Shoot the fuckin' things!"

"Don?" From a new direction, from the mist which seemed to devour the lost figures.

"Don? Please, Don?" Charlie's voice. And, faintly, Jeff's. "Please, Don? You can do it! Please help us! "

"Shoot!"

"Jesus H. Christ! Are you gonna shoot, or not?"

"I CAN'T!"

"Shoot the FUCKING DICE!"

"Don?"

If he did win this roll, he could get Jeff back, and then he could . . .

"Shoot!"

"Come ON!"

He bent for the third time and picked up the dice. They seemed even heavier than before, and he dropped one of them.

"S-H-O-O-T! S-H-O-O-T! S-H-O-O-T!"

He picked up the die, and, using both hands, brought both of them back to his right and forward. They left his hands and flew forward, heading for the gaming surface.

"Don?"

"Daddy?"

He jerked upright, his head coming up off the pillow and

his eyes flying open. It took a few seconds for him to focus, and during that time, he had no idea whatsoever where he was.

Ronnie! Where was . . . ? But he was in what appeared to be a bedroom . . . no . . . a hotel room. There were two big beds, the obligatory color television set, a table and four chairs, and draperies covering one entire wall of the room.

He shook his head in an attempt to clear away the fog which seemed to be obscuring his memory, and regretted the movement immediately. It felt like someone was standing on his forehead with track shoes, the kind with the sharp little spikes. He cupped his hands over his eyes and fell gently back. As he did, wisps of the dream came back, the looks on the faces, the shouted commands, the pleading voices. What the hell had brought all that on? As pieces of the previous night and early morning came back to him, he remembered his dietary habits and grinned wryly. Chocolate and scotch! No damned wonder!

Then, as the events leading up to his finally getting to bed came back fully, the grin faded. He kept his eyes closed, but suddenly his mind was frantically working, trying to analyze just what had happened. He had finally left the pot-limit game at about seven on Saturday morning, dead tired, about half drunk, and totally demoralized. After his initial two wins, it had been as if he was destined to come in second-best for the rest of his life. If he had a straight, someone else would catch a flush on the last card. If he had a full house, someone would have a bigger one.

After a period of that sort of treatment, he pulled back, trying to conserve his funds, waiting for the nut hands. Unfortunately, the nut hands never came. He folded several hands which would have turned out to be winners, had he stayed until the last card. Seeing this, he began chasing again, only to be beaten by the last card. He remembered buying in again and again, and he seemed to have a particularly sick memory of going for the remainder of his bankroll, only to find nothing there. Oh, Jesus! He hadn't lost all of it, had he? He couldn't have blown the entire . . .

He rolled over, sat up, and reached for his pants. He reached into the left front pocket. Nothing! The right front. A few coins, a comb. The back pockets produced a handkerchief and his wallet, which contained about thirty dollars in small bills. That was it.

The headache, which had receded under the panic of looking for the bankroll, came back with a vengeance then, closing his eyes. He just sat there for a long time, his head down.

It was gone. All gone! In somewhat less than twenty-four hours, he had managed to blow six grand! What had the one poker player said, referring to a friend of his? "From a hero to a zero!" Well, that pretty well described him, didn't it? Apparently Wes had been right after all. He came off the plane waving money around, and they had kicked his ass! Kicked his ass but good!

He got up and went to the bathroom. As he passed the other bed, he caught a familiar scent. He stopped and stared at the rumpled bedding, trying to place the odor. Then it came to him. Sex! The musky smell of sexual activity, mixed with the sweeter smell of a woman's perfume. "Why, Jeff, you sonofabitch!" he thought, "Apparently Wes wasn't the only one who got laid on this trip!" The only thing he remembered when he stumbled into the room had been Jeff sprawled out on the bed, sleeping heavily. He was surprised, although he had no idea why he should have been, and more than a little jealous.

He went on into the bathroom and relieved himself. He looked in the big mirror, and the visage staring back at him looked, for lack of a better term, miserable! He felt drained, empty. All of the gambling he had done yesterday and this morning had been exciting, great fun, but damn, it had been expensive! Maybe he should have started smaller, bet less until he got the feel of the . . . oh, bullshit! He couldn't do that, because he didn't want to appear to be timid, hesitant to Jeff and the others. If they had started with five dollar bets, he could have, too. But that didn't happen, and when he saw Jeff win so much in so little time on the first craps table, he knew that he wasn't going to be happy with five dollar bets. So, what . . . ?

His thoughts were interrupted by the ringing of the phone. He padded over to the side of the bed, sat down, and picked up the receiver.

"Hello? "

"Don? Don, is that you?"

"Hi, Barb."

"Don, Are you okay? You . . . I don't want to start anything, but you didn't call, and I . . . I was just worried."

"I'm fine, Barb. Just . . . fine."

"I'm glad! Are you having a good time? How is the weather?"

"It's . . . the weather is . . . nice. It's a lot warmer than at home. It feels good."

"I'm jealous! Promise me you'll take me someplace warm as soon as we can!"

"We will. I promise."

"The boys say hi."

"Tell them hi for me. Are you okay?"

"Oh, I'm fine! Thanks for asking. Are you having a good time?"

Don picked up his wallet from where it had fallen on the floor. "What? Oh, yeah. We're having a good time. I haven't won anything to speak of yet, but the trip is still young." He opened the wallet and was looking at the edges of his credit cards in their little pocket.

"Well, just so you don't lose all of our money!" She had meant it to be humorous, a flip comment, but it came across flat.

"I won't. I promise." His voice was a little distracted. He had the Visa card out and was turning it over in his hand.

"Are you sure you're okay? You sound . . . I don't know, funny, tired or something."

"Yeah, I am tired, I guess. I couldn't sleep on the plane, and I was up kinda late last night."

"Well, take some time for yourself and relax! You've been working hard, and you deserve it!"

"I will, I have, and I do!"

"Well, I'm glad I caught you! I'll see you . . . when? Monday night?"

"Yeah. We fly back into Denver on Monday, and I'll probably go to the office from the airport, so I'll be home Monday night. Love you!"

"I love you too, Don. Win lots, okay? Bye."

"Bye, Hon."

He hung up the phone and looked back to the credit card. "Win lots!" she had said. Well, he was certainly going to try. He was going to give it one helluva shot!

He picked the telephone back up and ordered coffee, a lot of it. The perky voice on the other end of the line inquired as to whether that would be all he required, and he decided to go ahead and have breakfast in the room. He knew that if he went downstairs and tried to eat in one of the restaurants or coffee shops, he wouldn't make it past the first table. He ordered bacon, eggs, toast, and tomato juice.

"No. Forget the tomato juice. Make that a bloody Mary!"

"Very well, Sir. Your order will be right up."

He hopped into the shower and was dried off and shaving when the knock came at the door. He tipped the man, leaving twenty-five bucks in his wallet. "But," he thought as he drank off about half of the bloody Mary, "I've got plastic, and that gives me all the money I'll need." The limit on his Visa was ten thousand, and he knew that the balance on the account wasn't more than twelve hundred or so. He would get a cash advance, and pay it back when he got home. No problem!

As he ate, he watched one of the Super Bowl promotional programs, this one aimed at comparing the high school and college football records of the starting offensive backfields of the two teams. Don knew that the statistics being touted meant nothing, the announcers knew that they meant nothing, and everyone else watching knew the same thing, but hey! If some beer company was willing to sponsor the thing, they would by God air it! Don was familiar with the circus-like atmosphere that the Super Bowl takes on each year, with platoons of media stepping all over each other to try and find some new angle, some bit of information they can use to justify their existence. This one was apparently to be no exception.

Fed, shaved, and dressed in fresh clothing, he was again ready to breast the monster. He came out of the elevator and took a quick circuit of the casino area to see if he could see Jeff or the others. There didn't seem to be any sign of them. A change girl happened by, and just for the hell of it, he took twenty of his remaining dollars and purchased metal dollar tokens. He then advanced on the Megabucks machines, and found an available chair. He fed the tokens into the slot three at a time, pulling the handle and watching the symbols roll past the viewing window.

The total of the progressive jackpot was up over four million eight now, and still climbing.

God, what he could do with that kind of money! Barbara wouldn't have a lot of room for bitching if he came home with something like that, would she? He could sell the damned accounting practice, quit burning himself out every tax season, quit fighting with the IRS on behalf of his clients. He could . . . they could move to someplace warm, maybe even Vegas! It would take some talking to get Barb to move here, but four million or so would be able to talk pretty damned loud!

He hit a few small payoffs on the machine, enough to keep him playing for some fifteen minutes. Every time he put three of the coins into the slot, he held his breath as he pulled the handle. Maybe this would be the time! Maybe the four proper symbols would line up on the right line, and the bells and lights would go off, and the casino executives would come out of their offices and shake his hand and take his picture and give him a great deal of money. Maybe.

Finally, the last three coins went down the maw of the machine, he looked at it disgustedly, and got up. On a whim, he walked to the roulette wheel, took out the last five dollar bill, and placed it on black. He looked away while the wheel spun, concentrating on the legs of a tall blonde in a short green skirt who was walking away from him. He watched her appreciatively until she disappeared into the crowd, and turned back to the table to see a red five dollar chip nestled next to the five dollar bill. He had won! Would wonders never cease!

He picked up the chip and the bill, and moved to the nearest blackjack table. He stood behind the only empty chair, and placed the ten dollars in the betting space. The cards were dealt face up, and his first card, a jack, was joined by an ace! Blackjack! The dealer paid him fifteen dollars, and he picked it all up and looked around. What next? He was on a roll, and the heart rate was coming up. He felt, not quite flushed, but marginally warmer as he walked through the casino area. Whether by design or accident, he looked up to find himself approaching the craps tables. Well, why not?

He considered taking his time, betting five dollars at a time, making the small stake last, but he just couldn't do it. He was down six grand, and he wasn't going to make that back betting five bucks at a time! Besides, he had to go home the day after tomorrow, and he was going to have to get his shit together and do some serious gambling if he hoped to . . . he put the twenty five down on the pass line.

"Eleven! Pay the pass line!"

He stacked it up, let it ride.

"Seven! A winner, seven!"

A hundred. It had been five dollars a few minutes ago, and now it was a hundred. If he had started with a five hundred dollar bet instead of the measly five bucks . . . he shook his head and again stacked up the chips. One more time! Just one more . . .

"Twelve! Craps, twelve! The pass line loses."

He didn't realize that he had been holding his breath again until he let it out with an audible whoosh. If only . . .

"If only what, you asshole!" he railed at himself. "If you would ever learn to take back some of your winnings, instead of letting it all hang out there . . ." But really, what the hell? It had only been five dollars when he started, and it had been kind of fun . . .

Well, it was time. He looked around for the cashier's cage, saw the neon sign, and headed that direction. As he walked toward it, he passed an area of the casino which he had not seem before. A poker room! Only about eight tables, not nearly as big as the Mirage, but he saw a sign over one of the tables advertising pot-limit Omaha. The table was vacant, but five of the other tables were jumping, and it was early. He decided to check it out after he completed his transaction.

A few minutes later, his entire attitude had changed. The six thousand and change he had lost didn't really matter any more. It had been, after all, money he had won from others. It had been free money! He regretted losing it, of course, but that wasn't really the point. The loss would in no way effect his life, and he was still in Las Vegas, still in the action. That was the important thing! And, thanks to his excellent credit rating, he was now possessed of a fresh supply of funds. If he didn't win any more at all, if he stayed stuck for six grand, so fucking what?

This trip had introduced him to a world that he barely knew existed until now. The only downer at this point was the fact that he was going to have to go back to reality on Monday. To leave this and go back to real life, the work and the office and the worries and the responsibilities and the . . .

But he had a good life! He had a wife who loved him and two wonderful sons and a big house and a good business and all that, but . . . none of that . . . none of that made him feel like he felt now, like he had felt since he hit town. Well, yeah, he had been pretty down there for a while until he remembered the cash advance feature on his Visa card, but . . .

He went back at the poker room, and talked with the manager. She said that the pot limit game didn't usually get started until around eight or eight thirty, but if he would care to sit in on one of the other games until then, she would be glad to put his name on a list. He agreed, and took a seat in a Holdem game. It was a ten dollar limit, so he relaxed and concentrated on playing a tight, solid game. The table seemed to be composed of a mixture of tourists and locals, so it was reasonably loose, and he did pretty well. He had been playing for about an hour when the elderly lady who had been sitting at his right got up and left. Don was involved in a hand when someone else took the vacant seat, so he didn't look that direction until he was pulling in his winnings and a female voice said, "Nice hand!"

He looked to his right and was momentarily speechless. Sitting next to him was one of the most striking creatures he had ever seen. She was obviously the result of a mixture of cultures, the slant of her large brown eyes revealing an oriental influence, and her skin tone showing a Hawaiian or Polynesian heritage. Her hair was jet black and straight, and she wore it long, almost to her waist. Her cheekbones were high and her nose was small, which accentuated her full lips. Her lower lip protruded just a bit, giving her a mildly pouting look. She was smiling at him, waiting for some sort of response from him. She looked into his eyes with a directness which he found somehow both disturbing and exciting.

"Thanks!" he said finally, hoping that he was not blushing.

He had always been an admirer of beautiful women, but so many of the truly beautiful ones were so full of themselves. He had never really considered himself to have the physical appearance necessary to attract a lot of attention. Barbara was very attractive, to be sure, but she was pretty in a girl-next-door, all-American way. The woman sitting next to him now was exotic, fascinating. And she was still looking at him, waiting patiently to see if he had any more to say.

"Well," he said, "once in a while I luck into one."

"That didn't look like luck to me! I watched you play, and I think you did it rather well."

"Thank you again! Do ... do you play here often?" Oh, God! So much for witty repartee!

"Well," she began, but then the cards were coming, and they looked away from each other. "Just a sec'."

He had nothing worth playing, but she called the opening bet and waited to see the flop. After the dealer placed the first three cards in the middle of the table, she showed him her hand before she threw it in. She had started with a pair of sevens, but the flop had been queen, ten, ace. No help.

"Yes," she said, again giving him her full attention, "I like to play here whenever I come into Vegas. The dealers are nice, and I've had pretty good luck."

"Where are you from?"

"LA. How about you?"

"Denver. We're just down for the weekend."

"Who's 'we'?" She was doing it again, looking deeply into his eyes.

"Oh. Just myself and three other guys. We've got rooms here." Now why had he said that?

She just looked at him for a few seconds with those eyes, and he was about to go on when she said, "So, you flew in?"

"Yeah. How about you?"

"Oh, I drove. It only takes me about four and a half hours. Of course, that's pushing it a bit!" She smiled. "I've got a little Saab, and it moves pretty well."

"Turbo?" he asked.

"As a matter of fact, it is! I just love the feeling when it kicks in. It's almost . . . I don't know, it's kind of a rush!"

They were off then, comparing car models, driving experiences, poker tales. They chatted like old friends for quite some time, one or the other of them occasionally playing a hand. He learned that her name was Mae, she was single, divorced actually, and that she was an advertising executive. According to her, a friend of hers was to have come along on the trip, but had become ill at the last minute. She had decided to make the trip anyway, and had driven into town late Friday night. She also had a room at the Bedouin, and would be leaving late Sunday for the drive home. She did not ask his marital status, and he did not, for some reason, share that information with her.

She had the nervous habit of shuffling her chips together. Her nails were long and lacquered a deep red, and what appeared to be tiny diamonds were glued to the nails of both index fingers. As she merged the two stacks of chips with tiny clicking sounds, he found that watching her fingers slide up the stack of chips was somehow erotic.

The manager asked Don if he would like to move to the pot-limit table. He looked over to see that six people were now seated around the table, waiting for play to begin. He turned to Mae.

"Do you want to play some Omaha? Pot-limit?"

"Oh, I don't know! I've only played Omaha a couple of times, and I've never played pot-limit. I'd better not. But you go ahead, if you want to." The eyes were on his again, but he couldn't read her thoughts. He was torn between his fascination with her and the adrenaline high he knew was waiting at the other table. He decided that the game would be there when he was ready to play it.

"No, thanks. I think I'll stay here for a while."

She reached over and touched his forearm lightly with her fingertips for just an instant.

"I'm glad," she said.

They continued to play and talk. As time passed, he thought he could detect a slight change in her. There was nothing he could have explained, but her mood seemed to be changing ever so minutely. She was just a bit less exuberant, her smiles were a trifle less frequent, and her card playing ability, which seemed to be quite adequate, deteriorated somewhat. Finally, after she had been beaten out of a nice pot by a tourist who refused to get out of a hand, she threw her cards toward the dealer and said, "Shit!" She slid her chair back and said, "Excuse me a minute." and walked out of the room. Don puzzled about her apparent change in attitude for a few seconds, but then there were two new cards in front of him, and he turned his attention back to the game.

He was again playing a hand when she returned. He glanced up as she sat back down and was favored by a dazzling smile. She leaned over, her shoulder pressing his, to see his cards. She stayed in that position as the hand came to a conclusion, the tourist again catching the right card to beat Don's flush.

"Well, bummer!" was her comment. She straightened back up, and her right hand went back to shuffling the chips. He looked at her and could see that her eyes were bright again, and she seemed to have been transformed. There was no trace of the mood she had exhibited before she left the table.

"Well, welcome back!" he said.

"Thanks! Nice to be back!"

"You okay?"

"I am just fine! I couldn't be better! At least that's what I've been told!" She looked away coyly and giggled.

Her mood was contagious. Don laughed and said, "Well, whatever you found while you were gone, I want some of it!"

She looked sharply at him, almost startling him. She hesitated for a few seconds, and then said softly, "Do you really?"

He was a little slow on the uptake. "Do I what really?"

"Do you want some?"

Then it hit him. He looked at her, his smile gone now. Was she saying what he thought she was saying? "Ah . . . excuse me for seeming like a yokel, but . . ." He leaned toward her, his voice low. "But what are we talking about?"

Cards came toward them, and they both glanced at them and threw them back away. She looked at him, her eyes narrowed fractionally, and she sniffed. He looked blank, so she frowned slightly, twin furrows appearing between her eyebrows, and she sniffed again. "Do you want some?" she asked again.

Cocaine! Coke, flake, snow, nose candy. That had to be what she was offering him.

"Well, I've never . . . never tried it!" he said.

"Never? You're kidding! Never, ever?" She was so excited that she was almost bouncing. Both of her hands were on his arm now, and she was grinning broadly. "You've really never . . . oh, my God, have you got a treat in store for you! I've got to warn you, the first time is always the best. For some reason, no one I've talked to has ever been able to recreate the feeling, the rush, of the first time."

He couldn't believe that she was actually suggesting that he try cocaine. He had led a very sheltered life, apparently, and cocaine was something he had never even considered. He knew that it was the drug of choice of the rising young executive set, but no one in his social circle was into it. Not that he knew of, anyway.

She was saying something. ". . . almost out, but I know where we can get some more." She saw his hesitation, and said, "Oh, come on! I really want to be with you when you try it the first time!"

Nineteen

They cashed out and left the poker room, her hand on his arm. While they were at the table, and even when she had stood to go adjust her attitude, he had not thought about her height. Consequently, he was a little surprised to discover that she was fairly tall, almost as tall as Barbara. That thought brought a quick pang of guilt, guilt at walking with another woman like this, and guilt at what he was planning to do. But he was a big boy, and he could do what he wanted to do, up to and including dabbling with controlled substances, thank you very much!

He put any other thoughts out of his mind, and brought himself back to the present. Mae's attractiveness did not stop at her facial features. She was slender, and her breasts were small, but well proportioned to her body. She had long, well-muscled legs, and quite probably the cutest little butt he had seen for some time. She wore a tight, fashionably short skirt and a blue silk blouse which set off the black of her hair beautifully.

He noticed and was secretly pleased by the glances she got from men as they walked through the casino. She led him to the elevators and thence to the underground parking area. Her Saab was black, and appeared to be immaculate. The overhead lights reflected almost perfectly in the roof and hood of the vehicle. She didn't ask him if he wanted to drive, but simply got in behind the wheel and popped the passenger door lock for him. He slid into the bucket seat and buckled the seat belt. As he closed the door, the shoulder belt traveled along the top of the door and clicked into place.

She drove quickly but quite well, dodging into traffic on the Strip and changing lanes as necessary to gain position. They traveled several blocks, and took a left on Sahara Boulevard.

"Where we headed?" He was enjoying the sight of the lights on the Strip, and the absence of illumination after the turn prompted him to turn toward her. God, she was gorgeous!

"Downtown." She piloted the little car up the freeway entrance and merged smoothly with the four lanes of vehicles. "I've got a connection down there, an old friend. He deals only in quality stuff, so he's a little expensive." She looked over at him suddenly, and then back to the highway. "Oh, gosh, I didn't even think! I don't have that much money on me! I left most of what I brought in the safe in my room. This is going to seem awfully presumptuous of me, but . . ." She was clearly embarrassed.

He smiled at her. He hadn't heard anyone say "gosh" in years. "How much do you . . . will we need?"

"Well, a gram will run about a hundred to a hundred and twenty, but if we want an eight-ball, that will cost three fifty to four hundred."

"An eight-ball?"

"Yeah, an eighth of an ounce, about three and a half grams."

"Well, we don't want to run out, do we? Let's go for the eight-ball!"

She again looked quickly at him, favoring him with another of her radiant smiles. "I like you, Don! You're a lot of fun!"

She shifted down to enter the off-ramp, and reached over and squeezed his leg just above the knee. He looked quickly at her, but she was concentrating on her driving as they came off one freeway onto another and almost immediately dove off to the right. They came out on a wide street which led into the heart of the downtown area. The downtown casinos were crowded much closer together, but they did their best to shine just as brilliantly as the larger properties on the Strip. The sidewalks were full of pedestrians, most of them walking quickly in ones or twos or small groups, heading somewhere, hurrying so that they could relax and have fun.

They pulled into the valet parking area of the Fortune Hotel and Casino, and Mae accepted the ticket from the attendant. She told him that they would only be a few minutes, and they walked into the casino. As he looked around, he saw that the interior was set up much the same as the Strip casinos, except that this one seemed older and more crowded.

Compared to the Bedouin or the Mirage, the Fortune seemed just a bit threadbare.

They walked the length of the casino, Mae now holding his hand and leading the way, weaving through the throngs of gamblers. She again drew admiring glances. The admirers also cast envious looks at Don, which he enjoyed tremendously. They stopped in the poker room and Mae looked around for someone. Then she waggled her fingers at one of the dealers, and he grinned.

"Twenty minutes!" he yelled across the room at her. She gave him a "thumbs up" sign, and then held up four fingers, clenched her fist, and did it again. He nodded silently and went back to dealing. Then, she turned back toward Don. It had not escaped his attention that she was still holding his hand.

"Jimmy says that he's going on break in about twenty minutes. What do you want to do? Do you want to play something?"

"Sure! Twenty minutes isn't enough time to get involved in a poker game, though. Do you like to shoot craps?"

"Well, why not? It's fun, and maybe we can win enough that you won't have to buy after all!" She said it as if she were talking about buying dinner. He glanced around nervously, but then realized that anyone listening would think that was exactly what they were talking about. If they cared.

There were two crap tables, both crowded, but they squeezed in at one of them, Mae standing next to the table and Don just behind her. She reached for her purse, but Don said, "My treat!" and threw four hundreds onto the table.

Mae looked back at him and laid one of her patented smiles on him. "Big spender! What shall we bet on?"

Of their allotted twenty minutes, one shooter held the dice for about fifteen, and they were with him all the way. This time, Don instructed Mae to pull back part of each win, and when the shooter finally sevened out, they were ahead over two thousand dollars! Mae was bouncing again, squealing in her excitement as she counted the chips in the rack in front of her. When she finished and announced the total, she leaned back against Don, her eyes closed and her breathing rapid. He leaned forward and put his arms around her waist. She reached up with her right hand, cupped her hand behind his neck, and pulled his head down and forward. As she did so, she twisted in his arms and kissed him full on the lips.

It was over in a second. She had turned back to the table and was gathering up the chips with both hands, laughing happily. "Here!" she said, turning back to Don and holding a double handful out to him. "Help me!" Don was still stunned from the kiss, but he covered it well, and the two of them stuffed chips into the pockets of Don's jacket. They walked back to the poker area, and got there just as Jimmy was getting up from the table at which he had been dealing seven card stud. He didn't look their way, but just lit a cigarette and walked out of the room, disappearing through a door beside the bar. They stood outside the poker room and watched the action for a few minutes, gloating over their win at the crap table.

"Do you want to give me back some of those chips?" asked Mae.

"Chips? Don't you want money?"

"No, chips are fine. You can buy almost anything you want in this town with chips."

"This is indeed a strange world."

"Do you mean Vegas?"

"Yeah."

"Oh, yes! It is that! I've been coming here since I was twenty one, which was ... a few years ago, and this town never ceases to amaze me."

He sorted through his pockets and came up with four black chips. "That enough?"

"That should be fine. Why don't you wait here?" Jimmy had reappeared, and was looking their direction. As she walked toward him, she unsnapped the small purse that she carried. The two of them met like old friends, embracing and laughing.

"Mae, sweetheart! How the hell are you, you handsome wench?"

"I'm great, Jimmy! How have you been?"

"Oh, you know. The same old shit! Just been dealing!" He grinned proudly as he said it, and her reaction was just what he wanted.

She laughed loudly at his statement, and they continued to talk for a few moments. Don watched them closely, but he saw no evidence of any exchange. The delay while they chatted gave him time to consider what he was doing, and he was just beginning to think that maybe it wasn't really such a great idea when Mae returned to his side.

"Shall we?" she said.

"What about . . . what about the . . . stuff?" He looked around guiltily as he asked the question.

She patted her purse. "All taken care of!" she said.

He frowned at her, and then shook his head. "You're good! You're really good!"

She looked directly into his eyes. "Thanks!" She took his hand and started toward the cashier's cage.

Don held back for just an instant, but she turned and, as he knew she would, smiled at him. And, as he knew he would, he smiled back and followed her.

When they again parked below the Bedouin, Don said, "Well, what now, my dear?"

She thought for a moment, and said, "Well, we could do it here, but it would be a lot nicer if we go somewhere else. How about my room?"

He looked at her for a moment, and reached out for her hand. She took it, and they turned and headed for the elevators.

He felt strange, vaguely uncomfortable as they exited on her floor and walked down the hall to her room. The maid had been there, and the room looked basically as if no one had ever occupied it. The room was smaller than the one he shared with Jeff, with just one king-sized bed. The curtains were open, and the window framed a spectacular view of the other hotels on the strip. He was really growing to like the gaudy display, not for any sort of esthetic reason, but rather for what the display represented.

When he turned away from the window, Mae was sitting on the edge of the bed, pulling a small plastic bag from her purse. She laid it on the bedspread, and dug out a small metal and glass device, about the shape and size of a lipstick. She unscrewed the glass end of the thing, and looked up to see Don watching her.

"A bullet," she said.

"A what?"

"A bullet. Also known as a carburetor." She was lecturing him, patiently explaining to the neophyte the mechanics of ingesting the magical powder. She filled the small glass vial from the bag, and screwed it back onto the metal portion. She then turned the device over and rapped it sharply on the heel of her other hand. She then twisted the metal part, revealing a cavity filled with the white powder. She held it out toward him.

He stalled, still not quite ready for whatever was awaiting him. He asked, "How . . . if you don't mind my asking, how much do you use?"

"I don't mind. I basically use it just on special occasions, like if I come here, or on weekends, like that. Sometimes I use it during the week, if I need to be sharp for a presentation, or if I have to go without sleep to get a project done. I suppose I do use it too much, but it helps me."

"Doesn't that get pretty expensive?"

"Well, yeah, but I make good money, and I'm single, and . . . I don't know, I just really enjoy the way it makes me feel. Like you said, it makes you feel like you can do anything!"

"So I've heard! How long does it last?"

"It really varies, with the individual, with the purity of the coke, with the size of the dose. With me, the real rush usually lasts about half an hour, forty-five minutes. Then I start to come down, and depending on where I am and what I'm doing, I either ride it out or take another hit."

"Ride it out?"

"Yeah, well, that's the down side. I guess everything's got a down side. After I've used for a day or a couple of days or whatever, and I quit, I get kind of anxious, depressed. It's like I could sleep for a week. Of course, I don't sleep much when I'm . . . when I'm high, so I guess it makes sense." She was looking away from his eyes while she spoke, contrary to her usual habit of direct eye contact. It was almost as if she was ashamed of what she was telling him.

"Well, " she said, brightening, "are you ready for your medicine?"

"Ah . . . you first. Okay?" He was extremely nervous, and he hoped it didn't show.

She smiled, understanding. "Sure!" she said, "I'd be delighted!" She brought the bullet to her nose, closed her right nostril with her finger, and inhaled the powder with a quick sniff. She closed her eyes, threw her head back and moaned softly. She took a deep breath, another one, and then opened her eyes and looked at him. The eyes held the brightness he had seen earlier when she returned to the poker table. She quickly closed the device, smacked it again, and twisted it to reveal a fresh supply of cocaine. She repeated the procedure, this time with her right nostril, and again squinted her eyes and moaned. It was obviously a moan of pleasure.

He could almost see the change occurring in her. She seemed to sit a little straighter, and he could see a faint flush to her cheeks that had not been there a few seconds before. There was just a trace of powder on the surface of the bullet, and she wet her finger, dabbed at it, and put the fingertip into her mouth. As she did, a shiver moved her slightly, and she crossed her arms across her breasts and hugged herself, her eyes closing again. Whatever reaction she was having to the cocaine, it was obviously a pleasurable one.

"Okay! Are you ready?" She went through the procedure of filling the cavity again, and held the bullet out to Don. He again hesitated, and she said, "Don't be afraid! You'll like it, I promise!"

He looked at her glowing face and her perfect smile, and made his decision. He reached for the device, their fingers touching for an instant, and he brought it quickly to his nose. He fumbled with it for a second, trying to figure out where to put all of his fingers, but he finally got it all organized, pinched off his left nostril, and positioned the cavity under the right. He inhaled sharply, as he had seen her do, and waited for . . .

Oh, shit! OhGodOhGodOhGod! He had closed his eyes in concentration, but the initial reaction snapped them back open. He looked at Mae, and she was still sitting on the edge of the bed, beaming at him. Something was happening to his eyes, she seemed to be more sharply detailed . . . he turned toward the window, and the lights of the Strip were absolutely dazzling! His heart was racing, he could hear it pounding in his ears, and he could feel perspiration beginning on his scalp and upper lip. Mae was saying something, and he had to concentrate, focus his thoughts to hear her.

" . . . side!"

"What?"

"The other side! Do the other side!"

"Oh. Oh, yeah!" He looked at the small device in his hand, saw that the cavity was empty, and rapped it on his hand as he had seen Mae do. He looked at it again, but the small hole was still empty. He pounded an it a couple of times, but he couldn't get it to work. He looked at her helplessly and she got up and took it from him. She manipulated it expertly, and offered it back to him, loaded and ready. He snuffed the powder into his other nostril, and was still reeling from the first blast of feelings when the second one hit him. He staggered, and moved to sit in one of the chairs by the window. He had never felt anything approximating the effects of the drug. It was a rush, an adrenaline hit, a euphoria that put any past experiences in the dark. This was a blackjack, a royal flush, a heavy win on the craps table, rolled into one, and multiplied by . . . by a lot! He giggled. Mae had moved around the bed and was now sitting on the side next to him, watching him closely.

" . . . it feel like?"

"What? I'm sorry, I . . ."

"What does it feel like, the first time?" She was leaning toward him, her hands on his knees, in the midst of her own reaction, but also trying to vicariously live through his. She was in a state of high excitement, and he could feel her nails digging into the sides of his legs, but it didn't hurt.

He grabbed her hands in his and said, "Oh, my God, Mae! I've . . . this is . . ." He took a deep breath and almost yelled,

"Whoa!" He threw his head back and laughed, great roaring peals of laughter. She squeezed his hands and laughed with him. He couldn't help it, the feeling, the exuberance was just too much to keep inside. He felt . . . what? "I feel great! I feel powerful! I feel like I could do anything! Is this what it's always like?"

"Like I said, the first time is always the best. Everybody has different reactions, but it sounds like you've got a good one going." She was up then, her heightened energy level forcing her to move. He stood also, feeling the rush of adrenaline or something very like it still coursing through his system. He glanced at his watch and saw that the entire transaction, the trip downtown and back and the buy had only taken about an hour and a half. The pot limit game should be heating up pretty well by now, and he was ready for it. Mae was obviously good luck for him, as evidenced by their performance on the craps table downtown.

"What say we take our two grand . . . our sixteen hundred and go terrorize the pot limit table? The way I feel now, we could destroy them!"

"I like that idea! Do you feel okay, in control and everything?" She was looking at herself in the mirror over the dresser, primping.

"You bet I do! I feel like I've just had about ten hours sleep, and I am ready to do battle! Let me use the facilities, and I'll be ready!" They grinned at each other like two idiot children, and he turned and went into the bathroom, closing the door modestly. As he relieved himself, it occurred to him that he was feeling extraordinarily horny. Just the touch of his fingers created a small degree of arousal, a slight swelling. He wondered if that was one of the effects of the cocaine. It must be, because all of his other senses certainly seemed to have been heightened. He thought of the desirable woman in the next room, but just as quickly, he dismissed the idea. He had never been unfaithful to his wife in all their years of marriage, and he had no intention of starting now.

Besides, Mae had shown no sign . . . well, that wasn't entirely true. His mind went back to the kiss at the crap table, the touching and holding hands . . . but that had just been the result of her excitement at winning, her natural way of showing friendship

. . . hadn't it? She just . . . but if the drug had given him this degree of sexual arousal, wouldn't it have done the same to her? And if so . . . !

He peered at himself in the mirror. His eyes were wide, the pupils dilated. He looked like a kid on Christmas morning, all big eyes and excitement. He grinned at himself, little Donny Curtis, all grown up into a big-time gambler and coke freak, locked in a hotel room with probably the sexiest creature this side of the Mississippi. His testosterone level was gleefully creating all sorts of fantasies, and he was considering more and more seriously the possibility of making some moves on Mae.

But what if she refused, or, God forbid, laughed at him. He did not consider himself to be the handsomest of men, and he knew that his ego was somewhat fragile. He couldn't bear the thought of her laughing at him. They were having a wonderful time together, and maybe it would be best to just go with the flow, roll with the punches, play it cool, keep a . . . keep a what? What were you supposed to keep?

He realized that he was babbling to himself, and he threw the door of the bathroom open, saying, "Well, milady, are you . . ."

The lights in the room were off, and he had unconsciously turned the bathroom light off, so that the only illumination was the glow through the window from the lights of the Strip. He was blind for a moment, but as his eyes began to become accustomed to the darkness, he could make out her shape on the bed. The background upon which she was outlined was white, and he remembered the bedspread as a dark blue in color. Mae had apparently thrown back the coverings, and was lying on the sheet.

"How much of a hurry are you in to get to that poker game?" she asked, her voice soft, quiet.

"Ah . . . well . . ."

"Come here."

His night vision was getting better, and he could now see that she was naked, lying on her back with her hands at her sides, the only movement coming from her right leg. The knee bent, drawing her foot up over the surface of the sheets along her other leg. Then the limb flexed again, the foot sliding back down, making a faint rasping sound against the cloth. The movement fascinated him, the foot sliding up and back down, up and back down.

"Come here." The voice sounded huskier now.

He walked slowly to the side of the bed, and just stood looking down at her. His eyes had fully recovered by now, and he could see that she was exquisite. Her clothing had covered no flaws. The strange combinations of lights outside the window gave her skin a darker, almost dusky appearance. She looked extremely exotic, and extremely erotic.

He began to unbutton his shirt, but she said, "Let me help!" She rolled up to her knees on the bed, and facing him, she undid the rest of the buttons and slowly pulled the tails of the shirt out of his trousers. The shirt dropped to the floor, and she put both of her hands flat on his chest. She slid her hands down over his stomach, around his waist, and up his back as far as she could reach. Then she brought her hands back down, raking his skin lightly with her nails. He arched his back and shuddered, reaching for her. He lifted her and their mouths met, opening. He could feel her breasts pressing against his chest. Without breaking the kiss, her hands came back around and began working on his belt and zipper. He was fully engorged now, straining for freedom. She helped him slip his trousers down, and he broke away and sat on the edge of the bed for a moment, tearing off his shoes and socks. When he turned back toward her, he could see that she was watching him, her breathing rapid, as was his.

A thought occurred to him, and he almost ignored it, but a small shred of reason forced him to say, "Ah . . . Mae . . . I don't have . . . I don't have any . . ."

"I do!" She rolled away, bounced off the other side of the bed, and pounced on her purse. She rummaged in it for a minute, and then was back at his side. "May I help you with this, sir?" Without waiting for him to answer, she pushed him back onto the bed and bent over him. She stripped his shorts off, dropped them off the side of the bed, and turned back to him. "My goodness, what a brave little soldier!" she exclaimed, "Look how he's standing at attention!" That sent both of them off into a fit of giggling. He stopped his snickering and caught his breath, however, when he felt her fingers begin installing the latex device.

He had not used a condom in a lot of years, and he had never considered the installation of one to be an erotic event, but Mae totally changed his concept on that.

He totally immersed himself in the experience of making love with her. She was all warm skin and taut muscles, constantly moving and making small noises of passion or contentment. She was both imaginative and enthusiastic, and he found himself trying moves, moves he had not used for years, moves he had only heard about. She was very responsive, which goaded him on to try even more.

Her breathing and her movements became faster, more urgent, and he joined her in the final struggle with renewed intensity.

He lay on top of her, panting. His face was buried in her neck and he was trying to keep most of his weight on his knees and elbows, to avoid crushing her. She lay still at last, her breathing also heavy, her body limp beneath him. He raised his head to look at her, and she kissed him again, very gently. "That was nice," she whispered.

"It certainly was!" he said, "If that's one of the effects of cocaine, I can see why it's so popular!"

They rolled over onto their sides, and she propped her head up on her hand, her abundance of black hair cascading over her shoulder. "They tell me that heavy use of coke can make a person dysfunctional, that the coke becomes more important than the sex, but I haven't had that problem."

"Apparently not!" he grinned.

She moved off the bed to use the bathroom, and his eyes feasted on her slender form as she walked away from him. Her hair swayed as she walked, brushing her bare back just above her waist. Just before she entered the bathroom, she turned back toward him.

"Don, I . . . I just want you to know that I don't do this all the time." She looked at him for a second, and then went in and closed the door.

He was still appreciating the view, but he barely heard her. His mind was already anticipating the pot-limit game.

Twenty

As it turned out, Mae was much more talented at making love than she was at pot-limit poker. She tended to be a little timid because of the amounts of money involved. Some of the players were pretty aggressive, and she let herself get bluffed out of several big pots. At the same time, Don, still hyper from the initial hits of cocaine, was in the thick of the battle. He was really enjoying the game of Omaha, with the two extra cards and the resultant possibilities of makeable hands. He was chasing cards, staying longer than he should, trying to bull his way through hands with big raises and aggressive play.

A couple of times, the two of them got involved in the same hand, and he dropped out in deference to her, only to see her get either bluffed out or beaten by a genuine hand. Between the two of them, they went through most of the money that had been won on the craps table, and her mood was beginning to deteriorate again. She had reloaded the bullet before they left her room, and she now excused herself and disappeared in the direction of the restrooms.

There was a patchwork of emotions. He was feeling guilt with Mae. It was almost an ache, a mourn- had been vital, alive, but which was no mises which he had kept for all the been broken. Of course, he had been ocaine, sort of, and he knew that not uld have turned down the invitation.

Besides, Barbara didn't have to know, did she? He had not shared the full extent of his gambling with her, because he hadn't wanted to worry her. Why should this be any different? What, exactly, would be accomplished by sharing this evening's activities with her? Nothing, as far as he could see! He did feel bad about straying, but he certainly didn't want to hurt her, so really, nothing would be gained.

He was disappointed with their showing so far at the poker table. He had been elated after the win at the crap table, convinced that his luck had finally changed after the severe drubbing he had endured on Friday night and Saturday morning. But Mae had proven to be too weak, too passive for this type of a game. The competition was just too stiff at this level. If they kept playing here, the possibilities of continued losses were just too great.

The problem was, he wanted to stay here, at this level of play! He was having a hell of a good time playing Omaha, immersing himself in the betting and raising activity. He had lost some money himself, but God, you had to love the action! But what to do about Mae? He felt that she had given him a lot, shared the incredible experience of the cocaine with him, shared her equally incredible body with him, made him feel virile and desirable and exciting. He certainly owed her something for that, but . . . well, how much did he owe her?

The money they had dropped at the poker table was still from the winnings downtown, but that was getting thin, and besides, he had been the one who had controlled the betting, pulled back part of the wins, built up the stake. He had put up the initial buy-in, he had suggested playing craps in the first place! If this continued, they were soon going to be into his money, the winnings would be gone, and just how far was he expected to go?

The elation, the surge of emotion brought on by the coke had been far beyond anything he had ever experienced! Yet, the feelings, the euphoria brought on by the chemical reaction of the white powder had not been entirely foreign to him. The effect had been magnified, to be sure, but the rush, the adrenaline high had been quite similar to the feelings he got while gambling. And now here he was, actually experiencing a combination of the two!

He knew that he was starting to come down, to lose the effects of the hits, and he was already missing it. He missed the excitement, the sharpness of mind and vision, the edge that he felt he had experienced. He was still playing poker, high-stakes poker, and the attendant rush was there, as it always was, but it was weak, pathetic, compared to the blast of emotion he had felt with the cocaine. He found himself looking out into the casino, waiting for Mae to return.

He was a little apprehensive, considering that the use of cocaine was, after all, illegal. He really knew little about the drug, but wasn't it also supposed to be addictive? From what Mae had told him, he suspected that she might be hooked on it, but what the hell did he know?

He was really starting to come down now. Where the hell was Mae? As he craned his neck, looking for her, he caught sight of Jeff coming toward the table. He stood up and waved, and the big man spotted him and came over.

"Don! Where the hell you been? Last I saw of you, you were in what closely resembled a coma up in the room!"

"Yeah, well, I got in a little late last night. Got involved in a poker game, and time sorta got away from me."

Jeff grinned. "Yeah, that happens! Did you do any good?"

"Not so you'd notice! I made a bit of a donation."

They were interrupted by the return of Mae. She had apparently made use of the bullet, as her eyes were bright again, the pupils large and round. She slid into her chair and smiled at the two men.

"Hi!" she said to Jeff.

"Hi, yourself!" Jeff looked at Don questioningly.

Don introduced the two of them, and as cards came out and Mae looked away, Jeff raised one eyebrow, his grin lopsided and lecherous. Don looked at his own cards and saw four cards that actually had some relationship with each other. He called the opening bet, and the flop gave him a medium straight and four to a flush. He got the flush on the next card, raised, and was beaten when some sonofabitch at the other end of the table caught a full house on the last card. He had blown off about two hundred dollars, and lost in front of Jeff and Mae. Crap!

He leaned over to Mae and whispered, "May I borrow your magical device, my dear?" She casually put her hand in her purse, and passed him the bullet under the edge of the table. He palmed it and slipped it into his pocket. "I'm gonna go to the john!" he declared, and got up. Jeff told Mae that it was nice to have met her and that he hoped to see her again in the future, and followed Don out into the casino.

"You bastard!" he said when they were out of earshot of the poker room. "You little bastard! She's beautiful! Is she a hooker?"

"No, Jeffrey, she is not a hooker! She's from California, and we've gotten to be . . . friendly."

"I'll bet! I'd like to get friendly with her! I have to pay a hundred bucks to get a little companionship, and you just sorta fall into it, you should pardon the expression."

"Yeah, I noticed that somebody had been making lust in your bed. Whoever she was, she had nice taste in perfume!" They entered the restroom, and Don went into one of the stalls and locked the door. "Be with you in a minute."

He quickly took the small vial out of his pocket and rapped the metal end on his hand, He twisted the end, and saw that he had succeeded in filling the little depression with coke. He sniffed it, and repeated the procedure. Just as he finished with the second dose, the first one hit him. He could feel the euphoria, the excitement flooding back. He waited a bit, until the initial rush subsided somewhat, and then pocketed the bullet and stepped out of the stall.

Jeff was standing, waiting for him, leaning on the opposite wall. He looked around to see if anyone was listening, and said, "First, you took a chance when she passed you the bullet under the table. Second, you made entirely too much noise snorting it in the stall, and third, always flush, whether you've used the stool or not. Fourth, always share with your friends." He grinned and held his hand out.

Don was aghast. He thought he had been so sneaky! The good mood didn't allow him to dwell on it, however, and he gave Jeff the device. As the other man ducked quickly into one of the stalls, it finally occurred to him why Jeff had never seemed to need a lot of sleep, why he could play poker until five A.M. and show up at the golf course at seven thirty full of energy.

Jeff reappeared and gave the bullet back to Don. He smiled happily and then turned away and sneezed explosively. He coughed and recovered, saying, "Damn! Good stuff! I didn't know you partook."

"Well, up 'til earlier tonight, I didn't! Mae introduced me to it."

"I'll bet that's not all she introduced you to! Well, have a good time! Thanks for the . . . ah . . . thanks!" He looked at the crowds around them, grinned once more, and was gone.

Don walked back up to the table just as Mae lost the last of the chips in front of her. She turned toward him, her face a strange mixture of excitement and disappointment.

"It's all gone, Don! I guess I'm not much of a pot-limit player!" She looked down at the empty felt in front of her and then back at him.

"I'm sorry!" he said, "What . . . what do you want to . . . do?" He didn't want to leave the game, but he also didn't want to stake her to any more money. "Are you . . . going to buy in again?" The next round of cards were dealt, and the dealer skipped her position. No money on the table, no cards.

"I did! While you were gone with . . . with Jeff, I ran out of chips and bought in again with the money I had brought with me. That was the last of it you just saw go away! Nine hundred dollars!"

"You lost all of it while I was gone?"

"In four hands! I had good cards! I really did, and I was feeling so good, so sharp, that I just knew I'd win, but I didn't! I just kept getting good cards, and I . . ." She looked to be close to tears. "They took it away from me!" She motioned toward the other players and then pointed at the dealer. "He kept giving me cards that I had to stay on, and then they took my money away!" Her voice was raising, and she was acting more and more nervous.

"Mae . . . " He put his hand on her arm, but she brushed it off like it was something dirty.

She rubbed her arm where he had touched her. "I knew I shouldn't have played at this table! I told you that I didn't know how, didn't I? I told you, but you didn't . . ." She was rubbing both arms now, trying to rid herself of something, some feeling. "You didn't . . ." She was close to screaming now, attracting the attention of players at the other tables. The manager was heading in their direction, and one of the security guards was looking toward her.

"Mae, please!"

"What's the trouble here? I'm afraid . . ."

Mae looked down at her arms then, and screamed. "Ahhhhh!! Oh, God! Get them off! Get them off!" She was staring at her arms, scratching them with her long nails as if to dig something out of the skin. Small droplets of blood appeared on her arms, and the scrabbling of her nails spread it, smeared it on her skin.

"Mae, for God's sake! What is it?"

The security guard was approaching them now, and Mae twisted out of Don's grasp, sobbing. She slipped past the guard, and ran out into the casino. She had stopped screaming, but her face was frozen in a look of abject terror. She raced through the crowd, dodging this way and that to avoid the masses of humanity, her long hair streaming out behind her. Then she was around a corner and gone.

Don followed her for a few steps, but then he stopped, uncertain what the hell he should do. He walked to the corner around which she had vanished, and looked down the long aisleway toward the elevators, but she was nowhere to be seen. He stood there for a few seconds, and then turned and walked slowly back to the poker room. He attracted some attention as he came back into the room, but most of the players were again intent on their individual cards. He gathered the chips that remained in front of his place, and started to leave when he was stopped by the manager. She handed him Mae's purse.

"I believe this belongs to the young lady?"

He almost told her to keep it, in case Mae returned, but a sudden thought made him take it from her.

"Thanks." he said.

"I hope she'll be okay!" The manager seemed genuinely concerned. "If you don't mind my sayin', that looked like coke hallucinations."

"Hallucinations?"

"Yeah. I went through them once, before I got my shit to-gether. It's real pleasant! Bugs under the skin, paranoia, chills, throwin' up, stuff like that!" She shuddered at the memory.

"Did you say bugs under the skin?"

"Yeah. And all that's just when you're high on the stuff. When you come down, that's when the real fun starts. I'm talkin' MAJOR depression, thoughts of suicide, the whole trip!"

"Jesus! Thanks for the help." He turned to leave.

"No problem! Like I say, I hope she'll be okay."

For lack of a better place to go, he put the purse under his jacket and headed back to the restroom. Back in the stall, he sat down and opened the little purse. As he had feared, the bag with the remainder of the coke was in there! Why the hell was she carrying that around?

While he was at it, he looked through he rest of the stuff in the purse. He found her car keys, driver's license, a handker-chief, a comb, some breath mints, and three more condoms. Her room key was also in there. What the hell was he supposed to do now? He really didn't feel like walking around carrying a purse, but he didn't dare turn it back in to the poker room manager with the coke in it. He considered flushing the whole thing, but . . . he didn't. He still had the bullet in his pants pocket, and he transferred the bag to his inside jacket pocket. He was still up from the last hits, and his heart was racing. He wanted to get back to gambling.

He was feeling strong, alert, and he knew that he could get back on a winning streak and stay there. The episode with Mae had been pleasant. Pleasant? It had been one of the most amaz-ing, most sensual things that had ever happened to him. He knew that, as long as he lived, he would retain the image of her lying on the bed in that room, her magnificent body illuminated by the lights from the Strip.

He thought that perhaps the right thing to do would be to go and look for her, check her room, her car. But what then? If he found her, what then? It was getting late on Saturday night, and he was going to have to leave on Monday morning. That gave him somewhat over twenty-four hours, twenty-four hours in which to gamble, to win back the money he had lost. He was going to have to sleep sometime, so that cut the available time down even further. He knew that it was probably selfish of him, but dammit, he had needs, too! It had all been very nice, but he was not her nursemaid, thank you very much! He left the purse with the poker room manager, and decided to walk over to the Mirage and check out the action.

As he walked out of the hotel and made his way along Las Vegas Boulevard toward the volcano and waterfalls which marked the front of the Mirage, he felt strangely at home. The traffic, the millions of lights, the twenty-four hour party atmosphere, the availability of the many forms of gambling that was Las Vegas seemed to embrace him, to welcome him.

He knew, if he would have stopped to think about it, that the overwhelmingly vast majority of the residents of the city, both permanent and temporary, couldn't have cared less if he lived or died. But he also knew, and this was the thought that was dominant in his mind, that as long as he had money, he could go anywhere, do anything he wanted. He could sit down in any game, walk up to any table, eat in any restaurant, see any show, as long as he had money.

As long as he had money.

And, thanks to the magic of his credit limit on his Visa card, he had money. He quickened his step and almost trotted past the tiger habitat.

He had become comfortable with Omaha poker, and he got a seat in the same pot-limit game as the previous evening. Two of the players looked familiar, and they glanced at him and then at each other as he sat down. He bought in for two thousand, and settled down to play. He still felt up, on top of the situation. He had had little sleep, and almost nothing to eat, but those things didn't seem to be important. He was feeling a little nervous, and he asked the dealer to summon the cocktail waitress. He was delighted to see Lori coming toward him, and shocked when she said, "Callanish rocks?"

He smiled broadly at her and said, "That'd be just fine, Darlin'."

She smiled back and turned away to take orders from the

next table, and he was admiring her legs when he heard the dealer say, "Would you care to join us, Sir?"

He snapped his head around to see that there were four cards on the table in front of him, and that the other players were staring at him, waiting for him to act. He grinned self-consciously and grabbed the cards. He had a queen and king of hearts, and a queen and ten of spades. It was an excellent starting hand for Omaha! Depending on the cards to come in the middle of the table, he could wind up with a straight, either of two flushes, a full house, or even four of a kind or a straight flush. He even had the possibility of making that most elusive of poker hands, a royal flush!

He glanced at the pot, saw that there was thirty five dollars in it, and raised that amount. The next three players folded, but one of the faces from last night re-raised. The next two folded, and the two remaining players to the right of Don called. Don reraised! By the time the dust settled, there was over a thousand dollars in the middle of the table, and the dealer dealt out the flop. The jack of hearts, the ace of spades, and the seven of hearts. He thought for a second that he had the ace-high straight, but then he remembered that he had to play only two cards from his hand. So, he had four cards to a straight, four cards to a heart flush, and three to a spade flush. They checked to him, and he bet three hundred. The others just called.

The fourth card hit the table. The ace of hearts. That gave him the ace-high heart flush, and a draw at a full house. He bet a thousand, and the others just called again. He would have bet more, but he wanted to see if anyone had the full house. Apparently not.

The last card was snapped down onto the table by the dealer. Yes! The queen of spades! He had the full house! Three queens and two aces! What a catch! He looked at the dealer inquiringly, and the man said, "Fifty three hundred." Don looked down at the money in front of him, and counted out five thousand in chips and hundred dollar bills. He pushed it toward the middle of the table, trying not to smile.

"Just five," he said.

"Raise!" The face at the other end of the table was also grinning, but making no attempt to hide it. He tossed a double handful of hundreds toward the pot, and the dealer counted it quickly.

"Raise ten thousand." The dealer might have been commenting on the weather.

The other two players folded, grumbling.

Don felt a cold something crawling up the back of his neck. He stared at the cards on the table. Oh, Christ! His opponent could have aces full! He must have an ace and a queen! He hadn't raised when the second ace showed, so he couldn't have had the full house then. Or had he been sandbagging, holding back, trying to let the pot build? Don looked at his cards again, and noticed that his drink had somehow arrived at his elbow. He took a long swallow, coughed, and almost threw his cards in.

But what if the grinning idiot across from him didn't have the full house at all? What if he was bluffing? There was about twenty seven hundred dollars left on the table in front of him.

He looked at the money, at the gigantic pot, and then up at his antagonist. The man was looking at him, his eyebrows raised in an insolent stare. Don glared back at him, but the man's eyes didn't waver. The cards were feeling slippery from the sweat oozing from his fingers, and he took a deep breath and was about to throw them in when the man said, "There's a lot of your money in there, slick!"

"Call! All in!" The twenty seven hundred joined the rest of the pot, and the dealer gave seventy three hundred back to the other man.

"Let's see 'em!"

Don threw his cards down, showing his full house. Everyone at the table looked at the cards, and then all heads turned. The bastard turned his cards over one at a time, drawing out the agony. The eight of hearts, the ten of hearts, the jack of diamonds, and . . . and . . . the ace of clubs! Full house, aces full of jacks! Son of a bitch! Don pounded the edge of the table in his frustration. Of all the rotten . . .

The dealer shoved the massive pile of chips and bills away from him, to the waiting arms of its new owner, and was again dealing. He hesitated when he came around to Don the first time, looking at him inquiringly. Don looked up and reached for his wallet, but then he remembered that it was all gone. He had gotten an eight thousand dollar cash advance from his Visa card, and it was . . . all . . . gone! He didn't even acknowledge the dealer's look. He just got up from the table and stumbled out of the poker room, walking quickly, blindly through the crowds and the noise of the big casino.

Twenty-One

The next thirty hours were a blur, an indistinct collage of images and emotions and sensations. It was a confusion of lights and chips and cards and dice and white powder and money. Lots of money. He was floating at the surface of a deep mixture of faces and bodies and noise and green felt. The coke was the only thing that kept him going.

There was no time to waste, no time to eat or sleep or anything else. The time was running, the time he had remaining to rectify the damage that had been done to him. He had tapped his Mastercard for ten grand. He happened across Jeff and Johnny and Wes and resisted their attempts to get him to eat or grab a nap. He had finally broken away from their unwanted attentions, but not before he borrowed five thousand from Jeff. He tried to put the arm on Wes and Johnny, but they were both losing heavily, and had declined.

He wrote a check which cleaned out his bank account, and another one which would overdraw the account by eight thousand dollars, the maximum the casino would allow. He planned to beat the check back to Denver and cover it before it could cause any problems.

He played blackjack and poker and craps. He tried baccarat, betting hundreds of dollars on the turn of a card, but he found the game to be too simplistic for his taste. It was possible to bet a great deal of money at the game, but he preferred the noisy camaraderie of the craps table or the psychological battles of the poker room.

As Saturday night ended and Sunday morning wore on, as every television set in every sports book in the city was turned to some sort of Super Bowl hype or other, his need for the effects of the cocaine began to increase in frequency. As his body required larger concentrations of the drug in order to maintain the "edge," he became more and more nervous, more and more edgy and irritable. He didn't know it, but he was flirting with cocaine delirium, the disorder that had pushed Mae over the edge into hallucinations.

As he grew more physically exhausted, he leaned more heavily on the coke to bring him back up. As the coke brought his nerves closer to the breaking point, he drank more of the Callanish to settle them. The alcohol, being a depressant, tended to increase his exhaustion. And so the cycle continued.

The Super Bowl game didn't begin until late afternoon, and whereas Don had planned to watch the game from the comfort of a poker room or sports book, he actually missed most of it. Poker had become too slow, too methodical. He was becoming more aggressive, and was beginning to suffer chills and nausea.

He only had about two hits of cocaine left, and he was a bit apprehensive about the after effects when he did run out. For now, though, he was still up, still in the thick of the action.

He had gone back to craps, the fast game, the game where it was possible to win or lose numerous bets on a single roll of the dice. He was attacking the table, betting on anything and everything. He was yelling, pounding on the edge of the table with his fist, and punching the air whenever the dice fell his way.

He had several incredible swings, winning and losing many thousands of dollars. The only time he had any concept of his position was when he would run out of chips and have to buy more. When the football championship game ended, and the word passed through the casino that Buffalo had not only failed to cover the point spread, but had actually lost by three, the news hardly impinged on his conscious mind. It was just another thousand, just a small part of the total.

He had once again gotten to the point that all of his chips were on the craps table. He had three bets out, and it took all of them to take odds on the numbers. If the shooter could only roll a few numbers, he could . . .

"Seven out!"

"SonofaBITCH!" He dropped his head and stared at the empty racks in front of him for a few seconds, and then reached for his wallet again. As he did, he became aware of someone standing just behind him. He turned and looked up to see Jeff Stevens.

"Don, we need to talk."

"Not now, Jeff! I've got . . ."

"I said we need to talk. Just for a minute!"

"And I said not now! They're comin' out with a new number, and . . ."

" Goddamnit, Don, they're not gonna take the fucking table away if you leave for five minutes!" Jeff grabbed him by the upper arm and tried to pull him away, but Don twisted away from him, raising his arm and jerking back toward the table. His elbow collided with the head of the man who had been standing next to him, knocking him forward. The man's glasses flew off and landed in the middle of the table. The man turned around quickly, ready to deck somebody, but the stickman stepped between the two men.

"Take it outside!" He was speaking to Don and Jeff.

Jeff again tried to lead Don away, saying, "Come on, Don. Please!"

"What do you mean, 'Take it outside!'? I've got a right to . . ." The stickman was saying something, speaking very softly. Don unconsciously leaned forward to hear his words.

". . . take it the hell away from my table, or I'll call Security and have them throw your ass out of here!" He glared steadily at Don, not blinking.

Don opened his mouth to reply, but the look in the man's eyes stopped him. He looked down, back up, and then turned and walked meekly away, Jeff at his side.

"You still puttin' that shit up your nose?"

Don turned on him, aghast. "What the hell do you mean? You used it!"

"Yeah, I used it! I took one hit, and it brought me up for a while, and it felt good, but I know better than to make a habit out of it! It'll fuck you up, man! It'll make you paranoid and impotent!"

"Impotent? It sure didn't have that effect on me!"

"No doubt! The first time you try it, you feel like fucking anything that moves, but you use it for a while, and that goes away. Goes away and then some!"

"Well, I'm not really planning on becoming an addict, if that's what you're worried about!"

"How much you got left?"

"Why?"

"How much you got left?"

"I don't know, enough for one hit, maybe two. Why?"

"Don, I'm not a psychiatrist, but I've seen how you took to gambling. I've played a lot of poker with you in the last year, and I'm sorry, but you're compulsive! You had your first experience with coke . . . what, twenty-four hours ago? The blast you get from coke is too much like the blast you get from gambling. You wouldn't be able to resist taking just one more shot, and then just one more, and . . ."

"Just what the hell are you saying, Stevens? That I'm a fucking drug addict?"

"No, Don. I'm saying that you've got an addictive personality, and you've gotten hooked on gambling. I'm also saying that, if you've got two hits left now, you've been snorting it every couple of hours since you started, 'cause you wouldn't be able to let it alone until you ran out."

"Bullshit! I don't need you to tell me how to run my life, thank you very much!"

Jeff looked at Don for a few seconds. Finally, he shook his head and said, "I'm sorry, Don!"

"For what?"

"I'm sorry I brought you to Vegas!"

Don laughed shortly and asked, "Why? Am I being that much of a pain in the ass? If so, why don't you just leave me the hell alone?"

"It's not me I'm worried about, Don. It's you! This town

has got you by the balls, and it's not letting go! How much money have you lost?"

The question forced Don's mind back over the losses of the trip. He tried not to think about it, didn't want to think about it, but the numbers came unbidden. The six thousand he had brought with him, the Visa cash advance, the Mastercard advance, the five grand he had borrowed from Jeff, the checks . . . he dug in his pocket and quickly counted the remaining bills.

There was just a little under two thousand dollars left! That couldn't be! Ten, twenty, twenty six, thirty one, thirty seven, forty . . . Jesus Christ! He went through his pockets again, frantically looking for more money, but there was none. He couldn't believe it! He was down over $43,000! His knees felt weak, shaky. He sat down in one of the chairs at an empty blackjack table and tried not to meet Jeff's eyes.

Jeff watched the expressions on Don's face as he went through the calculations. "That much?"

Don finally looked up, but his eyes were vacant, staring. "What? Well, yeah . . . I . . . ah . . ."

"How long has it been since you had any sleep?"

"I . . . don't know! I . . . I just haven't been tired!"

"That's the coke! That shit'll keep you up for days, and then when you do crash, it's like you died! I'll bet you haven't eaten, either!"

"Well, no . . ."

"I knew it! You wait 'til you come down! You'll eat anything that'll hold still long enough! Now come on! Let's get you something to eat, and . . ."

Don was on his feet again. "No! I told you earlier, I'm not hungry, and I'm not tired! We've got to leave tomorrow morning, and I can't take time to . . ."

"Don! Don, give it up! Cut your losses and get some rest! You're in no shape to be gambling!"

Don's right hand was in his pants pocket, and his fingers were wrapped around the bullet. He started to reply, but then his mouth snapped shut, and he turned and walked quickly away. Jeff just stood and watched him go.

Don made his way through the throngs of people, and entered the restroom. He quickly snorted the powder into his right nostril, and then the left. The rush was there, but not nearly as strong as it had been. Maybe he was building a tolerance, maybe he was really getting exhausted, but whatever the reason, it just wasn't the same. He tilted the little vial up and saw that there wasn't really enough for another full dose. He looked at it for a second, and then tapped the remaining powder into the metal end, and finished it off.

There! That brought him back up to where he wanted to be. He considered flushing the empty bullet, but he instead slipped it back into his pocket. As he stood and remembered to flush the toilet, he was hit with a wave of nausea. He turned toward the stool, but the feeling passed and he headed back to the action.

As advertised, when he came down, he really came down. He had been riding the cocaine-induced high for appreciably more than a full day and night, and his body and mind were starved for rest. He was also starved for food, but there just wasn't enough energy left to make the effort necessary to do anything about it. The way he felt, he could have easily gone to sleep face down in his food. As it was, he barely made it up to the room before he crashed.

When Jeff found him there, he was laying across the bed, his face buried in the pillow, and there wasn't any discernible sign of breathing. Jeff studied his still form, and finally walked to the side of the bed and rolled him over. His efforts were rewarded by a long, shuddering snore. He watched and listened for a few seconds, and then smiled and rolled the limp body back over.

They packed his stuff, propped him up and fed him toast and scrambled eggs, and tried to get him to talk about his adventures, but he was pretty much incoherent. He kept stuffing food into his mouth until the table was bare, and then drifted back off to sleep. He slept in the limo on the way to the airport, roused enough to devour four candy bars, and was asleep again as soon as he sat down in the plane. Jeff, feeling like he was caring for a very large, very retarded child, even had to fasten his seat belt for him.

He remembered nothing of the plane trip home, and only really woke up when a voice kept saying, "Hey! Hey Buddy! You wanta wake up?"

He came awake with a start, looking frantically around. He had no idea whatsoever where he was. His eyes focused first on the face that came with the voice, that of a cab driver. The driver was turned half around, staring at his passenger.

"Fifty three forty Palmer Court. That right?"

Fifty three . . . that was his address, the address of his house! How had he gotten . . . he shook his head, trying to remember. About the last thing that had stuck in his memory was somebody, he thought it was Jeff, walking him . . . walking him where? There had been lots of people, and . . . the airport! Of course! The airport in . . . in Vegas . . .

It all came back then, the memories tumbling over each other in their frantic efforts to gain the front of his mind. The trip down, and the gambling and the losing and . . . and Mae and the cocaine and the sex and then more gambling and more losing and more cocaine and . . . and then things got real fuzzy. He remembered having a great many chips in his possession at various times, but it wasn't completely clear whether he had won them or purchased them.

They had flown down on Friday morning, and it was now Monday . . . Monday sometime, and he remembered sleeping for about five hours all the time they were there. He had obviously slept on the return trip, but . . .

"Hey Mister! You in there?"

"Yes. Yes, I'm sorry! What did you say?"

"I said, the meter is twenty one seventy."

"Oh. Yes, of course. Just a minute." Don dug out his wallet and opened it to find . . . no money at all. Zip. He went quickly through his other pockets, and came up with a total of twenty-three cents in dimes and pennies. He held the coins in the palm of his hand and stared at them, and then looked back up at the driver, a strange lost expression on his face.

The driver frowned. "Ah, you maybe got some money in the house?"

Don looked stupidly at the man for a few seconds, and the

driver was about to speak again when Don said, "Ah . . . yeah. Just a minute."

"I ain't goin' nowhere!"

Don got out of the cab and turned toward the house, and then turned back. "Can I give you a check?"

"I'd really prefer that you didn't. You know."

Don looked at him. "Yeah, sure. I know." He made his way to the house and unlocked the door. As he did so, he glanced at his watch. It read one-forty. Barbara and the boys wouldn't be home until around four at the earliest. He stepped into the quiet house, closed the door, and just stood there for a minute. It was the same house he had left a little over three days previously, but it somehow felt different, chilly, almost unfriendly.

They didn't normally leave cash around the house, and he wasn't sure where he was going to get the money to pay the cab driver. He ran upstairs and rifled through the dresser drawers, but found nothing. As he started back down the stairs, he stopped, and then turned toward the boy's room. He tried not to think as he pulled the big rubber stopper out of David's piggy bank and shook it over the bedspread. He sorted through the coins and the dollar bills, counting. When he finished, he sighed and reached for the small gray elephant which housed his youngest son's savings.

After he got rid of the cabby, he considered calling the office. That thought lasted only as long as it took him to make it to the big couch in the family room. He brushed the TV remote control and some sort of small interplanetary vehicle onto the floor and collapsed onto the cushions.

A voice was calling softly to him, a voice that he knew very, very well. "Don? Don?" The sound was soft, somehow hesitant. Part of him tried to stay in the soft folds of sleep, but another part fought for the surface, tried to acknowledge Barbara's calls. "Don?"

He could see her now. He seemed to be standing in a field or a huge room or something. He couldn't see any details in the distance, only a kind of blending of colors. She was a short distance from him, but she did not approach him. Something seemed to be holding her back, some sort of fear or anxiety. Her face seemed to hold a mixture of expressions. Her mouth was curved in a half-smile of love and welcome, but her eyes and the furrows of her forehead conveyed a somewhat different feeling.

She glanced down, away from him for a second, and he followed her glance to see that the boys were with her. They were standing very close to her legs, almost but not quite hiding behind her. David had a firm grip on one of her hands, and Ronnie had one arm wrapped around her leg. They looked at him with expressions that he could not categorize. They were not exactly frightened or hostile, but then again, they were not the open, loving looks that he had grown to expect from them.

He held his hand out toward them, palm up, fingers gently curled, as you would offer your hand to an unfamiliar animal. They just looked at his outstretched hand and back to his face as if they didn't understand the gesture.

"Barb! Hi, boys! Come here and give Dad a hug!" He extended the other arm, and just stood there, waiting. None of the three made any move at all toward him. "Barbara? Are you okay? What's wrong?" He began to move toward them, but it was as if he were trying to walk underwater. He could make progress, but it took a great deal of effort, and he had only taken a couple of steps when he had to stop and rest. His wife and sons still made no move toward him. They just stood and watched. "Barbara! Answer me! What's wrong?"

He was about to start forward when he heard her calling again. "Don? Don?" He looked at Barbara's face, a few feet closer now, stared at her face, at her mouth, her lips, but they were not moving! "Don?" How . . . he looked again at her eyes, and saw that they had changed. They were wider now, staring as if she were seeing something strange and alarming. And, she was not looking at him any longer. Her eyes, as well as those of the boys were looking past him, beyond where he stood to something or someone else.

"Don?" Now the voice seemed to be coming from behind him, from whoever they were seeing. He turned slowly, against the resisting pressure of the air, or whatever the hell he seemed to be trapped in. As his eyes left those of his wife, he saw that hers seemed to get bigger still, and her mouth did move.

"Don?"

It seemed to take forever for him to turn around. He could discern a shape out of the corner of his vision for a few seconds before his head and eyes could complete the turn. The shape resolved itself into a tall figure with long black hair, wearing a short black skirt and a blue silk blouse. Mae reached one hand out to him, offering something. Her fingers were still curled around the object, and he couldn't see what it was. "Don?"

He stared at her for a long, long moment, and then shook his head at her.

"No!" he managed to cry. "I can't! Don't you see?" He turned back toward his family, gesturing at them. The three of them still stood huddled together, looking at the oriental girl.

"Barbara!"

"Don?"

"Daddy?"

"Don?"

Barbara slowly raised her own arm now, the one that David wasn't holding captive. She held her hand out toward him, silently asking him to come to her, to them. He began to lean toward them, his body preparing to move in that direction. As he did, the voice from behind him became louder, more insistent.

"Don! Look!"

He couldn't help himself, he couldn't resist looking back at Mae. As their eyes again met, she slowly opened her hand, and something small and round and yellow rolled off her fingers and fell toward the ground. His eyes followed the object, and just before it hit, he identified it as a thousand dollar chip! As the chip landed at her feet and bounced, there was a puff of white. He looked closer at the surface upon which Mae was standing, and saw that it was covered with white powder.

He was still staring at it when there was another puff, and another. The yellow chips were continuing to pour from Mae's hand, each splashing into the layer of white, kicking some of the substance into the air. There seemed to be a slight current of air blowing across the surface, picking up the disturbed particles and keeping them airborne. As he watched, a small haze of the powder collected and began to drift toward him.

He knew what it was, and he knew what awaited him if he inhaled it. He watched the small cloud with a mixture of excitement and dread. Beyond it, the chips were still falling, now making a small pile at her feet. There were many of them, seemingly an inexhaustible supply pouring from her hand, falling and bouncing and rolling. There was enough and more than enough to make up from his losses, to put him finally back in the position of a winner.

He needed those chips, needed them desperately! They would solve many, many problems. He had gone through his carefully hoarded bankroll, the collected winnings of which he had been so proud. That was a painful blow, but he had then gone on to lose the contents of his . . . their checking account, the credit limits on two different credit cards, the money he had borrowed from Jeff Stevens, and an eight thousand dollar rubber check! He had dug himself one hell of a hole, and the pile of yellow disks would bring him back to where he had to be. It would be so simple!

"Don?"

"Daddy?"

The voices pulled his head back around, his eyes leaving the bonanza of chips and the cloud of cocaine. Barbara still looked frightened, confused. A single tear spilled over from her left eye and slipped down her cheek. David looked stern, somehow disapproving, but Ronnie had clouded up, and the corners of his little mouth were turned down, his eyes also brimming. How could he think about walking away from them, away from his family, the people he loved? There was just no . . .

The scent caught him, jerked his head back around again. As he turned, his face buried itself in the cloud of cocaine, and he gasped, the powder entering his nose and mouth. He closed his eyes, the euphoria washing over him. God! This was as good as the first time had been! He snapped his eyes back open, and moved his head quickly, trying to inhale more and more of the cloud. Each sniff brought on more excitement, more of the feeling of power, of omnipotence.

"Daddy? Who is that lady?"

The small voice pulled him inexorably back down, and his

eyes followed the pointing finger. He heard a sort of strangled sound from Barbara, and when he again focused on Mae, he saw the reason. Mae had removed her blouse. The blue silk now trailed into the layer of powder from her right hand. She was not wearing a bra.

He spoke quickly, his voice strained. "'Mae! No! Not . . . not now! You can't . . . !

Mae seemed to be paying no attention at him at all. Her eyes were locked onto Barbara's. Her eyes were bright, her shoulders were back, and her breasts were thrust forward defiantly.

"Mae! Please . . . !"

He turned at see Barbara's reaction, to try and explain. He could feel the effects of the cocaine hit draining away already, and he blamed the embarrassment of Mae's brazen display. Barbara and the boys were again just staring. The boy's mouths were hanging open in fascination, but Barbara's face had drawn together in anger and defiance. Her lips were pressed into a thin line, and her eyes looked both sad and determined. David looked up at her as she slipped her hand out of his. She hesitated just a second, and then both of her hands went to the top button of her blouse.

Twenty-Two

"Don?" It was happening again. It was Barbara's voice, but he stared at her, and her lips did not move. "Don! Wake up! It's all right! You're having a nightmare!" He struggled upwards, trying to believe the voice, trying to escape the confrontation of the dream. He wanted to wake up, to come back to his family. However, a part of him, a large part, really wanted to stay in the place which boasted piles of large denomination chips, cocaine, and sex. He fought toward reality, but he dreaded what reality would bring.

The voice was that of his youngest son. "Mommy, can you have nightmares in the daytime?"

"Well, sure. I guess so. Don, what do you think?" He had managed to get his eyes partly open, and the three figures were swimming in and out of focus. "What? Think about . . . ?"

"Never mind, Don. It's not important." She smiled down at him.

"Is too 'portant!" Ronnie wasn't about to let his question get passed over. "I wanna know!"

"Ronnie, hush! I want to talk to your Daddy."

"Ah, Mom!"

"Ronnie!" Her voice raised at the end of the word, as did her eyebrows. Ronnie looked at her for a few seconds, and backed off. David, being older and wiser, just stood back and took it all in.

Don was awake by now, still quite groggy, approaching reality. He wasn't sure he liked it. "Hi, guys!"

"I'm glad you're back safely. I missed you!" Barbara sat down beside him on the couch, and kissed him soundly. The boys took her cue, and both landed in his lap. They hugged him and babbled about their weekend for a few minutes, and then their attention spans took over and they were gone, headed for the Nintendo. Barbara snuggled down beside him and laid her head on his shoulder. "So tell me, big boy, did you have a good time?"

He started to toss off some sort of flip answer, but his voice caught in his throat and he coughed.

"You okay?"

"Yeah. Yeah, I'm fine. I'm just . . . just tired, that's all."

"Well, tell me about it! What did you do? Did you win any money?"

"'Well, I . . . no, I didn't win. They beat on me some." He tried a smile, hoping it looked genuine.

"Well, that's all right. As long as it wasn't too bad." She smiled back at him, hoping for more information. There was a tiny crease between her eyes. "It wasn't too bad, was it?" She waited. "Don?"

"What?"

"Are you really okay? You're acting really . . . I don't know . . . down, depressed. What happened?"

"What do you mean? Nothing . . . I . . ."

She put her fingers on his lips, quieting him. She bowed her head for a second, and when she again raised her eyes to his, there were traces of tears. "Please. Please, Don. I've known you for too long. There is something wrong, and I need to know what it is. Please tell me?"

"Barb, I'm fine! I really am! Like I said, I'm just tired. I didn't get a lot of sleep in Vegas, and . . ."

She interrupted him again. "How much did you lose, Don?"

He tried for anger, again trying to take the offensive. "Is that what this is all about? Is that the reason for the inquisition? You don't care about anything but the money, do you? I am so damned tired of hearing about the evils of my gambling!"

"Why are you so defensive? You know that I worry about your gambling, but it doesn't seem to make any difference to you! I've tried to talk to you about it, about the fact that you're so preoccupied with it, but . . ."

"God damn it! Why is it that everybody in the fucking world thinks that I don't have the intelligence to take care of myself? I am getting so damned sick of people telling me how to live my life!"

Barbara got up and walked to the door of the room, looked to see if the boys were listening, and shut the door. As she turned back toward Don, her voice was quiet, tense. "I will thank you to watch your language in this house. Don't you dare subject those boys to that garbage!"

"Now listen . . ."

"No, you listen! I am sick to death of you going into denial every time I say anything at all about your gambling! You act as if you're ashamed of it!"

Don was sitting on the edge of the couch, his fists clenched. "Wait a damned minute! You're the one that acts ashamed of my gambling! You make me defensive about it, the way you're always yammering at me! I don't know why I can't be allowed to do something I enjoy, without having you all over my ass about it! I'm getting damned sick and tired of you trying to tell me what I can and can't do!"

"I am not telling you anything!" Barbara was standing with her hands on her hips, glaring down at him. "It wouldn't do any good for me to try, the mood you're in! All I'm saying is that you've changed since you started gambling! You never used to ignore me or the boys!"

"What the hell are you talking about? When have I ignored you? I happen to be very Goddamned busy, thank you very much, and sometimes I'm not able to devote the time that . . ."

"Oh, bullshit, Don! Bullshit! Bullshitbullshitbullshit! I know you're very busy, and you're a very good provider, and that's all just super, but all that has nothing whatsoever to do with what we're talking about! You are just not the same man that you were before, and I'm very, very worried! I think . . . I'm afraid that you're turning into . . . into a compulsive gambler!"

"A what?"

"A compulsive gambler! Charlie said . . ."

"Charlie? Charlie who?"

"Charlie Hardwick! Your friend, Charlie! He said that you were . . ."

"You talked to Charlie about me? God DAMN it, Barbara! What the hell right do you have to talk to Charlie, or anybody else, for that matter, about me? What right?"

"I didn't go to Charlie! He called me! He was concerned about your preoccupation with gambling, and he called me, and we talked about it. He agrees that you seem to spend a great deal of time talking about it, thinking about it, and, I guess, doing it! It seems like you can't leave it alone, and if that's true, that makes you compulsive!"

Don was standing now, his body leaning slightly toward her. "For Christ's sake, Barbara! I play a little poker, make a couple of bets on a golf game, and suddenly you and that little shrink have me branded as a head case! That's, if you don't mind me borrowing one of your favorite expressions, bullshit!"

"Don, don't lie to me anymore! It hasn't just been poker and golf! You've been betting on football games and basketball, and I don't know what all else! I don't know how much money you've gambled, I don't think I really want to know, but it just worries the hell out of me!"

"How do you . . . what kind of crap was Charlie telling you? Wait till I talk to that little bastard!"

"Charlie is your friend, Don! He's concerned about you, and that's the only reason he even said anything. He was really embarrassed by it, but I guess he thought I knew about the betting on sports, because he started talking about the bragging you and Jeff do during the golf game. He didn't go into details, but he indicated that the two of you talked about some pretty big money." She stepped toward him and took his hands in hers, but he didn't relax his fists. She could feel the tension in his stiffened wrists and arms. "I need for you to talk to me about this, Don. I want to help you, but I can't begin to do that unless you talk to me!" She was pleading, trying to reason with him, but he was having none of it.

"Well, I don't need your damned help!" He snarled at her and turned away, jerking his hands away from hers. "And I certainly don't need the help of a nosy little psychiatrist! I am not a compulsive anything! I could quit gambling right now! If I wanted to! Which I don't! And it's none of Charlie Hardwick's fucking business what I do with my time or my money! Come to think of it, it's none of your fucking business either! I work my ass off making a living for this family . . ."

His words were cut off abruptly as she slapped him. She didn't think about it at all, it was just a reaction to his words, the hurting words and the months of worry and the change in her husband that was inexorably pulling them apart. It was just like the involuntary swatting of a mosquito on her arm. It probably shocked her as much as it did him.

The blow brought red to his cheek. He just stood and looked at her for a long moment, refusing to give her the satisfaction of retaliating, although it did flash through his mind.

He pushed his lower jaw out at her and said, "Just leave me the hell alone!" He turned and walked out of the room, and she heard the front door slam as he left. She walked quickly to the front of the house, and was just opening the front door when she saw his car tear backwards out of the driveway. She started to shout his name, to try and bring him back, but she didn't. She just stood there, the tears running freely down her cheeks.

After assuring the boys that everything was all right, and that Daddy had gone to the office to catch up, she fed them dinner and settled down for a long evening of waiting. She thought of calling Charlie, but she had no idea what she would say to him. They had discussed Gamblers Anonymous, the group which was set up along much the same lines as Alcoholics Anonymous, but she had no idea how she would go about getting Don to even admit to having a problem, let alone attend meetings.

Charlie had done some research on the subject, and he had told her that the compulsion to gamble was very much like the compulsion to drink. It differed from alcoholism in that it was not a chemical dependency as such, unless you considered the desire for the adrenaline rush associated with gambling.

Compulsive gamblers were, according to Charlie, emotionally ill. Again like alcoholism, the illness was progressive in nature, and there was no cure. The only solution to the problems generated by the compulsion was abstinence from gambling in any form. Nothing else seemed to work. The literature from Gamblers Anonymous and from another organization called "The National Council on Problem Gambling" both stressed that the compulsive gambler tended toward immaturity, toward a tendency to desire something for nothing. The gambling is, to these people, a way to escape reality, to create and live in a world where they are powerful, important, comfortable.

Charlie said that the progression of the behavior disorder was quite insidious. The gambler places a bet and wins, the desire to win more arises, and another bet is made. When a loss occurs, and it will eventually occur, a bit of the dream collapses, and the gambler wants both the money and the dream back. There are usually fantasies of the "big win," which will enable them to buy and do all the things that will make them and their family happy.

The problem is, however, that no matter how much is won, it is never enough. The dreams tend to expand after a big win, driving the gambler on to bigger and bigger bets and more and more gambling, in an attempt to gain the bigger dream. It is an illness that feeds upon itself, gradually taking over more and more of the gambler's life until nothing else is left.

Barbara had recognized several of the danger signs as Charlie had read them to her from the literature. Don had taken time from the office to gamble, he had experienced a personality change in the last several months, and he had denied being as involved in gambling as it now appeared he was. He lied to her on several occasions, hiding the fact of his wagering from her.

She had made a vow to herself that she would not jump on him immediately when he returned from Las Vegas, but that hadn't worked at all. He had looked so down, so depressed that she knew something had gone wrong. As she told him, she really didn't want to know how much money he had lost over the past several months. He was right when he told her that his gambling hadn't effected her financial life. At least, it hadn't so far. She assumed from his mood that he had lost money in Las Vegas. Charlie had indicated that Don had talked about winning quite a bit at his various ventures, so she wasn't really worried about his losses over the last weekend. What she could not, would not take were the mood swings and the lies. Especially the lies.

She finally went to bed at about eleven-thirty, primarily because she didn't know what else to do. There had been no sign of Don, and she was becoming more and more worried, worried that he had been in other accident, or that she had pushed him too hard, had driven him away. She couldn't really believe that he would throw away all of their years together, but all of those years had been spent with the old Don. She wasn't really sure what the new one might do. She lay awake for a long time, and finally drifted off. She came awake with a start sometime later as she heard Don come into the bedroom. As he quietly slipped into the bed, the scent of liquor washed over her. She said nothing, didn't know what to say. Within minutes, he was snoring.

The two of them spoke very little the next morning. She was hesitant to start anything again, and he was in a hurry to get out of the house and to the office. The fact that he had put them fairly deeply in debt with his activities over the weekend kept nagging at him. The fact that he had also broken a couple of laws, having to do with controlled substances and adultery, faded somewhat in comparison to his concern with how he was going to cover the losses.

The money from the credit cards could be paid off at a few hundred a month, at ridiculous interest rates, but the eight thousand dollar check which he had written to the Bedouin, and which was about to bounce very high, was quite another problem. He could talk to Jeff Stevens about the five grand he had borrowed from him, but Barbara was really going to raise hell when she found out that he had maxed both of their credit cards and cleaned out their joint checking account. He was in the middle of tax season, with its resultant pressures and long hours. He certainly didn't need a bunch of people, including his wife, yelling at him about money. The office would bring in quite a bit of money in the next few months, but not nearly enough and not nearly soon enough to help his present situation.

"Jeff? Don."

"Hi, Don. Have you recovered?"

"Yeah, pretty much. Physically, at least. Financially, well, that's another thing."

There was a brief silence, and then Jeff said, "I had a feeling you were getting in a little deep. I'm sorry if I got on your case while we were there, but . . . well, I'm sorry."

"Don't worry about it," said Don, "Listen, about the five grand . . ."

"I'm not real worried about it. Pay me when you can."

"Well, that's the problem. I don't know when that will be. I over extended in a few other areas, and I'm going to have to come up with some money pretty damned quick, or the Bedouin is going to be unhappy with me."

"The Bedouin? Why the Bedouin?"

"Well, I wrote a check . . . "

"You bounced a check on the Bedouin? Jesus Christ, Don! That's something you simply don't do!"

"No, it hasn't bounced yet, at least not that I know of. That's why I need to get my hands on some money. Besides, what are they going to do, break me knees?"

"Not a joking matter, my friend! There are certain people you just don't fuck with, and casinos are right up there on the list! You better get that check covered, or they're gonna be pissed at both of us!"

"Why you?"

"Because I brought you in, introduced you to the place. They don't have much of a sense of humor when it comes to not getting their money. Any ideas on how you're gonna come up with the cash?"

"'Not really. I guess . . . I guess I was hoping that maybe you could help me out."

"I can't, Don. I was ahead when I loaned you the five, but the dice turned on me, and I dropped quite a bit before we left. I'm a little strapped right now myself. Can't you get a loan or something?"

"Yeah, but not quick enough to do any good. I've got to get that check covered."

"How about savings? Anything you can tap?"

"Yeah, there is, but everything's in tax-deferred stuff, and they'll penalize the hell out of me if I break any of it. I've got a couple of good bets on basketball, but I don't have anything to bet with. I seriously doubt that Sid would want to take any bets on credit!"

"You got that right! But, since you mentioned Sid, you might talk to him. I've heard that he's got some sources, but they're not cheap!"

"Sources?"

"Yeah, people that will loan money without a lot of collateral. But you're talkin' ten percent . . ."

"Ten percent isn't bad! Hell, that's cheap money!"

"Don, for Christ's sake, will you grow up? This isn't the First National Bank we're talking about here! That's not ten percent a year! It's ten percent a month!"

"What? But that's . . . that's a hundred and twenty percent a year! They can't do that!"

"They can do whatever the hell they please! Maybe you'd better just forget I mentioned it. I don't think they're the kind of people you want to get messed up with. These people don't play! You asked if the casino would break your knees. They might not, but these boys will, I promise you!"

"Well, yeah, but if you pay them back on time, there's no problem, is there?"

"No, there isn't, and everybody goes in thinking that they'll pay everything back on time, but pity the poor bastard that doesn't!'"

"Well, I'll see. Maybe I could borrow enough to cover the check and make a couple of bets with Sid. I've got to get some action going, get caught up! Hey, do you know of any other pot limit games other than the one Saturday night?"

"No, I don't."

"Well, if you hear of anything, let me know! Thanks for your help!"

"Don?"

"Yeah, Jeff?"

"If . . . ah . . . if you do talk to Sid, if you do borrow some money from his sources, do me a favor, will you?"

"Sure, if I can. What is it?"

"Borrow enough to pay me off too, will you?"

"What? I thought you said it was no problem!"

Jeff hesitated for a long time. Don was about to ask him again when he said, "I . . . I'm not sure how to say this, Don. I said in Vegas that you were acting compulsive about the gambling, and I'm still hearing it from you. So if you don't mind, I'd like to have my five grand."

"What the hell's the matter? Are you afraid I won't pay you back? Are you all of a sudden an expert on compulsive gambling, like everybody else I seem to know? I am getting so fucking sick of . . . oh, what the hell's the use! You'll get your damned money, Stevens! Have no fear!"

"Don . . ."

"Go to hell!" He slammed the receiver down and glared at the telephone. What was wrong with everybody? Well, to hell with all of them! He picked the phone back up and dialed Sid's number.

Twenty-Three

"Mrs. Montgomery, if you'll just calm down . . ."

"But I'm not calm, Mr. Curtis! I'm not calm at all! I am holding in my hand a letter from the Internal Revenue Service in Ogden, Utah, that tells me that I owe them four thousand six hundred and five dollars! I already paid them over six thousand dollars with the tax return you prepared, and I can't understand why I owe them so much more!"

"I told you, if you will just bring the letter into my office, I will see what . . ."

"This sort of thing never happened with our old accountant! Mr. Kelly prepared our return for years and years, and I never would have changed to you if he hadn't died! I am just very unhappy, Mr. Curtis!"

"As I said, Mrs. Montgomery, If you will bring the letter in, I will be glad to review it for you. There's a chance that the IRS just made a mistake, and . . ."

"I seriously doubt it! I thought that you seemed distracted when I came into your office to talk to you this year! It was as if you weren't really listening to anything I said! Maybe I should just pay it, so they will leave me alone! I'm sure it's right, but I can't really afford to send them another four thousand six hundred dollars! I just don't know what to do!"

"I'm trying to tell you, if you would listen to me! Bring the damned thing in, and . . ."

"Don't you dare curse at me, young man! I will not stand for it! I am going to take this letter and my tax return to another accountant, and if this is your fault, you will be hearing from my attorney!"

"Please, Mrs. Montgomery, I'm sorry! I . . ." But the line just buzzed at him. He glared at the receiver for a few seconds, and then slammed it down on the telephone. It hit crooked and skittered across the desk top, scattering papers. He grabbed it and his frustration exploded, narrowing his vision to a red tunnel. He raised the receiver again and again, slamming it down on the telephone. The plastic cracked, and a piece of the handset flew off, hitting the door. He sat, his shoulders slumped, staring at the jagged piece of black plastic still hooked to the phone by the coiled cord.

This was the third call of this type he had received in a week. The two which he had received last week had both turned out to be his fault, the results of omissions on the tax returns of the clients. He couldn't understand what had happened. Normally, he prided himself on the accuracy of the tax returns turned out by his office, and he advertised that he would pay the penalties and interest resulting from any of his errors. So far, that guarantee had cost him almost a thousand dollars in the past couple of weeks.

Was he losing it? What the hell was the problem? He had worked his butt off, putting in so damned many hours! And it wasn't as if he just had the office to worry about. It seemed like everything else in the known universe was conspiring against him. Barbara wasn't hardly talking to him at all, hadn't for months. Since the blowup after his return from Las Vegas, things had just gotten progressively worse between them, more strained, more distant.

She had gone on a real crying jag when he told her that the credit cards were not to be used, and that it would be a while before she could write a check on their joint account. She had again yammered at him about being a compulsive gambler, about not being able to control it. He was still very upset with Charlie Hardwick for filling her head with all that compulsive crap, and he fully intended to make his feelings known to the little psychiatrist. He had not found the time to call him as yet, but he certainly intended to do so.

Barbara had even been attending some kind of a support group thing, probably at the suggestion of the little neon shrink. It was called Gam-anon, or something like that. She had refused to talk to him about the meetings, but he had found some of the literature she left laying around. He had no idea whether she meant for him to find the stuff or not, but he had taken the time to look through the propaganda.

It had questions like, "Does your mate often return to gambling to try and recover losses, or to win more?" Well, who the hell doesn't?

"Have you noticed a personality change in the gambler?"

"Does the person ever gamble to get money to solve financial difficulties?"

"Does the person lie to deny his or her gambling activities?"

"Does the person try to shift responsibility for his or her gambling to you?"

Well, he had to admit that a couple of the questions hit pretty close to home, but that didn't make him a Goddamned compulsive gambler! Not by a long shot! He had taken some bad beats over the last months, starting with the trip to Vegas. No one else seemed to understand that he was behind, that he had lost so much that there was no way he could pay it off out of his normal income. He had no choice but to continue the betting, to keep it up until his luck changed back.

If he could have only a week, maybe two, of the kind of luck he used to have when he had first started, he could pay off the credit cards, pay back the money he had been forced to take out of the retirement fund and the profit-sharing plan to pay off Sid's "sources." He was going to get absolutely killed on the income taxes next year, with the extra taxable income and the penalties for early withdrawal from the tax-deferred plans. But that was next year. By then, he would be back in control again, he would be back on the winning side of the ledger. He had to be.

He had borrowed enough from the retirement funds to cover the bouncing check to the Bedouin, to pay off Jeff Stevens, and to place a couple of very heavy bets. He had spent the time until the basketball games were played in a state of high excitement, apprehensive about the additional debt, but high on the fact that, when he won, he would be well on his way back out of the hole.

But he had not won. The Lakers had failed to cover their spread by two points, and Chicago had one of the worst games in the history of the franchise, losing by over thirty points. One of the games had been televised, and he watched in horror as the Chicago Bulls went down to ignominious defeat. That fiasco had dropped him to a break-even situation at best, since he had bet the same amount on each of the games. When he heard the results of the Lakers game, he had just felt empty, used up. He had lost again, and he was in even worse shape than he had been. Instead of having the winnings to pay off the loan sharks, for that is exactly what they were, he had been forced to borrow from the pension funds to prevent the outrageous interest rate from ballooning the amount owed to them completely out of sight.

So now what? He hated the idea of having to go back to the sharks, hated the idea of being beholden to them. Borrowing money from them was flirting with disaster. The money was easy to borrow, but he had heard stories of others who had gotten behind on their payments. The highly illegal interest rate was a killer. Once someone got behind, it was almost impossible to catch up, as any payments were eaten up by the interest. The only hope was to pay off the loan all at once, which was what he had planned to do.

If those Goddamned basketball teams had paid attention, he would have been out of the woods by now, but they just buried him deeper than ever. He had tried to recoup the next weekend with the rest of the pension fund money, and he thought for a while that it had finally turned around for him. He won close to two thousand playing poker Friday night, and Saturday afternoon began with a win by Portland that gave him another three grand. From there, everything went to hell. Atlanta lost, Chicago lost again, and the Lakers fell short of covering the spread by one lousy point. With the exception of the win by Portland, every single team he bet on went down in flames.

His mood was approaching desperation. It was gone. The savings, the money for their retirement, the money from the credit cards. All gone. He had the feeling that he was running faster and faster, and still losing ground. Everything had been so good just . . . what? Not very many months ago. Everything had been going his way. He had been winning, winning a great deal of money, on his way to . . . to winning more, to becoming more independent, to having the means to get into the really big action. He still had fantasies about the big win, about how it would feel to make the big score, to have the money to go where he wanted to go, do what he wanted to do, buy the things for himself and his family that would show them that he wasn't a loser. It was exciting just to think about the money, the chips, the action.

But what the hell was he going to do now? There wasn't that much equity in the house, not more than a few thousand, and both of the cars were financed. The office had brought in pretty good money during tax season, but that had all gone to either gambling or to pay off the few bills that he knew had to be paid. He still received most of the mail at the office, and the letters and notices from those remaining unpaid were getting more and more hostile.

He knew what the answer was. It was obvious, but he really didn't want to admit it. There was only one place, one source for money left open to him. Without money, he couldn't live, he couldn't gamble. Without the gambling, he had nothing. He was nothing. He couldn't imagine not gambling at this point, couldn't imagine giving up the rush, the feelings of power and importance that didn't seem to come from anything else.

He was going to have to go back to the sharks, take the chance of losing again and having no way to pay them back, risk putting himself at their mercy. But he couldn't keep losing! He was so incredibly overdue for a win! At this point, winning a few bucks or a few hundred, or even a few thousand was not going to do much good. He needed money, a lot of money, just to get back to the position he was in several months ago, just to get even. He was never going to make the losses up by pushing a pencil, by doing income tax returns for people. There was only one activity, short of armed robbery, where he could get that kind of money. He knew that he could do it. He had done it before, he had won steadily at poker, at sports betting. There was no reason in the world why he couldn't do it again.

There was a tapping on the office door. He came out of his obsession and glanced around quickly, looking for someplace to hide the broken phone. For just a few seconds he was eight years old, expecting to be punished for the accident. Then he frowned and pushed the instrument aside, as if it held no further interest for him. "Come in!"

Becky peeked around the edge of the door. "You okay, Don?" Her eyes left his face and gazed at the remains of the telephone for a second. To her credit, her expression did not change. She just came on into the room and gently closed the door. "Don?"

He looked up at her and studied her face for a bit. She was just about to speak again when he said, "Becky my dear, I don't suppose . . . suppose that you . . ." He looked at her for a few more seconds and then dropped his eyes to his hands. They were clasping each other as if seeking mutual protection, the knuckles white.

"What? What is it, Don?" She sat on the arm of one of the chairs across from him, and leaned forward slightly. "What do you need?"

"I . . . I can't ask you . . ."

"You can ask me for anything, Don. I can always say no!" She was afraid of what he was thinking, but she had to know for sure. "What is it?"

"I . . . I need . . . money!" He took a deep breath, and spat the last word out, his eyes again falling. "I need a lot of money, but . . . but anything would help!" He was still staring at his hands, unable now to meet her eyes. She just sat and stared at him for a long time, unsure what to say. Finally, she spoke.

"What . . . what do you need the money for, Don?"

He looked up then, just for a second, and then quickly back down. "Well, I . . . I've had some bad luck, and I'm pretty . . . pretty far behind on some bills, and it would help me catch up a little bit, and . . ."

There was no answer. He finally looked up, and her eyes caught his and held them. Now she took a deep breath, let it out. "Don, I don't know how to say this, but Barbara has called me a couple of times in the last few months. She . . . she asked me not to loan you anything!"

She flinched as he suddenly sat straight upright, his face a mask of hatred. His eyes were wide open and wild, and she was afraid for a few seconds that he might come over the desk at her. She quickly stood up and moved around in back of the chair. "Don, I'm sorry!"

"You're sorry! You're sorry! The whole fucking world is trying to convince me that I'm some kind of Goddamned addict, and you're sorry! What the hell right do you have to talk to my wife or to anybody else about me? Just who the hell do you think you are?"

"Don, please. I didn't . . . I'm sorry! I shouldn't have said anything, but Barbara is really worried about you! She's scared, and she doesn't know what to do! She called me to . . . to just talk, I guess. She loves you, Don, and she . . ."

"She what? She can't keep her damned mouth shut? She just can't resist telling everybody about her failure of a husband? That's just wonderful! Did she tell you not to let me get close to a deck of cards or a sports page or . . . or a telephone or . . ."

He looked frantically around the office, and his eyes lit on what was left of the telephone. He reached over and grabbed it, jerking it back over his shoulder and breaking the cord leading to it. Then he turned and threw it. It sailed across the room, hitting and breaking a vase before it shattered against the wall.

He looked around for something else to throw, and was just about to go for the computer monitor when her movement caught his eye and stopped him. She moved quickly back toward the door and stood with her hand on the knob. She looked back at him, her jaw set and her eyes sparkling.

"You have my home number if you need anything, Don. I don't think I'll be coming in anymore. I can't watch you destroy yourself, everything you had. I care too much about you, Don. I'm sorry, but I just can't stand to . . . to watch anymore."

He glared at her. "Well go, then! Get the hell out! Who needs you? I don't need you or anyone else telling me . . . telling me what to do, how to live! You don't give a shit! Nobody does! Just get the hell out!"

She looked at him for a few seconds longer, and then squeezed her eyes shut. When she opened them again, the tears spilled over and slid down her cheeks. She opened her mouth as if to say something more, but then she just looked down and went out of the door, closing it quietly behind her.

When he stormed out of the office a few minutes later, Becky was nowhere in sight. The other two employees got very busy when he appeared, and didn't look up until he was gone. Then they went back to trying to figure out what the hell was going on.

He walked quickly to the lot where the Saab was parked, and wove through the downtown area toward the interstate. He was hot, extremely upset by the happenings of the past hour, and he wasn't thinking at all rationally. It was the middle of the afternoon, and he really had no place to go. He briefly toyed with the idea of driving to Central City or Cripple Creek and playing blackjack or poker, but he had very little money on him, and no quick way to get any more. He stopped at a service station and called the "sources," trying to make arrangements to borrow some more money, but the people he needed were not available. He drove aimlessly for a while, and finally headed toward home.

By the time he pulled into the driveway, exhaustion was setting in. He had been through too much, more than he could handle, more than he could stand. He was relieved to see that Barbara's car wasn't in the driveway or in the garage, because he desperately needed a nap, a little sleep to clear away the cobwebs. It was still early afternoon, and with luck, he could get two or three hours before anyone came home. He kicked off his shoes and laid down on the couch in the family room. He lay there for several minutes, the scene with Becky replaying on an endless loop in his mind. He felt very badly about losing her. He had considered calling her, asking her to reconsider, begging her forgiveness, but he just couldn't make himself do it.

He finally drifted off, and felt like he had been asleep only a few moments when Barbara's voice intruded on his subconscious. "Don? Don, are you asleep?"

He stirred, rolled over, and almost rolled off the couch. His anger flashed to the surface at being put in a position of looking ridiculous, and he lashed out at her. "Well, I was, but I'm certainly not asleep now!"

"I'm sorry I woke you, but I was afraid there was something wrong. I was really surprised to find you home in the middle of the afternoon. Is everything all right?"

He sat up and rubbed his eyes with the heels of his hands. They felt like somebody had put sand in them. Finally, he looked up at her. "Oh, everything is just great, thank you very much for asking. My head bookkeeper just quit, the IRS is trying to crucify me, and my wife. . ."

"Don . . . don't!"

"My wife is all over my ass about my vices, and I owe way too much money to way too many people! Other than those few small inconveniences, everything is just fucking dandy!"

"Don, cut it out! What happened to Becky? You said she quit?"

"Yes, she quit! She stuck her nose in where it didn't belong, and we had a few words, and the . . . and she just quit. Walked out!"

"But Don! Becky had worked for you for . . . how many years? I can't believe that she would just . . . just walk out for no reason."

He glared at her. "Oh, she had reason enough! It seems that somebody had been talking to her about me, about my 'gambling problem!' Seems this somebody told her not to loan me any money! Any idea who that somebody might be, Barb?"

She looked at him for a long minute, uncertain how to answer. Then she took a deep breath and said, "Don, you have to understand! You've got to stop! If you can't stop on your own, I've got to do whatever I can to stop you, and that includes trying to make sure that you don't, or can't, borrow more money! I'm really sorry, Don, but I had to talk to Becky to protect myself and the boys. And you!"

"Protect me? Protect me from what? From myself, from my big, nasty habit? Well, lady, has it ever occurred to you that I might not want your protection? Yours or anybody else's! I am so . . . !"

"I know, Don! I know! You're so fucking tired of everybody trying to tell you how to live! Well, let me tell you something, mister! Somebody needs to get your life back on track, and you've proven to me and to everybody else that gives a shit, that you aren't capable of doing it!"

"Now just a Goddamned minute! You can't . . ."

"Shut UP! Just shut up and listen! You have a choice to make! You either cut out the bullshit and start attending the Gambler's Anonymous meetings, and I mean now, or you are going to be trying to make it through the rest of your life without me and our sons!"

"Now wait . . . !"

"No, you wait! I mean it, Don! I will leave you. I've already talked to my mother, and she says that we can come live with her for a while. I will take the boys, and we will leave you here to do your worst. Sell the house and the furniture and whatever else you can sell and gamble it all away. I don't care about it, any of it! It's just stuff! All I care about is you! Please, for me, for us, just try going to the meetings! See if they can help you!"

"So I'm supposed to go sit in a church basement somewhere with a bunch of losers and pour my heart out? I hardly think so! If I can't make you understand, how the hell am I supposed to talk to a room full of strangers?"

"Don, it's not about making anyone understand! I understand what's wrong with you, and so do you, but you just won't admit it! You are addicted to gambling! You are a compulsive gambler, and the only thing that is going to help you is to stop gambling! You've proven . . ."

"Barbara, please . . ."

"SHUT UP! Just . . . just shut up. You've proven that you aren't capable of stopping by yourself, so the next step is to try and get some help. If you won't do it for yourself, will you do it for me? For your sons?"

"Barb, I . . . I can't . . ."

"Please, Don? Please just go to one meeting? If you never go to another one, if you still think I'm crazy, that the rest of the world is crazy, then you just go ahead and do whatever you have to do. But please just try it once? For me?"

"All right! All RIGHT! For Christ's sake, if it means that much to you, I'll go to the fucking meeting, and embarrass myself in front of a bunch of people, and then maybe you'll get the hell off my back! I don't suppose you would have an address, would you?"

She turned and almost ran toward the kitchen and her purse. "Oh, Don, thank you! There are meetings just about every night of the week, and I know I have the addresses here somewhere!"

He just stood and shook his head, his eyes looking toward the ceiling. "I thought you might," he said, "I thought you might."

Sure enough, she found the little directory, and there was a meeting that very night at an address in north Denver. He grabbed the little booklet from her and turned quickly, headed for the front door. He had no intention of actually attending the meeting, but he could disappear for a few hours, maybe find a little cash somewhere, and find a game. There was always Central City, just over an hour away.

As he headed north on the interstate, he kicked the Saab in the ass and wove through the beginnings of rush hour traffic. He was taking his frustrations out through speed, and the Saab responded nicely. As he flashed beneath an underpass, he noticed the pillar which held up the cross street. It was easily ten feet in diameter. It was protected by curved railings on each side, but it appeared that there might be sufficient room between the ends of the rails for a small car to pass through. If a driver hit the space just right, there would then be nothing between the car and the pillar. If a person were contemplating such a thing, he would want to be traveling at a high rate of speed, to preclude any chance of survival.

He shook his head, taking his eyes off the roadway for a second. He had surprised and frightened himself. Just the thought of . . . but one of the few things remaining after the fiasco of the previous year was several hundred thousand dollars of life insurance. With that kind of money, Barbara and the boys could pay off the debts, start over . . .

He slammed the gearshift lever into third and moved into the inside lane, winding the little engine out to a high whine before he again hit fourth. As he rounded a curve in the highway, he saw another underpass about three quarters of a mile ahead. He did his best to shut down the rest of his mind, and concentrated hard on driving, on trying to get as much speed out of the little car as possible.

He earned the glares of other motorists as he sped by them. There was a line of cars ahead on him in his lane, and he was going to have to slow down before he reached the underpass. He glanced quickly at the grass median strip, and jerked the wheel to the right. The wheels slid briefly on the surface of the grass, but then the front wheels caught and he was again accelerating toward the pillar.

It all seemed to happen in slow motion. The opening between the guard rails looked too small, he wasn't going to . . . but then he was through, only a few yards from what was rapidly becoming a wall of concrete. As he realized that he had passed the point of no return, he felt himself begin to relax, to welcome the conclusion of his life.

The front of the car collapsed, accordioning in on itself as it had been designed to do, trying its best to protect the passenger compartment. But an automobile, any automobile, that hits an immovable object at ninety miles per hour doesn't really have much of a chance of protecting anything. As the front of the car came to a stop, the rest of the car and its occupant continued ahead at ninety miles per hour. He was wearing his seat belt out of long habit, but the windshield and steering column didn't care about that. They came to meet him.

For a split of time, there was nothing. There had been a flash of brilliant, almost unbelievably bright color at the instant of impact, but then nothing.

Wait a minute!

How could he know that there was nothing?

How could he know anything?

He had just splattered himself all over the side of . . .

How could he be remembering that he had . . .

He couldn't still be . . .

Oh shit! Was this just another one of those Goddamned dreams? He fought upwards, feeling like a drowning man who had finally seen the surface, had seen the world of air and life above him, but so far . . . so far . . .

He came out yelling. He sat bolt upright on the couch and

looked around wildly. The back of his shirt was sodden with sweat, and the fabric stuck to his ribs under his arms. He was breathing rapidly, his lungs trying to keep up with his heart. The explosion of adrenaline jerked him to his feet, but his legs were shaking so badly that he couldn't control them and he had to sit back down.

He looked around the quiet room again, and actually squeezed his left forearm with his right hand to make sure that he was still whole. He seemed to still be alive, but the dream had been so real, the accident so vivid, that it frightened him to even think about it. But yet he couldn't help thinking, thinking of the dream and before the dream, his arguments with Barbara, the debts, the things and people he had lost along the way during the past year or so. It all came back, the incredible rush of the wins and the equally incredible crushing weight of the losses. So many losses. So much money. He had lost everything, the savings and the retirement funds and Becky and Jeff and Charlie and . . .

He heard the front door open, shut.

"Don?"

Was this still part of the dream? In the dream, Barbara had come home and found him, and they had . . .

Her voice went on, talking to someone else. "He must be here. His car is . . ." She appeared in the doorway of the den. And she was not alone. Standing right behind her and peering at him around her shoulder was the little neon shrink himself, Charlie Hardwick!

The three of them just stared at each other for a few seconds, emotions ranging from surprise to anger to embarrassment. Finally, Barbara spoke.

"Don? Are you okay? What are you . . ."

Don interrupted her. "What the hell is this, reinforcements? You can't face your lunatic husband without bringing along the damned cavalry?"

"Don, that's not fair! Charlie was out in his front yard when I drove up, and we started talking, and I . . . I . . . guess I was afraid . . . I don't know, I thought you might talk to him for a few minutes, listen to what he had to . . ."

Don could feel the back of his neck getting hot. He was still sitting on the couch, but he was now on the front edge, his feet under him, unconsciously ready to spring, to attack. "So now I need a psychiatrist? Has it really gone that far, Barb? Just exactly what the hell are you trying to prove?" He pounded on the arm of the couch with his fist twice, three times. He was so damned mad, so frustrated . . . why couldn't she, why couldn't anyone understand?

He started again, "You don't have any Goddamned concept of where I'm at, what I'm going through! I'm so damned far down that the only way I can get the kind of money I need to catch up is from gambling! And I can do it! I know I can! I . . . I've done it before! All I need is a little luck, a little . . ."

He stopped, surprised, as Barbara dropped to her knees in front of him. She reached for his hands with her own. He started to jerk away, but the expression on her face stopped him. Her eyes were wide, pleading. Tears spilled over her lower lids and traced twin paths down her cheeks. Her lips were moving, but she was having a great deal of difficulty getting the sound to come out. "D . . . Don? Please . . . would you just please . . . just listen to Charlie? Just for a minute?"

He started to pull back again, but her hands gripped his hard. "Please?"

"For what? So he can tell me that I'm some kind of a . . . some kind of an addict? That I can't control what I do? That I'm . . . I'm sick? That I . . . !"

Charlie had said something, but he spoke so quietly that Don unconsciously stopped yelling to listen. He frowned, staring intently at the lips of the little man, trying to make out the words.

" . . . know you don't feel like you're doing anything wrong. That's natural. That's part of the disorder. If the subject of an addiction felt worse when they used the drug or took the drink or placed the bet, then natural aversion would take over, and the problem would solve itself. Unfortunately, that's not the case. People smoke cigarettes because they 'taste good,' or they 'help me relax', or whatever. Alcohol helps to take away the stress or the loneliness or the pain, and cocaine, amphetamines, and gambling produce a 'high,' a 'rush,' that can only be produced by that drug or by that activity."

"But," Don protested, "I only gamble because I enjoy it! The . . . the only reason I . . ." He stopped, trying to gather his thoughts. "I only started gambling because it added . . . I don't know . . . added a little spice, a little excitement to the golf game, to the football and the basketball . . ."

"The excitement that you're talking about," said Charlie, "is the result of the adrenaline rush. Everybody probably gets that kind of a rush when they have something at risk. It, as you say, adds 'spice' to what are ordinarily pretty hum-drum lives. That's why the casinos do so well. But most people can let it go at that. They win or lose a few bucks, and they have a story to tell the folks at home, and they go back to their ordinary lives." Don started to speak again, but Charlie continued. "But a few people, statistics say about one in twenty-five, can't stop with the few dollars. They have to keep at it until the game is over, or the money is gone. Barbara tells me that you got in pretty deep in Vegas, and . . ."

Don's head jerked back toward Barbara, who still knelt in front of him, watching his face closely. This time, he did jerk his hands away. " Goddamnit! What right do you think you have to tell . . ."

She flinched at his new outburst and opened her mouth to reply, but again, Charlie's quiet voice silenced both of them. "She has the right of survival, Don! You've been acting like your . . . activities . . . haven't affected anyone but yourself, but that is far from true! The compulsive gambler is very good at gradually destroying his own life, his own reality."

"Charlie, what the hell are you trying to . . . ?"

"It's a fact, Don. The gambling takes over a little at a time, until it becomes the most important aspect of the gambler's life. In the process, everything else must necessarily fade into the background. Jobs, relationships, and most heartbreakingly, families become less and less important as the gambling takes up more and more of the subject's time and attention."

"That's not true! I . . . I haven't . . ."

"It is true, Don!" It was Barbara speaking now. "I've tried

to talk to you about it for months. The gambling takes over, and you don't have time for me, or the boys, or anything else! You know that."

"Well . . ." Don looked from one to the other. He was losing. He knew it. He hated losing, but he couldn't find the words to say what he felt, what he needed to say to convince them . . . "I . . . I guess I have been going at it a little heavy. But I know that I could cut back, maybe drop some of the sports bets . . ."

Charlie was just looking at him, his lips a thin line, shaking his head.

"What?" asked Don, "I just said that I could . . ."

"Won't work, Don."

"What? What do you mean it won't work? You don't know . . ."

"But I do know, my friend. I don't tell you how to do income tax returns; don't tell me about addictive behavior! It's common knowledge that an alcoholic, I should say a recovering alcoholic, can never, ever have another drink. There is something in their system that takes the tiniest bit of alcohol and uses it to tip them over into a binge. It just happens! Unfortunately, it's exactly the same thing with a compulsive gambler. Once you've stopped gambling, you can never again bet on anything! Not an office football pool, not a golf game, not even flipping for a cup of coffee."

Don looked at his friend for a long moment, realization slowly forming a large hollow place in the core of his being. "Never?"

"I'm sorry, Don. Never."

"But I owe so much . . . so much money! How . . . ?" The latest dream came back, jarring him. There was still the insurance money. That would . . .

Barbara took his hands again, gently this time. He folded her hands in his. "You still make good money, Don. We don't need a house this big, and if we . . . "

Her words faded as his world slowly caved in around him. The savings, the pension, the . . . the house? He tried to envision a world without poker, without craps, without football bets. He almost choked up at the thought. The gambling was a friend, a companion, a comfort . . . but he had once felt that way about cigarettes, hadn't he? And he had known for years that if he ever smoked another cigarette, he would immediately go out and buy a carton. His basic stubbornness had kept him off the weeds for quite a few years.

Don looked up. "Charlie?"

"Yes, Don?"

"Charlie . . . what . . . what's the success rate? Do you know?"

"The success rate?"

"Yeah. How many . . . ah . . . compulsive gamblers are able to quit, to stay away . . .?"

"I wish I did know, Don. Trouble is, it's such an invisible disorder that no one really knows how many people are affected by it. There may well be compulsive gamblers that are able to kick it, to stay away without ever entering any sort of a program."

"How about the ones that do go into a . . . program?" Don was still holding Barbara's hands. She had been watching Charlie as he talked, but now she turned and was staring at the side of Don's face, her eyes wide.

Charlie hesitated. "I wish I had an answer to that, Don. I truly wish that I did. The programs like Gambler's Anonymous are strictly voluntary. No one forces the members to attend the meetings, or to do anything else. They go to the meetings to get support from the other members, and to give support back."

Don started to speak, but Charlie held up his hand and continued, "I won't lie to you, Don. The dropout rate is pretty high. Gambling is just so available, so pervasive in our society, that it's tough to stick with it, to work the steps of the program, to stay away. But, I will tell you this! It's the ones with discipline that make it. It's the ones that are willing to work, the ones that are willing to admit that they've got a serious problem, and that the problem has them beaten down."

As Charlie stopped speaking, Don glanced at Barbara for a second, his face unreadable. He turned and stared across the room for almost a minute, his lips tight together, his eyes unblinking. Then, he turned back toward his friend and golfing partner. "Charlie, I . . . " He squeezed Barbara's hands and then released them and stood. He held his right hand out.

Charlie took Don's hand and pulled the taller man toward him. Don hesitated, but then he relaxed into the hug, the two of them patting each other's backs for a few seconds before they broke apart.

"Charlie, would you mind . . . I need to talk to Barbara."

"Of course, Don." Charlie turned toward the door. "Thanks for listening. If I can do anything . . ."

"I . . . we'll let you know, Charlie. Thanks for . . . for your friendship."

Charlie nodded and glanced at Barbara. Then he turned and quickly walked out of the room. As Don walked back to the couch, they heard the front door open and close.

Don stood for a moment and looked down at Barbara. She sniffed and rubbed a tear away with her knuckle, and then reached for his hands again.

He sat down facing her. She was just about to speak when he put a finger to her lips, stopping her. "Barb . . . I am . . . I am so sorry!" He tried to hold her gaze, but he couldn't. His eyes fell to their hands, and his head bent forward.

"I know, Don. I know. I . . . I don't have any idea what you've been through, what . . . what this had done to you, but you know that I love you, don't you?"

"I know you do, Barb. I also know that I don't deserve it!"

"Nonsense! Didn't you hear what Charlie said? It's a disease, Don! It's not your fault! It's . . . it's a disorder!"

"Yeah, well . . . it's something, that's for damned sure!" Don looked back up at her, his eyes moist and his jaw muscles clenching. "I just . . . I don't know if I can stop, Barb! I really don't know if . . ."

"Don, listen to me. I've known you for quite a few years, and we've been through a lot together. I've watched you build your business, I've seen you raising our sons. I lived with you while you were trying to get over cigarettes, remember?" He nodded. "I'm certainly no expert, but I really, really believe that you can do whatever you set your mind to!"

"I . . ."

"You can, Don, I know that you can!" She put one hand on each side of his face and kissed him gently.

Don felt like he had been wrung out. Barbara did still love him, he knew that. He didn't want to lose her. He couldn't stand the thought of losing her, of losing the boys. But he had done so much damage! The office was a mess. Their savings, everything that he . . . everything that they had worked for was gone; gone down the insatiable . . . !

He looked at Barbara's eyes, shifted his focus to her mouth, back to her eyes.

NO! No, by God, he had not lost quite everything! Try as hard as he could, he had been unable to lose the one thing that he now knew he had to keep. He had come close, frighteningly close, but . . .

He was still young! If he could stay away from the games and the bets and . . . and all that, he could . . . he could regroup, rebuild, get back to where they had been before . . . before! If he could stay away. Maybe, just maybe . . .

He got up from the couch again and walked quickly to the desk. Turning to the Addiction section of the yellow pages, he traced his finger down a page, stopped, and tapped the surface of the paper. He quickly punched out the number on the phone, spoke into it briefly, listened, nodding, and hung up. He scribbled something on a notepad and stuffed the page into his shirt pocket. He started away from the desk, but then he stopped and looked back toward the telephone. Walking back, he again consulted the directory, and called another number.

"Hello? "

"Becky?"

"Yes, Don?"

He spoke a little longer this time, but he was smiling when he hung up. Barbara just sat on the couch, watching him. Tears were still seeping from her eyes, but the corners of her mouth now turned up just a bit. As Don turned back toward her, she stood and held her hands out toward him. He walked quickly to her and they embraced almost desperately, clinging to each other.

"Thank you, sweetheart," Barbara said softly, "I really . . . I love you."

Don had his face buried in her hair. He started to speak, but then just sighed heavily and pulled back, looking down at her.

She studied his face, his eyes. "What, Don?"

"I'll try, Barb. That's . . . that's all I can promise right now. I'll try my best."

"And that's all I can ask."

* * * *

As he drove north on the interstate a few hours later, he kept well within the speed limit and avoided the inside lane. The memory of the latest dream was just a little too fresh.

"Anyone else?"

Don hesitated, his head pulled down into his collar like a turtle. He made no movement for a minute, but then he stood just as the speaker was about to go on. The man spotted him and stepped aside, offering the lectern. "Please!" he said.

He walked quickly to the front of the room and positioned himself behind the lectern before he raised his head to face the twenty or so people seated before him. Every eye in the room was on him, and he almost didn't say anything at all. He looked to the moderator for help, but the man just smiled at him and nodded as if he understood. He cleared his throat, and looked just over the heads of the back row.

"My name is Don, and I'm . . . I'm a compulsive gambler."